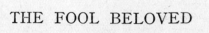

THE FOOL BELOVED

THE WORKS OF JEFFERY FARNOL

THE FOOL BELOVED

by

JEFFERY FARNOL

THE BOOK CLUB
121 CHARING CROSS ROAD
LONDON W.C.2

This edition 1950

MADE AND PRINTED IN GREAT BRITAIN BY PURNELL AND SONS, LTD.
PAULTON (SOMERSET) AND LONDON

To

The sacred memory of my brother

EWART

who was killed in action

Aged 19

at Vrieskraal, Africa

1901.

CONTENTS

7

CONTENTS

CHAPTER I

IN DIM-LIT chamber of the Black Horse tavern three men sat at wine: the first a gay-seeming fellow, ornate of person, bold of gesture and fluent of speech; the second a bewhiskered ferocity, slow of tongue though quick of eye; the third a pallid youth who leaned to peer from small, open lattice out upon the darkening road.

"Night!" he exclaimed, suddenly. "Night falls apace and yet no sign o' them! They should ha' been here ere this! Eh, eh—how say you, Annibal?"

"Well now," answered this first man, stretching booted legs to lounge more at ease, "as man of action, for this delay I curse, as gentleman I merely smile, but being a philosopher I say all's well, my Florizel,—is so, I say, and so shall be for that so be it must."

"Ay, we needs must," repeated Florizel, turning from the window, "being by evil compelled to this black evil——"

"Evil, quotha?" growled the scowling man ferociously. "Ha, now what puling chicken-hearted clack is this——"

"Hold!" said Annibal, with commanding gesture. "Temper thy so natural ire, my Rodrigo, for this our Florizel, being young, lacketh our much experience and smarteth to the prick o' conscience. Yet it shall blunt anon and irk him no more than doth thine or mine. He shall ripen——"

"Oh, mock," sighed Florizel, crouching in his chair, "mock me an ye will, yet do I protest this thing we are about to do is loathed and most detestable——"

"So now," growled Rodrigo, "he will dare miscall our trade, a notable profession dignified by ages and right gentlemanly calling——"

"Calling, ay truly!" retorted Florizel. "I've heard it called 'murder' ere now! And we presently compelled thereto by this damned Spanish lord Gonzago——"

"Peace, fool!" hissed Rodrigo, cowering. "Here is perilous name! Our lives do lie in his potent hand——"

"Verily! Oh, he hath us fast . . . for that one sin doth beget others! 'Florizel,' saith he, becking me aside, 'at such a time you did thus'—naming that me thought secret as the night wherein 'twas done. 'I've hanged men for less!' saith he, smiling——"

"Ay, yea," nodded Annibal, "my lord hath very wheedling way to woo one to his purposes——"

"So thus," groaned Florizel, "are we compelled to murder one that never did us wrong, a youth we've never seen, a hapless student all unsuspecting——"

"And the bee cried 'buzz'!" growled Rodrigo.

"A mere poor student," Florizel repeated. "I marvel so great a lord should stoop to harm such."

"Ay, but," said Annibal, reaching for the wine, "this same student is far more than he seems and therefore more worthy the—ha—attentions of such as we, my Florizel! He hath been oft assailed upon the road and lives yet!"

"Then," growled Rodrigo, "there was curst bungling!"

"Nay—there was featly play o' rapier and dagger wherefore our comrade Bandello lieth sore wounded! And dost mind that jovial toss-pot Vitry the Frenchman?"

"Certes. A merry, frolicsome fellow."

"Well, he will frolic no more."

"How—is he dead?"

"As mutton! And by this same well-managed steel! This student proveth notable man at arms, ha? Now I've heard tell our great Fortunio, this redoubtable fighter and invincible commander, hath a brother who, though a scholarly youth and lover of books, can twirl rapier featly as Fortunio's self, having learned the gentle art of that grimly old swordsman, Jacomo, his ancient. Well, is all plain now?"

"Ay, by the fiend, plain as these my hilts! Here's game worthy of us!"

"In verity!" nodded Annibal. "Thus, Vitry and the others failed! But we——"

"Aha—we," chuckled Rodrigo; "thou and I do never fail. So 'tis good as done and this lordly student no better than crow's-meat even now."

"Is this so sure?"

"As death, my Florizel, I warrant you this stripling shall

pass aloft so gently, so sweetly-swift he shall scarce know it."

"Ay," quoth Rodrigo, "we be marvellous expert, Annibal and I! We ha' sped many a weary soul heavenwards!"

"And thus," laughed Annibal, "are become benefactors o' mankind. For as this sorry world is full of all manner of hardships, sufferings and evils——"

"As murders!" whispered Florizel.

"Yea, murders and the like grievous necessities, it then follows—how good and noble are such as we to waft a soul from these vile haunts, this very doghole of a world, to that celestial kingdom, that sinless paradise, where is no contention save the throb of harps. Thus 'tis like enough this young Count Angelo, thus throned in bliss by our efforts, shall pour benedictions upon our heads anon for very gratitude."

"Oho!" chuckled Rodrigo. "Right excellent well said, Annibal! But since our student rideth with a friend, must we thus waft both to paradise?"

"This is as may be—so long as we do angelize young Angelo! For, and mark this well, 'tis suspected he bears dispatches, a letter of the utmost import; this we must secure! And that we may certainly know him I have his exact description—hearkee!"

So saying, Annibal drew a paper from the ornate pouch at his girdle, wherefrom he now read aloud: "'Neither tall nor short, and something slender. He is black-haired, dark of eye and pale complexion. Item: carrieth silver-hilted rapier whereon is 'graven the badge of his house, to wit 'Fidena'. Item: a black cloak, scarlet-lined and edged with oak leaves in silver. Item: a wide-eaved hat with feather o' scarlet."

"Good!" nodded Rodrigo. "I shall know him at a glance."

"Moreover, we are to take each some token for proof our business brought to happy finality. So, his cloak for me."

"And I his hat. Soho Florizel, and what's for thee, what?"

"Who knoweth? His sword belike! Now since he is brother to the great Fortunio that so lately freed our duchy from dread o' the Turk, why requite him thus vilely, why must we do this thing?"

"For reasons o' State, my Florizel, and for that we are so commanded——"

"Ay, by this Gonzago! And to what end?"

"The advantage of us all. We—being the very fingers of his hands, the toes of his feet whereby he climbeth to power; as he mounts so mount we. Thus shall our fortunes soar and——"

Annibal paused as to them shambled their host Tomaso, a fat man who sweated, breathed short and wheezed:

"Soldiers, my masters . . . there be soldiers . . . i' the village hard by . . . men o' the lord Fortunio's guard——"

"Ha!" exclaimed Rodrigo, leaping afoot. "A thousand devils! What now, Annibal?"

"Drink!" he answered, suiting act to word.

"Malediction!" snarled Rodrigo, clapping hand on sword. "Are they for us, Tomaso? Are we betrayed——"

"No, no, messires! I do but warn ye how there must be no shooting to rouse the village and bring these soldiers down on us. I do but warn."

"So?" nodded Annibal. "Then Tomaso, my fat one, bleat not so lamb-like. Content you, here shall be no blatant trigger-work nor hit-or-miss thunderous discharges; our steel by soundless insertion shall suffice. See therefore you keep us private here."

"I will indeed, sir."

"Hast set a watch upon the road to advise us of our travellers' approach?"

"Even so. You shall be duly warned, good master Annibal."

2

"Look up, old lad!" cried Count Angelo, clapping his silent companion on broad shoulder. "Yonder is the frontier at last, and beyond—my home country!"

"Good!" exclaimed Sir John Courtney. "Though in England, as you'll mind, are no frontiers, thank God, by His Grace we have the sea that is our everlasting barrier and sure defence."

"Ah," sighed Angelo, "would this ravaged land might have such barrier!"

"Nay, but, Angelo, this country, though fair, is not England, alas!"

"You are mighty proud of that same little island, eh, John?"

"Indeed, that am I, and with good reason. For though in this great world be many and divers countries, there is only one England! And 'tis of nature so miraculous that no matter how far an Englishman journey, even as I, or roveth hither and yon about this earth, yet is he forever at home; by cause he ever beareth England in his very heart."

"A fair thought, John. So here you shall be twice at home. For beyond those hills, that are nigher than they seem, is Celonia and my brother's castle of Fidena where you shall find such glad and hearty welcome that even your England and our years together at Oxenford will fade to a dream."

"Then 'twill be dream as blessed as our last days o' travel have been right cursed nightmare, what with bad roads, worser inns, thievish rogues and ruffians, sudden alarms, ambuscados and bloody onfalls!"

"Indeed," said Angelo, thoughtfully, "latterly our journey hath been something eventful——"

"Eventful?" exclaimed Sir John indignantly. "Good lack and God aid us—eventful, d'ye say? Here we've been shot at, cut at, stabbed at, ridden at, bedogged and bedevilled, and you call it 'eventful'! Here's me with a bullet-hole clean through my hat, and another very perilously through my breeches, and you with a rapier-thrust quite through that fine, Italianate cloak o' yours, and you call it—ha—that cloak! This gives me cause to ponder!"

"Why so, John?"

"By cause, Angelo, this same cloak is the only foreign thing about you! In all else—speech, look, dress and gesture —you are as English as myself and thus with no curst, foreign braggadocio flourishes, no feigned ferocity of rolling eye, scowling brow, flaring nostril, snarling lip, gnashing teeth or like futile fooleries. No, thou art, to all seeming, a very Englishman and right worthy so to be!"

"'Slife!" laughed Angelo. "This—and from such Englishman as you, John, is tribute wellnigh overwhelming!"

"Yet from my heart 'tis meant, i' faith. But now, Angelo, consider. As we are both English, seemingly, and as all travelling Englishmen are deemed vastly rich, shall this explain these repeated murderous attacks upon us? For by the Pyx, no two lone travellers ever fought for their lives harder than we! Though by Saint George we gave better than we took, of course; being the two best swords in all the colleges, this was expected. Howbeit, the question is: were these assailments merely by cause of our English showing?"

"Mayhap, John, and the fact that hereabout has been desperate war so lately."

"War," repeated Sir John, "and thy noble brother Fortunio the victorious champion a right notable soldier and most excellent commander by all accounts! The which sets me awondering, Angelo, why thou, being such joyous fighter, fought not beside him 'neath his famous banner."

"So I did, John, and repeatedly though he, as often, had me arrested and conveyed back to my then university at Padua and at last overseas to England and Oxenford. So thus, by my brother's will and most strict command, I have lived displeasingly safe until the warring ended. So now, here am I, by his will again, homeward riding with you, old friend, that helped to make the years of my inglorious exile less irksome. Though wherefore I am summoned so urgently and at such speed, I cannot guess."

"How long since last you saw your brother?"

"Five years."

"Good lack, Angelo, the whole world may change in far less time!"

"Why, so it has, John."

"Ay, faith, and these years that have so changed the world, and you from youth to man, shall have altered him far more. Today, by his mighty achievements, he has grown from man to titan, his fame a by-word!"

"And godlike titan, John, crowned with glory!"

"True, Angelo! Thus shall I be the more truly proud and honoured to meet him. But, and moreover, these years of such desperate effort, cares of office with hardship o' ceaseless battle, shall have changed him bodily also and, mayhap, quite beyond thy past memory and present knowing."

"Oh, never!" laughed Angelo, confidently.

"Nor," persisted John, doggedly, "in your new-come manhood and English tire and bearing, shall he know you."

"He will, John, he will," cried Angelo, checking his horse the better to speak, "for, since our parents died so many years agone, he hath been to me a father, ay, and mother also! Thus when brothers love as we, nought in this world, or the next, may blind each to other; our very blood would cry: 'Oh, brother, I am here!'"

"Hum!" exclaimed stubborn John. "Howbeit and nevertheless, Angelo, thou'rt so vastly changed, even since I knew

thee, that now and after these years of change and absence I'll
wager Lord Fortunio shall scarce know one of us from other,
t'other from which! I'll set you any wager that, dight in
your hat and cloak and feigning your walk, voice and gesture,
I could so confound him that he should greet me for thee
and John as Angelo."

"Never in this world, John."

"Dare you put it to proof?"

"Nay, 'twere mere foolery!"

"Why then, you are not so sure, eh, my old boy, eh?"

"John, I am sure o' this as—the grave, but——"

"Oho—'but!' So verily you fear 'brotherhood' might be
so deceived that my Lord should bestow his kiss o' welcome
on me?"

"No, I say—and no!"

"Well, then," chuckled persistent John, pulling up in his
turn, "since thou art so perfectly assured, my Angelo, take
thou my hat and cloak and, to prove thy belief, give me
thine." And so, after some hesitation and great unwillingness
on Angelo's part, the exchange was made and they rode on
again—to that which was to be.

Reaching the crown of a hill, Angelo halted once more to
gaze across a wide vale where, throned above ever-deepening
shadow, rose the embattled walls and lofty towers of Celonia,
a city just now mellowed and made beautiful by the last rays
of a blood-red sunset.

"Oh, Celonia!" he exclaimed. "Thou art lovelier even
than I deemed! How think you, John?"

"A right fair city and mightily strong!"

"In very truth, John! Too strong for the ravening Turk,
thank God! 'Twas there they besieged us, ten years agone,
when all save the city and Fidena, my brother's strong castle,
had fallen. 'Twas thence Fortunio drave them at last, fighting
battle after battle, out-scheming and out-fighting them until
—today, yonder is she, our mother city, unconquered and
immune, throned in glory——"

"And yonder is an inn!" quoth John. "Come, let's to't,
for I've a noble thirst. Come, Angelo!" Thither rode they
at speed and there dismounting were greeted by a fat man
who smiled and bowed.

And after they had seen their horses duly tended, they
followed this bowing, smiling fatness into a spacious, dim-lit

chamber where three other travellers sat in murmurous converse.

"Noble messires," smiled their host, forever bowing, "pray
how may I be honoured to serve your lordships? Will ye
bite, will ye sup? I can offer your nobilities a wine of Bur-
gundy richly rare and even worthy of your excellencies——"

"Good!" nodded Sir John. "Go fetch it."

"And speedily!" added Angelo, impatiently. "'Tis nigh
curfew, and we would reach the city ere its gates close."

"But, lording, they shall not close this night, for in the
city is marvellous rejoicing! Yea, in all the duchy folk cry
blessings on their great captain, the Lord Fortunio, for joy
o' their deliverance, their freedom won by his war-crafty
valour. So tonight for this victorious peace is high revelry;
folk sing and dance and ring their bells so lustily ye shall
hear 'em out yonder on the road—an you go hearken hard
enow——"

"This will I!" cried Angelo, starting afoot. "Go with me,
John; these bells shall cry us welcome."

"Nay, go you," answered stubborn John. "As for me, I'll
bide here and slake my thirst. Go list to your welcome, then
come you and we'll drink health, long life and enduring
glory to thy valiant brother."

"Ay, old John lad, and heartily!" Then away strode young
Angelo, spurs ajingle, and, being come out upon the road,
saw how the night-shadows gloomed and the glory fading
upon Celonia's walls and towers; but to him, faint and sweet
with distance, stole the glad pealing of her bells, like a dearly
familiar, oft-remembered, ageless voice, calling him home.
And lifting his arms thitherward with yearning gesture, he
whispered in answer:

"I come! Oh, Fortunio, my brother, God keep thee till
we meet. . . ."

And it was now, even as he uttered his prayer, that Annibal
unsheathed dagger and drew sword, whispering:

"Here now opportunity beckons—come!"

"Then," gasped Florizel, "I will not see it done!" and,
speaking, he dashed out the light. . . .

Then to Angelo, upon the darkening road, came a wild
distressful cry:

"To me! I'm beset . . . ha, for love o' God . . . help . . .
help me. . . ."

Out flickered Angelo's rapier and he sped, guided by this cry, into this place of darkness and murder where now ensued fierce ring and clash of steel, fury of unseen movement, a bubbling groan answered by a dreadful wailing, a jingling rush of spurred feet out and away. . . .

Then was ghastly stillness, an awful silence—broken suddenly by a frantic shout:

"Lights here! Bring a light! Ah, for love o' God—light!"

Thus presently came Tomaso, bearing in either shaking hand tapers, whose unsteady beams showed young Count Angelo backed to the wall, sword in hand, gazing down wide-eyed upon the shape asprawl at his feet, a motionless thing that stared up at him unwinking and sightless in death.

"O . . . saints and angels!" panted Tomaso. "O sweet saints . . . what to do is here!"

All unheeding and motionless stood Count Angelo, dumb with grief and horror; then, suddenly falling to a knee, he touched this pale, set face with gentle hand.

"John!" he whispered. "Oh, John, is it thus with thee? Ah, would I had not left thee! Art sped so soon, John? Nevermore to smile or laugh, thy young voice forever hushed? And all so pitiful soon! Oh, John, would I'd never left thee!"

"Woe and alas now!" wailed Tomaso, peering closer. "Noble sir, what's here?"

"Death!" muttered Angelo, stiff lipped. "See you—here leapt the murderous steel—to the joyous young heart of him."

"Yea, good my lord, 'tis even so! Ah, the poor young gentlemen is surely dead, alas!"

"Indeed—and in the blink of an eye!" murmured Angelo speaking like one entranced. "Then how frail a thing is life— to be snatched so swift away! So easily destroyed! An inch or two of steel, a drop or so of poison—'tis gone—and this body we so cherish is no better than senseless clod, a thing to rot . . . and rot! So now this that was my so-loved friend is become a thing to shudder at—ay, but what of the glad and valiant soul of him! Is this quite gone—like flame of out-blown taper? Can it, like gross body, perish? If this be so indeed, then what bitter mockery is life——"

"Oh and alas!" wailed Tomaso, louder than before. "Ah, what cruel, bloody business! Here lieth yet another meet for burial, one Master Florizel——"

"So!" exclaimed Count Angelo, rising. "You knew him then?"

"Not so! Not I, my lord, no no! I did but hear him so named by his fellow rogues."

"Canst tell me aught of them, their names, condition, whence they came? Speak!" And with the word, Angelo advanced his rapier-point so threateningly that Tomaso recoiled, gasping:

"No . . . no, most noble . . . gentle master, no thing know I o' such bloody ruffians; they be to me strangers all never seen afore! I hold no traffics with such, and this I do vow and swear by all the blessed saints! So, my good lord, prithee now put up thy sword."

"My sword!" Angelo repeated. "Now, for thy over-much vowing and swearing I am minded to use it, point and edge, on thy fat carcase, for thy every look proclaims thee liar. These murderers were here intent on our destruction!"

"Lord, how should I be ware o' this?"

"Rogue, how should you not? To what purpose were they lurking here—speak!"

"For rest, my lord, as I believed, for rest and refreshment—'tis so methought."

"So is my friend dead of them and thy so false thinking to my thinking—by thy damnable connivance."

"Not so, my lord, no—no! Here now upon my knees I do swear it by Holy Mother and all the saints of heaven! Guiltless all am I, my noble lord, guiltless and innocent as lamb!"

"So—up, wolf! Up now and summon aid to bear—this that was my friend—this that is now but sorry clay—where it shall be prepared for its last abiding place. See to it—go!"

"Yea, yea, good my lord, I will, I will!" And struggling up from his knees, Tomaso shambled away.

And now, kneeling once more beside his dead friend, Angelo made a sign of the cross above him with reverent hand; then, blinded by tears, whispered a prayer and thereafter whispered brokenly:

"Oh, John . . . John . . . here ends thy earthly journey ere it has well begun! So must earth to earth . . . but thou wert so young and sweet in life, kind Mother Earth shall cherish thee, transforming this poor clay to fragrant herb and flower. . . . But for the soul of thee . . . this I do think is even now with God in paradise . . . and yet . . . oh, John . . . I would I had not left thee!"

CHAPTER II

TELLS OF TWO THAT WAITED

THE CASTLE OF FIDENA being of no great size had therefore proved easier of defence throughout the late desperate war; against its massive walls the bloody tide of invasion, beating in vain, had been checked and finally rolled back in raving red confusion

Thus today, as evening fell, this stronghold, impregnable as the city itself, reared its battle-scarred walls, unconquered and mighty as ever, guarding the road that led by trampled vineyard, desolate village and shady woodland, to the chiefest gate of the city. But this evening the air was glad with the merry clamour of bells far and near, while in their ruined villages men, women and children danced, laughed and sang for joy that peace was come to bless them at last.

Meanwhile in spacious hall of the castle, where hung Fortunio's tattered banner with weapons of every sort, Jacomo, his ancient or standard-bearer, a grey-haired veteran grim and battle-scarred as the mighty castle itself, sat busily furbishing his lord's suit of armour, the various pieces of which littered the great table in gleaming disorder while all about him the riotous bells made joyous clamour; wherefore he scowled, cursed, and at last began to sing an old battle song, bellowing defiantly, and these the words:

> "See now thy sword its edge doth keep,
> Sa—ha! Sa—ha!
> That when it at the foe doth leap
> It biteth sure and smiteth deep,
> For men must fight though women weep,
> Sa—ha! Sa—ha!
> When loud their cursed trumpets bray,
> Sa—ha! Sa—ha!
> Then—out swords all and——"

Here a laughing voice interrupted him.

"What, my old war-dog, must you roar that old fighting ditty and now? 'Twas well enough to march and fight by in those evil times, but not on this of all nights!" So to him came Fortunio, this man of his love, limping somewhat by reason of an old wound, a man of no great stature, lean and worn by hard service, whose thinning hair shaded a scholar's lofty brow, but whose aquiline nose, firm mouth and jut of chin proclaimed the soldier and man of action quick to see and resolute to do; just now, instead of sword, his sinewy hand grasped a thick volume shut upon a finger to mark the place. "And why," he continued, "why in reason's name d'you scrub and scour that harness the which it glads me to think I shall never wear again. Have done, Jacomo; cease thy scrubbing and ranting and hearken to those bells that, like voice of choiring angels, do proclaim peace on earth and good will to all men."

"Ay, lord, but only to men of good will! And there be none o' good will was ever born Turk; ravening wolves rather! They are a plague, a pest, the everlasting bane o' this sorry world——"

"From the which God hath delivered us, Jacomo!"

"Ay, God heard our prayers—mayhap! Yet there needed ten years o' bloody fighting, and—thyself to lead us, Fortunio. As for peace—'twere well enough were every Turk dead and buried."

"Nay, live and let live, Jacomo."

"Ay, to fight again! So 'tis I thus cherish this good armour o' thine and shall keep it ready to thy need, the which may chance sooner than is expected."

"This I do nowise expect! So no more! Instead I now tell thee good news of our young Angelo, since thy love for him is great, well nigh, as mine own——"

"Ay, I'll warrant thee! What of our lad?"

"Tidings by express that he with his English friend came safe ashore and duly received the cloak from Morelli——"

"Eh, cloak, my lord?"

"As I say—and sewn within the lining of this cloak the writing you wot of, naming those traitors by whose contrive we twice came to nigh defeat——"

"Ha, by the bones! I mind well that time we with small following rode south to reconnoitre, and, thinking all clear,

were cut off i' the mountains, beset front and rear, half our
company slain, yourself desperate wounded, myself hurt and
saved i' the nick of time by young Ippolito's sudden charge o'
horse. This was one time; when was t'other?"

"In my tent the night before our onfall at Varenza."

"But Varenza was the first of our victories——"

"On that night, Jacomo, a thievish cur-dog stole and ate
my supper whereof he presently died the death intended for
me—that in the confusion of my dying, our camp might be
surprised and taken and our young war ended in defeat——"

"Mercy o' God! I knew nought o' this——"

"Nor did any save my squire Andrea—and the miserable
dog, poor wretch."

"But," gasped Jacomo, "how came this vile thing so nigh
thee—and in very midst o' the camp?"

"By the hidden hand, Jacomo! By this—this persistent will
to our destruction that I have sensed about me ever and anon—
this stealthy, all-pervading evil and remorseless menace."

"Ha! But, a God's name, who and what?"

"This we shall know, I pray, when Angelo cometh."

"The which should be now!" growled Jacomo, bending
to his self-imposed task again. "He should ha' been with
us hours agone!"

"Patience, man, patience! These be unchancy times for
travel. . . . Yet, though young, he hath a cool head."

"Ay, and thereto a ready hand and supple wrist, I'll warrant
him! With dag or rapier few shall match him—the which is
no wonder, for we learned him, thou and I! Howbeit, he
should be here. So the question is why——"

"Nay, Jacomo, the question is—should I warn the Duchess
of his return considering they are contracted and were betrothed so long since——"

"Ah—to wedlock, poor mites, and they then both i' their
cradles! And by will o' the Duke her father and thy lordly
sire that were brothers in arms. Yet today these Lords are
but dry bones, God rest 'em——"

"Yet their will lives and is known to her and the Council;
this betrothal holds."

"Oho!" laughed Jacomo, shaking his grim head. "Yet
will such will hold good with such wilful she that is so full
o' wilful life, high spirit and womanly whimsies, that she will
but to her will, let others will how they will? Have we not

known her, thou and I, as motherless babe, lovesome child, sweetly imperious maid, and today——"

"Proud and lovely woman, Jacomo, and our liege lady."

"That I've dandled o' my knees like small, dimpled Eve and never a figleaf withal! She was wildly wilful even then and would tug my hair with her little dimpled fists till my eyes watered, ay, and kick me i' the chops with her little rosy feet——"

"Keep these particularities for herself alone, Jacomo."

"Well, so I did last time we were alone, and i' faith she tugged my hair again till I cried her mercy, then, 'stead o' kick, she kissed me heartily, ay, heartily! Then a perches on my knee and 'Jacomo,' says she, 'those plagues that are my councillors tell me I must be wed and within one little year!' 'Verily,' says I, 'and by young Angelo according to promise!' At this, she gives me tweak o' the ears and 'Nay,' says she, 'no law and no promise shall compel me. I'll wed him only that I will and not for reason o' State but love.' 'Good!' says I. But then she said such thing that up rose I and shed her from my knee and with a plump. For she told me, and mark this, that our Angelo was to her abhorrent!"

"But she hath not seen him this ten years and more!"

"True—instead is this Gonzago, this lordly, smooth-spoken señor! Him she daily sees, or were blind, for he is forever to be seen, a most persistent courtier wooing her regard! And he a foreigner!"

"A grandee of Spain, Jacomo, and therefore noble gentleman."

"Yet I like him not."

"Nor I," said Fortunio, thoughtfully, "yet have no just cause for such dislike . . . except it be his too-fervent show of friendship."

"Ay, there it is! He is too intent on pleasing thee, courting thy favour and goodwill."

"Yet is this a crime, Jacomo?"

"Lord, such fawning homage may lead thereto! Moreover, he is great these days with Sebastian that is now chief o' the Council of Ten, these grave, so revered gentlemen! Well, how think you?"

"That your many and constant suspicions are a plague."

"Why, so they are since we are at peace! For bethink you how whiles we fought our last battles these same grave councillors accused Julio Morelli of treason so gravely that in grave he'd be but that he fled."

"Like guilty man, Jacomo!"

"Ay, or man unable to prove his innocence! And he was thy friend years agone."

"So he seemed!" nodded Fortunio, and began to limp to and fro as he ever did when greatly troubled and perplexed. "And I'm warned he is sending me this most secret letter!"

"And," Jacomo growled, "hid in young Angelo's cloak!"

"Now should this prove Morelli innocent, where then lieth the guilt?"

"Why, on these same so respected councillors ten, I'll warrant!"

"No, not all; this were beyond reason! Not all—one, mayhap, or even two——"

"Howbeit, m'lord, seize 'em all, hang 'em all, and so be done, say I!" Fortunio's anxious, care-knit brow smoothed, his firm lips curved to ghost of a smile as he retorted:

"Why, thou bloody-minded ancient, art so mortally wholesale?"

"Ay, thus would I for thy sake, to rid thee o' this 'creeping menace', this 'unseen hand'. For today, as thou in all the state art greatest, great is thy peril and greater my fear and care for thee. Thou art become the mark for all men's fawning amity or secret enmity. Honest warfare has none such perils as factious peace. Peace—with a wanion, a murrian on't, say I——"

Suddenly, high above pealing bells, rose the silvery notes of trumpets playing a long, happily familiar fanfare.

"Ha, the Duchess!" exclaimed Jacomo, rising.

"And she comes in state, mine ancient."

Together these old friends and much-tried comrades leaned to peer down from the narrow lattice set deep in massive wall, to look where through glowing sunset rode a splendid cavalcade; plumes and pennons fluttered, broidered mantles swayed, and amid it all, throned graceful upon white horse, the young Duchess Jenevra rode, waving slim, gauntleted hand to the joyful crowds that cheered so lustily as she passed.

Thus with majestic pomp she rode into Fidena's courtyard, there to be greeted in due state by Fortunio the victorious and Jacomo the grim. Between them she walked with gracious dignity until, being at last hidden from those many eyes, this stately Duchess became a happy, laughing girl who hugged and kissed them turn about, saying breathlessly:

"Oh, 'tis joy to see ye thus no longer armed in hateful steel! War hath made thee great, my Fortunio, so all folk honour thee—and so do I—yet most I love thee for the dear, gentle friend hast ever been since I can remember. As for thee, Jacomo, my old Jacco, hiding thy love for me in scowls and growls, stoop and let me pull thy hair for old times' sake! Oh, I joy to have ye thus safe home again!"

So she hugged, kissed and, clasping a hand of each, brought them into the hall. Here, seated between them:

"Now," said she, "I banish your Jenevra a while and speak as your sovereign liege lady. This night, my lord Fortunio, to honour you and the glory of your many achievements, is a banquet, a joy feast for this good ending to our long and bitter war, where ye twain are the honoured guests. And when I and all our court shall rise to pledge the future happiness and prosperity of our duchy, then, my lord, and you, Jacomo, with your hands in mine, I shall proclaim thee, Fortunio, not only Captain General but Lord Paramount of my Council of Ten and chiefest minister of our duchy. Also, Messire Jacomo, for your oft-proven valour, I shall name you Lord Warden of our southern——"

"How?" he exclaimed. "I—a lord, Jenevra?"

"My lord, 'tis the Duchess speaks!"

"Why then, gracious lady, of your grace spare me this! For well you know me unfit for such pageantry and show. Mere soldier am I, but also Fortunio's brother in arms and therewithal content."

"And," said the Duchess, knitting her slender brows at him, "my will is to ennoble you, Messire Jacomo."

"But," he retorted, shaking grim head at her, "my will is to be no other than I am!"

"Dare you so cross and deny me?" she demanded, long-lashed eyes flashing at him.

"Lady, in all timorous humility, I dare. Also, your noble banquet shall be the better without this clumsy, ungainly fellow that is myself——"

"My lord Jacomo, I command your attendance!"

"My gracious lady, accept my humble gratitude instead."

"S-S-So!" she hissed, clenching her fists at him. "Meaning you refuse me?"

"Meaning my place is here, and especially tonight!"

"Then you defy me?"

"Though with all submission, lady."

Her eyes flamed at him, brows contracted, fists smote at his broad chest as she panted:

"Ah, thou . . . thou graceless wretch . . . thou detestable runnion . . . thou ill-conditioned, snarling rebellious . . . oh——"

"Ay," he nodded, seizing her nearest fist in iron-like grip and kissing it very tenderly, "fetch thy breath, sweeting, then to't again! This reminds me how as furious babe thou wouldst kick me i' the chops and screech! Oho, happy days! So an wilt kick me now, let off with thy shoes, prithee." The young Duchess, struggling vainly, gnashed her teeth at him—but even then, seeing his adoring look, the whimsical smile that so gentled his harsh, scarred face, she became Jenevra, who, with sound between laugh and sob, clasped and kissed him, saying:

"Ah, Jacco, Jacco, I should have known thy doggish stubbornness! Yet will I honour thee despite thy surly, disobedient, long-loved self. Here, then," said she turning to Fortunio, "he shall bide with his self-sufficing self while tonight before all our nobility, with thy hand in mine, I shall proclaim him Lord Warden of—how, do you shake your head at me now, Fortunio?"

"Jenevra, dear lady," he answered, gently, "I needs must crave your indulgence that I cannot be your guest tonight."

"Cannot, my lord, or will not?"

"Madame, I am expecting a dispatch of the very greatest import——"

"It shall be brought to you."

Again Fortunio shook his head, and once again she raged, though now more bitterly than ever.

"You, too!" she cried, leaping afoot. "You also will defy me?"

"Dear child, here is no defiance——"

"Enough . . . oh . . . enough!" she panted. And now, being thus wildly furious, she said that which, womanlike, she knew would hurt him most:

"My lord, I have now to declare the marriage proposed so long ago betwixt myself and your brother Count Angelo shall never be . . . ah . . . never! I would rather die than

wed such craven as he that to avoid peril of battle fled safe
to England, there to read books instead of fight! So—he
shall never wed me, say or do what you will."

Fortunio merely looked at her and was silent; not so
Jacomo, for:

"Now . . . ha . . . now," he spluttered. "S'blood, here's
lie foul as the vilest deeps of hell! Shouldst be whipped,
Jenevra, smacked and slapped resoundingly for voicing such
falsity——" Speaking, he rose and so threatening of aspect
that, remembering certain undignified incidents of her not-
far-distant childhood, Jenevra had turned to flee when came
a loud, imperious knocking upon the door, which, at her
command, swung wide to admit a tall, handsome man in
prime of life whose rich attire served to offset his lithe shapeliness, a man this of such dominating personality that the
grim old hall seemed dingier by contrast with his splendidly
vital presence.

"Ah, Gonzago!" said the Duchess, reaching out her imperious hand. "My lord, you come as usual to my need."
He advanced gracefully to clasp and kiss this welcoming hand,
he bowed deeply to Fortunio, smiled merrily at Jacomo's
scowling visage and said in clear, strangely pleasing voice:

"Dearest Madame, and you my right good lord, I venture
this intrusion to inform your grace and you noble Fortunio
that the traitor Julio Morelli will trouble you no more——"

"What—is he dead?" Jacomo demanded.

"Perfectly, sir! The which, I dare to think, you must
agree is very excellent well, for as I——"

"No!" exclaimed Fortunio. "I denounce this as very ill!"

"But, most dear lord, the man was a traitor and——"

"Gonzago, this gentleman was never proved so!"

"And therefore," added Jacomo fiercely, "he was murdered! So I ask why and—who?"

"So you may, sir, but also to none effect, for I cannot
answer."

"However," said Fortunio, beginning to limp to and fro,
"this must and shall be answered tomorrow. Whence had
you this news, sir?"

"From that most worthy gentleman Sebastian, lord of the
Council, and he, as I guess, by special courier from the
south."

"The south!" repeated Fortunio. "And lately?"

"As I believe, my lord. Doth this happening so trouble and grieve you?"

"Murder is ever grievous, sir, and this especially."

"Indeed, Fortunio, I have heard vague rumour how this Messire Julio Morelli was friend of yours, the which I as your very true, most loving and faithful friend, instantly contradicted."

"Yet my friend he was, sir, and, as I believe, falsely accused. So tomorrow I will convene the Council and all concerned, and into this make close and strict enquiry."

"Very proper, my lord, very right and truly just—as is to be expected of our noble Fortunio. Shall I inform our good Sebastian?"

"Pray do. Bid him see all are present, also the courier who brought these ill tidings."

"My lord, I will. Indeed, Fortunio, I, as one who estimates your friendship at its true worth, pray you will believe me ever at your command to serve you how you will and as best I may."

"I thank you, sir!"

"Oh!" exclaimed the Duchess, fretfully. "Have done! For I weary and am sad, Gonzago; these my dear and life-long friends will not with us to our banquet. Thus, they grieve me—and this bare old hall is place of gloom, for groans and sighs 'stead of joy and laughter! Let us begone! Pray attend me to my horse. And so, my lord Fortunio, since you will thus flout my will and refuse my kindness—here shall you bide nor show yourself at court until I so command! Now, Gonzago, let us hence."

CHAPTER III

DESCRIBES A NIGHT OF DESTINY

"AHA!" EXCLAIMED Jacomo as soon as they were alone. "So much for our royal spitfire and right shrewish hell-cat! And 'Gonzago', quo' she, and gives him her hand most loving. Gonzago—pah!"

"Yet," said Fortunio, thoughtfully, "he is in every sense a man."

B

"That I now like less than afore."

"And night," sighed Fortunio, "falls apace!"

"Ay! And where is our Angelo?"

"God save him wheresoever he be!"

"Amen! And it seems God shall save him from wedding our shrewish claw-cat, the which is excellent well. For as she is proudly arrogant as her sire, Angelo is stubborn as thyself——"

"Am I stubborn, Jacomo?"

"As a mule, as a rock, ay, as this stout helmet o' thine that would yield nowise to heartiest buffets! Thus, as I'm saying, this marriage would be mere scratch and bite cat and doggery!" Here ensued a silence except for Jacomo's polishing and Fortunio's limping step, while the shadows slowly deepened upon them.

"Old friend," sighed Fortunio at last, halting in his restless walk, "he should have been with us long and long ere this."

"Lord," answered Jacomo, bending to his labour, "we hoped for and expected him at noon."

"Jacomo, what shall have stayed him, think you?"

"Lord," answered Jacomo, stooping lower, "the roads be . . . somewhat . . . perilous."

"Yet he rides not alone. . . . Ah, would to heaven I had sent an escort!"

"Ay, would you had!"

"Yet he is not alone . . . and hath a cool head!"

"Cool as thine own, Fortunio! Also with petronel and rapier few can match him—the which is no wonder, for we learned him, thou and I!"

"And yet . . . ha, Jacomo, my mind misgives me! I . . . feel a great despondency! There's evil abroad, Jacomo; I sense it i' the very air . . . this lurking menace that creepeth unseen . . . and ever nearer. . . ."

"Yet this is peace," growled Jacomo; "hark to those foolish bells! And the city full o' revelling fools and all unguarded, like this thy castle, though our gates be shut, I've seen to that! But in these walls we are alone save for old Bartoldi and a few other aged folk!"

"Well, what then, thou dismal, hangdog, growling misery? This is a night for rejoicing."

"True, my lord, and thus—whatsoever this night may bring, this is our comfort—we can die only once."

"Now out upon thee, Jacomo; what talk is this of death? Instead, go call for lights that I may read—old Plato here shall be far better company. 'Let there be light!'" Thus presently came old Bartoldi bearing tall candles in many-branched silver sconces; but even as he set them down, a horn brayed at the outer gate, whereat down went Fortunio's book again and he limped to the narrow lattice, eagerly expectant.

"Can this be Angelo—at last?" he questioned, in shaken voice; and in strangely gentle tone Jacomo answered:

"Dear my lord, I fear not. He would never summon us so, but come by the postern and secret stair i' the wall yonder."

"Ah, true, old friend," sighed Fortunio, bowing his head distressfully, nor did he look up when came Bartoldi, saying:

"My lord, a gentleman o' the court, one Messire Astorgio with message from her grace."

"The name is strange to me. Know you this gentleman, Jacomo?"

"Ay, for bedizened bladder o' lard that clacketh like a mill and to less account."

"And from the Duchess! I must see him. Go, bid him to me." So came this gentleman with small, very youthful page attendant. A very precious and extremely modish gentleman was Messire Astorgio, curled, perfumed and belaced, a creature of art from delicate shoe to stupendous ruff. He smiled, performed a complicated bow, struck an attitude and spoke:

"Right noble and most potent gracious lord, I greet you humbly yet passing well—my lord God keep you!"

"And you, sir."

"Noble and most excellent Fortunio, to thee I, as ambassador and envoy extraordinary, come from our gracious lady Duchess, this peerless paragon of all beauteous perfection, bearing unto thee for thy gracious acceptance this most precious thing yet more precious made by the lovely giver, to wit—our Duchess, no less! O page, present!"

The boy instantly kneeling, proffered his master a velvet cushion whereon reposed this gift of the Duchess, a silver goblet and a flask of wine. With beringed fingers, delicately spread, Astorgio lifted these tenderly, saying as he did so:

"Valiant Fortunio, glory-crowned victor and hero of our deliverance, lo—here within this crystal pent is wine of most ripe, most rare and notable vintage! This our gracious lady

sendeth thee, in token of her love and to thy later engorge-
ment, her loving command thus: that when creeping hand
of clock shall point the hour of ten of this most happy and
felicitous night of nights—to be forever remembered to thy
undying glory—that when at this same said hour, she herself
and all her court do rise to pledge unanimous our new-won
freedom—won by thy so valiant, potent, all conquering hand
—then, yea even then, thyself, here at thy cloistered ease, shall
also rise and thereupon drink, honouring this toast that doth
but honour thee. My lord, behold now my embassage
accompt!"

"My thanks, sir," said Fortunio, taking the flask and
setting it by. "To the Duchess my love and service. Tell her
that upon the stroke of ten I will drink this pledge." Then Fortunio saluted and limped away, leaving Messire Astorgio
gazing after him like one astonished.

"Now, by my beard," he exclaimed, caressing that silky
adornment with jewelled hand, "I do protest myself quite—
quite astonished and amazed!"

"Ah," growled Jacomo, "so am I! Sir, you have won-
derous gift o' words!"

"In faith, sir, I am something reputed therefor."

"And, sir, being such wonder 'tis no wonder. But, sir,
wherefore doth your beard so amaze you?"

"Nay, nay, sir! 'Tis not my beard, this is a familiarity.
My amazement is that yon gentleman can be the great lord
Fortunio."

"Sir, it can and is! Wherefore did he thus astonish
you?"

"For that he is so other than I, by report, expected."

"How 'other', sir?"

"Good sir, fame's loud-voiced clarions have so trumpeted
and englorified him that I protest he falleth sadly short of
my fond expectation."

"How short, sir?" enquired Jacomo, leaning nearer.

"By inches—this way and that. For meseemeth he should
to justly represent himself and justify popular expectancy, he
should, I say, be something larger of stature and more commanding of feature, form and presentment."

"Larger, sir?" enquired Jacomo, softly.

"Oh, infinitely! He should be greater to the eye as he is
to the ear; of bodily semblance vastly more heroical."

"He-roical?" said Jacomo, almost whispering.

"Even so! Heroical as Mars and as godlike! His eyes, voice, look and every gesture should command, compel——" Out shot Jacomo's powerful hand to seize the astonished speaker's delicate wrist in powerful gripe.

"So—now, sir," he growled, "I shall compel you somewhat—to use those bejemmed ears and purblind eyes. Look now upon this corselet, lo—here a lance-point smote him; there a bullet; here is dint o' sword and here an axe! Look now on this battered helmet, see—'tis nothing over-large. Yet in all this world you shall not find a head great enough to fill it. See you this plume, this handful o' sorry feathers broken now and faded all—yet many a man beholding them, 'mid shock o' battle and breaking ranks, hath forgot weariness, pain o' wounds and fear o' death, because 'neath these same feathers Fortunio fought. I've seen 'em stem defeat and, surging above the reeling press, show us the bloody path to victory. Sir, in this world be men great and small, but only one such as he. Wherefore, I had liefer lie dead upon a dunghill with Fortunio than feast with kings. And now, sir, I bid your lordly daintiness Good night."

Astorgio cherished his bruised wrist, made a half-bow, grimaced a smile and, beckoning to his little round-eyed page, departed with gallant swing of modish cloak and graceful play of slender legs.

Scarcely had this gorgeous person vanished behind closed door than Jacomo spat towards it with vehemence and exclaimed:

"That—for thee, thou thing—thou flatulent, bejewelled, ladylike no-thing!" Hearing a sound, he glanced up and beheld Fortunio smiling from the doorway of his bed-chamber.

"Truly," he nodded, "a dainty, too—too gentle man."

"Ay, by my blood! Too dainty for work, too delicate for war, too precious for aught save tripping and toeing it, bowing and scraping, primping and prattling—pah! And 'twas for such whim-whams we coarser wretches fought and endured what time they lay soft, slept sound, fed full and enjoyed the sweets o' life! As for ourselves, I am a blemish o' scars and thou goest with a limp and art besides a wifeless, childless, solitary man!"

"Not solitary, old friend; 'twere impossible with thee to plague me! Moreover, there is young Angelo——"

"Ay, but where? And the day quite sped. See at casement and loophole stealthy night peepeth!"

"Ah, verily night is upon us too soon!"

"And the clock yonder," growled Jacomo, "with its every cursed tick my fear grows, as it hath done since I heard on't."

"Heard? Of what, man?"

"The cloak! That damned cloak with its thrice accursed secret dispatch—ha, 'tis the very mark for murder——"

"Jacomo, bridle that tongue; it becomes a torment! Peace, I say! Never speak of murder and Angelo in the same breath."

"Ha, Fortunio, what a plague is this—to wait and wait! God's my life, in all our fighting I never felt the like o' this! To die in battle is clean, manly death! To be snatched by furtive shot or stealthy steel, ha—or poison, that weapon o' vile cowardice——"

"May also be manly death, Jacomo, and too often hath been ere now, alas! But no more o' this—no more, I say! I came seeking my book, my Plato."

"'Tis here, 'neath thy helmet, this good burgonet—and, Fortunio, when it fended thee in hazard o' battle, thy face never showed then so worn and haggardly as now—in this night of peace! For then, though battle, life and all were at stake, Angelo was safe! Here is thy book, and for pastime read or tell me of it, prithee."

"When didst ever incline to books, Jacomo?"

"Never till now, for mayhap in thy book is some thought may lift my mind above present care."

So Fortunio opened the book, saying:

"This was writ by the great Plato concerning his beloved teacher Socrates—one of the wisest and noblest men that ever lived—and yet he died by poison, Jacomo, and right manfully!"

"Ah! Was he murdered?"

"Ay, he was! And by his fellow Athenians after they had tried and condemned him for daring to learn them a new and better philosophy of life. And, like you and me, he had been a soldier and by account most valiant, not only in victory but defeat."

"Defeat—so!" nodded Jacomo, glancing up from the pauldron he was burnishing, "then right soldier was he! I'd fain hear more of him."

"Well, hearken to what he says before his judges!" And Fortunio read aloud: " 'When I was ordered by your generals to my post at Potidaea and at Delium and at Amphipolis I remained there at risk of my life, like other men—so 'twould be strange were I to desert my post for fear of death now—when God commandeth me, as I am persuaded he has done.' Then, Jacomo, here again: 'Athenians, I love ye right well, but I will obey God rather than you, so long as I have strength and breath, I will not cease from his work. Never will I do what I know to be evil or shrink from good—for fear of death. . . . In battle a man may 'scape death by throwing down his arms and kneeling to beg for life, and many other ways there are to avoid death—if a man be so contemptible as to say or do or promise anything, no matter how base.' "

"Good!" exclaimed Jacomo. "What like was he, this Socrates?"

"A very ugly man——"

"Aha! Good again, for I'm no Apollo! Prithee read more."

"Why then," said Fortunio, turning certain pages, "hear what he says after they have condemned him to die by poison: 'If death be absence of all sensation, a sleep untroubled by any dream, 'twill be a blessedness, a marvellous gain. But if it be only a journey to a better place where in a new life are all the noble great ones whom death has glorified —for this I am willing to die many times.' And here, Jacomo, are his last words to the tribunal: 'And since ye all, my judges, according to nature must die, I pray you shall one and all meet death with a good courage, believing this truth— that no evil can ever grieve a good man, in life, in death, or the hereafter.' And these last words, Jacomo, I have underlined because I think they are, or should be, an abiding comfort to all men!"

"Ay, truly!" nodded Jacomo. "And how did he take his death?"

"As he had lived—unfearing. For thus it is written by one who saw: 'When handed the poison-cup Socrates took it quite cheerfully, without trembling or change of feature, saying: "Now I pray my journey hence may be prosperous." Then putting the cup to his lips he drank the poison quite calmly. . . . And now my tears came fast and I covered my face, weeping not for him but for myself in losing such a friend. And all others of us lamented also until he spake us consolation, bidding us not to grieve. And this the while, to help the poison, he walked about until his legs failed. Then he lay down and the man who gave the poison began to examine his feet and legs, asking if he had any feeling there. Socrates answered No; and said that when the chill reached his heart he should be gone. And so it befell, for after brief space, he made a last, sudden movement. And when the man uncovered his face, his eyes were fixed. . . . Such was the end of Socrates who was, I am sure, the wisest, noblest and best man that I have ever known.' Well, here was a right noble end, eh, mine ancient?"

"Ay, faith!" growled Jacomo. "Poisoned like a cur-dog he died like a very man!"

Thus they talked, and with no further mention of Angelo, while the great clock above them ticked on remorselessly until came old Bartoldi to announce supper:

"Nought but cold meats, my masters, with a sallet."

"We've ate far worse!" quoth Jacomo, rising. "So bring us to't, man."

Thus presently seated in small, arras-hung chamber bright with the glow of candles, they supped together, talking of many things and events past and present, yet still without mention of Angelo, because of their fearful, ever-growing anxiety; while in the hall without, the hands of the clock crept on and on until:

"Hearken!" exclaimed Jacomo, pushing back his chair, "Ten o' the clock, 'tis the hour for our toast, Jenevra's gift—this 'most precious wine in crystal pent!' Ha, what precious fool is yon prinking Astorgio!"

So the wine was brought, the silver goblet filled and with this in hand Fortunio rose, saying:

"To the future welfare of this our State and happiness to all men, with abiding joy to those of us who died that this peace might be." Then setting goblet to lip he drank—choked and sinking back in his chair, shivered as with sudden chill. . . . Setting down the half-emptied goblet, he stared from it to Jacomo who had reached for it to drink in turn.

"Wait!" said he, in hoarse, breathless accents. "Jacomo—wait!"

"Why—how now, my lord, what's here?"

"Horror, Jacomo! The . . . hidden hand . . . again, but . . . it hath struck true . . . at last. I'm poisoned!

They have succeeded . . . this time! So, touch not the wine, Jacomo!"

"Nay, but, my lord . . . oh, God, Fortunio, this was sent us by the Duchess, our Jenevra——"

"Yet—poison, Jacomo! I'm . . . dying! See how . . . I shake . . . how I sweat! Ah, merciful Jesu . . . let it be . . . soon!"

Dumb with grief and amazement, Jacomo stared down into this so loved face now wet and drawn with the throes of swiftly approaching death. . . . The spasm passing, these pallid lips spoke again and less distressfully:

"To sleep, or perchance to meet all . . . those great ones whom death . . . hath glorified——"

"No—ah, no!" groaned Jacomo, falling to his knees. "Oh, Fortunio, my lord . . . Oh, loved master and friend, not death! And yet if this be so as now seemeth too sure, into death will I follow thee. As side by side we fought, so will we go together in a friendship which I do pray God shall be eternal."

"Nay, Jacomo, old friend, wait . . . wait God's own time. . . . Live on! Jenevra and the State shall need thee."

"Yet I need thee, lord! And being a selfish man, thee will I have to follow and serve in death as in life!" So saying, Jacomo brimmed the goblet and lifting it in steady hand, emptied it at a draught.

And now ensued a period not to be described, wherein the devilish venom did its cruel work on pain-racked, writhing bodies; but by degrees soul rose triumphant above perishing flesh, for, amid the gloom that deepened upon them, they talked, heartening one another so long as speech and strength endured:

"My lord . . . Fortunio, I . . . am with thee . . . now and ever——"

"Ay, I see thee yet . . . though, Jacomo, mine ancient . . . no banner have I for . . . thee to bear. . . ."

"Instead, lord . . . my hand."

"Ay, I feel it . . . and in this gloom. . . . Oh, I am . . . marvellous glad of thee . . . Jacomo, for I . . . have so truly loved thee. . . . Ah, now . . . it cometh . . . cold, cold and . . . darkness! But thou art here, my Jacomo, and . . . beyond is . . . light. . . ."

The bells rang on, though Fortunio heard not, and though Jacomo scowled, it was not now because of their merry pealing; for with hands fast clasped, these brothers in arms so long together in peril of life, were in death together still.

CHAPTER IV

HOW THE JOY-BELLS CEASED TO RING

"Gonzago, what . . . what o' God's name . . . hast done?"

"Sebastian, good my lord, sit and fetch thy breath."

Staring wide-eyed at the speaker's handsome, smiling face, Sebastian, lord and chief of the Council of Ten, tall, stately, and imposing, saw that which seemed to rob him of all dignity and strength also, for, sinking weakly into the proffered chair and quite forgetting his usual stateliness, he cowered back, saying in breathless whisper:

"Your . . . your message—if . . . if it be true——"

"It is true."

"Reckless folly! Oh, madman . . . madman!"

Still faintly smiling, Gonzago surveyed his agitated visitor feature by feature—the long nose, wide mouth and pointed chin, the sombre eyes deepset beneath jut of brow and high forehead gleaming wetly in the candle light.

"Gonzago, what has thou done?"

"All that was needed, Sebastian! Hearken to those joy-bells—tomorrow they shall hush to different tune."

"Forbid . . . forbid it, heaven!"

"My lord, heaven shall not trouble for such mere every-day earthly doing. Tomorrow's sun shall still beam on us— and on this duchy, the which tonight's doing shall have changed somewhat and—to our advantage."

"Did I not . . . and most expressly . . . forbid?"

"And did I not, more expressly, smile?"

"What . . . ha, Gonzago, how if this . . . this thing be discovered . . . how then?"

"What thing, Sebastian?"

"The——" Sebastian gulped, leaned nearer and whispered: "The . . . change o' flasks?"

"Then must we try again, with a difference."

"Not I, b'my faith, not I, no . . . no! Never this way, Gonzago!"

"Any and every way, Sebastian, to gain my purpose—and thine, to be sure!"

"Gonzago, I'll none of it! No more, never again! Thy too-reckless feet tread path too slippery——"

"And thine also, Sebastian! For thee now is no turning back, 'tis too late. Where I tread, thou must needs follow—up and up to the heaven of my desires, and thine, or down and down to perdition and the headsman's sword! 'Tis one way or other for such as we."   "

Sebastian rose and, like one distraught, took a hasty turn up and down the chamber while Gonzago's languorous-seeming eyes watched and upon his shapely mouth the same faintly-mocking smile as he said gently:

"My poor Sebastian, compose thyself. Sit down again and let us, like the highly virtuous fellow-conspirators we are, converse upon a lovelier theme—our imperious Duchess, this so feminine, delicious provocation to all the cardinal sins! Talk we of her, what time we wait together."

"Eh—wait? For what—for what?"

"Glad tidings, happy news of our success, how we this night have——"

"No no!" gasped Sebastian, hands violently out-thrown in horrified repulsion. "Not so! Whatever hath been done this night is thine—thy deed alone—of thy sole contrivance and done against my counsel."

"True, thou art a councillor, Sebastian, and honey-tongued orator beside. Thy business is the skilful use of words and subtle manage of phrases that, spoke or writ, they may be taken either or any way best suited to thine own advantage. Thou art by nature smoothly supple as an eel, a man so adroit that all other men esteem thee at thine own valuation. To all that do see and hear thee, my lord, thou art right noble gentleman of honour so impeccable they have made thee Lord of the Council, and our wilful Duchess ever heedful of thy advice. And so it is I use thee, my worthy lord."

"Use? Use—me——" Words failing him, Sebastian raised clenched hands; but even as he trembled, thus fury-choked, Gonzago laughed softly, beckoned languidly and said gently:

"Come, fellow-plotter, sit at ease. Waste not thyself in such pettiness as anger; 'tis the futility of fools! Come now, empty

me thy mind, speak me thy virtuous troubles, and if in thee
be any fear, I shall rid thee of it. Tell me the wherefore of
those trembling hands, that moist, care-wrung brow. Speak!"
And crouched again in his elbow-chair, Sebastian replied in
soft though furious voice:

"Gonzago, 'twas I, years agone, singled thee out, brought
thee to court, made thee known to Her Grace the Duchess and
by my influence and good-will made thee all thou art——"

"Nay, Sebastian, I am none of thy making; 'twere far
beyond thee! God or the Devil made me that I am, angel of
light or fiend of the pit, child of heaven or spawn of hell, one
or other, or both am I! As for thee, Sebastian, thou art neither
one nor other, being merely—thy so virtuous-seeming self!
Now how can such as I displeasure such as thee?—I that do
soar so high above all things that can but creep!"

"Thou?" retorted Sebastian, in tone very like a snarl. "Thou
art becoming my dis-ease and like to be thine own calamity!
There is in thee a fevered madness, a youthful hurry of the
spirit that by such ill-considered haste may ruin all!"

"Yet indeed," smiled Gonzago, "though warm and quick with
jocund youth, I am also man cold and resolute in action——"

"Thou art creature of impulse, Gonzago, ever running
blindly whereas thou shouldst walk circumspectly."

"I do neither, Sebastian; I fly! Like falcon to quarry I
stoop, hit or miss, and have never failed thus far."

"Yet there have been failures——"

"Ay, truly, by others! Even I cannot be everywhere. As,
for instances, being here I cannot also be—there, at the inn
we wot of—eh, my worthy lord—the Black Horse——"

"Hush!" gasped Sebastian. "Use no names——"

"Nay, be easy; we are private here, now as ever—as we
were, and in this very chamber, when thou, my Sebastian,
didst first propose and inspire me to——"

"Oh, never—never to such—such extremity as—this!"

"Why truly," laughed Gonzago, "being such master of
words thou didst lap thy meaning in such noble utterance
and with such high-sounding phrases that murder then seemed
a virtue and this night's work the very act of God!"

"Never—oh, never!" gasped Sebastian. "'Twas yourself
mistook me, misjudged me then as—as you do even now."

"Sebastian, I know how the magic of thy tongue can show
evil to be good, transform devil to seeming angel, hell to

paradise, and charm all to believe thee a
yet do so truly seem."

"Nay . . . not so. . . . I protest——"

"Thus I judge thee so rightly, my Sebastian, that
make thee great and greatly use thee when I am duke."

"Heaven's . . . light!" gasped Sebastian. "Dare thy—thy
vaulting, mad ambition leap so high?"

"Dost think aught else shall content me?"

"Nay, I—I know not what to think!"

"Then ponder our success."

"Nay there have been so many failures that my mind misgives me now for what is done and—is doing! Those—
others!"

"Which and who, I pray thee?"

"Thy—fellows—at the inn! Those—those instruments of
thine."

"Ours, Sebastian! Our murderers three! Now why blench
at the word? Come, be thy truest self with me. For do I not
know thee, Sebastian? Have I not followed thee and taken
thy measure, read thy most secret mind? Moreover, art thou
not deeply concerned with me in this most necessary shedding
of——"

"Hush! Oh . . . for love of God——"

"Fie! Call not on God, Sebastian, lest He blast thee! Cry
rather on the Devil, the Fiend, Santhanas and all his——
Hark!"

"What now?" gasped Sebastian, starting up. "I—I hear
nought!"

"Indeed, she is sweetly light of foot."

Came a tapping on the door, which opened to disclose a
woman, young was she though of dark and sullen beauty,
and, frowning, she said:

"There be two would see your lordship."

"Two only, Madonna?"

"Lord, only two."

"Well, bid them hither—when I summon."

"Two?" exclaimed Sebastian, so soon as the door had
closed. "There should be three! Ha, what shall this portend? Failure again! Failure, I say, and this time—disaster,
final and most dreadful! This hath been my dread ever since
Morelli fled our most intimate counsels——"

"Meaning our conspiracy, Sebastian! Yet, as we know,

id betray us. Julio Morelli

? How then?"

ian, the dead shall speak——"

o, our ruin! Shame and a dread-

retch, we shall die in fashion most
et us see and question our mur-

not be seen."

as with thee," said Gonzago; and, draw-
ing a   histle from the breast of his doublet, he
sounded a   elodious call, answered almost immediately
by tread of he y feet, then the door was set wide and, with
gallant swing of cloak, jingle of spurs and flourish of plumed
hat, Annibal presented himself, saying:

"Noble sir, most gracious lord, our mission is duly performed, truly achieved and perfectly accompt. In proof
whereof—behold this cloak of velvet black and with silver
broidery enriched."

"And here," growled Rodrigo, stepping forward, "this hat
with feather o' scarlet."

"Found ye any letter or despatch?"

"None, my lord, and we, as usual, were right marvellous
thorough and infinitely zealous."

"What of young Florizel?"

"My lord, the debate was something sharp, nay, I'm bold
to say of a bitter contestance and in gloom pitch-black, the
which ending, and Florizel not with us, 'tis to be presumed
he could not, ergo—that he is dead."

"I grieve for him, Annibal."

"We also, my good lord. Though his loss may be soon
made good and place filled by a better."

"Yet I mourn him," sighed Gonzago, laying three well-
filled purses on the table. "The young should never die; youth
and death should ever be strangers, save in cases most ex-
ceptional. Well, here is your promised fee, and Florizel's also
—share it betwixt you."

"Ha, gracious lord, here is princely wage!"

"So shall it ever be—whiles you be faithful. Now off with
you to yon clamorous revel, be merry yet watchful for my
interest. And so good night to ye." Scarcely had Annibal

bowed himself and Rodrigo away, closing the door, than out
from the arras stepped Sebastian, saying and in tone altered
as his look:

"So all is well; Morelli sent no message!"

"Indeed, 'twould seem we were in time, Sebastian, and
that death—that is to say—we, thou and I, Sebastian—
silenced him ere he could betray us by wag of tongue or twirl
of pen! And talking of death, see—this was Count Angelo's
cloak and most eloquently bloody! Lo—here went forth his
life and——" Gonzago's shapely lips were suddenly dumb.
Out flashed his dagger to rip and slash—then from this dreadfully stained garment he drew a small, folded paper, at sight
of which Sebastian cowered again.

"Ah!" he groaned. "I knew it—I knew it! My dread was
merited! Read . . . read! Let me hear! Read, I say!"

Slowly unfolding this paper, Gonzago read slowly and in
his strangely pleasant voice:

" 'To Fortunio, Captain General, these in all haste. Arrest
the lords Sebastian and Gonzago, these the chief conspirators.
Others there be though not personally known of me. This
warning, given and writ at peril of my life, should suffice.
Pray know me now for thy grievous yet assured friend, Julio
Morelli.' "

"Here," gasped Sebastian, "is our ruin and death! Burn
it! I say . . . burn it . . . let me see it no more than ash
. . . and ash, dust . . . and dust scattered to nothingness!
Gonzago, burn it, I say! Be rid of this fearsome peril; burn
it!"

"Not so, thou purblind, panic soul! This, with proper
manage and some small alteration, shall serve our future
interests right well. Let us suppose this so fateful missive be
made to read thus: 'To Sebastian, Lord of the Council these:
Arrest Count Angelo of Fidena for traitorous correspondence
with known enemies'—and so forth—ha? Thus, my Sebastian, when our lord Fortunio's death is known as—we hope
—it soon must be, the popular outcry will be 'murder' and
all men athirst for vengeance. Then publish this our amended
dispatch and this shall explain the why and wherefore of
Fortunio's dying! Now dost thou begin to see?"

"Somewhat, ay—yet be more explicit."

"Well then, our Great Fortuno, this high and truly noble
gentleman, learning of his young brother's death and shameful

treachery, and being himself so proud and godlike, shall prefer
death to such dishonour and himself by death translate himself above such infamy and——"

"Ha, this," exclaimed Sebastian, eagerly, "should serve—
were we but certain——?"

"Meaning certain of his death, Sebastian? I am, as thou
shalt be, and soon, I guess. But now of this letter, this most
precious dispatch that shall hush all cries of 'murder' and
stay the vengeful quest, we need but an able penman, a
skilled——" Gonzago paused to smile and lift one slender
finger—for the riotous bells were stilled, their joyous clamour
hushed, and in this sudden quiet was something awful,
though Gonzago yet smiled, saying:

"So, my lord, the bells have answered thee! Presently
they shall, as I foretold, be tolled for the grief of our Great
Fortunio's passing. For great was he indeed, a truly noble
man in deed and look and word, nor is there one in all the
duchy to honour him more than I, or cherish his memory
with greater reverence."

"Gonzago . . . when thou dost speak . . . and look as
now . . . then do I almost . . . fear thee."

"Howbeit, Sebastian, for us now—all is well; despite heaven
and all its power, crafty Roguery hath triumphed over peerless Virtue; Guilt is victorious! Thus at last our way lieth
open before us; all things to us now are possible; all our
fondest desires to be realized. Come then, my Sebastian, good
fellow-schemer; in this night of destiny, let us drink to ourselves, our golden future and—victorious Guilt. Drink!"

CHAPTER V

TELLS HOW, TOO LATE, COUNT ANGELO CAME TO FIDENA

IN THE city was tumult; rapturous joy gave place to grief,
despair and growing fury, for while some wailed and wept,
others raved and clamoured for vengeance instant and bloody;
brandished steel glittered and the air rang with shouts and
screams of: "Death! Death to the murderers!"

Through the wild hubbub of this frenzied multitude, two
soldiers, fierce-seeming, powerful men, forced their way until

at last, having won free of the clamorous city, they paused
to regain their breath, gazing round about and upon each
other like the utterly dismayed fellows they were.

"Andrea," said the first, "I'll never believe it till these eyes
do tell me 'tis so."

"Nor I, Manfred, nor I! 'Tis calamity too vast for belief.
For, an this be true, then here's an end to all—and woe to our
duchy!"

"Andrea, would I were blind ere my eyes do tell me such
fearsome thing! Come, let's on—to know the truth on't one
way or t'other and right speedily."

Thus, breathless and sweating with haste, they came to
Fidena, this castle where no man watched and no familiar
voice answered their distressful shouts. . . . From courtyard
to hall they tramped together, and from room to room until,
opening a certain door——

"Mother o' God!" gasped Manfred, reeling back.

"Ah, blessed Jesu!" groaned Andrea, falling to his knees.
And, after a while:

"Lookee," whispered Manfred, "how he sitteth—as he but
rested, all at ease!"

"Ah!" whispered Andrea. "And Jacomo . . . kneeleth as
in prayer."

"And their hands, Andrea, their hands fast clasped."

"Ay! They ever loved each other in life, so do they now
in death. Come away, Manfred; this place is by them made
too holy."

"And I . . . oh, Andrea, I am blind now . . . blind with
grief! Reach me thy hand."

So they left this chamber of death, closing the door with
reverent gentleness; and being come into the echoing hall,
they sank down, there at the great table, staring on each other
in a sorrow beyond words, and no sound to break the dreadful hush about them save the slow, solemn tick of the clock.

"So," groaned Andrea, at last, "'tis true! And a God's
name, what now? What must—what can we do?"

"Never ask me, Andrea; I'm heart-broke, spirit-broke and
lost! Nought can ever be the same again. This that was a
fairish world is now a cursed dog-hole!"

"But how—how came such death? I saw no blood."

"Nor I. Yet dead are they . . . by act o' God, or foul
contrivance o' the fiend!"

"Ah—murder!" exclaimed Andrea. "Yet—can it be so?"

"Ay, what other can it be?"

"Yet they showed no wound, no single mark of violence. Then in what furtive, dreadful shape came death, Manfred? How can men die and show so marvellous peaceful?"

"These were no ordinary men, Andrea! Thus—perchance death was the more kindly, I pray the blessed saints this was so—ay, even though murder crept sudden, unseen and——" Manfred's bearded lips stiffened to silence, but even then out flashed his dagger and he crouched, whispering:

"Footsteps!"

"I hear," breathed Andrea, drawing sword. Then, from somewhere beyond or within the massive wall, a voice hailed, faintly:

"Oho—within! Is there none to welcome me?" At this familiar voice sword and dagger were sheathed instantly and these two men, officers of Fortunio's famous, hard-fighting guard, rose to stare towards a certain curtained alcove with looks of very dreadful expectation; the curtain stirred, was drawn aside and into the candle-light, pale and dusty with travel, stepped Count Angelo. For a moment he paused to shade dazzled eyes, then:

"Andrea!" he cried, joyfully. "And Manfred, too! Oh, dear friends well met, indeed. Give me your hands. I came by the old secret stair yonder where we played as boys. But tell me—why is the castle unguarded? And wherefore so silent? Is not Fortunio here? Heaven forbid he is away when I so weary for sight of him! Ah—why look ye so? And both dumb! Is my lord away . . . on business . . . at the court? How—silent yet? Speak—is my brother here? Speak, Manfred."

"My lord, he is."

"Where then? And why this stillness, this—this dreadful hush? And why—why ring those mournful bells? Andrea, I charge thee—speak, answer me!"

"Lord . . . dear Angelo . . .!"

"Ha, why dost choke? Why do thy hands so gripe and shake? Is aught amiss? Is my brother sick? How is Fortunio?"

"Angelo . . . my dear lord," groaned Manfred, "all is . . . very well with him."

"Ah," whispered Angelo, backing from them, "if this be so, why show ye thus . . . livid . . . as corpses? What is the horror in thine eyes, Andrea? Why do I . . . all sudden . . . quake . . . as with a palsy? And . . . Oh, dear Christ, why . . . why do the city's bells ring a death knell? Oh, God!" he whispered. "Oh, God of mercy—not this, not this! Forbid . . . ah . . . forbid it——"

Speech seemed to fail him and for a moment he leaned weakly upon the table, then cried aloud in dreadful voice: "Fortunio, speak! Come to me! Brother, I am here at last! Fortunio, for love of God . . . let me hear thy loved voice . . . once more—speak!"

Ensued now a space of dreadful silence; a stillness which became so unbearable at last that, with sudden gesture, Angelo started erect, strode across the hall and, as if guided by instinct, turned aside to a certain door and, thrusting it open, entered that small, silent chamber of death. . . .

"Here," whispered Andrea, cowering, "here is most dreadful thing, Manfred!"

"Ah!" whispered Manfred, glaring about helplessly. "Here's madness, or mayhap—another dying!"

"He is far beyond our comfort, Manfred."

"Ay, and of all the holy angels, besides! What shall he be doing so long there with his dead?"

"Praying, I hope!"

"No prayer shall ever bring back our lord Fortunio! Nor shall we ever see his like again. As for young Angelo, we must——"

"Hist, man—yonder he is! And himself now like death!"

"So God and the saints help him!"

Angelo's head was bare now, his down-bent face hidden in his long, dark hair. Standing thus, he turned and twisted his hat in restless hands, gazing down at it with eyes wide though sightless, and when he spoke it was in drowsy, broken voice:

"Death, sirs, hath been . . . marvellous busy about me o' late and . . . in especial with those I most loved. . . . First, my English John . . . now Jacomo that would ride me on his shoulder when I was a small imp . . . and lastly . . . my brother that I am too late to see in life. . . . Far better I had died with John upon the road . . . than such homecoming as this."

"Angelo . . . dear my lord," groaned Manfred, venturing a step nearer.

"Nay, sir, grieve not for me. Save all your sorrow for this duchy; hers is the greater loss. Fortunio is dead—he that was our shield, our ever constant need and hope for the future, is now a senseless, silent lump for burial! This man of men! Yet there be thousands for whom the grave doth yawn, their dying a benefit to all—the Tyrant whose reeking, red, ambitious heel doth grind the face of a nation —traitors, hypocrites, friends forsworn and sycophants that wink upon iniquity—things of foulness, that, wriggling 'neath the wide arc of heaven, contaminate the very air whereby other vileness is bred! Thus, see you, Evil persists and Fortunio dies! Wherefore now I grope and grope vainly to find the hand of God."

"Oh," gasped Andrea, "my lord, Angelo—Angelo——"

"Indeed, Angelo am I, though truly of no deed being one of small doing and little worth—wherefore I live while yonder Fortunio sitteth dead! This man so mighty of deed and thought! This inspirer of other men! This conquer of armies and so resistless in battle, so wise and potent in council— yonder he sits now so pitifully helpless he shall fall at a push and lie to be trodden upon! Thus endeth our great and good Fortunio . . . and my loved brother! So—now come I to know the how and who of it, nor rest until I bring his slayers to God's justice or die of it."

"And, by God, we are with thee!" cried the two, almost in a breath.

Then Angelo tossed aside the hat and, coming to them, took a hand of each, saying:

"Andrea and Manfred, we that were boys together, tonight Fortunio's death shall make us brothers. Let us vow devotion to his memory and never to rest until God's justice is done upon his murderers. Amen!"

"Amen," repeated the two, reverently.

"Now sit, brothers, and counsel me, for these long years of absence have made me a stranger. Yet first—when was this evil wrought, think ye?" And Manfred answered:

"Scarce two hours since, I reckon, eh, Andrea?"

"'Twould be about then the bells changed their note."

"And how think ye it was done?"

"'Tis past our imagining!" sighed Andrea.

"Ay," quoth Manfred, "for there is no spot o' blood or——" He checked and averted his head, abashed.

"Nay," said Angelo, clapping hand on his broad shoulder, "speak forthright, Manfred; I were fool to be squeamish. Indeed there was no blood nor any sign of violence; instead there is a wine flask and silver goblet. Go fetch them, Manfred."

"Ah—poison!" exclaimed Andrea. "We thought of this and yet scarce dared so think or speak on it, for—Angelo, this same wine as we do know, Manfred and I, was sent by her grace and most expressly."

"So?" murmured Angelo. "The Duchess?"

"And this the very flask and here the cup!" said Manfred setting them upon the table. Angelo glanced from one to other with dilating eyes, then slowly reached for and took up the goblet; he peered into it, smelt it, probed the dregs in it with questing finger-tip, tasted, sipped, spat vehemently and, setting down this fatal thing, stared at it beneath drawn brows.

"Poison?" Andrea questioned, softly.

"A devil's subtle brew!" sighed Angelo.

"But . . . nay, but," stammered Manfred, appalled, "this was a gift . . . of the Duchess . . . bestowed by her own hand!"

"So Andrea tells me."

"But to . . . to suspect . . . our Duchess——?"

"Manfred, shall rank and high estate exempt her? Moreover, this may not be her gift."

"But, Angelo, alas—it is—in very truth. We saw, Andrea and I; we can swear to it."

"Then would ye swear like fools. This wine may have been changed on its way hither. Who conveyed it?"

"The lord Astorgio."

"I mind him for a prattling, pedantical whiffler. He is no murderer nor accomplice—none would trust such babbler."

"Yet 'twas he brought it."

"Yet shall braying ass turn tiger, prating jackdaw to stooping falcon? Who is there now at court or in the State that by this hellish deed hath most to gain?"

"None that I know."

"Nor I."

"Then who, now at court and beside the Duchess, is greatest?"

"The lord Sebastian Valetti."

"Ay, he is chiefest councillor of the Ten since Morelli fled."

"Mean you Julio Morelli that was once my brother's friend?"

"That same. But he was accused of treason, falsely as some do think, and fled for his life."

"So?" murmured Angelo. "And 'twas Julio Morelli sent me the cloak."

"Ay," said Andrea, taking it up, "'tis here, Angelo!"

"Nay, this was my friend John's! That I mean was stolen . . . stolen! And wherefore? Why should they take my cloak and leave poor John's?"

"My lord, what of this cloak?"

"So much, Andrea, that I fear my poor friend died of it! As briefly thus. Scarce are we safe ashore and at our inn, he and I, than cometh a dusty messenger bearing to me a black velvet cloak garnished with silver, saying 'tis a gift from his lord Julio Morelli. So, in this cloak I rode . . . then were we so often assailed by divers rogues . . . and as I now suspect, all by reason of that same cloak! Nearing home, it was my friend's whim to change habits with me and thus, he in my cloak and I in his, we came as evening fell to the inn of the Black Horse. And here yet again we were beset and my poor John killed, and, as I now believe, in mistake for me. Thus, 'twould seem he died of my hat and cloak, a most deadly and virulent disease!"

"Ah!" sighed Andrea. "Here was more villainy!"

"But why," questioned Manfred, "why should the rogues take your hat and cloak? That's the question!"

"Whereto I can find two answers: to wit, to prove their wearer was dead, or because hid in that cloak was something of value . . . a jewel of price . . . a secret message? One or other. Thus the question I ask is: to whom was this manifest proof of my death shown? Who employed these murderers? Have ye now any ideas?"

"None, Angelo, none!"

"Nor I, alas!"

"Yet, brothers, here somewhere about us is a stealthy evil."

"Ah," snarled Manfred, clenching hairy fists, "hither or yon is lurking Iniquity, creeping, bloody-handed Treachery!"

"True," said Andrea, with helpless gesture; "yet how may we uncover it, how come at it? We are lost i' the dark and all bemused! What shall guide us, show us light and point us the way?"

"Villainy itself!" replied Angelo, grimly. "For Villainy triumphant shall grow boastful, so overweening and malapert, it shall betray itself, especially to such as we whose eyes and ears shall be ever on the alert! Also, my brothers, we have this one advantage—Villainy believeth me dead, the proof my hat and cloak. Thus I who now speak to you am a ghost— and right ghostly will I act——" Even as the words were uttered, they started, all three, and turned as from somewhere nearby rose a soft, shrill wailing that died to a twitter and was gone.

"Saints . . . defend us!" gasped Manfred, clutching dagger-hilt. "What foul thing was yon?"

"Hush!" whispered Angelo; and after a brief pause the dismal sound was repeated nearer and plainer.

"Some . . . thing . . . comes!" whispered Manfred, and out again flickered his ready steel.

"Stir not!" whispered Angelo, with commanding gesture. Thus motionless and silent, they waited till once again came this desolate wail—that changed suddenly to the running trill of merry, liquid notes of a pipe and therewith a faint jingling like fairy bells, that grew ever louder until—into the hall on parti-coloured, capering legs tripped a jester or buffoon, a lean fellow whose comical visage was framed in a hood with cockscomb affaunt and ass's ears adangle and adorned with little bells like his escalloped cap; in one hand he grasped a pipe—in the other fool's bauble, which he flourished in airy salutation as, with ridiculously ceremonious bow, he cried:

"Sweet gallants, most noble lordings, hither come I to glad ye with dance, song, quip, quirk and quiddity in the fond and foolish hope that, being fool of parts, my folly shall befool ye for my part that ye shall, for your part, part, for my part, with such trifling fee or guerdon as may impart——"

"Off!" snarled Manfred, rising. "Lord, I'll see this fool out and about his business."

"Indeed," said Angelo, thoughtfully, "I'd fain see him about his business——"

"Fie—fie!" cried the Jester, approaching with fantastic dancing steps. "Such business can no business be, since Folly is too wise for such folly."

"Tell me," said Angelo, beckoning him nearer, "how long hast played the fool?"

"Since fool I was, sir, that's to say—since I could so think."

"Then shall thinking swell the list of fools?"

"Very! For since he that thinketh himself wise is a fool, and he that knoweth himself fool is, so thinking, wise, wise by ye by nowise so wisely thinking."

"Hast a nimble wit——"

"Ah, lording, I am a genius and there's my tragical sorrow! For though genius being of the mind, and therefore transcendental, may soar above base body, perch on a moonbeam, ride the wind, juggle with the stars and pierce the illimitable distances beyond, yet must it perforce sink back to earth to eat, alas! For here's the shame on't. Genius hath a belly! Thus, let him mount to heaven yet shall belly drag him down again. So, by reason of this baser part I am no better than I am, a poor, strolling Folly that must needs fool, since belly's need is constant and inconstant, alack, its filling." "

"So folly doth not pay then?"

"But poorly, sir, since every man is his own fool these days and we of the profession be out of place and ill served. This day I have taken so much money I might swallow it at a gulp."

Drawing forth his purse, Angelo emptied it upon the table, saying:

"Couldst swallow this?"

"At a gulp!" nodded the jester, patting the worn pouch at his girdle.

"Here be—eighty odd ducats. How like you them?"

"Like, quoth'a? I'm in love with 'em, yet would jilt 'em for eight hundred."

"These shall be yours for a consideration."

"Then, most beneficial lord, I'll sing ye, dance ye, rhyme and riddle ye——"

"Nay," said Angelo, beckoning. "Tonight I myself would play the wanton wag—hearken in your ear . . ." Then while his two companions watched gloomily askance, Angelo rose and, drawing the Jester aside, spoke him whispering and to such effect that the Jester, forgetting his antic drollery, grew solemn, staring like one greatly astonished.

"Come, take up the money!" said Angelo. The Jester's obedience was instant.

"What now, my noble master?" he enquired, closing his thus well-filled pouch with quivering fingers. "What now?"

"Go, wait me in the court-yard."

Now, when the Jester had departed, Angelo took up his sheathed rapier, loosed off his dagger and gave them to his wondering companions, saying:

"Brothers of mine, keep these in memory of Count Angelo who on this so fatal night was murdered at the Black Horse inn. Thus, when you hear mention of him and his sudden end, as you will ere long, then shall you with woeful visage shake your heads and sigh: 'Alas, poor Angelo, that he should die so soon!' And now, for the time, my right trusty ones, farewell."

"Nay, but, my lord," cried Manfred, "what's for us?"

"And," pleaded Andrea, "what wilt thou do now, Angelo?"

"Do?" he repeated, turning for one last look at that closed door. "Why now, being dead, what should I do but flit like disembodied spirit, and haunt as ghost should do? As for yourselves—remember we hence forth are a trinity of vengeance, a triune nemesis for remorseless justice, to do and dare all until this unseen, unknown stealthy evil shall be uncovered, rooted out and utterly destroyed! To the which good end I pray God strengthen us. . . . And so farewell."

CHAPTER VI

TELLS HOW THE FOOL UTTERED WARNING

IT WAS morning, and so early that birds, near and far, were carolling their first glad welcome to this new day, while the young sun, low as yet, sent his level beams to light small fires in dewy grass and deck every flower and leaf with sparkling gems, making this fragrant garden a place of glory; and amid it all, a girl was culling flowers while she sang softly-sweet as any bird:

> "The daisies and the violets
> Have op'ed their pretty eyes
> And to the young, new risen sun
> Do breathe their fragrant sighs;
> The throstle tunes his little pipe,
> The lark doth sing full clear,
> To call me from my drowsy bed
> For that glad day is here——"

"Fiametta!" The singer hushed and clasping the new-gathered flowers to her bosom, turned to say, breathlessly:

"Ippolito . . . my lord. . . ." Tall, strong and eager with young life he came to meet her, then paused and thus for a space they stood to gaze glad-eyed on one another.

"Oh, Fiametta," he murmured, "thou'rt all golden loveliness, sweetly pure and fresh as this happy day-spring!"

"But," sighed she, shaking lovely head, "we should not be thus glad, the morn and I—and our noble Fortunio so lately and so—dreadfully—dead! And the Duchess, my poor Jenevra, so grief-stricken, and all the court in mourning! Oh, and I so heedless to sing!"

"So do I thank God for thee, Fiametta! Thou'rt as these flowers and birds that bloom in beauty and sing thus joyfully because 'tis so their nature and therefore the will of God. Thou, like this fair world, art formed for joy."

"And yet," sighed she, "in this fair-seeming world is yet such wickedness that a noble gentleman dies and, as I hear, by—murder!"

"Ah, 'tis only too true!"

"But why should such as he that was so good die so cruelly?"

"For that Evil is ever at dagger-point with Good."

"Shall evil then vanquish good?"

"Never—or this world would sink back to barbarian savagery. Thus in the end Good hath ever been victorious and ever will be."

"Then why is our good Fortunio dead and buried?"

"Because Evil, being selfish, is forever intent on evil, while Good, heedless of self, giveth all care to the welfare of others. 'Twas thus and wherefore died my lord Fortunio."

"I grieve that I saw so little of him, for he was seldom at home or here at court."

"True! His life was spent fighting that others might live in joy of freedom."

"But you, my lord, fought in the battle beside him and so knew him well."

"'Twas so my honour."

"And saved his life, Ippolito!"

"Why now . . . how dost know this?"

"The lord Gonzago told me how at peril of thy life thou——"

"But Gonzago was in none of the fighting."

"Yet he spake me of it as he had seen——"

"Ha!" exclaimed Ippolito, frowning up at a lark that carolled above them. "Speak you often with him?"

"Indeed, my lord," she answered, quick to heed this frown, "as often as I will."

"So!" quoth Ippolito, frown deepening to scowl. "And how think you of this fine gentleman?"

"As do we all," she replied, smiling behind her flowers, "that he is very grand gentleman and—splendidly handsome!"

"True!" said Ippolito, scornfully. "I hear he is greatly esteemed by you court ladies! 'Tis even said he presumes to pay amorous homage to our Duchess! Yet this I will not believe."

"Oh, but 'tis verily so, my lord. And, 'twixt you and me, I think his wooing will not be in vain."

"S'life, Madame! You never mean she will stoop to wed him?"

"And why not, prithee? He is of a noble house, and was also lord Fortunio's dear friend."

"God's my life—here's news! Whence had you it?"

"Why, everyone at court knoweth how he was lord Fortunio's loved and trusted friend."

"Though seldom in my lord's company and by him never mentioned—this I know, for I was Fortunio's esquire! So much for your court gossip! And now you tell me the Duchess will wed him——"

"Nay, my lord, I tell you no more than this: that of her many suitors he is not the least favoured"

"And so I marvel!"

"At his good fortune?"

"At his audacity!"

"'Twould seem you have small liking for this fortunate gentleman?"

"I have none, Madame."

"My lord, neither have I."

"Oh then," said Ippolito, his scowl vanishing, "away with him! Instead, tell me of thy most dear self."

"Am I so dear, my lord?"

"Indefinitely dear, dear lady. Since that blessed moment when my eyes beheld thee for what thou truly art."

"Oh?" she murmured. "Now I pray thee . . . what am I, my lord?"

"Nay, first thou must name me for what I so truly am."

"Well, what art thou, my lord?"

"Thine own dear, most truly loving Ippolito. Nay, ask me so." And, meekly submissive, she enquired:

"Most dear and loving Ippolito, what am I?"

"The one and only woman I shall ever love!" he replied fervently. "The dear memory I have so treasured in my heart, the woman for whom I fought and would have died, the woman for whom I hope to live, the woman shaped to fill these yearning arms of mine! So, Fiametta, let them be filled—at last. Wilt thou, my beloved?"

She hesitated, glanced swiftly up and around—then, swift and graceful as a fawn, leapt to the shelter of a tall yew hedge nearby and, turning there, slim fingers on ruddy, smiling lip, beckoned him beside her and, as he joined her, whispered:

"Hush—yonder cometh my lord Astorgio!"

"Plague take him! What shall lure Sir Daintiness abroad at such hour?"

And pointing to her own lovely self, Fiametta whispered:

"Me! So let us to yon arbour lest he find us, for he is become my most persistent wooer!"

"So?" muttered Ippolito, fiercely.

"Even so!" she retorted, demurely. "He wooeth and sueth, moaneth and groaneth, peeketh and pineth; he wooeth by word, look and gesture, and of late—with sonnets."

"Ha, a bombastical dandy prat!"

"A worthy gentleman, my lord, of vast wealth!"

"Ay, a prancing money-bag! He so rich to dower thee like a queen and I so poor can give thee but this beggarly Ippolito, a very humble gentleman of small estate, yet one that might love thee right well with body and with soul—if such wonder might be!"

"Nay, thou poor gentleman," she mocked tenderly, "the wonder is thine arms are empty still. . . ." So saying, she turned and fled before him to the arbour, and in this fragrant bower his eager arms were filled at last. "My poor soldier!" she murmured, clinging to him.

"True, Fiametta, yet being thine—today the richest man in all this lovely world!" Thus for a while they forgot all save themselves until, roused by voices nearby, they peeped through their flowery screen and thus beheld Astorgio splendidly arrayed and so bejewelled that, like dewy flower and leaf, he sparkled with his every movement. Daintily he paced across the dewy turf with a young esquire behind to bear his embroidered cloak and long, bejemmed rapier.

"Ah—malediction!" he sighed plaintively. "And yet no sign of her, Luigi, no glimpse of this peerless she for whose beauteous sake I brave this dewy dampness, plague on't! Neither sight nor sound, eh, Luigi?"

"Alas, no, my lord!"

"Oh, dis-traction! Am I then astir thus early, bereft of my downy bed's voluptuous comfort and the sweet anodyne of slumberous content—and all, all to no purpose? Sweet Eros forbid! Tell me, Luigi, hast e'er known this tender pain called 'love' ?"

"No, my lord."

"Luigi, if thou liest I forgive thee, if 'tis truth, then I condole. For love is a tormentuous joy, a bitter sweetness, a blissful agony, a fire that consumeth not. 'Tis malady of the heart and stomach; the one leapeth athrob, the other rebelleth, scorning all good. Yea, by my beard, I have of late eaten no more than a mournful chameleon that liveth on thin air! And still she cometh not, Luigi, this she of shes that I wait and, waiting, yearn for—yet no sign of her?"

"Alas, none, my good lord!"

"Now this is strange and passing strange! For it hath been her sweet wont to walk here in sweet spring o' day out-dawning beauteous dawn with dawn of her own beauty. So will I, schooling passion to patience, wait a while. Spread me my cloak on the bench yonder and there seated I shall for pastime read thee my latest love-inspired sonnet."

"Your lordship honours me."

"I do, Luigi; in faith I do. For that, though young, thou art gentleman of tutored taste and refin-ed ear." Drawing a paper from his gorgeous bosom, he unfolded it, shook his head at it, sighed over it, and said:

"This day ere Phoebus peeped, I, by taper's wistful beam writ to my lady these lines, to wit—hearken and perpend." Here, in full-throated voice, be-ringed hand gracefully aflourish, Astorgio read:

> " 'When Phoebus young doth run to kiss shy Dawn
> And sullen Night his mantle foldeth up,
> Without thee, Fiametta, I'm forlorne . . .'

And there, Luigi, there I stick! And that's the pity on't, for what there is of it is excellent. 'When Phoebus young doth run to kiss shy Dawn'—'tis rarely sweet conceit, I think?"

"Quaint indeed, my lord, and rarely chaste!"

"I think so, Luigi! Ah, by my beard, 'tis truly so elegantly chaste it shall commend itself to every delicate ear! And again, this: 'And sullen Night his mantle foldeth up.' Here is yet another excellent concept! 'Tis line of absolute poesy save for the ultimate word—'up'. 'Tis small word 'up' and should be none so hard to rhyme. And yet by this same small word I am confounded! Canst find me a just rhyme for 'up', Luigi?"

This elegant young esquire, little dreaming of the eyes that watched him, glanced askance at his master's unconscious face with expression of contemptuous malevolence ere, bending supple back, he answered obsequiously:

"My lord, may I suggest 'pup'?"

Astorgio started, recoiled, shuddered and exclaimed indignantly:

"No—no, you may not. Out upon your 'pup'! A plague—a murrain on your 'pup'——"

"Your gracious pardon, my lord. I did but adventure——"

"'Pup'!" spluttered Astorgio. "As well give me such bawdy word as 'tup'——"

"Oh, never, my good lord. Instead, may I with all humility propose 'cup'?"

"Why, 'cup' is a good word . . . then we have 'sup' and yet these be out of place, and a good word out of place is worse than a bad one in. 'Up', 'cup', 'sup'? Confusion! Here's the very plague of poesy! Oh, I'm in the birth-pangs of most rare, fair sonnetic concept and 'tis a pang doth out-pang all other. Let us to it again,—do thou hearken perfervidly then suggest and propound, now:

'When Phoebus young doth run to kiss shy Dawn
And sullen Night his mantle foldeth up——'"

"Ha—ha!" laughed a strange, sudden voice:

"'One lieth dead by hand of friend foresworne
Ambition hath poured poison in the cup!'"

Even as these last words were uttered, out from the dense leafage nearby came a long, parti-coloured arm with hand grasping a fool's bauble that now tapped Astorgio lightly on plumed bonnet.

"Male-diction!" he gasped, leaping to his slender legs. "What's—here?"

"Jenevra!" cried this loud, strange voice. "Oh—beware!" Ensued a leafy rustling that became rapidly fainter and was gone; then as lord Astorgio and his esquire stared their surprise at one another, was sound of swift, light footsteps and, turning, they beheld the Duchess—Jenevra herself, who, with robe upheld in both hands, sped towards them, heedless of dignity but graceful as a deer.

"Where . . . where," she panted, "where . . . is he? Who . . . who cried my name?"

"Noble madonna, gracious lady," answered Astorgio, sweeping off jewelled bonnet and falling to a knee, "I cannot tell——"

"Someone called me! Who was it; tell me . . . who?" Where . . . what like was he?"

"Madame, ghost-like he came—so to vanish! I but glimpsed eyes amid the leafage yonder . . . a visage fierce, black-avised, dark as face of Moor or Zingari! It spake, it peered, cried and was gone."

" 'Twas voice cried my name . . . a warning and . . . what beside?"

"Madame, it spake a rhyme to mine ode, a jingle fantastic——"

"Indeed," said she, glancing about almost wildly, " 'twas rhyme of death—and a poison cup. This I heard . . . and yet more, one other word. Tell me, what was that word?"

"Lady, I heard none other."

"Then are those jewel-hung ears of small avail. Thou," she demanded, turning on the young esquire where he knelt, "did thine ears serve thee better to hear this voice that cried so loud—its every word?"

"Your Grace, methought this voice broke upon Your Grace's name, crying thus—'Jenevra,' and then 'Beware!' "

"True!" she sighed. "And . . . where stood this unknown speaker? Whence came and whither sped he? Speak, Astorgio."

"Sweet and gracious nobility, yonder, peeped he—but whence coming or whither gone, this, alack, I know not and therefore cannot tell."

"Why then," said she, frowning, "tell me instead why you show thus splendid, my lord, gemmed and bedight as for some gay festival, and Fortunio, my loved friend, scarce cold in his grave, and I myself thus sober clad for his too-soon dying!" And with angry though graceful gesture she spread the clinging robe of midnight hue that, moulding her shapeliness, served but to enhance her vivid beauty. "No jewel have I, my lord, nor garish broideries—while you are dazzling as the morn itself. Is it thus you show your grief?"

"Madame, most excellent lady, that dawnest upon my raptured sight like Grief beauteously personified,—of Your Grace I supplicate your belief that I grieve, have grieved and shall again, though for the nonce, this little hour, I as lover —woo, and for this am I apparelled. Yet since grief is the fashion, I shall sorrow in sable anon, black as any crow, lady——"

"Enough, my lord! Go put on your mourning weeds and therewith do your best to show what sincerity you may. . . . Oh, begone!"

Scornfully she turned and left him—in which moment she espied two figures stealing furtively away as if to escape her notice, whereat her anger flamed the hotter and she cried:

"Ippolito, Fiametta—stay! Now come you hither to me!" Mutely they obeyed and self-consciously made her their reverence while the Duchess, being young and therefore the more intolerant, looked from on to other with dark eyes aglow beneath close-drawn brows as she said and in bitter reproach:

"How can you so soon forget our grievous loss? Am I Fortunio's only mourner? Is there none to truly sorrow for him? Ah, what base ingratitude! Oh, 'tis graceless forgetful world——"

"Nay, Madame," Ippolito ventured, "not forgetful; I knew and loved him too well."

"I, too, loved him!" sighed Fiametta.

"Yet each other more!" retorted the Duchess.

"Madame, dear Jenevra, I do confess it!" said Fiametta, demurely. "Is love now become a crime?"

"At such time, Fiametta, 'tis an impertinence! But—let it

pass! Instead, tell me—did you see who it was cried my name hereabout a while since; did you see?"

"No, Madame!" they answered together.

"Having no eyes but for each other!" said the Duchess, sighing but disdainful. "As for my eyes, they are nigh blind with my long weeping."

"Alas!" retorted Fiametta, tenderly. "And thy poor pretty nose, Jenevra, thy lovely nose so pink, so——"

"Fiametta," snapped the Duchess, with imperious gesture, "you may leave me! You also, my lord. I go now to my private garden yonder to be alone with my sorrow. Let it be known I am nowise to be disturbed!"

CHAPTER VII

TELLS HOW GONZAGO WOOED AND THE
DUCHESS GAVE A PLEDGE

SLOW OF foot, hands folded and head bowed, walked the young Duchess, a dark though lovely shape in this golden morning —by shady alley, across marble pavement and dewy ling until she reached this sequestered garden where none presumed to enter save by her bidding. Thus she paused suddenly and in angry amazement at sight of one who stood as if himself the very figure of silent grief, a stately man black-clad from head to foot, whose handsome head was bowed and whose hands were reverently folded, like her own and who, as one dumb with overwhelming sorrow, uttered no word. Thus, when at last she spoke, it was less in anger than surprise:

"Gonzago, my lord—why are you here whence all are forbidden? How dare you thus trouble my grief?"

"Your Grace," he answered mournfully, "beloved lady, I thus dare that I may share it, hoping that grief thus shared may be the easier borne. Fortunio was my friend and thus I loved him, as he was great, greatly I honoured him, and now —oh, now that he is thus awfully snatched from life and our love, I ventured hither in all loving humility to share thy grief since thou didst love and honour him with fervour great as mine own."

c

"Ah, most truly!" she sighed. "He was the most dear friend
of my childhood, Gonzago. . . . And . . . oh, alas!" she
sobbed. "I parted from him . . . in my wicked anger! And
he so—so kindly gentle . . . with me . . . as he ever was! Yet
my last words to him were . . . harsh and cruel . . . and most
unjust! And minding this . . . my sorrow is . . . almost too
great for me to bear." Gonzago drew nearer, he even ventured
to touch her drooping, forlorn young head, saying tenderly:

"Alas, beloved lady! Here truly is cause for remorseful
grief. Yet old Father Time, the comforter of all sorrows, shall
heal and soothe even thine . . . and mine. And . . . ah,
Jenevra, thou art even lovelier for thy tears, so to my love is
added reverence and worship."

"He was young to die!" she murmured. "In the very zenith
of his powers and manhood! Our greatest soldier and mightiest
defence! Oh, why should we be thus bereft? Ah, God—God
of justice, take us in Thy care . . . give us vengeance—vengeance on his cruel murderers!"

"Amen!" sighed Gonzago, fervently.

"Alas!" she exclaimed. "In such time as this, God and His
holy angels seem very remote . . . so far beyond our reach."

"Yet, dearest lady, all men be created in His image for the
joy and comfort of one another—and I am a man doth live
only for joy of thee. So am I bold to declare how vast is my
love for thee."

"Enough, Gonzago! This is no season to speak me of love."

"Jenevra," he replied, lifting her unresisting hand to his
lips, "this is of all the properest time—that my humble adoration should cherish thy grief, lift thy sad heart and turn thy
thoughts from woeful shadow to dawn of light and a new, most
happy future. For, oh, Jenevra, by my soul and with every
pulse of my heart I do love thee—truly, passionately, yet in all
reverent humility. Pray you believe this of me, Jenevra."

"I do, Gonzago, and I will. But now my stricken heart is
far beyond reach of any love. So, by love, I conjure you to be
gone——"

"Gracious lady, humbly I obey. Yet, ah, Jenevra, there
shall dawn a day when joy of love shall banish vain grief
and——"

"Call it not 'vain', my lord! For in my every bitter, remorseful sigh, with every tear, is a prayer for my so dear-
loved, noble Fortunio."

"And yet—ah, lady of my adoration, there shall yet dawn a day when this soul and body that is me and that love hath made thine own shall——"

"Enough, my lord! I bid you go."

"Yet first, Jenevra, I crave of thee one word of promise and —hope."

"Without hope, my lord, I should die!"

"Then shall we live, Jenevra, thou in radiant beauty and I to worship thee. But now——"

"Now, my lord, hear this. Would you win my love and me to wife, seek out Fortunio's murderers, avenge me his cruel death, ah—vengeance to the uttermost! Do this and ask of me what and all you will . . . ! Ay, do this and I will make you lord of me and my duchy. And now, I pray you, be gone!"

Gracefully he bowed, sighing deeply he turned and slowly he went from her, handsome head down-bent, like one who felt a grief almost beyond his strength to bear; and very wistfully the young Duchess gazed after him until he was beyond her sight.

And now it was that she heard a sound like the chime of fairy bells.

CHAPTER VIII

TELLS HOW THE DUCHESS HEARKENED TO THE WISDOM OF A FOOL

GUIDED by this most unexpected sound, the Duchess hastened forward until once again she halted in angry surprise, for here in the very heart of this so private garden and leaning to gaze down pensively at the great marble sundial was a jester, a shabby fellow in worn and faded motley.

"Fool," cried she, wrathfully, "how came you here?"

"Woman," he replied, still intent upon the dial, "by setting one foot afore the other, as the custom is."

"What would you here?"

"The Duchess! I seek the Duchess Jenevra, woman."

"And wherefore?"

"To show her how this court that is her little, especial world, groweth ever baser, minute by minute and by the inch."

"Well, I am the Duchess and would——"

"Not so, thou art a better thing."

" 'Better', say you, 'better'——?"

"Indeed! For thou art a woman can sorrow and weep by reason of past iniquity."

"Nay, my tears are for Goodness lost to us and all suddenly banished by death."

"And thus, woman, Iniquity hath been, is, and shall be, alas! Come then, most truly gentle woman, and watch thy little world grow sinful inch by inch. Look now upon this dial, this ever-creeping shadow—'tis here, a while since—it was there, an inch or less, yet in this little space how many have sinned, what ills contrived, what future evils planned! Think on this and grieve, since thou'rt indeed such gentle woman."

"Yet am I the Duchess . . . and yet I weep for one whose loss is calamity for all and to me a grief abiding."

"So, Duchess? I heard somewhat of some such of some lord murdered, the which is nothing singular. But he was buried days agone and should be forgot ere now——"

"Oh, crass fool! Such as Fortunio are never forgot! For his great deeds he shall be ever remembered and . . . for his dear self I shall ever love and hallow . . . his memory."

"Then, most gentle Duchess, thy tears shall be his solace in purgatory and his glory added in paradise!" Now here she turned to survey this jester regardfully: his dark, gipsy-like visage framed in shabby, parti-coloured hood, with ridiculous cockscomb and dangling ass's ears; feature by feature she viewed this face, the keen, blue eyes, delicate acquiline nose and shapely sensitive mouth, while he continued to gaze down wistfully at the sundial.

"You are a marvellous strange fool!" she said at last.

"So I think!" he nodded.

"It was you made a rhyme concerning poison—a dreadful rhyme!"

"I did my poor best with it."

"What—ah, what know you of—poison?"

"What all the world knows, that 'tis deadly."

"Oh, this is folly!"

"True! I am a fool."

"Yet you cried my name, bidding me beware."

"I did."

"Of what should I beware?"

"Evil."

"What evil? And where?"

—"Every evil! Everywhere—especially hereabout and—most especially the evil that can greet us with smiling look, take us by the hand, speak us like a friend and we—all unknowing."

"Oh, what hateful, what foolish babble is this?"

"Such as a certain babbling brook babbled to me this morning—'tis brook well versed in evil for it floweth very nigh us yonder."

"Us?" she repeated, her bright eyes suddenly intent.

"Certes!" he nodded. "Thyself, myself, thy lords, thy ladies, all thy splendid court."

"Well, what said this talkative brook?"

"It chattered something on this wise:

> 'Beastly things that in the night
> Creep and wriggle out of sight;
> Soon as they see the cleanly sun
> To their holes do straightway run.
> Yet fouler things there be than they,
> That boldly strut in light o' day,
> That with smiling look do meet us
> And with friendly welcome greet us,
> Thus do they make us, every one,
> Blind to the evil they have done.' "

Now because these jingling rhymes voiced her own secret doubts and fears, Jenevra glanced from the speaker round about them, more like terrified girl than stately Duchess, and sinking weakly upon the seat beside this sundial she bowed troubled head between her hands, saying brokenly:

"Evil there must be . . . stealthy and merciless . . . or why was Fortunio killed . . . murdered . . . and to what dreadful purpose? And now . . . without his strong, gentle presence . . . I am all dismayed, so lost and terribly alone! Were I not my valiant father's child and Duchess of this realm with duty to my people . . . now should I be all . . . craven and most . . . dreadfully afraid. So now, O God, strengthen and help me!"

At this so desolate cry the Jester turned, leaned near as if to comfort her; instead he laughed loud and foolishly, struck a ridiculous attitude, but said in warning murmur:

"Duchess, play thy part, for yonder come those that expect it of thee." Glancing whither he directed, she frowned, sighing wearily:

"There be two of my chiefest councillors, and fools both!"

"Why then," said the Jester, striking another attitude for their behoof, "shall these fools banish Folly? Must I be gone?"

"No," she answered, lifting her proud, young head, "for by their looks and unwonted haste I judge they bear me ill tidings. If so, jibe thou and make a mock of their gravity; and should they plague me with their counselling, do thou outplague them with thy fooling."

Then sitting very upright, she waited steady-eyed and resolute to meet whatsoever might be.

So came these two lords, Sebastian, tall and dignified despite haste; his companion a plumpish, rubicund gentleman, somewhat breathless and perspiring.

"My lords," said the Duchess as they halted to bow, "I greet you not well and with no welcome that you dare this intrusion."

"Gracious Madame," said Sebastian, advancing a step, "the news we bring—my lord Count Emilio Calvacanti and I—must excuse us. For, alas, Madame, we, the lords of thy Council, long suspecting and ever watchful of thy precious safety and the weal of thy duchy, have uncovered a vile plot against both—black treason, Madame, and villainy most dire! Oh, horrible and most unnatural to utter or even think upon!"

"Yet speak it, my lord."

"Madame, I will, since I needs must. Know then that 'gainst this stealthy wickedness we have moved with such speed, such instant zeal and absolute devotion, that this foul menace, this iniquitous peril is now most perfectly quelled, the miscreants slain and thyself and the duchy secure! But—ah, Madame, among those so rightly and so justly killed is one whose name I scarce dare speak."

"How, Sebastian; dost fear to name such vile wretch?"

"My Lady, I do confess it. For, oh, Madame, dear Lady, years agone he was one well beknown to Your Grace——"

"His name, my lord; speak me this hateful traitor's name."

"Lady, he was—your childish playfellow, Count Angelo of Fidena."

"Count . . . Angelo?" she repeated breathlessly.

"Himself, Madame! Alas, 'tis but too true! Lo, here Count Emilio Cavalcanti to bear me out in this dire, this dreadful fact." Here Count Cavalcanti bowed and, wheezing slightly, said:

"I can, Your Grace, and do. For Truth being truth, I needs must——"

"Angelo . . . dead?" she said faintly. "Angelo . . . killed? Dead now . . . as his brother?"

"Alas, 'tis so, Madame, slain upon his evil way hither and therefore—better so."

"Better so?" she enquired; then up she leapt and stately Duchess became furious termagent. "Lies! Lies!" she cried, white fists aloft, eyes and teeth agleam. "Angelo may be dead . . . but traitor he never was—never, ah, never! He could not be so vile a thing, being Fortunio's brother, and the boy as I mind him . . . 'tis impossible and beyond imagining! 'Tis foul calumny I'll not believe, nor will I hear or permit its utterance."

"But, alas, Madame," mourned Sebastian, "here we have proof all too plain and most dreadfully manifest."

"Then I'll not see it."

"Yet, most gracious Lady, needs must I read it for justification of what hath been done. My lord Emilio, the letter, I pray you." From ornate purse at his girdle, the Count drew this fateful document, handing it to Sebastian, who, falling to a knee, tendered it to the Duchess, saying:

"Look, Madame, behold this damning evidence! Read, Madame; read and know how very just and providential was Count Angelo's death."

"Not I, my lord!" said she, walking distressfully to and fro. "Since it must be known, do you read it to me."

"As you will, Madame!" said Sebastian, bowing. Then, clearing his throat, gently though impressively, and, striking a dignified, oratorial posture, he read sonorously:

" 'To Sebastian, Lord of the Council, these in much haste. Arrest Count Angelo of Fidena for traitorous correspondence with the enemy while supposedly in England, and complicity with the known traitor Julio Morelli. Others are concerned though not personally known of me, wherefore I name them not. This writ at peril of my life by thy assured friend Antonio Friuli.'

Thus it runs, Madame. Deign now to see for yourself, I pray."

Unwillingly the Duchess took this letter and, having read, sank down again upon the bench as if her young strength had failed her even beyond speech; whereupon Sebastian continued and in gravely modulated accents:

"Furthermore, Your Grace, we have reasons for belief that our great, our noble Fortunio, becoming aware of this—his brother's most damnable treason, and thereby dismayed, quite distraught and heart-broken, chose the dark road of death rather than life with such absolute shame and dishonour!"

Now at this the Duchess, hiding her face in both hands, let fall the paper, in which moment Sebastian stooped for it, then snatched back his outstretched hand as down upon this paper came the Jester's worn shoe.

"So—ho!" he laughed. "Thus doth Folly tread down Villainy and trample lying Treachery underfoot!"

"Return that to me!" said Sebastian, imperiously.

"Right noble lord," retorted the Jester, taking it up and bowing with ridiculous play of arms and legs, "I beseech you have patience."

"Fool, give me that letter!"

"Most excellent, noble lord, I crave your indulgent attention that Folly may elucidate, excogitate, ruminate and animadvert upon this screed accusative and, by jocose comicalities, mayhap teach you to laugh Villainy out of countenance. As thus——"

"Madame, ha—Madame," fumed Sebastian, "shall a buffoon thus dare befool and flout us at such time and in matter of such high import? I pray you bid him hence or suffer me to rid you of——"

"No, Sebastion!" she answered and with very commanding gesture. "Instead, my lords, you may sit with me while I hear what Folly can make of this abomination."

"Ab—Abomination, Madame?"

"So I pronounce it. Be seated—both of you! So! Now, Folly, read and expound me this letter wisely as a fool may." The Jester approached, and with sly mockery at Sebastian's impressive dignity, struck an absurdly oratorical attitude, cleared his throat resoundingly and said in Sebastian's deeply sonorous tone:

"Here beginneth this screed accusatory-damnatory, by one Antonio Friuli of nowhere-in-particular, being of no stated rank, degree or station, to one, Sebastian, a right honourable lord and councillor, thus: 'To Sebastion, Lord of the Council, these

in much haste'—haste, mark you, and yet this letter is most
clerkly written and never a smudge or blot withal!—Antonio
thus in haste, thus continueth, to wit: 'Arrest Count Angelo of
Fidena for traitorous correspondence with the enemy. . . .'
Aha, Master Antonio, large in his indictment, troubles not for
'who' or 'when' or 'where', merely 'enemy', he writes. But
let it pass and hear him thus continue: 'for traitorous correspondence with the enemy while supposedly in England . . .'
Now here is a moot point as to which or who was in England,
the 'enemy' or this traitor Count Angelo. But let this pass also
and hear our Antonio further, thus: '. . . and complicity
with the known traitor Julio Morelli.' Thus, Master Antonio
damneth this Count Angelo as traitor double-dyed that should
have doubly-died therefore. Alack that he could die but once!
Now thus again, Master Antonio: 'Others are concerned though
not personally known of me, wherefore I name them not.' See
now what virtue is in our Antonio that he will accuse, and
condemn, only those he knoweth personally! And, herewith
he endeth: 'This writ at peril of my life by thy assured friend
Antonio Friuli.' Ho, Sebastian, most excellent gentleman, how
blest art thou in such friend! Well, well—so much for so little!
'Tis poor thing as letters go, with never a laugh throughout,
alack! Thus villainy keeps in good countenace, all assured!
Take it; Lady,—see an thy woman's wit can make more of it
than a poor Fool's folly."

"First," she demanded, glancing down at this letter, "how
and what think you of it?"

"Not I, alone, Lady, no! 'Stead of Folly a bird might answer thee, a bird of wisdom, thus:

'"Too-whoo," the owl doth cry,
    "Go to, 'tis but a lie!"
        Then so in faith say I——' "

"Madame," cried Sebastian, starting up angrily, "by your
leave, I'll go——"

"My lord," she retorted, "by my command you will
remain."

"But, Madame, this—this mountebank is my perfect
abhorrence."

"However, you may sit down again, my lord."

"Madame, this buffoon wastes my time and——"

"Your time is mine just now, my lord. Sit and you shall hear me instead. Sit, I say!"

Speechless and pale, Sebastian obeyed. Then the Duchess flipped open the letter with scornful finger, frowned at it and said:

"If this indeed was writ in haste, here is no sign of it! Whence had you this thing, how and when?"

"From the south, by special messenger, three days since Madame."

"Then why have I not seen it ere now?"

"I thought it wisest to first let your Council deliberate upon it, Madame."

"Well, and what then?"

"It was instantly published, Madame, posted up and cried in every town and village."

"And this without my knowledge."

"Madame, it was decided to be thus instant to stop these popular tumults and clamours."

"Why do my people so clamour?"

"By reason of Fortunio's sudden death the people cry 'murder' and 'vengeance'——"

"And very rightly, my lord. So would I have them do until his death be avenged and his murderers dragged to light, and justice done."

"But now, thank heaven, we are assured this was no murder."

"As how, my lord?"

"By the evidence now in Your Grace's hand."

"Call you this evidence, my lord? Tell me, who is Antonio Friuli?"

"A—most worthy gentleman and my honoured friend."

"I would fain see and have speech with him."

"Nay, but, Madame——"

"You will therefore summon this gentleman hither to Celonia."

"But, Madame, he is fled in peril of his life, none knows whither."

"Then, Sebastian, neither will I believe this letter with its vile accusation of Count Angelo, who, being dead, cannot defend himself. However, my too credulous councillors on their own authority and without my knowledge have dared publish this infamous thing, have they, Sebastian?"

"Infamous, Madame?"

"So infamous that I shall so proclaim it. Today at sunset you will convene the Council and in full assemblage I will pronounce this for base and slanderous lie. God's light!" she cried, leaping afoot so suddenly that Sebastian, forgetting his dignity, recoiled. "Ha, dare you think that upon the unsupported testimony of this man Friuli, and he unknown and so conveniently fled, I will believe or suffer others to believe our noble Fortunio murdered himself for his brother's shameful villainy?"

Sebastian, no longer impressive, seemed to cower as he glanced from this passionate young speaker round about him like one, for the moment lost and quite confounded. Then slowly he arose and fronted the Duchess with eyes narrowed to gleaming slits and expression so unexpectedly menacing that she in turn recoiled; yet when he spoke it was in tone as unexpectedly soft and gentle:

"Madame, are you determined to so declare?"

"I am, and I shall!"

"Then as your chiefest councillor and one that truly loves and honours you, I now, and from my heart, advise against your so doing, and this for the best, the greatest and dearest of all reasons."

"Well," she demanded, "tell me this reason, Sebastian."

"Yourself!" he answered, almost whispering.

"My lord," said she, leaning slowly nearer, "you must tell me more . . . yes, you shall tell me why and how I am concerned."

"Lady," he replied, speaking now below his breath, "the venom that killed Fortunio and Jacomo was in the wine you sent—your gift of wine wherein, by your expressed will, they were to drink and pledge our——"

"No!" she cried, and then in hushed and awful tone: "No! It cannot be . . . 'tis too dreadful to even think upon . . . no . . . no."

"Dear Lady, it is proved beyond all doubt! The flask and silver goblet were submitted to Friar Clement for analysis, and in both he has found—poison most virulent."

"Oh . . . now!" she gasped. "Oh, God help me . . . for here is terror and unimagined horror. . . ." Then, turning, she went from them through the golden morning, swift of foot and purposeful, yet pale now as death itself.

And presently the Jester, turning also to be gone, glanced over his shoulder at the two very silent gentlemen, pointed to a lark carolling joyously above them, tossed up his bauble, caught it and said in foolish chirruping lilt:

"Hark—the lark that heavenward wingeth,
'Tirra—lirra—lirra' singeth;
But wise owl, 'Too—hoo!' doth cry,
'Go to—go to, 'tis all a lie!'
And so, in faith, my lords, do I."

"Presumptuous rogue!" said Sebastian in cold, still fury. "Hie you from court or I'll have you whipped and that malapert tongue cropped shorter!" The Jester laughed foolishly, flourished his bauble, stepped into the leafage and was gone.

CHAPTER IX

TELLS OF FATHER CLEMENT, A LEARNED FRIAR

IN REMOTE and sunny corner of the inner defences where the embattled palace wall made a wide curve was a little oratory, and beyond this, set within a fragrant very orderly garden, Friar Clement had his lonely dwelling.

A somewhat aged man was this Friar, greatly experienced and therefore wise, having been in turn student, soldier, philosopher, scientist and physician, but ever and always a servant of God and thus a very gentle man and humble.

Famous as a scholar among scholars, and respected for his learning and discoveries in scientific research, he was feared by the vulgar as a wizard, but loved by all such troublous ones as sought his help, for to these he gave comfort of mind and sometimes healing for pain-racked body.

This morning he sat in the small chamber he called his workshop, crouched upon a rough stool between cold furnace and sooty forge, his strong clever hands empty and idle for once, his gentle, wide-set eyes upturned to a shelf crowded with retorts of many shapes and sizes, crucibles and all the paraphernalia of chemical research; but it was upon two objects that his gaze was fixed so intently while, over and over again, he spoke aloud like the solitary man he was, voicing those words that have been the prayer of knowledge-seekers since ever man could think:

"Almighty God, give me light! Show me the truth, O God!"

And after some while, as if in answer to his prayer, was sound of light, quick feet, a flutter of draperies, and into the dimness of his grimy workship sped one seeking his comfort, one who cried in weeping voice:

"Oh, Clement . . . Friar Clement, dear Father Clem, help me, for today I am a child again . . . so desolate, so lonely, that I am . . . afraid at last! So, holy father, pray for me, comfort me now as you did when I was a child lonely and motherless. . . ."

"Come then, child of God!" said he, rising with gaunt arms outstretched, and like a child she nestled to the strong, gentle comfort of him. Then lifting her head, she looked up at him with aweful eyes, saying breathlessly:

"Oh, the wine . . . the wine I sent! They say it was . . . poisoned! That you found the poison. . . . Ah, holy father, dear Clement, tell me it is not true."

Now finding him silent, she drew away to gaze at him in wide-eyed horror.

"Oh," she whispered, "then it is true! The wine I sent . . . killed them . . . Fortunio, Jacomo . . . both! And they my dearest, best-loved friends! Was the wine I sent . . . death to them . . . death sent by me?"

"My child," he answered gently, "I can tell thee only this —the wine they drank was poisoned, this I have proved, an herbal distillation called, as I think, Aqua Megara."

"Oh, but how . . . how can this be?" she faltered. "The wine I sent was such as I and others drank on that dreadful night . . . 'twas waxed and sealed, but in special flask of Venetian crystal."

The Friar turned, reached from the shelf a certain object, and placed it upon the table before her, saying:

"Was this the flask?"

"Yes! Yes!" she whispered, shrinking from it with look of horror. " 'Twas this I sent."

"Art thou sure, Jenevra, perfectly sure?"

"Too—too sure!"

"And yet, my child," said he, placing a second flask beside the first, "this one is the truly fatal thing! This was Villainy's weapon wherewith the murder was wrought!"

"Oh, then . . . you mean . . . the flasks were changed?"

"I do. For here stand these two vessels, the innocent and guilty, and yet alike as two peas."

"Horrible!" she whispered. "For . . . oh, Father Clement, here was such devilish craft, such wicked cunning that I am all adread!"

"Indeed!" sighed the Friar, setting these objects back on the shelf. "It seemeth a devil walks among us, a demon of murder, unseen, unheard and all unknown—as yet. But God the Father is here also, His protecting love all about us if we will only be aware of His presence. He is our safeguard and salvation, child!"

"Then why—oh, why did He suffer my two dear friends to be so cruelly murdered and my heart nigh broken, why?"

"Perchance because, their work being done so well on earth, He hath raised them for greater employ in a better life, Jenevra. For these our beloved dead be more gloriously alive than we. As for thyself, Jenevra, I think God hath thus afflicted thee to make thee nobler, stronger, gentler and more able to rule this State."

"Then," sighed she, "in this thought is some meed of consolation. Ah, but they say now, my father, that Fortunio killed himself for shame of his brother Angelo's villainy! And besides, Angelo is dead likewise, so who now is left alive to tell the truth of it all?"

And Friar Clement answered, gently: "God, Jenevra." Then, taking her nerveless hand, he led her out from the gloom into his sunny garden to show her where and how his beans were clambering aloft in their pride of green and scarlet, and then his peas all abloom, with noble leeks and corpulent onions all asprout, talking of them with pride; he showed her also his very many herbs and simples, discoursing learnedly on their diverse properties and virtues, until her woeful-drooping head lifted, the slim hand in his cherishing clasp grew vital with new life; and looking up into his strong, gentle face, she murmured:

"Oh, my father, now truly I thank God for the comfort of thee; thou wert always my consolation, yet never so much as now. And . . . dear Clement . . . there was another gave me comfort and he, of all creatures, a—sorry Jester! And yet in his look and the . . . seeming folly of his talk was a something . . . almost . . . noble."

'And he a Jester, my child!"

"Indeed. Though at times . . . he seemed . . . Oh, come, let us sit in the shade yonder and I shall tell all that chanced this morning."

Thus presently seated on rustic bench made by the Friar's clever hands, Jenevra, like the eager, clean-hearted, lovely troubled girl she was, told of Gonzago's wooing, of the Jester's odd behaviour, and of her scene with Sebastian, though oftenest she spoke of this Jester, his high, bold look, strange dark face and cultured speech. And the wise Friar, heeding every intonation of her soft, rich voice, the ever-changing beauty of this face he had watched grow more lovely with the years, uttered no word until her story seemed finished.

"So, Jenevra," said he, when she paused for breath, "'tis a mannerly creature, this Jester?"

"Mannerly and manly," she answered, "and withal very shabby."

"And dared to ridicule and denounce the letter, say'st thou?"

"Oh, he did, and so aptly it was joy to hear! and to watch Sebastian, his face turn red as fire, then pale as ashes, and himself in such fury he could scarcely speak! As for me, I could have laughed, and yet . . . oh, Father Clement . . . I dared not, for in the Jester's mockery and Sebastian's rage was something . . . . dreadful! Here now is the letter. I brought it for thy wise judgment; read and tell me."

So Friar Clement took the letter, read it carefully, shook his head at it and said gently, but with the utmost conviction:

"Lies, my child. I marvel Sebastian should give credence to such nonsense! Though, to be sure, he scarce knew Count Angelo."

"But we did, thou and I," said Jenevra, taking back the letter. "I mind him as a shy boy except with other boys, for he would fight any that I bade him and all his thought was to be valiant and honourable and worthy of Fortunio's love."

"And I," said the Friar, smiling, "remember him as mischievous imp . . . broke one of my best retorts and spoiled an experiment! Yet he would never tell a lie to 'scape punishment, and was apt at his books. I mind how he learned Jacomo to read; they were great friends. Yes, even as an urchin he was honourable and worthy his noble brother, ten years agone."

"Ten years!" she repeated. "'Tis a long, long time, my father! Think you ten years may change such boy to villainous man?"

"Never such boy as was Angelo! And now that he is a man . . . ah, no! Alas, he is dead, you tell me?"

"Aye, so 'tis reported, my father. 'Killed on his evil way hither' they say of him."

"Then may God rest him!" sighed the Friar. "He shall be in my prayers henceforth."

"So, dear Father Clement, he passes for me like scarce remembered dream or I should grieve him more. But I have known overmuch sorrow of late, and trouble is yet heavy upon me. Also today at sunset I front my Council of Ten to proclaim this tale of Fortunio's self-murder a foul calumny."

"Well, thy councillors have my pronouncement on the poisoned wine——"

"And I," she exclaimed miserably, "oh, 'twas I sent it! Poisoned or no—I sent it! So thus for aught I or anyone can prove to the contrary I am a murderess! I that so loved them, may be accounted their slayer. Oh, Father Clement, I had not thought of this . . . and now that I do . . . I grow all faint and sick."

"Then think not so, Jenevra, but with faith in God and thine own innocence, take courage, my child. And know that I and such as do love thee for what thou truly art, shall never rest until the truth is made plain and manifest. Ah, there sounds the matins bell. Come, my loved daughter, let us go speak to God our Almighty Father." So, hand in hand, they came to the little oratory and there, side by side, they knelt awhile in silent though passionate supplication until, lifting her head at last and with hands still folded:

"Oh, dear my father," she whispered, "now let me hear thee speak one small prayer for this troubled me." And forthwith, Friar Clement voiced this, his constant prayer:

"Almighty God and Father of us all, comfort and strengthen this Jenevra, this child of Thine and, of Thy mercy, give us— light!"

Now when at last they came out into the sunshine, Jenevra stooped and kissed the Friar's work-roughened hand or ever he knew, saying:

"Ah, holy father, dear Father Clement, thou hast brought me so nigh to God that my fear is gone and I am bold for whatsoever is yet to be. And now," said she, bowing her head, hands folded reverently, "give me thy blessing, for I must go."

And when he had touched this lovely head, and spoken the divine words of benediction, she went her way, no longer the terrified girl, but with young head erect and resolute like the ruling monarch destiny had made her: though Friar Clement, for all his brave words, gazed after her with look of wistful anxiety until she was gone. Then back went he to his garden and, being thus troubled, took a spade and, tucking up his threadbare frock, began to dig lustily.

For some while he laboured thus vigorously and had just driven his spade a full spit deep when he heard a sound that, by memory's instant magic, swept him back ten years through time,—yet this no more than three or four flute-like notes whistled softly. Loosing his spade, Friar Clement turned swiftly and beheld, perched upon his garden wall, a Jester who flourished his bauble, saying:

"Greeting, good Friar!"

"Was it thou—whistled?"

"Even so!"

"Then—who—who art thou?"

"A fool, good sir, a poor wandering Jester that calls himself Bimbo, a name the which should fit such fool as he that I seem; this or a ghost am I—choose thou."

"There was," said the Friar, slowly, "a boy I loved—long years agone—used so to whistle."

"Aye, faith, Friar, I knew him well, he was thy pupil, a mischievous imp that loved not his Euclid and had much ado to cross the 'pons asinorum' and his name was Angelo."

Step by step the Friar approached and with such look upon his thin, gentle face that when he paused as if troubled and unsure, down leapt this Jester and held out his arms.

Then Friar Clement went to him and, putting back his hood, kissed him on the brow, gazed at him very earnestly and kissed him again, saying thereafter:

"Now God be thanked and glorified! Thou art back from the dead, Angelo."

"Verily, dear father, dead Angelo am I and must so remain!" said Angelo, returning the Friar's kiss of welcome very heartily. "I'll warrant me thou hast never been kissed by a ghost, a grimly phantom, a grisly spectre ere now, so there's for thee again—and again, most revered father. For, ah, Clement, dead and damned is Angelo and now proscribed as accursed traitor. So thus instead of Angelo is Bimbo a fool, that with his fooleries and fooling shall perchance do more than ever might Angelo for all his schooling! So now prithee let us to thy den of smoke and grime—how I loved it as a boy—and there, with none to spy or hear, we will talk, for much is there to say."

CHAPTER X

INTRODUCES ONE, PEDRILLO, A MIGHTY MAN

"WELL, THERE'S my tale, Father Clement. Truly more of ill has befallen in these few days at home than in all my years abroad! And of this vile and ghastly business, this much have I learned. First, that 'twas Messire Astorgio Ferranti, this too-rich fool, conveyed the deadly wine, and with him his esquire one Luigi and his page Beppo. By these, one or all, I suspect the wine was changed or poisoned, unless 'twas done beforehand by the Duchess——"

"Ah, canst thou believe such evil of her, Angelo?"

"Oh, never—yet others may. And thus is she suspect. Secondly, I know that one Gonzago, whom I have yet to meet, woos the Duchess—a something audacious fellow——"

"What dost thou think of her, my Angelo?"

"Thirdly; I know the lordly councillor Sebastian for a liar. And this so little is all I do know—as yet."

"And now," repeated Friar Clement, his gentle eyes twinkling, "answer my question: what of our Jenevra that was thy childish playfellow, how think you now——"

"So much so that I think of her little as I may lest such vain thinking cloud my purpose. For, oh, father, she is all and more than I dreamed possible—dark as fragrant night and as gentle, yet again, passionate as thundercloud! Hers is a beauty dignified by intellect and this tempered by wit. She is, in fine, a gracious woman and such as I dreamed yet never thought to see."

"Verily she is all this, Angelo, unspoiled as yet by the gross flatteries of her courtiers and adulation of her suitors, and yet that way trending."

"As how, father?"

"She, like the Duke her sire, is something proud and arrogant, and the fawning homage of all about her is, I fear, daily aggravation thereto. Wherefore I am heartily glad of thee for her sake; the sooner she is thy wife, the better——"

"Nay, father——'—"

"Yea, Angelo. This marriage was decreed by her sire and thine, they being sworn brothers in arms. So are ye betrothed to each other still, and as I say,——"

"No!" exclaimed Angelo. "The world is direly changed since then; all the cardinal sins are loosed, up and raging."

"Not more than aforetime, my son, for, alas, sin is ever with us though more active of late——"

"Ay, murder! I know, I know! Thus am I all distraught by Fortunio's dying."

"And this marriage was his fond hope and expressed wish——"

"This also I know, yet to win her I must woo; and how, in heaven's name, may any man woo in cockscomb and dangling ass's ears? Look on them; these alone would make her wooing a mockery! An amorous fool in such motley sighing his love would be thing to laugh at!"

"Yet in thy motley would be thyself and thy true self thereby the more truly manifest. And spite thy ass's ears thou'rt always Angelo and he the boy she loved in years agone!"

"Think thou she loved me—then?"

"I do know it. And by her own telling!"

Angelo, having risen, instantly sat down again and, propping elbow on table and chin in fist, gazed at the radiant sunlight flooding in at the small, unglazed window, and slowly in his sombre eyes dawned a light not of the sun; perceiving which, Friar Clement continued:

"Angelo, if ever she needed a strong arm and cool wise head beside her—it is now! And if this head weareth cockscomb and this arm be clad in motley—so much the better. For somewhere an unseen evil moveth, and because of this unseen thing she that was never fearful is afraid at last."

"Said she so, father?"

"She did, and sitting in that same rickety old chair."

"Oh! Happy chair!" exclaimed Angelo, embracing it. "And Jenevra—afraid! Said she aught else?"

"This, Angelo, that amidst all her many courtiers she was alone and very solitary. So now, what of that head to scheme for her, that arm to fend for her?"

"By my soul—yes!" said Angelo, so vehemently that his bells jingled. "To counterplot and outscheme secret Villainy until it shall betray itself, itself unknowing it is known!"

"But, my son, is that Folly's bauble thy only weapon?"

"Not so, Father Clem, for an this poor fool's wit lack point—here is thing more trenchant!" And from somewhere about him, even as he spoke, Angelo flashed a broad-bladed, needle-pointed poniard; whereat the Friar nodded and thereafter sighed deeply, saying:

"Alas that I, a man of peace, that goeth to and fro preaching love and gentleness to all men, am yet glad of that deadly thing for thy sake! For too well I know how perilous will be the path before thee; once thou'rt suspect 'twill be steel in thy 'fenceless back or sudden bullet."

"Verily," nodded Angelo, with wry smile, "I must be the butt, the mark, the popinjay for all to shoot at. Ah, but— he that so shooteth must so—discover himself."

"Pray God he shoot amiss, Angelo."

"I shall be wary, father. Though life is none so precious without Fortunio and dear old Jacomo. So should I die I shall be in right good company."

"And what of Jenevra?"

"Ay, faith—Jenevra! To woo her in this humble guise— such proud lady—a poor, sorry jester, a thing for mockery and laughter, to be kicked and cuffed for the sport of any! To woo her so, were wildest folly! To win her so? Ah, Father Clement, this should be such wonder—indeed the very miracle of love! None but merest fool would attempt it—a feat greater than all the labours of Hercules—yet that fool am I!"

"So art thou blessed fool, my son, and shalt, I think, be fool beloved. For love that is purely true is certainly of God and therefore such love cannot fail."

"Except for lover who loveth one that loveth another, for then such lover may go hang, and she he loved shall love her lover the better therefore."

"Ho!" murmured Friar Clement, blinking those mild eyes of his. "Was it at thine Oxenford college thou didst learn so much of women and love, my son?"

"Enough to know that few men be worthy of the best, and most men better than the worst, good father."

"Hum!" quoth the Friar, rubbing bristly chin. "Here is a philosophy in the which I am little versed."

"And I," said Angelo, "am scholar enough to know sweet-souled truth when I see it. Moreover she could still weep for Fortunio so truly that her lovely eyes were all swollen; even her precious nose was pink, bless it! Nor cared she, but fronted her lords proud in her grief. Thus did I know her, then and there for true woman, as then and there I told her."

"Ah, and what said she?"

"Made to look arrogant and spoiled it with a sob. And so when Sebastian—this noble lord—dared suggest she herself might be suspect of this crime and she fled to thee, I followed unseen and unheard, for I can silence these bells with care, and here she found consolation. So God love thee, Father Clement, our gentle comforter in our childhood, thou art so even now."

"So with God's grace will I ever be, my son. And among other subjects we talked of Angelo the boy that was her playmate."

"What said she?"

"That he was shy except with other boys, and so honourable she wondered if ten years could change such boy to villainous man."

"'Tis so I am reported. Doth she believe it of me, father?"

"Not she, my son."

"Then here is some small comfortable hope. Spake she of the Jester?"

"Often!" answered Friar Clement, the twinkle in his eyes again.

"Well? Well? What said she of the poor fool?"

"That he was shabby!"

"True enough, for so I am. What more?"

"That in his seeming folly was wisdom—that in him was strange comfort." Up rose Angelo joyously as if to be gone, and as instantly sat down again to ask:

"Said she aught of my jingling rhymes, and doggerel rant, father?"

"Indeed! She repeated them and laughed for the first time—so did I."

"Did she mention Sebastian's letter?"

"And she gave it me to read."

"Oh, excellent. Well?"

"I pronounced it nonsensical lying, my son."

"And, father, 'tis thus towards Sebastian suspicion's finger points me. And therefore him shall I watch."

"Then take heed to thy every step, Angelo! For besides being high in office and public esteem, he is of large possessions and hence very powerful, with servants and agents a many."

"Is he an ambitious man?"

"He might have been, but now, save for the Duchess, he is greatest in the State."

"So?", murmured Angelo, chin in hand. "He might have been ambitious . . . had Fortunio lived to thwart his will and check his growing power! So Fortunio died—ah, and so doth my suspicion grow! Verily I shall watch this potent lord——"

"And verily it will be at thy peril!" sighed Friar Clement and, rising, crossed to a vast oaken chest in dingy corner, presently returning with a padded, close-fitting shirt of fine link-mail exquisitely wrought and lined with soft doeskin.

"Angelo," said he, rather sadly, "until we, for I am with thee heart and hand—I say, until we have uncovered and extirpated this hidden evil, thy life must be at constant hazard and perchance be attempted. Now therefore, though as servant of God I believe His love will protect thee, yet having been also a soldier of God I believe in taking every possible precaution. So here now is one of woven steel that shall turn any sword or dagger-point ever forged and once a caliver-ball, or I should have died young—indeed it hath been well tried. So off with thy doublet and shirt and on with this! Thus thou shalt be doubly armed and guarded." And when Angelo had donned this man-made defence, they knelt, and Friar Clement implored the surer protection of God, saying:

"Almighty Father of all men, we Thy soldiers are about to do battle with the powers of darkness. Give us therefore eyes to see the hidden evil, wisdom to out-think and strength to out-fight and vanquish them. And if any should die, take them, we beseech Thee, home to Thy everlasting peace, Amen. . . . Come now, my son," said he, rising, "let us go eat, though I can offer thee but plain fare, a smoked ham

with a sallet." So forth to the garden went they to pluck the
needed herbs and vegetables and thence to a small, bare
chamber, its only furniture a rough table, two chairs, a very
splendid crucifix of ivory and ebony and beneath this a long-
bladed sword. Towards the crucifix Angelo bowed reverent
head; at the sword he smiled, saying:

"Ah, now here is an old friend! For, like the mischievous
urchin I was, I'd oft steal behind thy back to handle this old
sword of thine, and my wrist then scarce strong enough to
bear up its point. And 'tis bright as ever, father."

"Eh, bright," repeated the Friar, busy preparing his "sallet",
and giving all his mind to it, "bright? That is Pedrillo's
doing."

"So he is yet with thee?"

"He is, thank God. Without him I were solitary indeed!
He cooketh, washeth, cleaneth, diggeth, yet mostly helps in
my workshop—he becometh well skilled in the chymic arts.
He also helps me physic such as seek my aid."

"Ay truly, a marvel is Rillo!" said Angelo, taking down
the sword and twirling it in much-experienced hand. Thus,
while Friar Clement prepared their meal and Angelo made
intricate feints and passes with the sword, they talked thus:

ANGELO (*making a circular parry with the sword*): Ah, verily
a marvel is Rillo; thy marvel, father; a hunchback, a
cripple and one of thy many cures. I mind folk said at
the time he was healed by thy arts magical.

FRIAR (*breaking up a lettuce*): 'Twas by mercy of God and
some skill in medicine, my son.

ANGELO: Do they still call thee wizard and magician and
sorcerer as they did?

FRIAR: Ay, they do, in their pitiful ignorance, poor souls!

ANGELO: And 'tis no wonder, since by thy wondrous doing
Pedrillo became the strongest man anywhere hereabout—
and he a cripple! Where is he now?

FRIAR: First to the early market and then to the court stables
to physic a sick horse.

ANGELO: So you even cure animals.

FRIAR: My son, we seek to comfort all God's creatures.

ANGELO (*making a thrust with the sword*): 'Tis noble weapon
this—though something ponderous and therefore not so
speedy as our modern rapiers.

FRIAR (*snorting contemptuously*): Call not your rapiers swords; spits are they rather. A sword should have edge as well as point.

ANGELO: Yet point is swifter and more deadly than edge.

FRIAR: With that good blade I would shiver you a dozen of your niminy-piminy rapiers!

ANGELO: Well, 'tis good sword this, and was my boyish admiring awe especially when thou wouldst tell me of how and when thou hadst used it.

FRIAR: Then was I blameable to fill thy young head with such tales.

ANGELO: Ah, but 'twas then I loved thee most, father. (*He replaces sword upon the wall*). And now, seeing I am become a stranger here in Celonia, ay, in all the duchy of Segovia, by ten years' absence, tell me, father, who besides my old friends Andrea and Manfred are to be trusted? So far we are but five, namely: thyself and Rillo of course, Andrea, Manfred and myself. Then there might be Ippolito that was Fortunio's esquire and did so well in the war; what say you of him?

FRIAR (*measuring oil to vinegar like the expert chemist he was*): Count Ippolito is young, though of approved courage, clean of heart and trustworthy.

ANGELO: Then he shall be listed.

FRIAR: There be very many I could summon, stout fellows and faithful all. Yet I think the fewer the better—at present.

ANGELO: So think I. Six, then, let us be until we may see and know our way. But, good father, I, as chiefest concerned——

FRIAR: Nay, we be all concerned, Angelo.

ANGELO: True! Yet Fortunio was my brother. And thus I would not have thee anywise peril thy most precious life in this cause—nay, I forbid it.

FRIAR: My son, I shall help thee in mine own way and as God shall direct. For there be powers I could loose more terrible than any known weapon.

ANGELO: Aha, thy sorcerer's spells of magic and wizardry?

FRIAR: Call them so. And now do I call thee to dinner, so come—eat! And drink—though only rough wine of the country have I.

So down they sat, this one-time master and pupil, like the men and life-long friends they were, eating in that blissful silence that true hunger inspires, until:

FRIAR (*cutting another slice of ham with the delicate nicety of a skilled craftsman*): Angelo, should God spare thee to be our Duke, I would have thee build and endow a new, great hospital for the poor with spacious laboratory furnished with all instruments needed for chymical search —and furthermore——

ANGELO (*bolting a mouthful*): Hold, father, hold! To be Duke, supposing I'm not untimely killed, I must win Jenevra—and in this most vile, unheroical, right damnable motley——

FRIAR: Swear not, my son! Instead, pass me the sallet— take thou and pass. Now, tell me how and where dost propose to live.

ANGELO: At Fidena—though secretly.

FRIAR: Impossible! For, since Angelo is so dead, the castle of Fidena, having no owners, reverteth to the Duchess.

ANGELO (*rubbing his chin perplexedly*): Good lack—I had not thought of this! Well, Andrea or Manfred must find me some lodgement; any hole or corner shall serve.

FRIAR: Good! Then I have a corner for thee here, indeed several. Shalt have thy choice.

ANGELO: God bless thee, Father Clem; this will I.

FRIAR: Then, my son, when not haunting the court, shalt dig with me, help in my workshop or play me music on thy pipe yonder.

ANGELO: All other will I do for thee except pipe, for I cannot pipe a note. Were it a harp now—faith, I think I will get me one. A harping Folly should be something new.

At this moment a voice was heard upraised in song, a sweetly rich man's voice, coming nearer.

ANGELO: Why, what marvellous songster cometh yonder?

FRIAR: Pedrillo. Some three years since this power came to him—hark!

The singing drew nearer, was suddenly hushed, and into this small room strode a crooked man, broad as he was long, but with a face whose harsh ugliness was softened by great luminous eyes,—which eyes now beholding Angelo widened in amazement.

ANGELO (*reaching out his hands*): Pedrillo! Ah, Rillo, dost not know me? Look now, 'spite my cropped hair, this vile wig—away with it—and dark stained face—who am I?

Uttering shout of joyous welcome, Pedrillo set down the huge burdens he carried, reached out great arms and lifting Angelo as if he had been a child, hugged him to his broad chest, crying in his splendid voice:
"Angelo! 'Tis little master Angelo grown to manhood! Nay, but . . . Angelo is dead . . . killed for treason and so proclaimed. I heard it today i' the market——"
Here and very briefly Angelo explained the why and wherefore of his supposed death, whereat Pedrillo rejoiced the more.
So now, instead of two, were three in eating, drinking and fellowship, for Pedrillo, this crook-back, was not only mightily strong of body but cultured in mind, having learned much from his scholarly master; and thus they ate and conversed, all three.

PEDRILLO: In truth, Angelo, I should never have known thee.
ANGELO: Nor any other, I hope. Whence come you now, Rillo?
RILLO: From tending a horse at the court stables, and what a horse! 'Twas gift of the Duchess to my lord Gonzago— a right noble creature.
ANGELO: Which creature, the horse or man?
RILLO: Both! For each is beautiful as other! Eyes never saw handsomer, lovelier man—all slender shapeliness and hidden strength of body like his face, for in those lovely features is a latent power——
ANGELO: For good or evil, Rillo?
RILLO: This I cannot say—only that I, being creature so hideous, do love all creatures beautiful, man or beast. And for this lord Gonzago, this splendid man, in him I read power of mind besides beauty of body! Ah, 'tis no wonder he is favoured of the Duchess. They do say she will wed him——

ANGELO: Do they so? S'life, I grow urgent for sight of *this* gentleman, this paragon of manly perfections.

RILLO: Mock not, Angelo, for indeed, though beautiful, he is very man.

ANGELO: Well, he is new here since my time. Whence came he and when?

FRIAR: Some five years since and from Spain as I've heard.

RILLO: It was from Spain, master. Yet 'stead of showing darkly Spanish he is clear-ruddy of complexion, grey of eye, and his hair—for he weareth no beard or moustachio to mar his face—his hair, I say, is of that rare colour, named auburn.

ANGELO: That's to say—red! Well, for my part, I like not red polls, and a beautiful man is a disgust——

FRIAR: Judge no man unseen, my son.

RILLO: And by all at court this man is deemed matchless at play of rapier and dagger——

ANGELO (*mournfully*): And my weapon a fool's bauble! Yet mayhap he shall be matched anon.

FRIAR (*anxiously*): Be not too forward in quarrel, my son! Thy life henceforth is dedicate to nobler purpose! Therefore waste not thyself in selfish broil with such as he.

ANGELO: Never—except he cross my wooing. Thyself said 'twas my duty to woo, as I now do certainly believe, and no man shall come 'twixt me and such duty. My duty—my lovely, pleasing, joyous, most difficult of duties! This reminds me—today at sunset the Duchess meets her councillors in public, and there will I be, though not in motley. I must have some other guise—a butcher's bloody smock should best suit me, seeing Angelo is a corpse so lately.

RILLO: Well, this I could provide from Jovani the butcher.

ANGELO: Excellent! And therewith a good, stout quarter-staff. Thus equipped, I'll raise such clamours, if necessary, as shall set lying Villainy by the ears and silence its slanderous tongue! At sunset then?

FRIAR: At sunset, my son.

RILLO: And if thou shout, Angelo, I'll warrant I will out-shout thee.

ANGELO: This, perchance, we shall prove—at sunset.

CHAPTER XI

TELLS HOW GONZAGO COUNSELLED THE CHIEF COUNCILLOR

MY LORD GONZAGO, a splendid figure in his rich suit of mourning, took his gracious way through the palace gardens athrong with lords and ladies of the court who, old and young alike, very aware of the profound grief of their Duchess, reflected her sorrow, as courtiers should, in the sombre ostentation of their persons: they echoed it in muted speech, and, if thoughtless youth dared a laugh—such irreverence was instantly stifled by frowning reproach.

Thus amid them all Gonzago, who was never known to hurry, made his leisured way, pausing frequently to bow in stately greeting or to smile with softly uttered word; for since it was thought their Duchess favoured him, her courtiers sought his favour for themselves and their own possible future welfare.

Thus, graciously aware of all their flattering homage, Gonzago bowed and smiled his way until he came where Astorgio, newly arrived, stood with his young esquire behind him, peering about, amid this ever-moving concourse, for the lady Fiametta who at that moment was deep in murmurous talk with young Count Ippolito in a green alley discreetly remote.

Now if Astorgio's thoughts were all of love and joy, his garments were eloquent of the deepest woe; from the raven plume in his bonnet to the toes of his elegant shoes he was completely funereal, no gleam of gold or glitter of jewel anywhere about him: even the hilt of his rapier was of ebon hue. Thus Gonzago, beholding him, paused to bow and say in that very pleasing voice of his:

"Messire, you are the very image of Grief, a mirror of Melancholy, a perfect spectacle of Infelicity! And, 'twixt you and me, it is well you should appear so."

"Oh—my lord," tittered Astorgio, with bow of many complications, "I vow, I protest your commendation transmutes my grief to joy woeful yet—a joy!"

"And," continued Gonzago, gravely, "I repeat 'tis well you should appear such figure of dolorous gloom, since yourself is the direct cause of our widespread lamentation."

"I—I, the cause—I?" gasped Astorgio. "God's my life—how?"

"For that you, Messire Astorgio, were the very agent of—Death!" Astorgio started back so suddenly as almost to collide with his esquire whose furtive gaze was ever upon Gonzago's handsome face as if watching for some meaning glance or signal, while his astounded master bleated:

"How . . . who . . . what . . ."

"Messire," continued Gonzago, "is it not the fact that upon the fatal night you were the bearer of certain wine to Lord Fortunio at Fidena?"

"Indeed . . . from . . . from Her Grace . . . 'twas so mine honour . . . a most precious gift of the Duchess——"

"How, my lord, from the Duchess say you? Dare you so aver when 'tis now known that in this same wine was some venomous infusion, some vicious drug whereof our great and most lamented Fortunio presently died?"

"The . . . the wine . . . poison . . . Fortunio——"

"And not only he, but that faithful soul and valiant soldier his ancient—Jacomo! Dare you now accuse the Duchess of this——"

"No—no! As . . . as God's my witness, I know nought . . . nought in the world . . . of this!"

"Yet, alas," sighed Gonzago, mournfully, "it is but too direly true, whereof I doubt not you will be questioned anon" —here for a moment Gonzago's glance met the young esquire's ever-watchful regard—"questioned, Messire Astorgio, concerning that fatal wine you bore so faithfully, whereto I am happy to think you will find a just and convincing answer." So, with smiling bow, Gonzago passed on, leaving Astorgio a very shaken gentleman indeed, with no thought now of love, joy or anything in the world except his hapless self.

Meanwhile, up the broad, marble steps of the palace went Gonzago, passing the armed guards with kindly word and smile for each, through spacious ante-chamber and great hall of audience, along noble colonnade with its famous groups of statuary, and so at last to the council chamber, vacant at this hour except for Sebastian and his four secretaries.

"Ah, my lord," said Gonzago, gayly, "I greet you humbly well and as humbly crave speech with your lordship—alone!"

Sebastian sighed pettishly, frowned wearily and dismissed his satellites imperiously, saying the moment they were gone:

"Gonzago, be brief, for, as you see, I have much business."

"Business?" murmured Gonzago, sinking languidly into the nearest chair. "Some world-shaking matter of village market dues? Ah, well—let it wait, for my business is of life—and death! Thy death, Sebastian, or perchance—even mine."

"Hush!" whispered Sebastian, rising hurriedly. "Go with me to my chamber where we can at least be private."

Thus presently seated behind closed doors in small but sumptuous apartment, Sebastian demanded angrily:

"Well? What new recklessness? What rash desperate scheme engages you now?"

Smiling, Gonzago selected the easiest available chair and leaned back, and still he smiled, though in his eyes such malevolent glare that Sebastian, about to speak, was dumb with shocked amazement; then Gonzago's long, thick lashes fell, and when they lifted, his eyes, somehow matching his smile, showed their usual languid amusement.

"Sebastian," said he gently, "upon that night when the joy-bells changed their tune—our night of destiny—you asked of me—or rather demanded my answer to your question, thus. 'Gonzago,' said you, 'what hast thou done?' Well, now I return that question: Sebastian, what hast thou done? I also ask and demand an answer. Where is that letter, the dispatch signed Antonio Friuli?"

And after momentary hesitation Sebastian answered:

"I thought proper to leave it with Her Grace——"

"Ah, you thought proper——"

"I did and do. Consequently it is in her charge So for the moment she has it, but——"

"And, my poor Sebastian, just as surely will she have thy head, thy blood, thy life, except thou produce this same Antonio Friuli!"

"How? Will you presume—will you dare to—to threaten me?"

"Not I, thou muddlesome conspirator; not I, but circumstance and by reason of thine own ineptitude——"

"Enough!" exclaimed Sebastian furiously and, rising with what dignity he might, "I will not hear you——"

"Sebastian, you will sit down and harken with both ears lest the last earthly sound you hear be hiss of the executioner's sword or creak of gallows. So—pray sit and hear me—do!"

Sebastian sank down rather than sat, lying back in his great cushioned chair as if bereft of strength, while Gonzago continued in the same gentle tone:

"Why must you to the Duchess with that quite accursed letter and—without me?"

"She being head of the State I was bound to bring it to her notice."

"Assuredly, but in proper time, place, manner and—in my presence. Now, is there such person as Antonio Friuli?"

"Most certainly there is!"

"Who is he? What is he? And—where now?"

"A very honest man that farms part of my estates in the south."

"So? A rustical fellow, and honest? Better have chosen any other, or none, than such as he."

"Ah, and why so?" demanded Sebastian, frowning.

"Think now—being a farmer he shall seem too rustical to act the part he must, and being honest he will not—unless you corrupt or compel him thereto. For indeed he must carry perfect conviction by look, word and seeming when he swears to that letter."

"Ha, that damned letter!" fumed Sebastian. "This was thy contrivance—thine!"

"And thy performance, Sebastian! And should have served excellent well, properly used! As 'tis, should the Duchess refuse its testimony today and damn it before the Council and others, then my too venturous Sebastian will be in sorry case unless he promise to produce his Antonio Friuli——"

"And why not yourself, Gonzago, and your friends? Why myself more than any other of you?"

"Because," answered Gonzago, in tone soft as caress, "I am a friendless wight. But thou, dear Sebastian, art such woeful bungler, such grave, stately, pedantical fool that I begin to fear nature meant thee for honest and virtuous soul. Nay, be not aggrieved nor protest thyself co-villain with Gonzago, for this thou canst never attain unto. Therefore, let thyself be, as ever, thine own content, and this evening at sunset before this assembly seem thy seemliest and most virtuous self and by the magic of thy tongue make all thy hearers so believe thee. Well now, having thus warned and counselled thee as loving friend should, I will leave thee to thy much business." But as he made to rise, Sebastian stayed him with a gesture, saying:

"Suppose the Duchess should . . . refuse Friuli's testimony . . . even on oath?"

"Then, alas for thee, Sebastian!"

"And what—of thyself?"

"I shall grieve for thee!"

"Thou grieve—for me? Thou!"

Sebastian rose, trembling with such fury as for the moment held him speechless, while Gonzago, taking out a small gold comb, began smoothing his long, glossy hair—until his hand was arrested by Sebastian's clutching, icy fingers:

"Gonzago," he whispered in strangled voice, "should danger threaten me . . . never think I'll suffer thee to . . . stand aloof and all immune! Should disaster shame and crush me, I will not die alone! Ah no, my fate shall be thine, since thine was the hand that swept Fortunio from our path. . . ."

Gently Gonzago freed his hand, then, looking up into the pale, contorted face above him, said in his very kindest tone:

"My poor Sebastian, thou art thine own torment! Yet here is no reason to so plague thyself with such dire phantasies. Instead sit down and tell me of thy new scheme to make a scapegoat of the Duchess and——"

"'Twas no scheme of mine! I say it was not! Cavalcanti or Fabriano first spoke of it, one or other, and these lately in thy company, and, like as not, inspired by thee. As for such scheme—'twas madness."

"Yet therewith you threatened her this morning——"

"It was no threat. I but spoke her gentle warning as one that loved her."

"May I hear thy warning?"

"'Twas how she herself might be held responsible for or even suspected of Fortunio's death."

"Whereat she fled in a panic, ha?"

"Neither one nor other. She is not so readily affrighted!"

"Alas, no! And panic fear can be so useful, being a power so infinitely—persuasive!"

"Ah, you mean?"

"That she must be so persuaded—and by thy perfervid oratory, Sebastian."

"Gonzago, what mean you? How persuaded and whereto?"

"To a discreet silence in regard to that letter and her belief in Fortunio's murder."

"Well and good, but how, man, how?"

"You shall to her make great ado of public clamours, paint in lurid words how Fortunio's veteran soldiers be astir and armed for vengeance on his murderers and plotting their discovery. Say this spirit of vengeful unrest is spreading in town and country and nought to stay it but proof he died by his own hand. Then show her how and why she herself may be imperilled by this blind and growing menace of revenge. As first, her known wilfulness and love of power wherefrom none might dare to stay her, save—Fortunio. Secondly, her pride that will suffer none greater then herself, and no man strong enough to challenge this save—Fortunio. Thirdly, how in her determination to rule alone none was great enough to forbid or withstand her ambition, save— Fortunio. Hence and wherefore, the poisoned wine and—exit Fortunio! Thus stands the indictment against her, the which, by thy special pleading and craft of wordy eloquence should be made so damning that even her bold spirit may quail and she thus be—persuaded to silence or, at least, to make no public utterance today at sunset. And now," sighed Gonzago, stretching lazily and rising. "I'll leave thee to thine own so important business."

Being alone, Sebastian sat awhile in profound meditation, and gradually his gloom lifted, his eyes brightened, his lips curled in a smile that he instantly hid with a white, well-cared-for hand. Presently he rose, donned hat, cloak and sword and, going forth, sought and was granted audience by the Duchess, this harassed girl, and contrived to seem even more gravely impressive than usual. And thus he set forth his case with an eloquence so terribly convincing as to afflict her, first with troubled doubt and then—such dread as appalled even her resolute spirit.

So thus it befell that at sunset her ten lords of Council met not in great crowded hall, but in the dignified seclusion of their own chamber; there the letter was read, discussed, filed among the archives, and the business done. Sebastian, relieved of all fear and anxiety, passed serenely through the dispersing townsfolk who, though disappointed by the absence of their Duchess, cheered her chief councillor for the noble lord he so truly seemed.

D

CHAPTER XII

TELLS HOW THE JESTER WOOED AND WHY
THE DUCHESS LAUGHED NOT

COMING into her garden, and even earlier than usual, the Duchess glanced askance yet expectantly towards the great, carved sundial and, seeing there nothing except the sundial, caught herself sighing, frowned pettishly, turned angrily and— beheld the Jester leaning against a tree within a yard of her.

"Oh!" she exclaimed, girlishly, then, remembering her dignity, became the more stately and aloof, surveying his shabby person with the utmost disparagement like the proud young potentate she was, saying coldly:

"Dare you intrude here again, fool?"

"And with all my heart, lady!" he answered meekly, yet with a sparkle in his dark eyes. "And I came, as aforetime, by setting one foot——"

"I know, fool, I know. But why must you creep upon me like sly-crawling cat or horrid ghost?"

"Were I a ghost, then with phantom finger I would touch and wake thee to memory of happier days. As it is, I am but poor Jester that was here with the sun, waiting until thyself came, to help him light the world, stealing upon my vision like——"

"Fool, I never steal!"

"This then leaves us—'creeping' or 'crawling' upon my sight like——"

"Don't dare say 'cat'!" she warned him, with swift up-glance and ruddy lips that almost smiled.

"I would say aught in the world to win of thee a smile; thou poor, unsleeping sadness."

" 'Tis true I sleep little of late," she sighed.

"And thus art abroad so early—which is good!"

"How 'good'?"

"Excellent good—for the birds and such other happy creatures blessed with eyes to behold thee! And yet 'tis sad thy sleepless hours be wasted on woe for past ill, rather than on joy for that which is surely yet to be."

"Well, but what is 'yet to be'?"

"Love and——"

"No!" she exclaimed, fiercely. "Never mention this to me; 'tis most hateful word."

"By overmuch repetition, thou much be-suitored soul? Then will I attempt thy laughter with a tale, thus. There was a poor Folly, that, being froward fool, dared love his lady and she a dame of proud and high degree—and there's the pity on't!"

"Where is the pity and why? Mean you she had this so presumptuous fool whipped?"

"Alas, no!"

"Then stripped and turned away to starve?"

"Nor even that."

"Then what did she?"

"Married him, thereby losing a good fool and winning but indifferent fool of a husband."

"Oh, futility! Such witless fooling shall never make me laugh."

"Indeed I had some doubt of it myself."

"Then why tell such nonsense?"

"Lady, I know the fool."

"Oh! And the lady, know you the silly love-sick wretch?"

"Nay, fie—let us talk of fish!"

"Fish, fool?"

"Fish, lady. There was, on a time, a fish feminine, frocked in gold and purple splendour, that lived in certain placid pool, and she, being fool of a fish, though feminine, loved the eldest son of a swineherd that fished this pool, his angle baited with such fulsome flatteries besides the wily worm upon his hook, that this fish, being as I say so femininely foolish, would certainly have been caught but that fish masculine leapt first and, leaping, was lost."

"This," exclaimed the Duchess, "is merest absurdity!"

"True, lady! And on thy lips peeps ghost of a smile."

Jenevra laughed, then, turning, crossed to a marble seat nearby and sank down there; but now though the rising sun's level beams made a glory all about her, they showed, instead of laughing girl, a very troubled woman who surveyed him with keenly-questioning eyes, from worn shoe to dark, lean face which just now seemed so preposterously at variance with its ridiculous cockscomb, coarse, black elf-locks and shabby hood; this sensitive face whose delicate features could change from wistful sadness to grimmest mockery in as many moments. . . .

"Who," she demanded, at last, "are you? What is your name?" And glancing up at a lark that carolled high above them, he replied:

"Bimbo."

"And suits you not at all!" she retorted.

"Yet 'tis most excellent foolish name," he murmured.

"Then, Bimbo Fool, whence come you?"

"From hither and yon, near and far, lady, though lately from a right saintly friar, a very man of God, which, seeing me all friendless, needy and forlorn, sheltered me, fed me and called me—his son!"

"This must be Friar Clement."

"Ay, truly! And he called me his son. Thus as son I love and obey him, wherefore I am—here."

"So then 'twas dear Father Clement bade you hither to me?"

"Even so, and bearing his love with hope of seeing you in the oratory for matins today. Here also—this script to witness my truth!" And from breast of his shabby doublet the Jester drew a small, folded paper which he presented, saying: "My reverend father thought you might perchance read it to me." Thus when she had scanned this missive she read it aloud in voice softened to very tenderness:

"'Beloved daughter, God be thy abiding strength and comfort, Amen. He that beareth this, shall prove less foolish than he showeth and is one thou mayest trust as myself. Clement.'

"Now truly," said she, refolding this paper, "my reverend father must know thee passing well to so write."

"And truly," answered the Jester, "my reverend father is very wise and blessed with vision. Moreover, friendship is not always a matter of years. Sometimes, like true love, 'tis born in a moment—a word, a look, a sigh, and 'tis there forever."

"So I am to trust thee, Bimbo the Jester?"

"Ever and always!" he answered, fervently. "To death—and beyond!"

"Here now is strange talk for a fool!"

"Nay, 'twas the reverent son of Father Clement spake then."

"So let him often speak—and comfort me—if he only may." She sighed. "For I, that ever scorned fear, am greatly fearful

at last! Though I am child of my valorous sire that was
called 'The Fearless', yet am I also—a woman."

"God be thanked!" murmured the Jester.

"Oh—why?" she demanded.

"That in good time others as nobly valiant may call thee
'mother'. Meanwhile, may I know the reason for thy new
fear?"

"Oh," she exclaimed, with hopeless gesture, " 'tis all about
me! My whole world seems falling in dreadful ruin since my
loved Fortunio died and left me desolate. He that was so
strong and able—murdered! And with him, my dear Jacomo.
This was my bitter grief! But now—that I should be held
suspect of their deaths! Oh, this is my horror! And later,
perchance, to be . . . accused . . . and proclaimed . . . their
murderess——"

"No!" cried the Jester, angrily. "This can be no more
than vile court gossip——"

"Ah, would indeed 'twere so! But my courtiers would
never dare—they do and say only that they think will pleasure
me; Sebastian alone dare speak me the hateful truth——"

"Aha—Sebastian!" exclaimed the Jester, seating himself
cross-legged upon the grass. "Now, prithee, what sayeth this
so truthful lord?"

"That Fortunio's veteran soldiers be stirring my people
in town and country to suspect and cry vengeance upon me
as his poisoner."

"So—ho!" cried the Jester, tossing up his bauble and
catching it. "There sits the wind, ha? The good Sebastian
shows thy danger and how it may be readily avoided by
agreeing this wished verdict—that Fortunio murdered himself. Is it not so?"

"Yes," she nodded, miserably, " 'tis so he urges, yet to
this I will never agree, never!"

"Howbeit, lady, this should still all vengeful clamours,
end all suspicions and—Fortunio is safely dead and buried."

"Oh," cried she bitterly, "think you that now his voice
is hushed I will suffer his glory to be so dimmed or his
memory dishonoured—to shield myself, or any other, by such
base lie? Dare you think this of me, most hateful fool?"

"Not for a moment, most noble lady and right valiant
woman——"

"Rather will I die!" she cried passionately.

"So shalt thou live," said he, gently, "live to be honoured and loved as such woman should be—and is!"

"To be—loved?" she repeated. "Yet 'tis said I am arrogant . . . 'twas so Jacomo would oft reprove me for my pride. Ah, would he were here to so reproach me now— my old Jacco that used to ride me on his shoulder—my earliest playfellow, alas!"

"And alas!" sighed the Jester. "Yet, here now sitteth one Bimbo a mountebank-folly that, 'stead of bearing thee shoulder-high, shall now do his foolish best to lift thy droop-ing spirit high as yon soaring lark and banish thy melan-choly—according to the behest of my Father Clement and his instruction concerning thee."

"What were his instructions, Bimbo?"

" 'My son!' quoth he sighing—thus: 'Alas, she is a Duchess and therefore solitary, since all greatness must be lonely; she is a woman and therefore changeable, but she is young and therefore should be joyous. So, Bimbo my son, let thy foolery banish solitude and sadness, lifting her troubled mind above present cares. . . .' "

"Ah," she sighed, "would indeed you might!"

"Duchess, I both will and can. Lady, I shall! So, woman perpend! What in all this world can be so comical, so laughable, such object for side-splitting merriment, as a Jester, a Folly that is such foolish fool as in his folly should dare to love? Surely nothing, since he is but thing for jape and jest and universal mockery. A Jester in love—oh, rare spec-tacle; his heart nigh bursting with love, his eyes brimful of pleading, wistful worship 'neath ludicrous, flaunting cocks-comb and dangling ass's ears, his every sighful, soulful utter-ance mocked by his jingling bells, his very reverence made ridiculous by his motley, himself a creature to be kicked or buffeted for scorn or brutal merriment! Thus now to woo thy laughter, I, like froward fool and fooling Jester, do thus woo thee, list now and laugh. Oh, lady of all loveliness, fair embodiment of dream, thou woman of my reverent worship— here Folly kneels—and flip-flap goeth cockscomb, wig-wag his ass's ears what time his jingling bells mock his adoration and thy laughter smites him dumb for pain of thee and his own poor futility."

"But," said she, looking down on him where he knelt, head bowed, "I have not laughed—yet."

"Why then, oh woman, our foolish Jester, hands thus
meekly folded, dareth to proceed. It was but chance of birth
made thee a Duchess, but God made thee a woman. Chance
of fortune made me this thing of mockery, yet nonetheless I,
too, am God's handiwork; and we, thus divinely equal, I
dare proclaim my love divine likewise, and so great to fill
the universe and make for me this sorry world a glory. Here
our fool, in the fervour of his passion, throws wide his arms—
thus! whereat is flip-flap, wig-wag and jingle-jangle. And
then since this cruel mockery is beyond endurance, he leaps
afoot—while I sit down—and flyeth, poor wretch, to whisper
his love to birds in lonely wood, and dream himself, instead
of fool, a man beloved of her he loveth."

"Then, Bimbo, this fool is fool indeed since dreams be but
emptiness."

"Not so, woman; no and no! For think, how the poor
prisoner in black gloom of dungeon, shut out of life and hope
may dream how once in dawn of day he stood mid dewy
green to watch the young sun rush through the gates of
morning to kiss the earth to wakefulness. Thus, though
prisoned, he may weave him dreams whereby his narrow
walls and cruel shackles vanish all, and—he is free! So
dreameth our fool, ay—and to right marvellous effect!"

"How, Bimbo?"

"That his motley is such prison wherefrom he may 'scape
into a world of dream wherein his beloved cometh to meet
him . . . and upon her lips, within her eyes and in all her
sweet body is love ineffable whereby his foolish motley is
transformed to a glory, and himself to all he would be."

"And yet all this is but a dream," sighed Jenevra, "but
this world, alas, a most troublous reality!"

"Why, so it seems," he nodded; "wherein thou art a
Duchess, a ruling monarch and I a motley wag and creature
of none account. And yet methinks I have the better part,
and so 'tis I grieve for thee thou royal poppet."

"Oh?" she demanded. "And wherefore wilt thou so
dare?"

"That destiny, making thee so great, thus spoiled God's
sweet handiwork. For what fool is she would choose to be a
Duchess to live prisoned in a palace, to be forever watched,
spied upon, harassed, grieved and bemused by courtiers and
councillors with their petty jealousies and lying policies?

Better a goose-girl singing to her hissing charges, or milk-maid paddling barefoot in the dew."

"I have thought the same of late," sighed Jenevra, "for I am now so lonely and desolate, save only for my dear Father Clement."

"Yet, lady, I have heard tell of suitors amany."

"So many they become my plague."

"Also, Duchess, there is one—Gonzago?"

"Gonzago?" she repeated. "Him I shall wed . . . mayhap, since wed I needs must."

"How 'must'?" enquired the Jester sitting upright and very suddenly. "Why and wherefore 'must'?"

"My councillors have lately revived an old law how that no woman may rule alone longer than five years. Thus in six months I must wed or abdicate."

"Aha! And which seems to thee the lesser evil?"

"This I shall know six months hence. And because this law would so compel me, love is become hateful."

"Yet thou shalt love anon—I pray God!"

"Oh? and why so pray God?"

"For thine own sake and—one other."

"Oh!" said she again, and very softly, glancing up in her turn at the lark, or its mate, still carolling high above them. "One other, Bimbo?"

"Nay," he answered, looking at this lovely upturned face, "there is but one Bimbo, and he thy faithful fool of comfort."

"And doth my fool of comfort think love shall find me—if I wed this lord?"

"Never!" exclaimed the Jester, so vehemently that she glanced from lark to fool beneath raised brows.

"Oh!" she murmured, for the third time. "How then may one find love and where?"

"Nowhere!" he answered, and with the utmost finality. "None may ever find the love that is true and everlasting—until it find them. For this cometh all unsought and when least expected. Yet once it hath found us then with us it abideth, through life and beyond death, since True Love, being of God, is immortal."

"Ah, Bimbo," she murmured, "I never thought, I never dreamed love could be thus sacred, such holy thing, for it hath ever seemed so very—otherwise. This is why I have

scorned and driven it from me hitherto, and this, mayhap, is
why they call me proud and arrogant. But this love you tell
of is very strange, Bimbo——"

"Ay—in princely courts!" he nodded. "For there be so
many ogling, sighful shams and cozening counterfeits calling
themselves love that True Love, for very shame, hath fled
to hide in——" He paused as his keen, ever-watchful eyes
beheld one approaching with leisurely grace, a tall person
whose rich though sombre attire served only to offset his
lithe shapeliness to perfection and whose almost too handsome face was framed in lustrous auburn hair.

Now glancing whither Bimbo looked, the Duchess frowned,
then smiled, saying, as this magnificence drew near:

"Tell me, my lord, what is love?"

And smiling, this gentleman answered, forthwith:

"Gracious loveliness, some do name him Eros, others call
him Dan Cupid, but his true name is—Gonzago."

The Duchess laughed again.

CHAPTER XIII

WHEREIN BIMBO THE JESTER JINGLES—AND
TO SOME EFFECT

"So you, my lord, like this motley impertinent, dare trespass
again! Yet this morning I make you welcome, Gonzago."

"Most loved and gracious lady," he murmured, bending
to kiss her yielded hand with passionate fervour, "then to
sweet Venus be my thanks that I should win of thee such
greeting——"

"Not you, my lord; 'twas won for you by this Folly. So
'stead of Venus, thank him."

"Heartily!" said Gonzago, glancing where the Jester
sprawled, plucking idly at the grass. "So, come, thou thing
of waggery, rouse thee and accept my thanks and therewith
this gold for winning me such priceless welcome; look up,
I say!" And, speaking, Gonzago stirred this shabby figure
with toe of his delicate shoe. . . . Slowly the Jester turned
and, leaning on an elbow, looked up at Gonzago, who gazed
down upon him—and thus they met. . . . For a tense,

silent moment dark brooding eyes looked up into blacklashed
eyes of grey that gazed down as keenly.

Then the Jester saluted with airy flourish of his bauble,
saying:

"Hail, Apollo! Greeting, Hyperion! Come, make thy
gold pieces two and I will jape or jingle ye, rhyme or riddle
ye or cut a caper." Gonzago laughed and tossed a second
coin, saying:

"Thus then even Folly is never content? 'Twere fool of a
Folly were he so, for he that is content is poor, base wretch
predestined to servitude."

"And yet, oh lovely Hyperion, he that is content with
little, possesseth all."

"So thou'rt a stoic-philosophical Folly—a follower of
Epictetus, ha? Well, he was a slave."

"Ay, that won to freedom, fame and an enduring memory,
my lovely lord."

"I'faith, dear lady, methinks I shall love this fool; 'tis
folly original, an erudite Jester, a buffoon versed in the
ancient wisdoms——"

"And he calls himself—Bimbo!" said she musingly as she
glanced from Gonzago's radiant face to the Jester's dark,
clean-cut features.

"And, pray thee, Jenevra, is this same Bimbo he that
flouted our stately Sebastian and even dared—oh, thunder of
heaven—to give him the lie direct anent—a certain letter—
is this he indeed?"

"Truly and indeed, and, oh,"—she cried with sudden trill
of laughter—"for once in his life my so impressive chief
councillor was quite, quite out of countenance, and, forgetting his grave dignity, he stammered and stuttered, grew
red, grew pale and finally to raging fury."

"So?" exclaimed Gonzago. "Then now do I love this
fool! And the more that, by his means, I have heard thee
laugh again, Jenevra—to me the sweetest, loveliest sound in
all this lovely world. Thy laugh hath waked my very soul to
gladness—with promise of joy that is to be and——"

"Enough, my lord! Such protestation for one small laugh
is fulsome. Instead talk we now of Sebastian. You must
know that last night I sent him word how I will never permit
use of that false letter to so dishonour my loved Fortunio's
sacred memory, nor allow this hateful, lying verdict of his

self-murder; no—not even though I die for it! This I wrote him last night; know you how he received it?"

Gonzago sighed and shook his handsome head, saying:

"I would not have told of this, but, since you so demand, I will say no more than—that he took it nothing kindly."

"How so, my lord? Be explicit, Gonzago! What did he, what said he of my letter?"

"Madame, ah, Jenevra, it woke in him that which was my dreadful amazement."

"Ah, you mean he raged and cried out against me—dared he so?"

"Worse! He was silent and very still. If he raged 'twas too deep, too dire for mere utterance——"

"Yet 'twas 'gainst me and my decision?"

"Dearest lady, I make no accusation 'gainst one so high in Your Grace's favour and the public esteem. Also he—was—my friend!"

"Was, Gonzago?"

"Jenevra, beloved lady, I set the Duchess and her welfare above friendship and all else."

"Are you suggesting that Sebastian has changed towards you of late?"

"Alas, 'tis so my grief!"

"And aha," exclaimed the Jester, juggling his two gold pieces very dexterously, "so God protect us from our friends!"

"Fool, be silent!" said the Duchess, frowning and distressful. "Indeed, my lord, this matter of Sebastian troubles me greatly."

"Nay fie, why should it?"

"I am—so lonely!" she sighed, wearily. "I feel so lost and helpless without Fortunio. And now that he is gone, Sebastian is the most powerful lord in all Segovia, as you know."

"'Tis beyond question, Madame."

"Gonzago . . . think you he means to be . . . greater yet?"

"Who knows? But this reminds me! Do you recall to memory one, Count Francesco Loredano?"

"Very well; he was banished by Fortunio for treachery. What of this wretch?"

"He is stolen back from banishment and hath been recognized."

"Then, if he is taken he shall die. Let this be known. But now as for Sebastian, how think you?"

"Nay, Jenevra, look not so woeful, for though he be so powerful, neither am I a weakling! And love shall make me able and strong as giant to thy defence—if need be. But no more of this! Give me thy hand, dear lady, and let us walk a while and I will tell thee merry tale of——"

"Nay," said she, rising with weary, almost hopeless gesture, "the morning hath lost its gladness, and would this fretful day were done and I lost in the blessed peacefulness of sleep——"

"Oho!" cried the Jester. "Yet sun shineth, birds sing and Folly, thy fool of comfort, percheth on sward to pity thee Jenevra, thou poor, pestered, princely poppet! Cry plague on court and councillors and consort with birds and beasts o' the field that, being creatures of no reason, no reason shall give thee to sigh for sleep and forgetfulness of life that should be joy. . . . Ha, but—lo, what stately and embattled trouble marcheth on thee yonder to thy further woe!" And he gestured where Sebastian was approaching with Astorgio, closely followed by Andrea and Manfred, their burnished armour flashing back the sun. The Duchess uttered sigh like a groan, yet lifted her chin resolutely. Gonzago's slender brows knit in momentary frown, while the Jester from his lowly posture watched all.

"Madame," said Sebastian, advancing to bow, "early though the hour, I think it well that here in the privacy of your grace's garden you should hear me question this gentleman Messire Astorgio on whom suspicion rests touching the grievous and mysterious death of the late lord Fortunio. To the which end you here behold us."

"But, my lord," said she, wearily, "I have never suspected this gentleman."

"Howbeit, Madame, needs must suspicion darken him since in the bearing or conveyance of that . . . supposedly poisoned wine, Your Grace's own gift, he was thus Your Grace's known agent——"

"My lord," murmured Gonzago, "may I very humbly beg leave to suggest 'messenger' instead of 'agent'——"

"Oh," cried the Duchess, "what matter the word? You all know I did send the wine and by this gentleman, openly and before you all, as . . . mark of my dear love——"

"And yet, Madame, 'tis known he died of poison——"

"Ay!" exclaimed Andrea, impulsively, stepping forward and saluting. "Wherefore, as captain of Your Grace's body-

guard and by Your Grace's leave, I now demand of this gentleman—how came poison in the wine he bore?"

"Ah!" growled Manfred. "Let him answer that now!"

Astorgio glanced from the bleak, fierce eyes of Andrea to
Manfred's scowling visage, gulped nervously and replied:

"Madame, my . . . my lords and gentlemen, I now swear
before Almighty God and . . . and . . . yourselves, I, as I say,
do vow and protest my complete ignorance of all, and innocence most absolute of any poison soever. Nought know I of
such . . . nought, I say, in all this world . . . as I'm a
gentleman . . . nought."

"Aha!" exclaimed the Jester; and then, beating time with
his bauble, he intoned or chanted:

> "Why then most nought-y innocent
> Say now—was it alone you went
> As nought you say, since nought is known
> Went you your nought-y way alone?"

"Well, my lord Astorgio?" the Duchess demanded.

"Oh, but, Your Grace," he demurred, "of Your Grace I
beseech . . . must I stoop to heed this . . . this thing of
motley?"

"Instantly, messire."

"Then, my lady, I inform Your Grace, I went with mine
esquire Luigi and page Beppo attendant as——"

"Were you horsed or afoot?"

"Honoured nobility, we rode all three. As Your Grace's
ambassador extraordinary, especially chosen and so honoured,
I went in due estate, thereby honouring Your Grace——"

"Stayed you anywhere or spoke you any person on your
way to Fidena?"

"Sweet and most gracious ladyship, I rode direct with no
let, pause or hindrance, nor spake I with any, being upon
Your Grace's mission bent, the which——"

"Oho!" exclaimed the Jester, flourishing his bauble:

> "Now, being mere fool, it seems to me
> This squire and page should questioned be."

"This they shall!" said the Duchess. "Andrea, go you
with Manfred, summon them in my name and bring them
hither—to me!"

"Nay, Madame," exclaimed Sebastian, with forbidding gesture; "with all submission I must protest—this is neither the place nor time for such inquisition, I suggest——"

"On the contrary, my lord, I protest no time or place could be better. So here they shall come and here will I question them. And fie, Sebastian, look not so unkindly upon my Jester, this fool that is, it seems, my wisest councillor."

Sebastian turned from the Jester to gaze after the two glittering, stalwart figures already striding towards the palace, and Sebastian's lofty brow showed moist and haggard as he paced restlessly to and fro, while Gonzago, leaning gracefully against the sundial, watched him—and smiled. Noting all of which, the Jester presently favoured them with another jingling rhyme:

> "Although no seer or prophet, I
> Will, for your pleasure, prophesy:
> Of young esquire and page Beppo,
> E'en though ye seek them, high and low,
> Seek them here, and seek them there,
> On land, on sea, or in the air,
> Seek them up and seek them down,
> In village, countryside and town,
> 'Twill soon be manifest and plain
> That, seeking, ye shall seek in vain.
> The question now that I propound
> Is: are they ever—to be found?
> Thus I, the prophet of a minute,
> Ask: are they on the earth, or—in it?"

Sebastian, halting in the middle of a stride, turned to gaze with a fearful intentness, first at the Jester and then at Gonzago, whose lounging form slowly tensed while the Duchess gazed wide-eyed upon the Jester, who was looking up at the radiant heaven again. Thus for a space none stirred or seemed to breathe, and in this unnatural stillness was something inhuman and therefore dreadful; then Gonzago laughed, Sebastian fell to his pacing and the Duchess spoke almost whispering:

"Ah, Bimbo, what—oh, what new horror are you suggesting?" and, shaking his cockscomb, he answered:

"Not new, alas—'tis old as this poor mortality—'twas policy of Cain and hath been much in practice ever since."

Here again Sebastian halted suddenly, while one of his fumbling, restless hands, chancing upon his dagger-hilt remained clenched there, nor moved he until Gonzago, laughing once more, said lightly:

"Our Jester hath gift of rhyme, it seems. So, good motley knave, I'd fain have more of thee. Canst jingle us rhyme now of, say—our right noble lord Sebastian, ha?"

The Jester nodded, saying:

"Eftsoons, Apollo, at a price." Gonzago tossed him a ducat, with the query:

"Will that inspire thy muse?"

"No!" quoth Sebastian, indignantly. "I say no, my lord; I will not be made subject for this—this pert buffoon's fooleries——"

"Tush, my lord; fie on thee, Sebastian! Why so peevish at mere jest, and we in her grace's lovely presence! 'Tis but mere pastime until Astorgio return and——"

"None the less, Gonzago, I will not suffer it. If you must stoop to such folly—be yourself its subject."

"Ay, with all my heart!" said he gaily. "So come, Folly, have at me, jingle and rhyme of me at your antic best." And forthwith the Jester did so, thus:

> "As for thee, my lord Apollo,
> What is not yet is yet to follow.
> And that which follows, as it will,
> Be it good or be it ill,
> Will, at the last, since all things must,
> End thee—in nothingness and dust—
> Since man is dust and dust is man.
> Yet soonest dust—Sebastian!
> For, though unmarked he seem to be,
> Yet marked by deed indeed is he—
> And, for that earth to earth returneth
> There is, methinks, a grave that yearneth
> For——"

"Oh, abominable!" exclaimed Sebastian. "This . . . Madame, I protest this miserable insolent . . . this pestilent jackanapes is past endurance——"

"Oho, admirable!" laughed Gonzago. "Lady, I protest thy jingling Jester delights my heart! As for thee Sebastian, to so waste thy dignified contempt, to be so ruffled and roused, by mere merryman's rhyme, the which—ha, but yonder Astorgio returns at last and—by the Mass—with only his page, Madame. Now what shall this portend? What of his esquire? Can thy Jester's prophecy be true: 'not on the earth, but—in it' ?"

"Gonzago, I dread to think!" she answered, watching where Astorgio came, his little frightened page between the tall, glittering forms of Andrea and Manfred; hardly were they in speaking distance than Astorgio burst forth in wordful torrent:

"Your Grace and most excellent gracious lady, all is vain; our search none availing since him we sought is not, that is to say he, mine esquire Luigi, is from my lodging in the palace removed and from my house also, vanished, and thus our questful diligence unrewarded all——"

"When saw you him last, Astorgio?"

"Madame, he was, as wontedly, attendant upon my bedward ascension whither Beppo, my page, lighted me, thereafter Luigi aided my disarrayal and retirement, since when I have nought heard and nought of him seen."

"Andrea, how say you?"

"Your Grace, that this gentleman Luigi is indeed nowhere to be found. Failing him, we bring the boy Beppo that saw him last."

"Beppo," said she gently, "come you to me."

"And, boy," his master warned, "forget not thy reverence! Be supple in thy homage, sirrah! Flex thy young knees, bare-headed bend and bow thee and with gracious——"

"Leave him alone, Astorgio, lest you fright him beyond speech. Come hither, Beppo, and answer my questions." Timidly the boy approached, twisting his broidered cap in nervous hands, looked up, looked down, and, plumping to his knees, nodded curly head.

"Nay, stand up, Beppo, and tell me when last you saw this Luigi?"

"Madame, 'twas when he boxed my ears, last night."

"Why did he so?"

"For trying to peep through the lattice, Madame."

"Why did you peep?"

"To see who tapped."

"And did you see?"

"No, Madame—yes, Madame, only she was all hid in a black cloak."

"So it was a woman you saw?"

"Ay, Madame."

"Well, what of Luigi?"

"He climb out of the window and so he and the woman they go away together——"

"Aha!" laughed Gonzago. "A right gallant esquire, thine—eh, Astorgio? Like master like man, ha? So, gracious lady, 'twould seem here is no more than nocturnal amour, Venus in the ascendant. All this to do for so small and very ordinary matter! What now sayeth our motley wag, our poetical merryman? How wilt rhyme us on this, Bimbo?"

"Thus, gossip," answered the Jester.

> "Since squire's away
> He nought can say,
> But then—he may,
> Some other day.
> Ah—but
> If dead is he
> Then dumb he'll be
> Eternally.
> But as for me,
> Better to live poor fool, thinks I,
> Than be a young esquire and die.
> Lo, yonder now in sweating haste,
> Cometh fine gentleman red-faced.
> A different tale mayhap to speak
> Of this esquire ye vainly seek."

And he pointed where, fanning his rubicund visage with plumed bonnet, came that buxom, frequently-perspiring gentleman, Count Emilio Cavalcanti.

"Your Grace . . . my lords," said he, saluting them, breathlessly, "aware whom you seek . . . I come with news of him . . . most urgent and of dire suggestiveness."

"Ah, mercy of heaven!" exclaimed the Duchess, clasping her hands. "What now—what more?"

"Gracious lady, I must inform you—this vanished Luigi is brother to that vile traitor banished during the war by Fortunio, to wit—the Count Francesco Loredano!"

The Duchess's clasping hands became white fists, up went her indomitable young head and, firm-lipped, she demanded:

"Are you sure, perfectly assured of this?"

"Alas, too sure, Madame!" sighed the Count, dabbing at rubicund visage with dainty handkerchief. "For this morning, 'neath certain window of Messire Astorgio's lodging, was found—a letter——"

"Holy saints!" exclaimed the Duchess. "Another letter? Show me—nay first read and let us all hear." And so, after some fumbling, the Count produced this letter and, unfolding it, read aloud:

> "'Brother F. Having put F. to bed and forever asleep, none stands now 'twixt our vengeance on her save only S., which lord shall soon slumber as deep. To the which desired end move thou, summon thy powers and know me ever thy devoted L.'"

"So!" exclaimed the Duchess, between shut teeth. "Now give me that hateful thing."

Flushed and perspiring, Count Cavalcanti obeyed; and when she had frowned over this letter she read it aloud with her own interpolations, thus:

> "'Brother F. (this I take it should mean Francesco). 'Having put F. to bed and forever asleep,' (having murdered Fortunio) 'none stands now 'twixt our vengeance on her' (meaning me) 'save only S.,' (meaning Sebastian) 'which lord shall soon slumber as deep' (meaning your death, my lord). 'To the which desired end move thou,' (I wonder how and where) 'summon thy powers' (shall this mean an army?) 'and know me ever thy devoted L' (for Luigi)."

"Treason!" exclaimed Sebastian. "We must act and at once, Madame!"

"Francesco," she cried, striking the letter passionately, "this would prove 'twas by his means and will that Fortunio died! Francesco—and I can well believe it of him!"

"And worse!" said Cavalcanti fiercely. "Ah, noble lady, worse; for he and his accursed brother, this Luigi, do now threaten even thee!"

"And this," sighed Sebastian mournfully, "all this by reason of Fortunio's most unwise mercy! 'Twas thyself, royal Jenevra, doomed Francesco to shameful death; it was myself, and thy Council, pronounced and confirmed thy sentence; but alas—'twas Fortunio overruled all and merely banished him. Thus Francesco lives to be thine and our menace yet, and make too evident the arrant folly of mercy."

"And now," demanded the Duchess, "what is to do? Thou, Astorgio, what know, what say you of your esquire Luigi?"

"Nought, gracious Nobility; nought say I since horror of soul and ferocity of heart smite me speechless . . . such monstrous evil, such soul-shattering wickedness, such impious treason 'gainst thy princely self is profanity beyond my poor expressment; Madame, I am dumb!"

"Indeed, Astorgio," said she, red lips quivering to ghost of a smile, "never heard I dumb man so eloquent! Well, my lords, how must we counter this threat? Counsel me—you, Sebastian."

"Your Grace, all roads shall be watched, night and day, the city patrolled hourly, every gate double-guarded and all strangers strictly interrogated."

"This sounds very well, my lord. And you, Gonzago?"

"Beloved lady, not a word until I have heard Folly here pronounce and in rhyme——"

"Not so!" exclaimed Sebastian, indignantly. "Here is no time for buffoon's foolish babble. Madame, I protest——"

"Yet will I hear him," said she, turning where lay the Jester plucking idly at the grass. "So now, Bimbo, what say'st thou of this letter, this hateful thing?"

And smiling up into her lovely, troubled eyes, he answered lightly:

"Sweetest of poppets, I think of one word, a very small yet potent word, for thinks I—'if'."

"Well?" she enquired, stooping to look down into these darkly-blue eyes that now gazed up at her with such expression that she felt a sudden, strange comfort. "What of thy 'if', Bimbo?"

"And," demanded Gonzago, "canst speak us thy 'if' in couplets, good Folly?"

"Verily, Adonis—at a price!" Gonzago laughed and tossed another coin; the Jester took it up, spun it and nodded, but ere he could speak:

"Oh, this," fumed Sebastian, "this and at such crisis is beyond my patience or further endurance; it shames all reason! So, Madame, by your leave, I'll away and act——"

"Sebastian," she retorted sternly, "by my command, you will remain! Mayhap I shall need your grave wisdom to temper my Jester's folly. Bimbo, speak me thy 'if'."

And forthwith he did so, thus:

> "If this esquire so foolish was to write,
> If truly he this letter did indite,
> If he such deadly secret dared to pen,
> If, having penned it thus so plainly, then
> If, as 'twould seem, he let it fall indeed,
> If there it lay for all the world to read,
> If this he did that on his head alone,
> If thus he'd take the blame for evils known,
> If this be so—why then what doubt can be
> If in this world is greater fool than he?
> If by my 'ifs' this letter false I've shown,
> Jenevra—laugh! Nor shalt thou laugh alone,
> For I'll laugh with thee and, with laugh, proclaim
> Here is poor shift, a shift to shift all blame
> From one, or many, that the guilty be,
> Upon this sorry 'scapegoat', Squire Luigi.
> Who are the guilty, time alone shall show.
> Thus here I end and, ending thus, I go
> Lest peradventure, I should end also,
> Since ye are you, and I but poor Bimbo——"

Uttering his name, the Jester leapt afoot, bowed to the silent company with many absurd, complicated flourishes and stalked majestically away.

CHAPTER XIV

TELLS HOW JENEVRA SOUGHT COMFORT OF FRIAR CLEMENT

THE DAY being fair and very apt for digging, Friar Clement was performing vigorously with a mattock, when to him sped Angelo to clasp motley arm about this stalwart form, then lead and seat him, willynilly, beneath the great mulberry tree; then:

"Father, oh, father," he exclaimed in joyous ecstasy, "what a woman is she! Her lovely body a beauteous casket to hold the bright jewel of her soul! She is all perfection within and without—mind, soul and body she is all and more than I ever dared dream or hope——"

"Ha!" exclaimed the Friar, his shrewd eyes twinkling. "If all this meaneth Jenevra——"

"Who else, Father Clem? In all this world for me there is but one woman and her beloved name is Jenevra. For, upon my life, she is truly——"

"A mere woman, my son, and very human and, so being, hath her blemishes, since nothing human can ever be perfect, alas! Therefore, my Angelo, be warned and——"

"Of what, prithee?"

"She is passionate and given to sudden furies——"

"So was she ten years agone, and so—I love her."

"She is by nature something too proud, and arrogant, headstrong and wilful, moreover——"

"To win her shall be greater glory, therefore; ay, and by love to tame her shall be joy——"

"Ay, but to win her, Angelo, thou must woo and——"

" 'Slife, father, I've been wooing her this two hours and more."

"Eh? Wooing? So soon?"

"Most urgently and right sedulously, with art tenderly suggestive and craft of gentle innuendo!"

"Oho! And what did she?"

"Well, first the sweet soul opens her lovely eyes on this fool in disbelieving wonderment, then would smile, but checks it, then views this fool askance, asks his name, he tells her 'Bimbo'—a very fool of a name—and then, God love her, she knits her lovely brows and vows it doesn't suit him; whereat I yearned to kiss her—and very nearly did!"

"Yet did not?"

"Alas, no! For, though a jesting Folly, I'm not such fool of a Jester! And, oh, Father Clem, to think she is my predestined wife!"

"And she beset by princely suitors, Angelo! And thou such mean-showing, shabby creature and sorry wretch!"

"Why, so I am, and right glad therefore!"

"And yet, my son, were it not better I made thee known to her?"

"No and no—except in the last extremity; for, being this poor, jingling Folly, my fool thought is—to woo until very love, her love awaking, shall give her choice 'twixt the emptiness of her princely state, with all its pettiness and idle shams, and the joy of freedom and glory of a poverty hallowed by such love as shall make the meanest cottage the home that no palace may ever be."

"Nay, my son, here is merest dream of a fool's paradise!"

"Yet a paradise, my father!"

"Alas," sighed the Friar, shaking his head, "this asketh too much of any human love, my Angelo, and especially of such proud, young monarch and born ruler as Jenevra."

"Howbeit, as poor fool will I woo her . . . so long as I may . . . and even though I may not live to enter this dear Paradise of Fools, yet 'tis something to have lived and striven for. Thus strive I will nor shall she know me until true love shall make me known to her . . . in life or death."

"Be it so, my son. But now what is this talk of death?"

"Merest talk! Instead, my father, do thou tell me of Jenevra and these last ten long years——"

"Nay, forget Jenevra a while and——"

"Impossible, for she is become so much part of me that, should I lose her, life would be empty, a hateful weariness, a broken thing I'd toss away right gladly."

"Shame on thee, Angelo! Say not so, my son! For our lives belong to God to be used for sake of our fellows and to the glory of Him that made us. So let not this love blind or turn thee from God's work—to vindicate innocence and unmask evil. . . ."

"Nor shall it ever, my father. For 'spite this joy of love, to this purpose I'll live and for it die, an need be. To the which end I have been something busied this morning. I have lit a spark shall presently become a flame to show us this hidden evil, and then a cleansing fire to consume it. . . . I have in doggerel rhyme cried 'Treason!' 'Lies!' and 'Villainy!' I' faith, I have defied Roguery and challenged murder, as thus." And forthwith Angelo told very fully all that had transpired that morning in the palace garden, while Friar Clement listened with profound interest but ever-growing perturbation.

"And thus," Angelo ended, "what with my quips, quirks

and jingles I have given them cause for profound thought
and no little anxiety—I hope!"

"And thyself," groaned the Friar, "now in direst peril,
Angelo!"

"Yet, father, God is in heaven, thou art on earth to watch
and pray for me and 'twixt my life and murder is thy good
link mail——"

"Ay, 'tis comfort to remember this, my son. Yet from
henceforth thou art in constant jeopardy!"

"Why, this was expected, father. I am the mark, a popinjay
to draw their shot. 'Twas to this purpose I challenged Villainy,
and thus compel them, for until they move in their own defence
we cannot attack."

"Nay, here was rash doing, Angelo, for they will surely
attack thee."

"'Tis so I hope, father, and therefore am duly prepared,
being greatly minded to live—for Jenevra's lovely sake. So
now I pray thee tell me of her—nay, first, didst get word
to Andrea and Manfred and Ippolito?"

"I did and they should be here anon. Also I hoped to
see Jenevra at matins, but doubtless her angry councillors
shall keep her—after our Jester's outrageous and too reckless
versifying."

"True!" nodded Angelo, smiling grimly. "My jingle of
'ifs' smote them to a dumbness should find fury of words
aplenty, thereafter. And she—oh, strong, valiant soul—the
one 'gainst the many to front them undaunted! For I must
tell thee, my father, thy letter so commending the Jester won
me her kinder notice and later her trust. Yea, by all the
saints in heaven—faith and trust looked on me from her
lovely eyes, 'twas in the tones of her voice! And so, as the
Jester adores her, Angelo loveth thee! Now of this Gonzago,
doth she, can she, will she ever love him, think you?"

"Nay, how shall I know this, Angelo? The common report
is that she favours him more than others, but as for love,
who shall say?"

"She told our Jester she might wed this fellow, yet, in the
telling, frowned, God bless her! What think you of this lord?"

"A most seemly, gracious gentleman!"

"Seemly?" repeated Angelo, with rueful frown. "The fellow
is a perfect Adonis! Ay, lovely-seeming as Hyperion to catch
a woman's eye and sweet-voiced as Apollo to charm a lady's

ear! And in his splendour a right potent rival to our poor, mean swart-faced, sorry Jester, alas!"

"Verily, Angelo, he is so much all this that I would have thee confess to her thy true identity, or suffer me——"

"Nay, Angelo is dead and his memory accursed as proclaimed traitor——"

"Yet Jenevra shall never believe thee thing so vile?"

"God love her, no! And for this alone I could die for her, Father Clem. Her faith in me is precious as her lovely self——"

"Then why not declare thyself?"

"Should I do so—might not this knowledge be for her an added care, seeing I must needs run some little hazard——"

"Alas!" sighed the Friar. "Alas, 'tis but too true."

"Thus, father, did she know that Angelo was quarry for Evil to stoop and fly at, might she not be troubled—a little? Such being my hope—such trouble therefore will I keep from the sweet soul! As to this Gonzago I confess he confounds me! I know not if to hate or love the fellow, for——"

Here was a rapping on the door that pierced the massive wall, nearby, whereat the Friar rose, saying:

"These should be our trusty Manfred and Andrea."

"Then, father, to make on them final test of my disguisement, I'll up into the tree and drop on them suddenly!" So Angelo swung himself lightly aloft and, lying prone on a great branch, lay thus securely hidden while the Friar, drawing bolt and bar, opened this stout door and was instantly embraced by Jenevra, who clung to him, saying breathlessly:

"Oh, Father Clement . . . such to do . . . such talk of wars, rebellions, blood and treachery . . . and all by reason of . . . that Jester of thine! Sebastian hath convoked the Council of the Ten and would have me there, but instead I fly to thy comfort. Close the door . . . and bolt it! So! Now come and let me tell thee something of my new troubles." And speaking, she led him to that shady seat beneath the great tree and there, nestling to him as she had so often done as a child, she told of Luigi and his brother Francesco. "And all—all by reason of thy Jester and a letter, yes— another letter! I brought it for you to see—though much against Sebastian's will! Thrice he demanded it of me and once methought he would have dared force it from me, had not Gonzago intervened! Here is the hateful thing! Read it, father, and judge you of it. Though first you must know 'twas writ by Astorgio's esquire and found 'neath a certain window, lying as if intended to be found, or so I think, and yet . . . oh, read and tell me how you judge of it, of Luigi and of Francesco who they tell me hath returned from exile." So Friar Clement took and perused this letter, slowly and very heedfully, word by word, while Jenevra watched him speechlessly until he looked up; then she said:

"The Jester made of it a scoff, a mockery and proclaimed it false! He said this was never writ by Luigi, but was 'poor shift to shift all blame, from one or more, upon this Luigi, making him the helpless scape-goat'. He said 'time alone will show the guilty'. More also he said to the same purpose and in a rhyme with every line beginning with 'if'—and this methought so wonderful I would have fain heard more but that he sped away, leaving fury and confusion behind him . . . and myself direly amazed!"

"Why so, my child?"

"For that whereas Gonzago laughed and Count Cavalcanti scowled yet was dumb, Sebastian raged and, like one distraught, laid hand on dagger, crying death on the Jester! And . . . oh, Father Clement . . . in that moment he showed so murderous I was appalled. . . . Murderous!" she repeated softly as if pondering a new and very terrible possibility. Then turning to the Friar with look of horror, whispered that dread word yet again: "Murderous!" And then: "Sebastian! Oh, father . . . Father Clement . . . could this be?"

The Friar hesitated in troubled perplexity and, chancing to look upward, beheld a face down-peering amid the leafage, a head that nodded so vehemently that a bell tinkled faintly; whereat the harassed young Duchess, roused from her dreadful speculation, glanced upward also, but saw only leaves and the great bough outstretched above them; wherefore she continued distressfully:

"Oh, Father Clem, if this be possible . . . if it be . . . true? Oh, I am all acold with dread! That he of all men! This man of my trust! This man so long familiar! This so honoured and . . . honourable-seeming man, so eloquent, so wise and gravely virtuous. Is it possible? Can it be—true?"

"Alas," sighed the Friar, "many dire things are possible in our fallen humanity! Yet lacking proof positive, on suspicion only——"

"Yet, as I tell you, my Jester so believes and so dared proclaim in verse and prose very boldly plain——"

"Ah!" exclaimed Friar Clement, in frowning anxiety. "Then was he madly rash——"

"Yet is he most calmly sane and most courageous indeed, his motley clothes a very man; 'neath his ass's ears is head so wise that I confide in his strength and wisdom . . . and he a Folly, a Jester, yet is he also my stay and comfort. So, dear Father Clem, I thank thee now with all my troubled heart for sending me my fool of comfort. And this mindeth me to ask how you found him, when and where?"

"Why, truly, Jenevra, 'twas he found me."

"How, where? Tell me!"

"Over yon wall he came to me a homeless, friendless wanderer."

"Dear Father Clem, so you fed and sheltered this poor shabby creature, this friendless, jingling Folly, and called him 'son'. Oh, I know, for so he told me. But whence came he and——"

"Hearken!" said the Friar, hand upraised. "There soundeth the call to matins."

"Then," said she rising, "let us go and pray God to show us if this . . . this man be guilty or no—and, oh, Father Clem, at mere thought of this . . . horror chills me!" Then slipping her hand into his strong, work-roughened clasp, away they went across this wide and lovely garden to where, bowered in trees and close against the city's massive wall, was the little oratory.

And prone on his branch the Jester watched in a sort of ecstasy until they were beyond his sight. Then he spoke low-voiced and very reverently as if he, too, were praying:

"Oh, Fortunio, loved brother, thou bright angel of God that by death art become in all things wise, thou knowest how I do love her body and soul, yet for love of thee am willing to forgo the joy of her. . . . So, if I must die so soon for what I must do, then, dear my brother, do thou intercede with our Almighty Father for my sake, that hereafter in some better life we may be reunited, she and I. And now even while she kneeleth in prayer, so pray I that, come life or death, I may vindicate thy fame, my Fortunio, and bring thy slayers to judgment and the justice of God. Amen."

And now in the garden ensued a hush, a deep silence save for the drowsy hum of insects, the sleepy twitter of birds and the chirp of crickets in the hot sunshine. . . . At last, with clash and clink of steel, was sound of approaching voices raised in disputation.

"Andrea, I say thou'rt fanciful as any woman."

"And I tell thee, Manfred, thou'rt a very purblind numps, a cloddish dullard, a thick-pated noddy not to be 'ware of him! Where be your eyes not to see. Your ears not to hear. Your fat-witted noddle not to——"

Here a ponderous fist thundered on the door, then:

"Andrea, those gogglish eyes o' thine see more than is to see; thy besotted ears——"

Here another thunderous knocking; and thus these two brothers in arms disputed and pounded to no purpose until:

"Ho!" growled Manfred. " 'Twould seem we are afore our time, Andrea."

"Nay, we are precise to the minute; I heard the matins bell but now."

"Why then certes the good Friar will be at his prayers. Yet he summoned us here, us and the Count Ippolito. Well now, since door won't ope us'll e'en escalade—give me a hoist, Andrea; heave now!"

Thus next moment above the wall rose Manfred's helmeted visage to peer about this blooming, fragrant garden; then, reaching down, he hauled Andrea beside him and together they dropped, with jingling clash.

"Cocksbody!" exclaimed Manfred, glancing around. "A howling desolation!"

"A fair, sweet-smelling haven of peace, thou base, material clod! Would all the world were so. There be rare flowers to bless the eye and herbs the belly, Manfred——"

"And nought else, never a soul, not one. So a plague o' thy needless haste, Andrea, we might ha' stayed to rid us of our harness—a murrian on thy plaguey scurrying——"

"And did not Rillo say the Friar would have us here strictly o' the hour?"

"Well, here are we, but where's Rillo? Nowhere! Where's Friar Clement? Nowhere neither! Where the Count Ippolito? and this my burgonet hot as the hoofs o' Satan, and stifles me!"

"Well, so doth mine, but do I mewl and pule therefore?"

"Howbeit, an we must wait we'll do't out o' this heat i' the Friar's dwelling yonder; mayhap they are there waiting us. Come!"

So away they clanked, still disputing like the old and tried friends they were.

After some brief while came another vain knocking, then over the wall rose a gay feather a modish bonnet and the comely face of Count Ippolito, who, mounting the coping with effortless ease, dropped gracefully into the garden and, seeing nobody, came and seated himself in pleasant shade of the great mulberry tree. Scarcely had he done so than a twig, dropped unerringly, struck and bounced lightly from his shapely nose. Ippolito started, glanced up and beheld a face leering down at him from the leafage, a bauble that tapped his astonished and indignant head—and down from the tree swung the lithe, shabby form of a jester, who bowed, pirouetted, struck a ridiculous posture and said:

"Noble sir, of thy wisdom, tell me the difference 'twixt wedlock and death. Aha, you cannot? Then I, of my folly, inform you—the one is soonest over. So who but fool would choose wedlock?"

"Ha, thou pert jackanapes!" exclaimed Ippolito the lover. "What do you here?"

"As doth your high nobility—I breathe."

"Then go breathe otherwhere. Away, I'm in no mood for thy fooling; off, I say!" But now to them came Andrea and Manfred, clashing in their haste.

"Ha, fool," growled Manfred, "get thee hence——"

"Oh, my lord," said Andrea, very wistfully, "be right gladly welcome, for my heart telleth me thou art our Angelo."

Back went cockscomb, off came wig and, reaching forth his hand, Angelo answered:

"Thy heart speaks truly, Andrea."

"How . . . how then . . . God's my life!" gasped Manfred, while Ippolito leapt afoot to stand speechlessly at gaze, wherefore Angelo turned to him saying:

"Well met, Ippolito! Time hath sped since I charged beside thee to Fortunio's rescue; take my hand old friend, and with it my love. We saved Fortunio's body that day; now we are here for counsel how best to rescue his fame from false accusation of self-murder and to uncover the hidden hand that struck him from life, so——" Angelo paused and glanced up swiftly as from the little oratory, hidden in shady grove, a sweet-toned bell tolled once; at which signal, he donned wig and cockscomb and, drawing his friends close, said very earnestly:

"Hither presently will come the Duchess and she must not know me for other than the Folly I seem—this on your lives! Now, command yourselves, for yonder she is."

Thus as Jenevra approached with Friar Clement she beheld the three grouped about the Jester, who seemed telling them some tale; now though aware of them all, she saw only the one dark leanly aquiline face 'neath foolish, dangling ass's ears and instinctively quickened her step with sense of such deep gladness that she flushed selfconsciously and, becoming furious with herself, instantly vented it on all and sundry:

"How now, sirs, must you dally with this—this jingling Folly, wasting your lives to such idle purpose and none effect?"

Andrea and Manfred clashed each to a knee. Bowing his curly head Count Ippolito did likewise; only the Jester stood, head bowed, regarding her; and meeting this sadly-wistful, questioning look, she parted ruddy lips to speak, sighed instead and, turning to the Friar said, quick breathing:

"Go with me, Father Clement, for I must to the council chamber and there I shall have need of thee." And now as they went together, she sighed again yet in that same moment, frowned as in troubled perplexity, but the wise Friar, quick to heed and guess the reason, smiled.

CHAPTER XV

TELLS HOW ANGELO SCHEMED AND THE PAGE BEPPO WAS SAVED FROM DEATH

"Nay, but," cried Ippolito in wide-eyed dismay, "this were to invite thy certain death, Angelo."

"Death?" he repeated. "Say rather this were merely to adventure life for knowledge—truth at last and proof absolute. Howbeit, to be done with this hidden evil thus shall I act and this do——"

"Ah, not so!" groaned Andrea. "I beseech thee not this: the hazard is indeed too desperate!"

"Ay, by the bones!" exclaimed Manfred. "Certes there would be a secret grave for thee, Angelo; grief for us——"

"And our Duchess!" murmured Andrea. "So would Villainy triumph and she and ourselves be utterly confounded."

"True!" nodded Ippolito. "So wherefore hazard thy life so lightly? Art so weary of it?"

"Ippolito, all my will is to live—I was never so passionate for life as now."

"Then must we scheme a course less perilous, Angelo."

"Ay, with all my heart, but what? Think and tell me now." Here these three old and trusted friends gazed anxiously at Angelo, stared at one another, down at earth and up at sky in a very ecstasy of troubled thought until at last Ippolito broke this painful silence to say somewhat diffidently:

"But, Angelo, nought have we whereon to base our actions save only thine own suspicions . . . and to dare believe such base dealing, such foul treachery——"

"And bloody villainy!" growled Manfred.

"As I say, to believe such monstrous evils of—such noble-seeming lord as——"

"Seeming—ay!" exclaimed Angelo, nodding so that his bells rang a small chime. "A noble-seeming lord! Hast said it, Ippolito! Ay, faith, golden-voiced Villainy, cloaked in virtue, may charm Doubt to sleep, show like very angel of God, yet do like very devil! I tell thee, Ippolito, I have glimpsed this same devil oft of late, and today, for a moment, I saw him uncloaked, heard golden voice crack to demoniac stridency, beheld stark murder glare on me from fearful eyes, for that he knew I was 'ware of him at last—there before me I saw Guilt stand manifest!"

"Ay, to you, Angelo, to you—but who else?"

"To me!" said Andrea.

"And me!" growled Manfred.

"Even so," Ippolito demurred, "what proof have we? Not one jot, never a tittle or iota, and without this, suspicion, howsoever strong, is but merest futility, so proof evident we must have!"

"Ah, verily!" sighed Angelo. "In this world poor Truth must ever be propped 'twixt the crutches of Fact and Proof. like hobbling cripple."

"Angelo," sighed the Count, "let me die if I see any way of gaining such proof!"

"Because there is no way, Ippolito, except the Guilty be made to speak or by some act betray himself. So needs must I compel such speech or act as, God aiding, I will."

"Yet not at such madly desperate hazard! For, Angelo, I tell thee——" Here a voice deep and richly sweet hailed, and towards them with his long, ungainly stride came Pedrillo, this crooked, mighty one, this skilled physician of minds and bodies whose renown was second only to that of his learned master Friar Clement; and when they had greeted him heartily:

"Pedrillo," said the Count, "thou'rt right welcome to our council, for this Angelo, this my friend, will be done with life!"

"Rillo," growled Manfred, "here's our Angelo will be his own destruction and our ruin!"

"In fine," said Andrea, "he will dare prison and death to win entry to lord Sebastian's lodgings at court, ay, and his palace i' the city."

"Well, so he shall, 'tis so agreed," quoth Pedrillo, nodding. "Nay, sires, why stare ye in such amaze? For there is no dwelling I may not enter by reason I am my great master's servant to bear and administer his precious salves, his wondrous elixirs and medicaments. I have them here in my budget—potent drugs may cure or kill. And, what's more, I am the lord Sebastian's physician and dose him as well as his horses, dogs and servants. Thus when next I go, thither goeth Count Angelo as my assistant."

"Aha," laughed Ippolito, "there is subtlety that promiseth well."

"But now," said Pedrillo, shaking his great, ugly head, "I must tell ye that i' the city I heard whisper how the great Fortunio was poisoned by the Duchess her command!"

"'S blood!" gasped Manfred, clapping hand on dagger. "Here's lie and foulest treason!"

"The Duchess?" repeated Ippolito in horrified amazement. "Who would so dare?"

"And who," demanded Andrea, "who set this whisper a-going?"

"Her bodyguard shall be doubled!" growled Manfred.

"Yet shall not check this whispered evil, these accursed tongues; these vile whisperings mayhap shall grow to murmur, to shout and so to roar, tumults and rebellion——"

"Civil war!" sighed Ippolito.

"God and His saints forfend!" groaned Pedrillo. "My lord, oh, Angelo, how think you?"

For a space Angelo sat mute and utterly still, as if listening intently, then answered softly:

"I think our lord Sebastian is true prophet since he foretold this, and to the Duchess herself days agone. Hist all—heard ye aught a moment since?"

"Nay, what should we hear?"

"A distant cry."

"Ay," nodded Manfred, "'twas a squeak, a squeal, someone mayhap killing a pig. But—ha, what now?"

"I'd fain see this pig," said Angelo, rising. "Bide ye all!" Then he was across the garden and, unbarring the ponderous door, began running very fleetly towards a sombre grove of cypress trees whence now came another breathless scream with sound of light, scampering feet; then out from that dark grove sped a small figure of terror—mouth agape in blood-smeared face, eyes wide and fearful, for close upon him was a man with hand outstretched to clutch the little fugitive's black curls. Angelo hurled his bauble; the pursuer stumbled, glanced round and, espying only a Jester, made to leap at him, but seeing this Jester's hand suddenly armed with glittering poniard, checked, turned and made off very nimbly. Angelo would have followed, but two small desperate arms were clasping his legs and a breathless voice implored:

"Don't . . . suffer they . . . kill me?"

Now looking down at these glossy curls and small, blood-stained face, Angelo stooped, saying, kindly:

"Oh, Beppo, my child, what have they done to you?"

"Tried to . . . kill me——"

"Why?"

"By cause of . . . the dagger——"

"Whose dagger?"

"Luigi's——"

"Boy, can you walk?"

"No, but . . . I'll try."

"Nay," said Angelo, smiling as he sheathed poniard, "instead, shalt thou ride upon my back. Come, mount—so! Now hold fast and try not to bleed on me too much." Now as they went Angelo enquired:

"Boy, what is that betwixt us that irks me?" And still breathing distressfully, the child answered.

"Only Luigi's dagger, an it irks me too, but I can't move it yet, cause it's tied up in my shirt!"

"Aha!" said Angelo. And after some while Beppo ceased trembling and having regained his breath, began to talk a little boastfully like the very boy he was:

"Yon rogue would ha' killed me, stabbed me i' the arm he did an' it hurts, but I fought him I did and got away and——"

"Who was the man; did you know him?"

"No, and I'm glad you are the Jester because I like your face and the things you say. So may I call you Bimbo, please?"

"Ay, surely."

"And I wasn't feared o' yon man, I wasn't—not very. And all my blood on me do make me feel like a soldier, so I don't mind it—much."

"Then you're very brave!"

"Yes, I am. Yes, like my father, he was so brave he got killed in a battle . . . Oh!" he gasped suddenly, clutching Angelo tighter, for they had entered the garden. "Who be all those men, and him, the great ugly one?"

"Friends all, Beppo. And here," said Angelo to these astonished friends, "here is your pig, Manfred, and though somewhat bloody well in life by God His grace. Take him, Rillo; he needs thy skilled ministry, so——" But at mere sight of Pedrillo's ugliness the boy clutched his rescuer in such panic that Angelo turned to the still astonished three, saying:

"Brothers, all, here is small witness whose testimony shall perchance alter our scheme. Therefore I go now with Pedrillo to tend his hurts and question him. Meet me tonight at ten o' the clock by the sundial in that most private garden, and so till then God keep us all."

CHAPTER XVI

THE "MOUTH OF A BABE"

His HURTS comforted by Pedrillo's great, gentle hands, washed and bandaged, Beppo lay naked in Angelo's small truckle bed, glancing from one to other appraisingly; then nodding graciously at Pedrillo, he announced:

E

"I like thee better now, for though nowise good to look on, thou'rt very strong and I love strong men I do—sometimes." Pedrillo's smile was so strangely compelling that the boy, smiling also, instinctively reached out his hand and began to talk while Angelo, seated near, inspected this small, exquisitely fashioned dagger from keen point to delicately chiselled pommel.

"And so," said he, thus intent, " 'twas in your master's garden you found this beautiful thing, Beppo? But how are you sure this truly belongs to Luigi?"

"He showed it to me and I've seen it oft-times at his girdle, and there's an 'L' on it for 'Luigi'."

"Ay, so there is. And do you mind just where in the garden you found it?"

" 'Twas in the grass where 'twas all torn."

"And where was this?"

"Nigh the droopy tree that Seppi the gardener do say be adying."

"And why were you beaten?"

"For that I saw a light amid the trees and thought 'twas ghosts and when I asked of it Vincentio he beat me."

"Who is Vincentio?"

"My lord's Steward."

"Was it he stabbed your arm?"

"No, 'twas the tall, dark man that smiles."

"Ha, smiles does he, Beppo!"

"Ay, even when he tried to kill me."

"Know you his name?"

"Nay, but 'tis only he do so frighten me that I do forget to be brave."

"And no wonder!" said Angelo, leaning to smooth the boy's glossy black curls, at which caress Beppo looked up with eyes suddenly tearful, saying:

"Oh, Bimbo, 'twas so my . . . mother touched me just afore she died."

"My poor Beppo! And thy father, too."

"Ah, but he was one of Lord Fortunio's bravest soldiers and died in battle."

"And what of thy master, Count Astorgio?"

"We lived in his village anigh his great palace, so he then took me to be his page."

"Is he kind to thee, Beppo?"

"Not so very."

"Dost love him?"

"Not much, so will you take and keep me please and learn me to be like you—wilt hold and keep me safe?"

"This will I, though first promise me never to stir from this garden alone and never to unbar the door till dost know who knocks. Wilt promise me this on thine honour, boy?"

"Yea, yea, on my honour, and wilt learn me to be a Jester like as thou?"

"Mayhap. Now close thine eyes and try to sleep."

"Well, but—an I do—he won't creep and kill me, yon smiling man?"

"Not while I am with thee, Beppo, never fear."

"Oh, I be nowise afeard—much! 'Tis only I don't like the way he do smile. And when Luigi do come back he shall be kinder to me mayhap and very glad I found his dagger for he did tell how 'twas very rare and precious. And prithee, Bimbo, when I sleep—wilt not leave me?"

"Nay, I'll have thee in care and so shall our good Rillo here. Now hush thee!"

"Rillo," the boy repeated drowsily, "I think I shall love thee like as I do Bimbo—tomorrow."

The mighty one smiled, touched this little speaker's black curls, closed the dark slumberous eyes with light, caressing touch of great sinewy fingers, and so presently the boy slept; then, nodding at Angelo across their little sleeper, together they rose and stole silently away.

And now while Pedrillo prepared the midday meal, Angelo sat awhile profoundly thoughtful and sighing; at last he spoke:

"Thus, Pedrillo, by testimony of this our innocent yonder, we are to know Luigi the esquire lieth buried in Messer Astorgio's olive grove, 'neath a fading tree—the dying above the dead. . . . Of the which I might versify, thus:

Here, beneath a tree fast dying
Luigi, faster dead, is lying.
But Luigi dead may yet arise
A shape of doom for guilty eyes.

At dead of night, a shape of fear
If to the guilty he appear
Shall then his death-wound bleed anew
To prove——"

Pausing at gladly-familiar step, he opened the door to welcome Friar Clement with the eager question:

"Well, Father Clem, how doth she—Jenevra?"

"E'en as thou sayest, my son—well, yea and passing well! For never did she bear herself more princely before the ten, fronting these grave councillors boldly as ever her valiant sire might have done."

"Ah truly," sighed Angelo, "in that most lovely body is right valiant spirit, her winged soul can soar 'bove all doubt and fear—and yet she can be marvellous tender! A Duchess, yet a very woman, God be thanked! So thus it is that I— ah, but how now, is aught amiss?" he cried, in sudden anxiety, for, being come within-doors, Friar Clement stood, head bowed, like one greatly troubled and perplexed.

"Angelo," said he, putting back his cowl with weary gesture, "today in full council, was read a verbose indictment charging thy noble brother, yea, our great Fortunio, with— his own murder! How that he, and Jacomo also, sought death for shame that Count Angelo was proven traitor!"

"Ay, I've heard as much ere now. But what of her? How looked she? What did she?"

"Cried 'lies', my son! Denounced this indictment as basely craven expedient to stifle truth for very dread of it, since the truth was murder and nothing else. Declared Fortunio the victim and as innocent of his own death as was his brother Angelo of treason. And when her councillors rose, crying on her for proof of this, she retorted on them with reproaches and scoffs bitterly scornful that they, these so wise councillors, should prove indeed such blind fools and simpletons to be so readily deluded by tale so idle. At this, they cried on her again, louder and fiercer: 'Proof! Proof!' And then, Angelo, with leisured grace, she rose and, standing in majesty gazed slowly round upon them, each and every—and all hushed and speechless; at last: 'My lords,' says she, 'the proof is among you and so, for your discovery! Indeed,' says she, and once again her bright, slow gaze searched them, face by face, 'even now I may be looking upon Guilt!'"

"Oho!" whispered Pedrillo smiting brawny thigh. "There sped shaft to mark!"

"Ah, Father Clem!" murmured Angelo. "The wise and valorous soul of her! Would God I had been there to see and hear! And what did Sebastian?"

"Showed stately, my son; looked wise and said nought."

"And was so wise as he looked!" said Angelo. "But who were they cried on her for proof?"

"The Count Cavalcanti was one, lord Juliano Fabriano another, with Messer Nicola Podi; others there were, but these loudest and most insistent."

"Who was he read the indictment?"

"Fabriano."

"How stand these gentlemen in the council?"

"Foremost and very——" At this moment from the inner chamber a voice shrill with childish terror cried:

"Bimbo! Ah—Bimbo!" Then was swift patter of bare feet and in upon them sped little Beppo naked as Eros and as shapely, who leapt at Angelo to clasp and cling, saying brokenly: "I dreamed thee gone . . . oh, and me left . . . to the smiling man."

"Nay, instead, lo now here is the good Friar Clement— and my cape to cover thee, so—now make him thy reverence." This Beppo did, muttering:

"Thy blessing, holy father, and, Bimbo, I'm hungry likewise." So, their simple meal being ready, down they sat to eat and talk in all good fellowship until hunger was appeased.

"Now, Beppo," said Angelo, as the boy nestled to him, "tell me this. When thy master the lord Astorgio took thee with Luigi bearing that flask of wine from the Duchess, which of them carried it?"

"They did, both of them."

"Both, say'st thou—both of them?"

"Ay, my master had one and I spied the other 'neath Luigi's cloak as he got to horse, and I rode, too——"

"So then—there were two flasks, Beppo?"

"Yea, and my horse was the dapple grey named Pluto——"

Friar Clement, leaning back in his chair, sighed deeply; Pedrillo craned eagerly across the table, and neither moved nor seemed even to breathe as they waited the next question:

"So you rode to Fidena; and when thy master made to dismount there, what did he with his flask?"

"Gave it to Luigi to hold whiles he dismounted." And now it was Pedrillo who leaned back, sighing, while Friar Clement, starting forward in his chair, exclaimed softly:

"So! This is how 'twas done!" And Beppo nodding brightly, answered:

"Yea, holy sir, like this; I pulled Pluto's reins, so! I freed both feet o' the stirrups, cocked my leg and was down with never a stumble—almost. 'Tis easy done when you know the proper manage o' horses like I do." Here he yawned suddenly, blinked sleepily, and said drowsily: "Now, Bimbo, I think I'll get me back abed."

"Then so be it, but first, didst ever tell any one of these two flasks?"

"Never—nobody—only Luigi, and he kicked me he did."

"And when you told him—where were you?"

"In my lord's garden chamber, by the lattice."

"Was it open?"

"Yea, always."

"Saw you anyone in the garden?"

"No, only my lord talking of his olive trees. Oh, that was the first time ever I saw him!"

"Who?"

"The smiling man, but he can't kill me now with you here and the holy father and Rillo so big and strong. So I'm nowise afeared to sleep any more."

"Well, Rillo shall take thee to bed, and sleep sound. Thou art in good care, Beppo."

"So this," sighed the Friar, so soon as they were alone, "was how 'twas contrived!"

"And this," said Angelo, "is why young Luigi died!"

"Art so sure he is dead?"

"So I believe, and tonight I shall make sure. For I am persuaded 'tis thus they have sealed his lips—because they are afraid. So they move at last; 'tis now for us to counter them."

"As how, my son?"

"First by means of spade and mattock."

"Ah—dost mean——"

"I mean to uncover their handiwork and perchance make it rise against them. To front stealthy murder with its victim, ay—to give this poor, misused clay a semblance of dreadful life; to make of it a thing of reason-blasting horror whose sightless eyes shall seem to glare upon its slayers, what time its dumb lips shall find a voice to utter that the which only Murder may hear, the wailing screech of untimely death for justice, the hue and cry to all the powers of heaven calling down vengeance upon Guilt."

"And by the justice o' God," whispered Pedrillo, who had returned unnoticed, "we, holy father, thou and I, reverend master, do know how this might be contrived! And terror is a right potent weapon!"

"Nay," said Friar Clement, in troubled voice, "the dead belong to God and should therefore be sacred and immune from such usage; 'twould be a profanation."

"Howbeit," said Angelo, grimly, "if by such usage, Guilt, through terror, may be compelled by act or word to betray itself, then I hold such profanation justified. So, lest Murder strike again, as it surely will, I am bold to ask, nay demand, thine aid." The Friar sighed again, shook his head and, beckoning Pedrillo, forth they went, leaving Angelo crouched at the table, chin in hands, so profoundly thoughtful that he started violently to find Pedrillo beside him again.

"Dost know the properties o' phosphorus, Angelo?"

"Somewhat. Ay, enough to think it might serve my purpose, properly used."

"It shall be!" Pedrillo nodded. "Though my noble master is troubled——"

"So am I as to how we may gain entrance to a certain castle——"

"By a certain small door, called postern, Angelo, that shall open to my tap by reason of the lately sick young wife of an oldish and therefore doating husband. He is one Pietro Vanni, chief verderer to the lord we wot of, and his young wife is to live of my wise master's wondrous elixir by me administered, and thus her oldish spouse so grateful that, as I say, watchmen shall sleep and door open whenso I will."

"The watch shall sleep, sayest thou?"

"Soundly, Angelo! And the wherefore of their slumber here!" and he touched the large wallet at his girdle.

"This promiseth well, Rillo!"

"Ay, for whiles sentinels sleep Terror shall wake and haunt to right good purpose, I'll warrant thee!"

"And yet," sighed Angelo, " 'tis but a chance, a hope that may prove vain, a shaft that may not bring down the quarry, though truly aimed. For, Rillo, this fearsome ghost may smite guilt dumb, alas!"

"This is as maybe, Angelo. Howbeit, I do love this thy scheme and will now away to its furtherance. Also there be many sick and ailing ones do look for me and such relief as I

can bring them, God aiding. Hast any commands for me i'
the town?"

"Ay, seek out Andrea or Manfred and say that 'stead of
the palace garden they shall meet me here, soon after sunset
as may be. And so the blessed saints aid us all in that we go
to do this night."

"Amen!" quoth Pedrillo; then, catching up his ponderous
staff, away he strode.

CHAPTER XVII

WHICH IS, FOR THE MOST PART, A CHAPTER
OF SHADOWS

AND SO it was as heatful day faded to glimmering, star-shot
dusk that the three devoted friends, seated in Friar Clement's
fragrant garden, listened speechlessly while Angelo told of
that which was to be done.

"Saints of heaven!" exclaimed Ippolito in hushed tone.
"'Twill be horror—on horror!"

"Most ghastly!" murmured Andrea, shuddering.

"And most excellent tactic!" quoth Manfred. "A right
fiendly manœuvre and likes me well. Aha, this shall stir
them, heart and liver!"

"Yet such ghoulish labour!" muttered Ippolito. "The
mere thought appals me! And dost think it shall succeed,
Angelo?"

"Who shall say?" he replied, gloomily. "If Terror can
give dumb Guilt a tongue, or compel hidden Murder to
reveal itself—'if' and yet 'if' alas! We must needs wait the
event."

And now they were silent all, and each profoundly gloomy
until—towards them through the deepening shadows strode
Pedrillo, humming blithely to himself in his richly-sweet voice.

"God love ye, my bretheren," said he, cheerily, "and by
this same token all's well, as witness this key, and divers
watchmen snoring or shall be anon. Ah, but—the lord ye
wot of will, this of all nights, sup with divers other noble
lords in his great tower-chamber at ten o' the clock! And
how sayst thou o' this, my Angelo?"

"Excellent well!" he answered, leaping nimbly afoot. "Ay, faith, this is indeed passing well an these same lordly visitors be blessed with good eyesight, for by ten o'clock the moon will be riding high."

"Eh?" exclaimed Ippolito. "Now a God's name what's all this of 'eyesight', and the moon?"

"That these same gentlemen having eyes shall see, by light of moon, a furtive-creeping Jester intent on mischief and give such alarm, I hope, as shall bring their host to attempt his capture——"

"Or death!" growled Manfred.

"I hope not this, but that, in close pursuit of this errant Jester they shall all suddenly come upon—that which, new-risen from grave, shall challenge, demanding truth at last—at ten o' the clock!"

"But," Ippolito demurred, "to show thyself thus boldly—how an they shoot or——"

"I can but hope they'll shoot amiss——"

"But to so hazard thy life——?"

"Needs must I, being bait to the hook——"

"Ah!" groaned Manfred. "A live bait that may be dead bait by twitch o' trigger or bite o' steel——"

"The which God forbid!" said Andrea.

"Amen, my brother! And yet what He will—will be, will we how we will. So will I dare this hazard right willingly, trusting that what will be must be will of God. But now I, thus willing, will thou take this spade to use with a will this night and, I pray, to good purpose. Come ye, night falls apace and we have much to do——"

"Ay," growled Manfred, "and a full moon rising yonder!"

"Good! The better to see by."

"Ay, and be seen, my lord!"

"Good again—so long as none other is seen save only this Jester. So, brothers all, let us to our ghostly work and silent as ghosts—come!"

Thus as the moon rose, they left this fragrant, peaceful garden, stealing forth amid the shadows and as silent, or very nearly.

On they went amid a sultry darkness, through glooming cypress grove pierced here and there by shafts, these radiant arrows of the rising moon, on until they reached a wall which though lofty, was no impediment to these men who were up and over with scarcely a sound. On they went, silent as so many flitting spectres, until in shady grove of trees Angelo halted them, stealing forward to quest here and there pausing at last beneath a young sapling whose every leaf showed dismally adroop; hither he beckoned his companions, and at a spot where the ground showed uneven directed them to dig. Silently they wrought and yet so speedily that presently Manfred whispered:

"What's yon?" And as softly Pedrillo answered:

"A hand!   Be gentle now!"

Spade and mattock scraped cautiously awhile and then:

"A foot!" growled Manfred. Ensued more gentle scraping until spade and mattock were suddenly arrested and Pedrillo muttered:

"Look!"

Now peering down on that which now sprawled so horribly plain shaming the pure moonlight, Angelo sighed:

"Ay, this was Luigi!"

"And," whispered Pedrillo bending down, "killed by dagger-thrust."

"The silent steel!" nodded Angelo. "'Twould be so."

"The cloak," whispered Pedrillo, "the cloak—so! Now stand away, Manfred; I have him."

And after a brief while Pedrillo stepped from shade of this dying tree, bearing the dead, a muffled, awful shape.

Silent as they had come, they crossed the moonlit shadowy garden, over lofty wall, and, stealing ever within the shadows, followed Pedrillo with his ghastly burden until before them rose another wall, but this pierced by loopholes and topped by scowling battlement; in the grim shadow of this wall they advanced until they halted at a door deep-set in glooming arch.

"Now!" said Pedrillo, and tucking his dreadful burden lightly beneath one arm, he rapped upon the door which, opening almost instantly, showed a man who peered forth by light of flickering lanthorn held up in shaking hand.

"Is't thou, good master?" he muttered.

"Myself and the friends ye wot of. Is all well?"

"Ay, none stirs—so far! But for dear Mary's sake beware!"

"Didst give the watchmen yon wine, Pietro?"

"Ay, I did—and they sleep——"

"So shall they till cock-crow."

"Yet have a care, reverend master, and be speedy for sake of all the dear saints——"

"And thine own sake, Pietro, and mine—this will I. So off with thee to thy Bianca and sleep sound to see nought, hear nought and nothing know—away!"

"I go—and may the blessed saints shield thee well, good and dear master!" So saying, Pietro set down the lanthorn and vanished silently amid the shadows.

On again went the speechless five, across a small, paved court to a place of sombre trees, tall, clipped hedges and dim-seen, mazy paths along which Pedrillo strode unfaltering and soundless until before them, pillar and portico gleaming in the moonlight, they beheld a small, marble temple, mellowed by ages, a thing of such beauty that Angelo drew a deep breath for very joy of it; within this ancient fane was an altar, wonderfully carved, and here at last Pedrillo laid his burden, saying:

"Now leave me a while, yet bide within call; leave me to do what I may with this poor mortality!" And he began to unfold that swathing cloak.

And so, hidden again within the shadows, these four waited, gazing where above motionless tree-tops soared a great grey embattled tower, its massive walls pierced by arrow-slits, and high above this a row of narrow, scowling casements, from one of which a golden light beamed—and it was from this that a man leaned suddenly to glance up and around, while with snowy kerchief he mopped at brow and cheek, for the windless night was very warm; thus stood he a while as if for air, then, sudden as he had appeared, was gone.

"Didst see who that was?" Ippolito whispered.

"Cavalcanti!" answered Angelo, as softly. And then, from the temple hard by, Pedrillo called to them.

CHAPTER XVIII

TELLS OF A TERROR BY NIGHT

IT WAS not so much because of this very close, sultry night that Count Cavalcanti was perspiring even more profusely than usual, as extreme perturbation; instead of sitting or sprawling at his wonted ease, he was striding up and down this spacious, luxurious chamber, breathing short and flourishing his dimpled fists, while Sebastian, stately as ever, regarded him beneath drawn brows, saying irritably:

"Sit down, Emilio, sit down, my lord, and be at ease."

"No! No!" panted the Count. "This is no time for ease. I can but think and think how yon most devilish Jester dared us this morning, flouted and jibed at us! Ah, and why dared he so presume? Because Gonzago, damn him, set him on us, encouraged, ay—and paid him to do so! I can but mind how the Duchess, hearkening to this Motley's audacious fooling, frowned on thee, Sebastian, and, what's more, on me! We are out of favour, thou and I, Sebastian, and all—all by reason of Gonzago."

"Nay, my lord, I——"

"And this very afternoon i' the council chamber she defied us as never afore, denied our will and thwarted our purpose, and then—ha then—she, looking on us one by one and eye to eye, said how even then she might be looking on the guilty! And all—all by reason of Gonzago and this fiendly Jester!"

"And thus," sighed Sebastian, "this same Motley shall presently cease his fooling and be suddenly dumb, for 'tis a mischievous rogue and——"

"Mischievous? By these hilts he is perilous! Those accursed rhymes of 'if' and 'if'! I say he, like Gonzago, is a menace it behoves us to be rid of, ay, and soon, or we are undone! Gonzago and his Folly!—'tis them or us, and, for my part, I say it must and shall be them or all's amiss!"

"Emilio, here's wild talk——"

"Sebastian, I talk sense, having eyes that see withal, whiles you, remote in high authority, sit wilfully blind and deaf——"

"Think you so, my lord?"

"Ay, I do! As do the others, Fabriano most especially, and with too good reason! Why i' the devil's name did you so trust Gonzago—why and why?"

"Circumstances compelled me thereto and——"

"Meaning he did—being aforehand with us by lightning-stroke or ever we knew—in the matter of Fortu——"

"Silence!" exclaimed Sebastian, low-voiced but with such look that the Count, in the act of sitting down, started erect, while Sebastian, leaning slowly towards him, continued:

"Speak no names, thou blatant, vociferous fool, and this, of all names, I will not hear!"

"Ha, wilt name me 'fool'—me?" demanded the Count, mopping himself ferociously.

"Never, my lord, except with just cause. So pray heed—this is name shall not be uttered in my hearing."

"Ha, well, 'tis name whose echoes are adying, soon to be hushed and so—forgot. But, Sebastian, this our present accursed menace is yet in life! Ay, faith, Gonzago is all too much alive for my comfort and well-being. Ever more the Duchess favours him and thus ever more he waxeth in power! Also, as the Duchess favours him so favours he this Motley by whose wit he now wooeth her and jeers us—especially thee, Sebastian, despite the dignity of thy high office, as, for instance, to him Gonzago, thus: 'Good Motley, make us a jingle on my lord Sebastian'—and fees him thereto with a gold piece! Again, think how this Jester made rhymes anent young Luigi: 'Not on the earth but in it'! And yet how—how should he know that, even then, Luigi was——"

"Emilio, again I command your silence!"

"Why so you may, yet mark this—except you act, silent we all shall be and forever dumb! Oh, sweet saints forefend! Thus, saints or no, prudence and thy friend Emilio bid thee—act!"

"What would you have me do?"

"Not I, Sebastian, no no, 'tis Destiny commands! The fate of all compels—that you, as chiefest lord in the duchy, should act, and, as I suggest, by impeachment, public trial and execution end him—or—by means less public!"

"Meaning Gonzago?"

"Assuredly! Ay, and this Folly, this devilish Jester, his disposal should be trifling matter."

"It will—and shall be, Emilio. But . . . for Gonzago——"

"There be many and diver methods . . . he is wary and very cunning . . . a notable swordsman . . . thus, I deem a banquet surest and safest, a noble banquet, Sebastian, with—more of thy Vittorio's so rare and most especial wine! Well, well?"

"Emilio, could I be perfectly assured that one, himself so deeply implicated, would dare betray——"

"Dare, Sebastian? I tell thee he would dare all the flames and fiends of hell! And, for all his seeming languor, he is busied on somewhat, for I know he hath agents questing abroad——"

"How know you this?"

"We have had him watched, though his purposes we know not—yet! Howbeit, thou and I with Juliano Fabriano, Nicola Podi, Giovanni and Benevento, six gentlemen well beseen, of fair estate, fame impeccable and health abounding, may by his will and word—become loathsome carrion for flies to breed in—and of memory most shameful! Think on this and—act! And how better than—saints and angels defend us—what's yonder hubbub?"

"Those we expect, Fabriano and the others——"

"Then wherefore that clamour?" gasped the Count, starting afoot and clutching dagger-hilt as excited voices were heard rapidly approaching, then the door swung wide to admit four very heated and somewhat breathless gentlemen who together cried:

"The Motley——"

" 'Twas the Jester——"

"We spied him astride the wall——"

"Podi nigh had him——"

"So did I——"

"But he 'scaped us——"

"Yet is still below——"

"I' the pleasaunce and may be taken an we're speedy——"

"Good! Ha, excellent!" cried the Count, unsheathing dagger. "Let us down and seek him forthright! Sebastian, turn out your guard, sound the alarm——"

"Neither!" said he, rising. "We be six, friends all, and that we go to do were best known only to ourselves. So, follow me, sirs, and by my private stair."

Down they sped and in this wide and shadowy garden, halted to peer and listen, and in the hand of each steel glittered. Thus stood they themselves mute and still as the death they meant to inflict; then from the leafage, and unexpectedly near, was a rustle, with faint tinkle of bell and thither they leapt—to espy the Jester who seeing them close upon him, uttered a fearful, wailing cry and fled though not so fleetly but that they kept him in sight; thus they sped, pursued and pursuers, through vivid moonlight and sudden pitch-black glooms, until before them gleamed the little temple whereto he turned and, stumbling like one weary and spent, staggered beneath the looming portico and vanished.

"Aha!" panted the Count, breathless but flourishing his sword, fiercely triumphant. "Now . . . now we . . . have him!"

And so came these pursuers to the temple; they entered it, and within its darkness beheld a thing that seemed to flame at them . . . death in awful life new-arisen from burial . . . Luigi's remembered face . . . glaring eyes, mouth agape, teeth, tongue and every livid feature aglow, lit by a smouldering green fire . . . a gaunt arm upraised against them to point with flickering fiery hand.

Someone groaned. Weapons, loosed from nervous fingers fell clattering upon the marble pavement. Then was a strangled cry, a wild stumble and scurry of feet in panic flight—out and away. Thus deserted, Sebastian remained fronting this horror —rigid, dumb, breathless he stood at gaze, but after some while, from his stiff lips issued sounds like a child's whimpering that changed to a wordless gabble, then to a man's horrible screaming as backward he reeled out into the moonlight, there to fall suddenly as if down-smitten by an unseen hand, and so lay mute at last and very still. . . . But presently, drawn by this shrill outcry that seemed to find an echo in this sultry night, came one who in turn beholding the ghastly thing that glared on him with fire-shot, smouldering eyes, this that flamed yet was not consumed—this one also shrank appalled, but, instead of screaming, shouted for servants and lights so commandingly that very soon they came and with them— realization.

CHAPTER XIX

WHICH IS A SHORT, THOUGH PREGNANT CHAPTER

SHUDDERING to consciousness, my lord Sebastian opened unwilling eyes to find he was in the comfort of his own private chamber—but with Gonzago seated at ease near by watching him with that seemingly slumberous gaze and who now enquired with kindly solicitude:

"My poor Sebastian, art awake at last? Art thine own stately self again—eh, not quite? Well, take thy time, for——"

"How came I hither?"

"By my care. I found thee lying moon-struck and sum-moned divers of thy people. So here thou art with thy Gonzago who is fain to ask question or so——"

"Nay, I—not now, Gonzago—I, 'tis late and I am in no mood for question or company. I am not myself—I——"

"He was full young to die, Sebastian, our Luigi—to have the cup of life snatched ere he had well savoured its sweetness. Glad youth and grim Death should never meet, had I my way. But, alas, I am neither god nor devil and, though myself, I am merely finite and there's the pity on't!"

"What—ah, what do you here, Gonzago?"

"Gaze on thee, my noble Sebastian, and marvel at our motley prophet, our japing seer who saw, 'twould seem, a certain hidden grave and the youthful dead therein, e'en poor young Luigi—'not on the earth but—in it!'"

"You—you saw that—that thing in the temple, that— fearsome corruption——?"

"I beheld Luigi, so lately slain, so newly buried, so very dead—and yet stolen from his secret grave—to visit thee?"

"No! No—there were—others! But you—you also saw —it?"

"I beheld Luigi radiant as heavenly angel or aglow with fire of hell, new risen from his secret grave to sit, or rather sprawl, in judgment upon his too-ready slayers——"

"Gonzago, how—how came it thither, think you—and in such dire—such dreadful shape? By what unearthly power— what infernal agency?"

"Fie, Sebastian! Canst thou, a scholar, a student of books and men, believe the dead may rise and walk—putrefaction stir unaided? Is this thy philosophy?"

"Alas, I—tonight—oh, Gonzago, I know not! This night I know not what—or how to think! God aid me, I——"

"Speak not of God, Sebastian, He is not of our affinity or we of His! We are men to do and think alone and, for ourselves, be gods shaping our own destinies."

"And how—how an disaster smite us and—a shameful death?"

"Hail them as fellow gods, Sebastian, as indeed they are, and like gods endure."

Now slowly Sebastian's nobly moulded features lost their deathly pallor, his vaguely wandering gaze steadied, his listless-drooping hands clenched and, rising to his majestic height, he said, in strangely gentle tone:

"The Jester! I heard the jingle of his bells!"

"So—ho!" Gonzago murmured. "Then all is explained! 'Tis thus the dead arise and walk! But as for the fiery glow, that truly Satanic emanation——"

"Merely an alchemic compound," said Sebastian in that same small, still voice. "'Twas the Jester! I heard the jingle of his bells! I saw him . . . flee before us . . . into the temple——"

"Nay, Sebastian, what manner of Folly is he that dealeth in alchemy?"

"The Jester! I saw him . . . 'twas he led and lured us . . . to the temple!"

"Well, and what then? Here was no awful miracle to wonder at, no corpse, animate by demoniac juggle, to cry damnation on his slayers! Yonder was no more than Luigi's soulless body, his poor flesh untenanted and soon to rot. So noble lord, content thee."

"The Jester!" Sebastian repeated, in the same dreadfully stifled voice. "I saw him! I heard him!"

"Faith, Sebastian, certes thou'rt Jester-haunted, Motley-harried and Folly-ridden! But—of young Luigi so apt to serve our turn in that our night of destiny—pray, why didst thou murder him——"

"I?" Sebastian demanded, in furious amazement. "Never dare so to think, Gonzago! This was by no will or act of mine."

"Then I pray, whose the will and act?"

"Let be—ah, let be! 'Tis past and done—and I all unknowing, so name it not to me."

"Whose was the act and will, Sebastian?"

"No more, I say, no more! Be done! I am not well, I say, I—am not myself. Tomorrow—ay, tomorrow ask what ye will, but for this night—no more!" Here Sebastian sank back in his chair as though overcome by great weariness, staring before him sightlessly and so very still he might have been asleep but for those wide, fixed eyes, nor did he stir or heed when Gonzago, rising, said:

"Sebastian, if there be a God, He meant thee for a virtuous petty-man, so art thou a lost soul wandering 'twixt heaven and hell." Crossing to the door, Gonzago paused there, for, once again that hushed voice spoke, hissing now between hard-shut teeth:

"The Jester——!"

Then Gonzago opened the door and went his way, a man now very thoughtful.

CHAPTER XX

IN WHICH GONZAGO AND THE JESTER CONVERSE WITH GOD AND SATAN

THOUGH the morning was bright and joyous, Messer Astorgio was quite the reverse, for, being out of favour at court, he was also completely out of courage and bore himself like the fearful gentleman and dejected courtier he was. His daintily-shod feet, instead of lightsome trip, shambled heavily; his slender legs neither skipped nor postured; his little, silky beard was crushed and obscured in the belaced immensity of his ruff; the very plume in his jewelled bonnet seemed to droop abjectly. But as he went thus disconsolate, a richly pleasant voice hailed him and, glancing up, he beheld Gonzago, who smiled, saying:

"Well met in this fair morn, I give you joy of it—nay, but how now, what ails thee, man?"

"Alas, my good lord," moaned the unhappy gentleman, clutching at his bosom and bowing with a mournful humility, "though you greet me so graciously well, and I grateful therefor, yet, sir, you in me behold a poor gentleman so well-meaning that nought is well with him—I peek, my lord, I pine and droop despairing by reason of stress of circumstance."

"Sir, how so?"

"Oh, my lord, 'tis this matter of the poisoned wine and I —I, alas—its most innocent purveyor! Thus am I out of favour with the Duchess—in disgrace with Her Grace and, therefore, to all grace—less and viewed askance! Whereso I come, others go, they flee me as I were plague-smit. And, ah my lord, this very morning my lord Sebastian scowled me from his presence!"

"So?" murmured Gonzago, shaking that handsome auburn head of his. "Truly I fear our Sebastian, this so potent lord, loves thee not and shall further disfavour thee with Her Grace, but——"

"Ah, then, woe is me!" groaned Astorgio. "Sebastian my dispraiser? Then out goeth sun and I walk henceforth in night of black despond! Sebastian mine enemy? So am I the merest mournfullest dog that ever howled!"

"Nay," said Gonzago, kindly, "howl not, for though Sebastian would blast thy fame, yet he is—merely Sebastian, whiles I am—myself, and whoso is my friend may walk boldly i' the sunlight, jut his beard at Fate, dare Circumstance, nor fear—even Sebastian. Well, Astorgio, art thou my friend?"

"I, my lord, I—thy friend?" he gasped, in a sort of ecstasy. "Yea, yea, this am I henceforth, heart and soul, Gonzago, body and mind, with my every breath! And this I do swear by——" He checked suddenly and seemed to cower, as towards them came Sebastian in stately pomp, followed by divers of his armed retainers each of whom bore their lord's cognizance of a sun in splendour, on breast and back, twelve men-at-arms these—and one in rich, though sombre garments that bore no such device,—a tall, lean gentleman, whose close-set eyes gleamed below a pent of brow while his lipless mouth curled in perpetual smile beneath down-trending nose. Sebastian, pale and haggardly pensive, would have passed by had not Gonzago hailed him cheerily:

"Greeting and fairest greeting, Sebastian! I trust your nobility slept well? As for myself, I beg your kind regard and consideration for this my poor, misjudged friend Messer Astorgio whose worthiness I proclaim and will maintain."

Sebastian looked at this smiling speaker and inclined his stately head, glanced at the bowing Astorgio, frowned, nodded and said:

"Gonzago, I am but now from the Duchess and desire instant word with you in private."

"Impossible, Sebastian, for I am even now seeking audience of Her Grace, thus, alack, your lordship's word must wait!" At this, Sebastian turned away, but with such look that Gonzago enquired lightly: "Fie, Sebastian—is that scowl for me or for Astorgio? My lord, we wait your answer." And speaking ungraciously over his shoulder Sebastian replied:

"I shall expect you, Gonzago, within the hour!"

"Why then," laughed Gonzago, "by Venus you are like to be disappointed."

"Then by Sathanas you are like to rue it!" Sebastian retorted in voice that was almost a whisper, and so continued his stately way; and now it was not at him that Gonzago gazed so keenly, but at the tall, lean man who smiled.

"He acknowledged my reverence," sighed Astorgio, "yet he frowned on me, alas!"

"And yet," Gonzago repeated, his gaze still intent, "he shall smile on thee anon—mayhap! But—of that other, yon narrow-eyed, too-smiling gentleman, know you ought of him?"

"Not I, my lord, nor will I, for his aspect liketh me not."

"Yet mark him well, Astorgio, to know him again, for I would have you inform me as to his motions at court in so far as you may. Wilt do this as a friend for thy friend Gonzago?"

With a rapturous eagerness Astorgio was still protesting himself willing to serve this most powerful friend to the best of his ability when they came to one of the many small, bowery arbours that adorned these wide and beautiful palace gardens, and into this pleasant, sequestered shade Gonzago led him, saying:

"Now of Luigi, thy sudden-vanished esquire, hast any news of him?"

"Never a word, friend Gonzago, neither sight, sound nor faintest whisper."

"The which doth nowise surprise me. Didst know him for brother to this banished rebel Count Francesco?"

"Not I, sir, no no, for, since learning he was so brothered, I am, as 'twere, astounded beyond astonishment, since I had believed him son of an impoverished though worthy gentleman that neighboureth me on one of my estates, Cavanesa, to wit——"

"So?" murmured Gonzago, with slow yet pleasant smile. "And yet our Sebastian and the Count Cavalcanti do proclaim him brother to this rebel Francesco! And Sebastian, as we know, is most virtuous and noble lord! As for Cavalcanti, he sweateth overmuch——"

"Nay, Gonzago, by thy good leave I must needs contradict thee how 'twas neither of these gentlemen so affirmed, they but produced the letter that so did."

"Ah, certes—the letter! How think you of it, Astorgio? Could you swear 'twas writ by Luigi?"

"Nay, sir, all I dare affirm on oath is that it certainly may be so—yet if as certainly it be not so, no man can hold me blameworthy or impeach mine honour——"

"Then you are not sure?"

"Gonzago, for thy sake or to pleasure thee I would fain be sure most assuredly, but, being unsure, sure am I I should win thy dislove were I, thus unsure, to make oath of assurance even though to gain thy favour. Sir, I can say no more."

"Nay, faith has't said enough——" At this moment from some bosky remoteness came sound of a lute with murmur of feminine voices and then sweetly clear as soaring lark one began to sing, and these the words:

> "Oh tell me now, ah tell me, pray
> Whither doth my loved one stray,
> Where is he I love today?
> Oh, pretty bird upon the spray
> Thy pinions spread and wing away,
> Find him for me, then tune thy lay
> And with thy sweetest warbling say:
> 'He that so from me doth stray,
> He that will not when he may,
> When he will, shall then have "nay"!' "

"And there," said Gonzago, as the singing died upon a chord, "there's the woman of it, the philosophy of feminine contrariety! Yet never sweeter sung and by that essential sweetness feminine, the lady Fiametta, Her Grace's dearest gossip—and thine own adored plague, eh, Astorgio? Well, to her, man; I'll not keep thee; yet first, to gain her pretty ear and set her little, pink tongue aprattling, here's item of news known as yet but to one other—the Duchess shall dismiss her princely suitors. Query: Wherefore? Answer you: Her choice is fixed! Query: On whom? Answer I: Astorgio, use thine eyes!" Astorgio did so, for, opening them very wide, he gazed awestruck on this smiling, handsome speaker and, in tone matching his look, exclaimed:

"My lord! Ah, Gonzago, and thou—thou art my friend?"

"Be assured! Now away to thy lady, thy torment in petticoats—ha, and shouldst espy the Jester on thy way, bid him to me here,—off to thy wooing, talk, laugh, sigh, prattle and plead, show alternate fierce and tender, master and slave, yet ever forceful since ever woman so expects—go, and my friendship with thee."

Stammering gratitude, Astorgio bowed deeply, turned blithely and tripped away, feet light, legs graciously nimble, small beard manfully outthrust, cloak and bonnet plume fluttering with his joyous haste while Gonzago watched and smiled—then started as a voice unexpectedly near said softly:

"A mouse! A sprightly mouse shall squeak and scurry anon!"

Slowly Gonzago turned, surveyed the Jester languidly and said, low-voiced:

"Well, thou japing corpse-monger, thou jingling resurrectionist, how now?"

"At your service, sir!"

"How long hast been eavesdropping, thou sly, motley knave?"

"No longer, sir, than a piece of rope."

"A rope may be cut, fool."

"Verily, gracious sir, yet verily it may first hang a man!"

"Ay, rogue, even though he wear cap and bells."

"Oh sir! To hang poor fool were act o' folly and waste of good rope!"

"Not for such purposeful fool as thou, for in thy fooling is so much reason that for this reason thou art as reasonably suspect, wherefore I suspect, and with reason, that fool and foolery alike are like to be cut short and shortly! This being so, I would have thee sit in this seclusion and talk with me a while."

"Willingly, Apollo! Now let us, seated, thus cheek by jowl, converse of blow-flies that, being so by nature, do gloat on carrion."

"Indeed and verily, Bimbo—thus may a too-wise and speechful food become flyblown anon."

"And, sir, flies buzz and poor Jester, yet in life, crieth: Oho, will such as your high nobility stoop to threaten such lowly wight as this same Motley?"

"Not so, I warn!"

"Grand merci, sir! Of whom?"

"Last night should tell thee, and—an open grave. Well, am I plain enough? Art warned? How sayest thou, Bimbo?"

"Sir, I say again, Oho and likewise, Aha, being fool, and wonder wherefore such as thou shouldst trouble for such as I."

"For one reason because, all unwitting, thou hast served my turn, right well, and for another because I love that nimble tongue o' thine, and yet another for that I've heard thee win our lovely Duchess to laughter and brief forgetfulness of her too-persistent sorrow and I know she esteems thee right well—and I would have her ever happy—for these reasons and her precious sake I would not have thee fly-blown —yet awhile, nor such—grave man as young Luigi! Above all the Duchess, her welfare is very dear to me. . . . I would as I say, have her forever glad and joyous——"

"So would God, sir! For she is young, and youth is made for gladness, like this fair world where is no sorrow save man that is his own grief and plague perpetual——"

"Nay, what man would plague himself, Bimbo?"

"He that plagueth his fellow! For evil ever begetteth evil— whence cometh fear, hate, lying, treachery, murder and revenge, and since these all proceed from man alone, ergo, man's only torment is man."

"Or the devil!"

"Verily, sir, since man is part angel and part devil in more or less degree." Here for a space they were silent, for Gonzago's arrogant head was bowed, his handsome face gravely pensive, until he demanded suddenly:

"So, Bimbo, you believe in God?"

"Sir, having eyes, I needs must."

"Ha? Is thy God so manifest in this evil world?"

"Indeed, sir, in tree and flower, in friendship and all things that be simply true."

"And, Bimbo, the simple truth is that man born in sin is therefore sinful by nature—thus 'tis the devil is lord paramount, king and master of this foredoomed sinful carnality! My potent Devil hath dethroned thy meek God and maketh the world his wanton toy and plaything. . . . Well, art dumb? What say you?"

"Buzz, my lord; I say buzz! The which bringeth us back to our blow-flies and this most pertinent question, to wit: if these foul flies must gloat upon dead corruption wherefore not on corruption alive that goeth upon two legs, hath reason and thus, being more actively vile than things dead, do breed more active evils. Aha—and talking of such—what thing of evil crawleth yonder?" Now glancing whither the Jester pointed, Gonzago nodded, saying below his breath:

"Verily hast said it, Bimbo! Yonder cometh a two-legged, smiling thing that I have lately been at pains to learn—and know for Evil Incarnate! So—and with six of Sebastian's men-at-arms! Now what shall he be after, canst guess?"

"So well, sir, that I'll begone——"

"Too late, Bimbo, our smiling Evil hath espied thee! Bide still therefore and await the event. Moreover, I am here!"

The six armed men halted and their leader now approached the shady arbour, this tall, lean gentleman who bowed, hat in hand, smiling, of course.

"Ah, my lord," said he, teeth aglint, "I am Vittorio Manucci, at your service—you know me, I think?"

"Yes, monsieur," replied Gonzago, speaking in French, "I think I do, and better than you think. Well, monsieur, what would you—and these six armed fellows?"

"No more, sir, than conduct yon Jester unto your most assured friend my lord Sebastian."

"Indeed, monsieur—to what purpose?"

"Oh, sir, for my lord's pleasure, as I dare guess——"

"Oh la-la, monsieur! How then, would Sebastian, our so sedate and gravely dignified councillor, consort with Folly, now? Go to—pish and fie, I'll not believe it!"

"None the less, sir, he wills this Jester shall be brought to him——"

"Nevertheless, sir, I will he shall remain with me for mine own pleasure. Here now be two wills and but one Jester, wherefore Jester will abide with me."

"How, sir, how—must I believe you will gainsay, indeed actually venture to thwart my lord Sebastian's most expressed will and——"

"Joyfully, monsieur, since I am an adventurous soul. Howbeit, I will not my will be crossed by will of any man, for though your wilful lord be Sebastian, I, by nature, the devil and my own will, am my more wilful self. So, mon cher, monsieur, you may now return to our Sebastian and say that 'stead of this jingling Folly I send him a far better thing, to wit—my love."

Vittorio's narrow eyes glittered, his arching nostrils quivered and his lipless mouth curled in such smile that his sharp teeth gleamed again as, bowing lower than ever, he said, gently:

"Then, noble sir, I must remind you that in all the duchy my lord Sebastian is paramount, his will and word do override all other——"

"Save that of Her Grace the Duchess, monsieur, and most certainly mine own! And this, as her loyal subject, I will maintain right gladly and to extremity!" So saying, Gonzago rose gracefully and, unsheathing his long rapier, stepped lightly from the arbour.

"Six!" said he, glancing around. "Six men in arms against Her Grace's peace, and all wearing the badge of lord Sebastian! Six men who——"

"Seven, my lord," smiled Vittorio; "you behold me yet, I think?"

"Indeed, monsieur, I am aware of you, but I said—men!" For an instant Vittorio's smile vanished—only to return with yet wider show of teeth.

"Well, my lord," he demanded, "will you compel me? Must I command violence?"

"Ay do, monsieur, and with my last breath I'll cry 'treason'."

"Alas, sir," smiled Vittorio, moving beyond reach of Gonzago's steel, " 'twould indeed be thy last breath—thyself slain as traitor and so proclaimed. So, my good lord, for thine own sake be dumb and suffer us to depart with this knavish Jester, unmolested——"

Gonzago's answer was a ringing blow on the nearest soldier's burgonet—then, as he retreated before the counter-attack, a hideous screeching shrilled upon the air:

"Oho—treason! Aha—treachery! Dogs, Sebastian, cry down thy ban-dogs! Call off thy murderers——" and forth of this shady arbour the Jester tripped—a wild figure, who pranced and postured and screeched, beating time to these horrible outcries with his bauble. "Ha, thy dogs, Sebastian, thy dogs—call them to heel!"

So very hideous were his cries and so frantic his gestures that for a moment all turned to stare on him, and in that moment, before pike could thrust or sword smite, rose an answering shout and towards them Manfred hastened, clashing in his armour, with chosen men of Fortunio's veteran guard.

"S'blood!" he exclaimed, somewhat breathlessly. "S'bones! What be this ado? What hellish outcry was here?"

"Nay, Sir Captain," answered Gonzago, flourishing rapier in gracious salutation, " 'twas verily a cry of salvation since you come so aptly, almost as by signal prearranged!"

"Sir, I heard cry o' treason."

"Certes, captain, for here stands Treason seven times manifest and wearing our noble lord Sebastian his device! These six men led by this Vittorio Manucci, here treasonably in arms, would have slain me but for this so harsh-throated Jester——"

"S'death!" exclaimed Manfred, gesturing with his sword. "Arrest me these bloody-minded rogues——"

"At your peril, captain!" smiled Vittorio. "For my lord Sebastian will exact——"

"Silence, thou dog, yap not at me!" growled Manfred, and then to his company: "Disarm the cursed, treacherous knaves—so! Now, form up, quick march!"

Hardly were these gone than came others all and sundry: first, Count Ippolito running, sword in hand, with Fiametta following, she hampered by her petticoats crying on him to wait and screaming when he did not; behind her sped others, gallant gentlemen who shouted, fair ladies who screamed in chorus; lastly came the Duchess, for she, because of the general hurry, checked her own impatient feet and approached with a gracious, leisured dignity. At her coming all were hushed, and in answer to her question, Gonzago, sinking to a knee, made brief though such vividly-eloquent narration, that scarcely had he ended than she glanced up and around, bright-eyed, demanding:

"Well, where now is he—the Jester?"

At this, voices cried and called for him, here and there; search was made for him everywhere, yet all in vain, for it seemed that amid the general stir and confusion this elusive Jester had stolen away . . . And yet not so furtively but that eyes, unseen, had watched his going; feet, unheard, had followed, and Murder, with ready steel, waited to strike.

CHAPTER XXI

DESCRIBES ONE USE FOR A FOOL'S BAUBLE

ANGELO sat alone, for the Friar was abroad on his unending ministry; also, this being market day, Pedrillo, now young Beppo's devoted slave, had taken him to the city.

The drowsy afternoon was very hot and still; through the small lattice, open upon the garden, stole the mingled sweetness of herb and flower with the hum of insects and sleepy twitter of birds.

In this peaceful solitude, Angelo sat nibbling the feather of his pen and staring down at the blank sheet on the table before him; and after he had sighed distressfully, he at last began to write this woeful letter:

"To the learned and honourable Faculty at Oxenford, these:

"Right worshipped sirs, it is with much grief that I write to inform you and all whom it may concern, of my loved friend Sir John Courtenay, his death . . ."

Here Angelo's usually facile pen faltered and stopped, for this was tale so difficult to set down in adequate words that he lifted troubled eyes—in time to see and just avoid death as it leapt at him through the open doorway, a long rapier blade that grazed his throat. Dropping pen, he leapt afoot, caught up his bauble and with this contrived to parry this ever-darting point as he retreated, step by step, before this figure of Murder whose face was hidden in hideous white mask. Thus Angelo gave back before his unknown assailant, his only defence bodily agility and the bauble which was being hacked to pieces each time it met and turned aside this glittering menace. Backward thus and back he went, step by step, until at length he came where hung Friar Clement's old sword, then, even, as he snatched it down, he reeled, gasping, to a thrust that would have transfixed him but for that hidden shirt of good link-mail. Armed now, he attacked his attacker, ponderous sword against light rapier plied so deftly that again it bent double against Angelo's unseen armour, whereat from behind that white mask a hoarse voice gasped:

"Sorcery!" In which moment sword smote rapier from lax grip and, thus defenceless, the unknown leapt backward, turned and sped for his life. Angelo sprang to pursue, but, tripping over the fallen weapon, fell heavily and, knowing further pursuit vain, lay to regain his breath and thus espied upon the lintel of the door a splash of blood.

After some while Angelo rose, rubbed elbow and knee, replaced Friar Clement's sword and, taking up his assailant's rapier, examined it with some faint hope it might afford clue to the identity of its late user; but, finding none, set it in reach and sat down to finish the writing of his letter; he was still thus engaged when Friar Clement came, trudging heavily like a weary man, and who, sinking into a chair, sighed:

"Angelo, the Jester must vanish, for he is denounced and proclaimed as the murderer of Luigi, the young esquire!"

"The which," said Angelo, signing his now finished letter, "doth not surprise me, Father Clem. And Sebastian the accuser?"

"Not so; this was the Count Cavalcanti, and before the Council, in full assembly!"

"Was she there—Jenevra?"

"She was, and I with her."

"And what said the Count?"

"He told how one Bimbo, a vagrant Jester, with divers other rogues unknown, brake into Sebastian's demesne and there deposited the dead body of one Luigi——" Here the Friar pausing, Angelo nodded, saying:

"All precisely true! What more said the Count?"

Sighing again, Friar Clement continued:

"He then described how this said Jester did actually and positively declare Luigi to be dead and buried long before such fact was known or could possibly be thus known to any save the murderer himself!"

"And there," nodded Angelo, "he made a point reasonably conclusive and therefore damning, eh, Father Clem?"

"So much so, my son, that upon this, the whole Council was agreed and forthwith denounced the Jester guilty of this crime, pronounced him outlawed and called for his instant capture and execution!"

"Said Jenevra aught, father?"

"She did, for at her bidding the royal trumpeters sounded a rouse and then, having silenced thus all clamorous tongues, she spake forthrightly, saying: 'My lords, last time I sat here ye cried on me for proof—today I echo that cry and demand of you proof absolute or ever I will permit such indictment. Also I forbid your ban of outlawry! In this, my duchy, shall be justice for all alike, rich and poor, high and low. As for this vagrant Jester, let him be taken unharmed and brought to me and my jurisdiction, and'—here, Angelo, she rose to look down upon us all—'let none do him hurt on pain of death. This Jester shall be tried in open court, but, except he be proven guilty, should his life be attempted by any man, howsoever high his estate, that man shall die shameful death. Such is my declared will, let it be known——"

"And so," exclaimed Angelo, clasping his hands, "so will I be her adorer, soul and body, and love my fetters for her dear sake! Surely never was such glad prisoner as this thrice happy Jester, this poor wretch that shall rely upon her justice and princely strength! Oh, valiant lady—the sweet and lovely soul——"

Now when Angelo, eyes gladly bright and cheek flushed, would have risen, all eager youth and love, Friar Clement stayed him with upflung hand and shake of grave, wise head.

"Indeed, my son, as Duchess she is strong and above all fear, yet by reason of her high estate she is solitary—the one 'gainst the many. Thus today, though she bare herself so princely, yet afterwards, alone with me, she wept like the troubled woman and tender maid she so truly is! And wilt thou add to her cares, Angelo?"

"God forbid!" he answered, fervently. "I'd fain lighten her griefs and perchance win her to laughter; she needeth her fool of comfort."

"Verily 'twas thus she named thee, and with tears, knowing thy life now in direst peril and fearing in her woman's heart lest the Duchess have strength to protect thee——"

"Said she as much? Oh, Father Clem, what said she?"

"That in her heart she knew the Jester all innocent."

"In her heart? Oh, lovely, gentle heart! What more?"

"That this fool was of all her councillors the wisest."

"Oh, gracious lady! What more?"

"That should they kill this Jester she would be most desolate——"

"Oh, beloved woman! More yet, father, her every lovely word, I beseech thee."

"Then, my son, she bade me kneel with her and implore our merciful God to have this Jester in His most especial care now and evermore."

"Oh, Jenevra, thou sweet and gentle loveliness! Oh, Father Clement, am I presumptuous to hope, to dare believe this proud Duchess, this glorious woman, this tender thing of all lovely perfection—she that is all this, and more—can she, hath she, doth she stoop to love this so perilous Jester, this lowly wretch, this most reverent, adoring man that is—me? Can it be possible? Is it true? If this be so, then the proudest,

humblest man I in all this happy earth. See—thus upon my
knees I wait thine answer! Speak, I do conjure thee."

Friar Clement rose and, having paced the narrow chamber,
paused where Angelo knelt.

"Dear my son," said he, gently, "this only can I tell thee
—that she wept for thee, prayed for thee, named thee wise
and her comforter. This she said and no more. But in her
tearful eyes, in voice and look was that whereby I dare to
think love hath indeed stolen upon her and she, I guess, all
unaware as yet. And thou, Angelo, for her sake, thine own
and—that the which I pray shall yet be, I say again—the
Jester must vanish, must be seen and heard no more."

"Well, but how then, my father, what of me——?"

"Assume other guise and bide here in safety where no
enemy may suspect——" Rising from his knees, Angelo
took the rapier and therewith pointed to the blood-splash
on the lintel, saying:

"Murder followed me today and but for thy good mail and
noble old sword I should now be thing for burial." Briefly
he told of his masked assailant, laughing grimly as he ended:
"So 'twas thanks to thee and thy arts magical I yet live, for
when his point refused to pierce me, the fellow cried 'Sorcery!'
and fled—in terror of thee, Father Clem! But alack, our
Jester's bauble is ruined beyond repair—so, reverend father,
thy wizardry and arts of Sorcery shall conjure and transmute
this jingling motley wretch into an airy sprite to flit hither and
yon. But first this night he shall bid farewell to—her."

"How, Angelo? The Duchess? Wilt so dare thy life——"

"Dear Father Clem, I would dare a thousand lives—for
this night with the spirit of reverent love to aid me—she—
shall yield her lips to this Jester, kiss this jingling Folly and
thus make of love—a glory."

CHAPTER XXII

TELLS OF NIGHT, ENCHANTMENT AND A KISS

A NIGHT bird in the shadowy garden below was piping to the
full-orbed moon, but it was not these plaintive, liquid notes
that brought the young Duchess to her dimpled elbow so

suddenly,—her quick ear had caught another sound—and
this like the faint, sweet chime of fairy bells. Silently she
rose, swiftly she dressed, turned hastily to be gone, paused
uncertainly, took up a jewelled girdle where hung a small,
gold-hilted dagger, frowned at it, hesitated, then, clasping it
about her shapeliness, stole past the pallet where Fiametta
slumbered—out and away. Avoiding silent watchman and
tramping sentinel, she opened a certain door and, light of
foot, descended a narrow, winding stair and so—forth into
this fragrant, midsummer night. But now she paused and
stood, lovely face uplifted to the moon as though listening
entranced to the notes of that sweet-throated bird of the
night, though her every sense was aware of the so familiar,
shabby figure coming towards her and now with no sound
of bell or footfall; nor did she move or seem to notice him
until so near he might have touched her, then she started
and turned upon him, saying angrily though in hushed tone:

"What do you here at hour so—unseemly? How passed
you my guards?" And softly he answered:

"Like a shadow, my lady, a shadow that must soon pass and
vanish as it had never been. Thus come I seeking thee——"

"And wherefore—at such time of night and with such
hateful—such detestable secrecy?"

"For that at such magical hour as this, whiles all save we
lie drowned in sleep, our dreams, like holy angels, may meet
us——"

"Or murder!" she retorted. "And thou art murderer proclaimed! So should I shudder at mere sight of thee—as I
do—see how trembles this poor hand!"

"I also!" he answered. "See—both these poor hands how
they shake because of thee. Yet thou art all guiltless of
murder as I. Then wherefore should we tremble thus at
each other?"

Instead of answering she turned and began to walk, though
very slowly; and after thoughtful pace or so, she echoed his
question:

"Why?"

"Enchantment—mayhap!" he replied. "For this little while
we are so blest—to walk together in world of enchantment
where no thing evil can be, where hope burgeons to fulfilment and dreams take on most glorious reality." And after
brief pause, again she questioned softly:

"How?" and as softly he made answer:

"Thyself—of such blessed dream the fair embodiment—art now no more and no less than woman and with moonbeams tangled in her hair; myself a man with lips unsealed to speak at last that which——" But here, with passionate stamp of foot, she turned on him to say as in sudden fury of scorn, though in voice subdued:

"A man? Thou art no more than Jester, a buffoon, a zany, a vagrant motley—yet hatefully presumptuous—and accused of murder beside! Oh, what do I here, at such hour, with such as thou?"

And, bowing with extravagant humility, he replied:

"You berate this poor, meek wretch like any virago, most gracious of ladies. And what doth he, think you? Madame, he cocketh eye aloft, thus, and winketh at the man up yonder i' the moon, for his lunar majesty, seeing much, is passing wise."

"And now," said she, between white teeth, "now should I summon my guards to drag and dungeon thee for—for impudent rogue should lie in fetters awaiting my justice!"

"Then, right noble and gentlest of ladies, then should I with index finger trace in the slime of my dungeon the sweetest of all lovely names—Jenevra."

Now at this, having frowned and bared her teeth at him again, she walked on and, being angry, more quickly until he enquired in tone humbly plaintive:

"Most gracious Your Grace, of Your Grace pray tell this motley-meek humility—whither do you take him and at hour —so unseemly?"

"I?" she demanded, indignantly. "I take thee?"

"Even so, highness, for see—yonder gleameth the sundial! 'Twas there at spring of day you first dawned upon a poor Jester's raptured vision fresh and fair as Aurora's very self, bringing with you memory of other and better days when the world was younger and therefore less evil." Now after they had gone a little further, she sighed and questioned, wistfully:

"Think you the past is ever better than the present?"

"Ay, I do, lady—though far less glorious than the future may be, or so I hope and pray."

"The future?" she exclaimed, clasping her hands. "Oh, I dread it and hate it! At dawn of day and fall of night I dread it ever more and more."

"Yet God is in heaven, Jenevra, and thou art thyself."

"But heaven is so remote and I, at such times as this, do know myself indeed for no more than merest woman——"

"Even as God made thee, Jenevra! Thus at such times thou'rt at thy sweetest best."

"And yet, alas—a Duchess!" she sighed. "So needs must I show valiant when most fearful and—and in—other ways seem far other than I truly am."

"Except," said he, very gently, "in such most sacred hour as this and—to such as I!"

Now here she turned and looked at him very narrowly, eye to eye, scanning his every feature, and the moon very bright above them.

"Put back your hood!" she commanded. "That foolish cockscomb!" Mutely he obeyed, and, drawing nearer, sne enquired:

"Are you a Moor to be so dark, or of the Zingari, the gipsy folk?" And as from his very heart he answered, reverently:

"I am, and ever will be, all thou wouldst have me to be, soul and body! To live for thee with my every breath, or die for thee an I must; though God knoweth how fain I am to live—for thee." Slowly she turned and went on until, being come to the sundial, she sank down on the marble seat thereby.

"And wilt be faithful to me—till death?"

"And beyond!" he answered, fervently.

"Oh!" she exclaimed with pettish gesture. "Why didst give thyself such ridiculous name . . . Bimbo! 'Tis discordant absurdity and sorts not with this night or thee. So, for this little while I will name and call thee Fidelio. Now as for thyself, Fidelio, I know thou art a scholar and, by thy speech and bearing, judge thee of gentle birth; then wherefore stoop so low—to the ignominy of bells and ass's ears?"

"I would stoop lower to stand—thus—so nigh to paradise!"

"Is it by reason of past sinning you go in this ignoble guise, for penance or fear of pursuing justice?"

"Canst so believe, Jenevra, even though I am accused of murder?" Again she gazed at the face above her, this dark yet handsome face lit by brilliant, long-lashed eyes, the dominant nose and chin, the mobile, sensitive mouth that could be so grimly sardonic and yet so ineffably tender, as now; and thus gazing, she murmured:

"And yet they do accuse thee—Fidelio!"

F

The sensitive mouth tightened; the delicate nostrils expanded; the brilliant eyes, half-closing, glittered.

"'They'!" he repeated, almost whispering. "And these that are 'they' do, by such false accusation, proclaim their own guilt."

"Of—what?" she demanded, quick-breathing. "Of what are they guilty?" And bowing his head, he answered:

"Upon a night, as I hear, one . . . Fortunio was murdered . . . by poison——"

"Oh, alas!" she gasped. "And by wine, sent by—my most unhappy self . . . 'twas my gift——"

"Not so, Jenevra; never think of it! Not thyself, but—'they'! Thus now thy fool of comfort shall jingle thee the truth of it:

> This most pernicious wine
> Was no death-gift o' thine;
> Instead 'twas other wine that they
> By slight exchanged upon the way——"

"They?" she exclaimed, starting afoot. "Ah, whom do you mean?"

"They that would silence me as they did young Luigi."

"Thy accusers?"

"Even they!"

"Oh, now . . . God aid us!" she whispered, brokenly. "If this indeed be so . . . these lords of my Council . . . 'tis nightmare . . . horror . . . this uncertainty! Do but give me proof——"

"They shall themselves afford this——"

"Oh, but how . . . when?"

> "Lady thy fool of comfort I,
> Do now foretell and prophesy:
> Fear shall haunt them, night and day,
> Till they themselves—themselves betray
> These that be guilty—even they——"

"Oh, have done with thy jingles!" she commanded. "For this brief hour be thy best self. The truly gentle man that I trust and have therefore named Fidelio. So, Folly, hush thee!"

Here for a moment one slim finger touched his lips that quivered to the joy of it. "Now sit you here beside me,

Fidelio, and let us take counsel how this wickedness may be so proven. And you shall tell me of your verses of 'If' and how you could have known Luigi dead and buried—how and by what means?"

"By no means," he answered, now sitting as she bade him, " 'twas bow drawn at a venture."

"And like to harm thyself!" she retorted. "For this will be held as proof of guilt—when thou art brought to trial."

"That is—to my death! For I am foredoomed; thus Innocence must die lest Guilt perish—as it must and shall! Wherefore I come not to judgment. This sorry, lovesick Jester thy adoring fool of comfort shall be seen and heard no more!"

"So?" she exclaimed as in sudden anger. "Dare he not trust to my jurisdiction; will he flee like a—a base and most contemptible craven?"

"He will do more, noble lady; he shall vanish like a phantom."

"A craven!" she sighed. "A poltroon! And, despite cap and bells, I deemed him a valiant gentleman!"

"And because of his cap and bells, this adoring poltroon is proud and infinitely grateful for thy so deeming."

Faint and sweet with distance a church clock began to chime the hour. . . .

"Midnight!" she sighed. "So flitteth life away! In a little while, pray God, I shall sleep—yet only to waken to another day of care for the present and dread of the future, a fear I must not show."

"Oh, Jenevra," he murmured, with instinctive gesture infinitely yearning, "would to God I might comfort thee——"

"Nay," she retorted, between sob and laugh, "thou art soon to become mere phantom! So talk not of comfort when, for craven fear, thou wilt leave me in my greatest need . . . for now, as they tell me, even my people begin to murmur against me and——"

" 'Tis but 'they' do tell thee so and so do lie! As for me, —phantom-like I shall be nigh to watch over thee unseen——"

"Then shall I be haunted!"

"Ay, lady, by an adoring spectre called Fidelio."

Jenevra turned to gaze upward, saying very plaintively:

"Even the moon will desert me now! See how she sinks

and the shadows deepen upon me! Oh would this cruel world were gentle and peaceful all as this quiet garden—or that I might walk a little while within thy world of enchantment . . . and yet—even thou wilt soon be a phantom to affright me——" Even as she spoke, he was down upon his knees before her, saying:

"What is to be is not yet. These be no phantom hands; touch them and see! These be no phantom arms, and thus —with the moon above us and God over all to watch and bless—come to my heart, Jenevra!" And his hands were strong, his arms compelling, and his mouth, the gentle, sensitive mouth now so vitally urgent . . . Jenevra closed her eyes and for a while forgot all else. . . . At last she broke from him, panting:

"Oh! Shame! Oh, base—thou to talk of God and—force me to—thy hated kiss!" And out flashed her dagger.

Now being yet upon his knees, he looked up at her as she crouched to strike, and shook his head, saying:

"Jenevra, beloved, shame not thy noble love for shame of this motley. For as I revere thee I dare to think God also loveth thee for that kiss, since 'twas the angel in thee dared bestow it! Yet now, if for empty pride's sake, the devil in thee would have my life—take it and make of me a phantom indeed."

The dagger fell and lay between them, its small, cruel blade agleam in the moonlight until he took it up and set it in her unwilling grasp."

"Take it," said he, "most gracious of noble ladies and most beloved of women, take it and with it myself, heart, mind and body, to have and to hold to thy loved service so long as life be permitted to me. And now, Jenevra, here by this sundial, this sacred place where first we met, I bid thee farewell until, an God be so merciful, I come back to thee. . . . Wilt kiss me then, I wonder? There—thy steel in its sheath— so! Now give me thy hand—this dear, small, strong hand that I would fain kiss yet will not. Come, I will see thee safe, for though I am not yet a phantom, things there be more evil that haunt the night—and day, alas!"

Hand thus in hand they went, nor spoke nor even looked at each other until they came where tower and battlement loomed above them; in this shadow they paused, neither speaking, upon her hand she felt the touch of his lips, then as speechless still, she turned to be gone, he murmured:

"Some day, an God be merciful, these arms shall hold thee closer yet."

Being again in her great bed and in shadow now, for the prying moon was no longer at the narrow casement, Jenevra lay very still with no thought or wish for sleep; Fiametta, lying so near, sighed once or twice in her slumber, but Jenevra, thus wakeful, sighed far oftener and much deeper until at last, hiding her face in the pillow, she uttered this whispered prayer:

"Oh dear God, Almighty Father, be merciful!"

CHAPTER XXIII

TELLS HOW VITTORIO MANUCCI CHANGED MASTERS

IN HIS small though beautiful garden Gonzago sat so intent upon the closely-written papers before him that he was quite unaware of the eyes that watched him until, hearing a silken rustle, he glanced up swiftly, and as instantly smiled at the vision before him, all glowing provocation from the blue-black tresses framing the oval of her face to the small, proudly-arching foot apeep below her broidered robe.

"Carlotta mia!" he murmured, setting down the papers to reach out both hands. "By Venus thou art my joyous refreshment——"

She advanced one slow, graceful step and paused, saying in soft, husky voice:

"For how long, my lord? Thy many promises! Break thy word and my heart and I will not live——"

"My bewitching madonna, I do but counsel patience."

"Nor will I suffer thee to live."

"Carlotta, sweeting, wherefore trouble that most lovely head, wherefore plague thyself—and me with such idle doubting?"

"Thou art my life, Gonzago; take it not from me, for I would fain live for thee; also thou art young to die."

"How, my Carlotta, is this a threat?"

"My lord, no, it is a promise. Death cannot take either without the other since love hath made us one——" With leisured grace he rose and took her in his masterful embrace and for a moment she clung to him wildly, saying in hushed, dreadful voice:

"Oh, Gonzago, seek not death when life might be so passing sweet."

"It shall be!" said he, kissing her silky hair; then very gently he put her from him, saying gaily:

"Hold faith in thy beauteous self, in the future and, above all, in me. Now I pray thee, sweeting, bid the man Annibal hither and suffer none intrude." For a moment her great eyes flamed rebellious, then, sullenly obedient, she turned and went to do his will.

Thus alone, Gonzago walked amid his roses and, choosing a great scarlet bloom, cut it deftly with his dagger and was inhaling its sweetness when, with prodigious jingle of spurs, flutter of cloak and sweep of hat, Annibal presented himself; but Gonzago, savouring the fragrance of his rose with delicate nostrils aquiver and eyes half-closed like the voluptuary he was, seemed wholly unaware of anything else until Annibal ventured to cough.

"Ahem!" quoth he, and struck an attitude, left hand poised gracefully upon the hilt of his long rapier, right hand wafting his hat in airy salutation. "Ahem!" quoth he.

"Cough not!" sighed Gonzago, caressing his rose. "I am sufficiently aware of you. But for the moment when I consider the exquisite beauty of this flower and enjoy its heavenly sweetness, beholding the wonder of it, one might almost believe it the work of God. Believe you in God, Annibal?"

"Oh, most infallibly, my lord!"

"And thou my paid assassin, Annibal! Thy hands so oft imbrued in, let us say, ichor. Art thou such hypocrite?"

"Not so, my lord. A true son of Holy Church, I—that do make full confession of my every act and, doing penance therefore, receive absolution."

"True, thy sins are remitted and thyself freed to—sin again."

"Nay, but, my lord, what is sin? For God made the world and all therein, thus I am His handiwork and live and do by His will——"

"So, wouldst make thy God the author of thy deeds! Well, 'tis comfortable philosophy. But, now to business." So saying, Gonzago sat down at the small table set in shady bower and, laying white hand upon the papers before him, enquired:

"There is a certain Vittorio Manucci that serves the lord

Sebastian in his most secret—enterprises; you know him, I think?"

"Sufficiently, my lord, that, knowing him, know him I will no more than I must."

"Certes," nodded Gonzago, smiling, "there be degrees in villainy. Thou, my Annibal, art a gentleman of the profession, bold of hand and heart; this Vittorio a furtive creeper! In a little while he will be here—came Rodrigo with you?"

"Ay, my lord, and waits your summons."

"Very well. You and he hidden in the arbour yonder shall wait the while I question Vittorio, and when you see me enjoy the fragrance of this rose, thus and thus, you shall steal upon him and, standing beside him, right and left, touch him with your daggers to speech or silence as I shall direct. Is this understood?"

"Perfectly, my lord. Are we thereafter to rid the world of this two-legged pest?"

"Not today, but hereafter, mayhap. And now, Annibal, hear me say I am pleased with thee, hast served me so well that, to serve me better, thou shalt to court as mine esquire."

"Ha—grammercy, my good lord!" exclaimed Annibal, sweeping the turf with hat-feather. "Indeed to thank your lordship duly is beyond this my grateful-faltering tongue——"

"Then spare me and thyself, Annibal. But now, and heed me well, as my gentleman thou must be entirely retailored and something remannered."

"How so, my lord?"

"Thy present attire smacks too much of everything. Thy gentility too obvious. Thou must be richly-unremarkable, showing a luxury restrained, for profusion is vulgarity and therefore damnable! The ferocity of thy moustachios must be tamed, thy voice schooled to dulcet sweetness, thy gestures to a gracious languor. Since thy teeth are good, smile readily; laugh seldom; talk much, but say little; be quick of eye and ear. Observe these rules of conduct, Annibal; be faithful, and thy fortunes shall soar with mine, or, like poor young Icarus, plunge headlong to ruin irretrievable."

"Never, my lord! I cannot think of thee and ruin together, for in thy every look and gesture success is manifest."

"A fair thought, Annibal; hold it fast, for thought begets action and action is life, so—ah, yonder is madonna to say this Vittorio waits—go summon Rodrigo and with him to the arbour yonder, and watch!"

Thus presently Gonzago's sleepy-seeing eyes were surveying his visitor, who approached, hat in hand, with a series of bows.

"Most gracious lord," he smiled, "suffer me to express my humble thanks for your lordship's interest on my behalf. My enlargement from prison is, as I learn, owing not to my lord Sebastian but your more potent influence and good will towards me——"

"Let us say my influence, monsieur. As to Sebastian now—well?"

"'Twould seem his power wanes, my lord, while you go from strength to ever great strength. Thus I rejoice you should have summoned me hither and humbly beg your lordship will command me."

"I think I shall," said Gonzago, nodding at his rose, "but not as Vittorio Manucci; at least, I shall think of you by your true name."

"I laugh, my lord, for I presume you jest?"

"Not at present, monsieur."

"Then might I venture to enquire your lordship's meaning?"

"The truth, monsieur! As for instance—fifteen years since you were Jean Francois Collet, a French officer with such knowledge of chemistry that you were condemned to the galleys for being concerned in the death of your paternal uncle. Is this not truth?"

The narrow eyes glittered, the sleek head was shaken gently, and from that lipless, ever-smiling mouth a serenely confident voice replied:

"Not so, my lord. I am indeed Vittorio Manucci, a Florentine. As for these charges, they are so absurdly false that——"
Gonzago lifted the rose to his delicate nostrils and Vittorio, starting about, beheld Annibal leering on one side of him while Rodrigo scowled upon the other and in the fist of each a naked dagger.

"Fifteen years since," Gonzago repeated, "having been justly condemned for this crime, you were branded with hot iron—the fleur-de-lis, according to custom. Is my word enough or must I see this mark of infamy? Touch him to speech, Annibal?" Instantly the two dagger points were at Vittorio's throat, whereat his smile widened to glint of teeth as he replied and with the utmost composure:

"Your lordship's word suffices."

"Escaping from the galleys," Gonzago continued in gentle though remorseless tone, "you were later suspect of other murders, one of which was proven against you, whereupon you fled France and inflicted yourself upon this country where you took service with your present master and have on several occasions—served him, let us say, since, as I mentioned before, you are something of a chemist. Is my knowledge still sufficing or must I name each, how, when and—whom?"

"My lord, your profound knowledge is all-sufficing."

"Well, Vittorio, as you were so instant to perceive, your master's power is waning, his sun shall set ere long and—not in glory. This being so—well, Vittorio?" Gonzago paused to fasten the rose very tenderly in the breast of his resplendent doublet, while Vittorio bowed again, saying:

"This being so, my lord, I shall at once seek other and, I hope, nobler service."

"Meaning mine, Vittorio?"

"Such is my profound ambition, my lord—to be yours absolutely henceforth, most humbly and obediently to command."

"This would be expected. Now to try you, tell me this: has your master and my avowed friend suggested my death yet?"

Vittorio hesitated and for once that mouth of his lost its smile; so long he stood thus hesitant that at last Gonzago murmured:

"Touch him to speech, Annibal."

And instantly Vittorio flinched from the prick of those ready dagger-points, saying:

"Your lordship will pray forgive my deliberation, seeing my situation is so invidious."

"And perilous!" sighed Gonzago. "For verily, Monsieur Collet, few would grieve, many applaud, and none question your sudden demise and total disappearance."

"My lord, I am aware of it; few could and none would. And for your question, truth alone would compel me to answer in the affirmative."

"So then my death is ordered?"

"Not as yet, sir, merely considered and debated."

"Ah—so! By the four we wot of?"

"Even so, my lord."

"And by means of—your specific?"

"It has been suggested, sir."

"Well, I had suspected as much; 'tis as well to be assured——"

"Dare I hope, my lord, that now I may also be assured of your favour, the privilege and honour of your lordship's employ?"

"'Twas to this end I troubled to free you from prison."

"Then, my good and most gracious lord, how may I serve you?"

"By serving your present master."

"Ah—you mean——?"

"Be and do all he expects, but—keep me informed."

"Constantly, sir! You shall know all that transpires."

"Very well. Take now your earnest money, this guaranty," said Gonzago, laying a purse within his reach. "In my service zeal and loyalty are well paid, but none hath ever lived to betray me twice. Now you may go and—fail not!"

"Never doubt me, my lord," said Vittorio, taking up the purse; "you shall find me devoted and faithful to the death!"

"Ay, but—whose death, Vittorio? Ah, well, this we shall resolve soon or late."

Then at Gonzago's languid gesture of dismissal Vittorio bowed, smiled and departed.

"And there," murmured Gonzago, looking after him, "there goeth the deadliest thing in all this duchy!" Then beckoning the two::

"Hearken, both!" said he, sinking his voice. "There be three noble gentlemen I would have ye watch and report on: you at court, Annibal, and you, Rodrigo, in the city. And these are, Count Cavalcanti, secondly Juliano Fabriano, and thirdly Nicola Podi. Also in taverns and other places of resort set going a whisper how the lord Sebastian is out of favour at court by reason the Duchess suspects him of Fortunio's murder. Let it be further known that he is scheming to put off this crime on Her Grace since the poisoned wine was her gift though she is innocent as angel of light. Be vague though persistent; say, for instance, you've heard tell such and such. That 'tis common report. That word goeth of this and that —and such like. Now is this perfectly understood of ye both?"

"Yea, sir!"

"It is, my lord!"

"Then here's guerdon, and for the present fare ye well."

CHAPTER XXIV

CONCERNING A HAIRY GARDENER THAT WAS A PHANTOM

IT WAS evening and the young Duchess, entering her private garden, glanced instinctively towards the sundial and round about very wistfully, but saw only a middle-aged gardener, a rough-clad, very hairy, rustical fellow plying a scythe in shady corner and using it very awkwardly.

Slowly she came to the sundial and, bowing stately head, leaned there, her prideful beauty gentled by something more than mere cares of state. Motionless she leaned thus, only her eyes, ever and anon, glanced up and around with that same wistfully searching gaze, at which times she sighed distressfully. Thus stood she musing and disconsolate until, roused by very harsh, unpleasant noise, she frowned thitherward and saw this was caused by the gardener sharpening his scythe, wherefore she called to him angrily:

"Wretch, what do you here?" And with floundering bow he replied, hoarsely:

"Which, me leddy, I sharps me scythe."

"Then go away this moment."

"Which can't nowise be, leddy, being nowise possible nohow."

"How?" she demanded, amazed and indignant. "Will you disobey me?"

"Ay, m'leddy, which seeing as how."

"Impudent man, will you defy me?"

"Ay, m'leddyship. Which seeing as how I can't nowise haunt 'ee proper except I be wheer you be, for Jenevra, behold in me thy own very humble, ever-adoring phantom."

She started erect, recoiled a step, and then—why must her cheek, so suddenly pale, show as suddenly flushed? Why must her bright eyes veil their light 'neath down-swept lashes, and wherefore did her breath catch, so that for the moment speech was impossible? When at last her ruddy lips parted it was to a sound which in any other than this stately Duchess would certainly have beeen termed a giggle.

"Who—whoever heard of phantom with such whiskers and a scythe and such very—horribly hairy face?"

"No one," he replied, gravely, "for of all phantoms, spectres, ghosts and apparitions I am rarest and most original."

"Oh, Fidelio," she exclaimed, impulsively, "I am marvellous glad of thee, for though new troubles menace me, yet thou canst so banish them that already I have laughed!"

"What is thy new menace, my lady?"

"The old one in more threatening guise. Last night certain of my councillors even dared to threaten me, seeking to daunt me to their purpose by talk of sedition, a rising of the citizens against me! And this by reason I still refuse to agree their verdict that Fortunio murdered himself for shame of his brother Angelo's perfidy. 'Twas then Sebastian denounced me as a menace to the public welfare, and 'twas then that I, in righteous anger, dismissed him from his high office. How say'st thou of this, Fidelio?"

"That these be they of whom thy vanished Jester warned thee—and yonder cometh one even now!"

"Oh!" she whispered, clasping her hands to stay and hide their sudden trembling. "And one of the most vindicative, Cavalcanti!"

"Howbeit, I am with thee, Jenevra."

"Alas, and thou'rt but a phantom, a poor, mere ghost!"

"Nevertheless," said he, smiling grimly through his grizzled whiskers, "I am thine own phantom and most original ghost."

Count Cavalcanti approached in rather higher state of perspiration than usual; he bowed, mopped, breathed short, and thus before he could speak the Duchess demanded:

"Sir, what means this intrusion? Why will you trouble my privacy?"

"Madame," he replied, mopping, "I would dare, yea and do, much to save you from the consequences of your too-prideful will. For I must tell you——" Here his words were lost in harsh grind, clash and clatter of sharpening-stone on scythe-blade, whereat the Count turned upon the gardener in perspiring fury, crying:

"Have done, thou knavish clod! Go hence—remove, I say —begone; dost hear me?"

The gardener stared, gaped, shook grizzled head, and replied hoarsely:

"Noble sir, which I do but sharp my scythe!"

"Knave, hold thy peace—begone!"

"Which I ax 'ee, m'lud, wheer away?"

"To the devil and be damned!"

"Sir Count," cried the Duchess in high indignation, "you forget yourself! And in my presence!"

"Oh, Madame, I humbly crave Your Grace's pardon—but this witless clod——"

"One of my gardeners, sir, and therefore in his proper place whiles you, being an intruder, are quite out of place here."

"On the contrary, Your Highness, I am here most rightly, to plead with you for your own good and welfare of the State."

"Well, what is your plea?"

"That you shall reconsider your sudden dismissal of Sebastian and——"

"I have, sir, and do now confirm it. If you be come from him you may return and tell him so."

"But, Madame, you must surely be aware how your Council is 'gainst you in this——"

"As in most other matters, sir! Now you may go and say my decision is final."

"Then, Madame, you compel me to inform you how this most unwise sentence 'gainst such worthy gentleman as Sebastian is by all regarded as——" Here again was grind, clash and clatter of stone on scythe-blade; and thus, fuming with fiercely restrained anger, the Count was forced to wait until, this detestable noise ending, he was able to continue:

"Your Grace, such unjust, nay—tyrannicalus age of our noble Sebastian hath caused uproar, fomented riots! There be clamours in the city for his immediate reinstatement——"

"Then, my lord, you shall go and make it known how this very afternoon I will meet my people in the market-place to hear and answer them. Let this be cried throughout the city and all things made ready."

"Alas, Madame, this shall not serve you; 'twould but lead to further riot and——"

Here yet again clash, grind and rattle silenced him; and, stamping with fury, he turned to scowl where the gardener was even then whetting that very noisy scythe of his. The Count, at a loss for adequate words, clutched at his dagger-hilt, and crouched threateningly. The gardener goggled and sniffed. The Duchess spoke:

"Count Cavalcanti, you weary me and to none avail! I bid you depart."

"Madame," he cried, gesturing wildly towards the gardener who had approached and now stood leaning on his scythe, staring open-mouthed, "this—this dolt, this most accursed shog, mads me. Bid him hence or I shall be——"

"My lord!" exclaimed the Duchess. "I will no longer endure you——"

"Madame," he retorted, straddling his chubby legs resolutely, "noble lady, you needs must, for with all submission I beg you to believe me one who, for the good of all, will dare even your displeasure and even more! I am by nature a man so bold of purpose that I tell you again——" Here his plumed bonnet was whisked from his astounded head to fall yards away.

"Ha, what—what," he demanded in stammering amazement, "what's here——?"

"M'lud," answered the gardener, "which I says 'tes ghostesses or specaters—mebbe they do tell as phanitums do haunt hereabouts——" Dropping scythe, he crouched suddenly, for, with frenzied cry scarcely human, Count Cavalcanti plucked forth dagger and leapt at his tormentor, who, stooping very nimbly, seized that armed hand—then, breast to breast, they closed in silent though deadly combat, but the Count had eaten and drunk too well for such relentless violence, insomuch that after brief, desperate struggle he was thrown so heavily that his dagger fell, to be caught up by the gardener who, thus armed, set his clumsy shoe upon the gasping Count, a merciless foot that not only held him thus prone and helpless, but spurned and trampled him so viciously that the Count groaned at last and the Duchess, eyes wide and hands clasped upon rounded bosom, cried breathlessly:

"Enough—oh, enough! Let him up!"

Unwillingly the gardener removed his foot, but, dagger in fist, showed so menacing that the fallen man instinctively shrank behind lifted arm.

"Rise, my lord!" said the Duchess, stepping lightly between him and this threatening dagger. "Rise, I say, and, for your own sake, go nor trouble me again!"

Slowly and with painful effort Count Cavalcanti got to his legs and for a moment stood gazing down at the place where he had fallen; and his usually too ruddy face was now too pale, his heavy lips showed pallid; then, his gaze thus abased, he turned without word or backward glance and trudged heavily away. Only his plumed bonnet remained and this the gardener forthwith kicked into the bushes; then, thrusting dagger into girdle, he took up his scythe; but now, hearing a stifled gasp, he glanced thitherward and saw the Duchess had sunk down upon the marble bench, head bowed, and face hidden in her hands.

"Jenevra?" he murmured. "Oh, my lady, shed no tears for such——" She glanced up; gasping with stifled laughter, she wiped lovely, tearful eyes, and, controlling her merriment with an effort:

"Oh!" she sighed as if now in an ecstasy, "Cavalcanti of all men! So vicious, yet so plump! And he fell with such a—flounce! Heels above detestable head! What joy! What rapture! Oh, Fidelio, truly my ghost, my haunting phantom, is very blessedly and most comfortably strong! Surely never was spectre so powerful! Nor more provoking! For indeed you teased and tormented the hateful wretch beyond endurance—'tis no wonder he yearned to slay you! And then—you trampled him so cruelly!"

"Nay, too tenderly, Jenevra, for he is one of your chiefest troubles and therefore to be trampled. But why are not these troublers prevented, denied this private garden by your guards?"

"Alas, my counsellors have right of entry and audience at all times."

"Then who would choose be a Duchess?"

"That I am was no choice of mine. God made me so."

"Nay. He made thee merely a woman."

"Then who made me a Duchess?"

"Chance, lady, chance. For though God indeed made you of His handiwork the perfection, apt for love and the joyous wonder of motherhood, blind Chance condemned you to be a Duchess enslaved by state and foredoomed to wedlock, willing or no."

"Fidelio, I will never—oh, never will I wed any I do not love!"

"Ah, but—can a Duchess wed for love? If so, well and good; if not—let her cast aside empty pomp, shake off her ducal fetters and be free—and lo, thou poor, harassed Duchess, yonder Trouble returneth four times multiplied!"

"I see them!" sighed she, wearily. "So am I the more glad of my phantom—see that he haunt me close and hover near."

Led by Count Cavalcanti, these gentlemen approached, bowing with sweep of hat or bonnet, except the Count, who had neither, and who now, gesturing towards his three companions, spoke full-throated:

"Highness, we, thy hearty lovers and well-wishers all, are here to plead——"

"And supplicate," said Lord Fabriano, tall and saturnine.

"To sue," sighed the Marquis Grimani, pale and languishing.

"And exhort," added Messire Podi, small and pompous. "I repeat, Madame, to exhort you, though most humbly, first in the matter of lord Sebastian and—that you will——"

"I will not, messires!" said she, rising the better to say it. "I will neither recall Sebastian nor ever agree your wished verdict concerning my lord Fortunio! Waste not your time therefore or my patience in these matters."

"Gracious lady," sighed the Marquis, "we yet dare to hope——"

"Do not!" said she. "Such hope is vain!"

"Your Grace," said lord Fabriano, "you are so young and therefore little experienced in governance wherein we your councillors, being so much elder, are thus the more practised. Hence we, speaking for the Ten, propose you shall, for your own ease and for the commonweal, vest in us your full authority to act for you until such time as you be wed. Here, Your Highness I have the document for your acceptance whereby you free yourself of all State cares so ever—it needs but your signature."

"And here, Madame," said Nicola Podi, stepping briskly forward, " pen and ink-horn!"

"Give me the paper!" said she, gently, though with gesture so commanding that Fabriano instantly tendered it with deep obeisance.

Slowly the young Duchess read this document, then, glancing round upon her intently watchful councillors, she as slowly tore it across and across and, tossing the pieces scornfully towards them, said in the same dispassionate tone:

"There is your answer, my lords. Now you have my permission to leave me; this audience is ended." But instead of going, these four gentlemen drew slowly together and nearer the Duchess, whereat the gardener, leaning on his scythe hardby, stole ready hand to the naked dagger in his girdle.

"Madame," cried Count Cavalcanti, pointing fiercely to those scattered shreds of paper, "by this wanton act you affront us and the whole Council, and I, being the man I am, demand"—here he advanced a threatening step—"I say I demand that you——" He checked suddenly, as from the leafage very near him stepped Gonzago, followed by his now smooth-shaven and newly-equipped esquire Annibal.

"Noble and dear lady," said Gonzago, stooping gracefully to kiss the white hand outstretched to him so readily, "dare I hope my sudden appearance no intrusion?"

"Indeed," she answered, smiling on him very kindly, "Gonzago, you are most truly welcome."

"Though, dear lady, 'twould seem you are troubled by matters politic; those right noble gentlemen, councillors all, by their so portentous gravity, would seem engaged on matters of import. Shall I retire?"

"I bid you wait, for the audience is ended and these gentlemen about to go. But," said she, turning upon the four, "ere you depart, be it known to you now, as it shall be to the Council this night, that here and now I name my lord Gonzago chiefest of my councillors in room of Sebastian and also seneschal of the city. Go ye now and bid the Council in full assemblage meet me tonight at nine of the clock, when I will so proclaim."

"And most gracious lady," said Gonzago, sinking before her on his knees, "let all hear me say I thank Your Highness for this signal honour and vow myself yours for life or death, and to so act, and from this moment, that Villainy shall hide fearful head and Treachery be stamped out. And so, my lords," said he, springing lightly afoot to front the four dismayed gentlemen, "as chiefest of the Ten, I counsel ye, each one, to take such instant measures that, for the good and safety of all—and the State, of course, as each of you shall deem proper. And, my lords, as seneschal, I shall command the city gates to close each day one hour after sunset."

Dumbly the four made their reverence to the Duchess and, speechless, they departed.

"And not one of them," murmured Gonzago, as he watched their silent departure, "never a one but needs a halter!" Then, turning to the Duchess, he bowed, saying: "Most dear lady, suffer that I present my esquire, Annibal who, by thy gracious leave, will abide with me at court. . . . And, oh most noble, beloved lady . . . ah, Jenevra, how may I thank thee for so honouring me——"

"By loyalty to me, Gonzago, and faithful service to the State."

"On my life, body and soul, I swear it!" he replied softly, yet with such passionate fervour that none, not even the gardener, could have doubted his deep sincerity. Again he knelt, once more she gave him her hand; and thus together they went away talking in muted voices, leaving the gardener, a most forlorn wretch who leaned dejectedly upon his scythe and scowled at the grass he had mowed so very badly.

CHAPTER XXV

WHICH, BEING OF NO PARTICULAR IMPORT, IS BRIEF

SEATED this same evening in Friar Clement's shadowy garden, Angelo frowned up at the rising moon, sighing dismally, like the unhappy wretch he was; then, elbows on knees and chin in hands, scowled down at his dim-seen, clumsy shoes.

Now after some while, to him came Friar Clement to sit beside him, set long arm about his drooping shoulders and enquire in that deep, so gentle voice of his:

"Angelo, my son, what aileth thee . . . to eat no supper and sit thus solitary, so forlorn and sighful? Is it, as I guess, this youthful unease, this passion of love? Check now thy groaning and answer me." And in bitter, snarling voice Angelo replied:

"Gonzago!"

"Ah, by cause she hath so honoured him?"

"Ay—and no! But—he so gallant . . . radiant and lovely as Apollo! And I, with my vile, hairy visage a very satyr by comparison! No need was there for Pedrillo to make me so hideous!" Friar Clement's powerful arm tightened and he chuckled, softly deep.

"Oh love!" he murmured. "Oh jealousy!"

"'Tis neither!" groaned Angelo. "Only that now I must be such vile, repulsive thing—for dogs to howl at!"

"Why then, my son, go to her as thou art now—smooth o' face and no wig—or, better, let Angelo come back to life! Go to her as thine own best self; what is there to let or stay thee?"

"Fortunio's murderers, father! And this beside—as the

poor creature I seem, I may pervade the court, too mean for notice, but as Angelo I should be watched and mayhap slain or ever my work be done. My work! Ay, Fortunio's slayers, his memory to be vindicated . . . and my own good name! Fortunio's murderers—one I know, three I suspect and one I can but guess at. Thus, for my loved brother's dear sake, I must be the vile wretch I seem."

"Well, my son, but what of thy love for Jenevra?"

"My love?" Angelo repeated in groaning voice. "Oh, Father Clem, it filleth the very universe . . . and yet . . . Fortunio must come first! I must serve him in death ere I serve myself in life."

"Dear, my son, even so!"

"Ah, but—Jenevra!" he sighed, despairingly. "Until my duty to Fortunio be done, she must love me for the thing I seem or—not at all! But . . . oh, my father, if only she may . . . if only she can . . . if she doth indeed, ah, then——"
Here he gazed up at the moon again, no longer frowning but in a speechless ecstasy of yearning.

But now came Pedrillo to say:

"Our small imp will not sleep till he hath kissed thee good night, Angelo."

Forthwith indoors they went, all three, the Friar and Pedrillo to their chemical mysteries, while Angelo, sitting beside Beppo's little bed, told a taie of faerie, as had become his wont. But when the boy was asleep, Angelo wandered forth into the now moonlit garden and, seated beneath the mulberry tree, pondered on what had been and was yet to be. But, as the moon rose higher, he grew restless, and after some while went to seek the Friar and Pedrillo busied together in their dim-lit, grimy workshop.

"Ha, sorcerers!" he exclaimed. "What spells conjure ye? —foul by the reek!"

"My son, 'tis a salve for poor, suffering humanity——"

"And," said Pedrillo, stoking a small fire beneath bubbling pot, "a right marvellous specific worketh such healing wonders, we be ever short of it. But what's for thee, Angelo, and—hey, why that rapier 'neath thine arm?"

"I'm for—the garden ye wot of, dear my friend, and to-night I've the whim to go armed."

"Then, my son, God keep thee!" said Friar Clement, loosing pestle and mortar to lift hands in benediction.

"Amen!" said Angelo and Pedrillo, in a breath.

And so, presently having donned his abhorred face-hair and wig, Angelo turned to be gone; then, espying Pedrillo's massive staff in a corner, laid by the rapier and, taking this instead, fared forth to the night's adventure.

CHAPTER XXVI

TELLS OF MURDEROUS STEEL AND A SILKEN NOOSE

CLASH of steel beneath the moon . . . a gasping, broken cry for help. . . . Thitherward sped Angelo and thus beheld one beset by four—a man who fought, back to a wall, a very nimble man whose single blade opposed, checked and countered the four blue-glittering points aiming at his life. To them, unheard, and upon them, unseen, leapt Angelo, plying both ends of Pedrillo's heavy quarterstaff heartily and to such effect that the four, thus smitten, and now assailed front and rear, broke and fled, leaving one who lay very still and silent.

"Ha . . . good fellow . . . well struck!" gasped the one, and out from looming shadow of the wall that had been his protection stepped Gonzago. "So—so?" he exclaimed gaily though breathlessly, as he sheathed his rapier. "Is it the gardener fellow?" And hoarsely his rescuer replied:

"Ay, m'lud, which that it be!"

"Then i' faith and upon my life, my life I owe thee, thou lusty knave. And though my life is to me in life the most precious thing and beyond price, I, for this that is priceless, bestow my purse. Take it, fellow, and herewith my gratitude. So, for that no money may buy, take now this money—come."

Thrusting the purse into breast of his ill-fitting jerkin, the gardener reached out his long staff to touch that which lay so mute and still in shadow of the lofty wall, saying:

"Sir, be this yere a dead un?"

"Faith he should be," nodded Gonzago. "I ran him deep enough."

"Which, sir, he do wear a mask!"

"So did they all. Help me to drag this one into the moonlight—so! Now—off with his mask—well, dost know him?"

"Which, sir, I dunnot."

"Alas, a boy!" exclaimed Gonzago, stooping above the dead. "A rogue, yet a very youth—'tis pity! Now were I God, youth should never die or weary to hideous, unwanted old age! So alas for humanity that I, though myself, am but finite man. Yet, good fellow, I am Gonzago the Lord Seneschal, so thus thou shalt price my life accordingly—well?"

"Which, m'lud, I be paid and content."

"Fool, he that is ever content is mere spiritless clod! Be not content, fellow, for this night in saving me alive you have wrought far better than you know. Ay, truly, for tonight is yet another night of destiny and—I live, thanks to thee and fair Luna yonder!" Here he bared his head and wafted a kiss to the moon. "So, good fellow, for my so precious life I will nobly requite thee when I am duke."

So saying, and with gracious gesture, Gonzago turned and strolled away, leaving Angelo gazing after him above the dead, and the word "duke" yet ringing in his ears.

Gonzago, walking leisurely, reached the palace, paused beneath the shadow of its frowning, embattled gateway, gave the pass-word to the steel-clad night guards, saluting them graciously, and so by wide antechamber, noble hall and stately corridor, came at last to that small, secluded chamber or cabinet wherein Sebastian had been wont to transmit his more private business; but tonight in his stead and in his great chair, bowed above table, quill in hand, sat Vittorio Manucci. At Gonzago's entrance he started so violently that the quill pen escaped his suddenly nerveless fingers while he stared wide of eye and his now unsmiling, lipless mouth opened, then closed to a gasp.

"Pick up thy pen," said Gonzago, smiling down on him. "I am no ghost, Vittorio, so pick up thy pen. I was delayed somewhat on my way hither and am a little late. Yet we have all night for—what we have to do. I see the letter still occupies you."

"My lord, it lacks but final words and signature. I dare to think you will be pleased by its exactitude."

"I hope to be so indeed, for it must bear conviction in its every dot and comma, every twist and flourish."

"Will your lordship see what I have done thus far?"

"Not until it be finished," said Gonzago, sinking languidly into the easiest chair. "The sign manual must be facsimile, Vittorio, therefore pray take due time."

So Vittorio stooped to his careful pen-work again while Gonzago, taking out a small, gold comfit-box, helped himself to a sugared almond. Thus for a space was silence except for the gentle scratch of Vittorio's busy quill, for the great palace above and around them was hushed in slumber. At last Gonzago enquired:

"May I talk, Vittorio, or will it distract you?"

"No, sir, this work needs but hand and eyes; mine ears attend your lordship."

Now watching his companion with those sleepy-seeming eyes of his that yet saw so very much, he murmured:

"The moon, Vittorio, yon serene goddess of the night, is waxing in splendour—tomorrow she will be throned in full glory and—at such times I am ever at my best. This, mayhap, shall explain why tonight they failed to murder me."

"Murder——?" Vittorio repeated, pen suddenly arrested.

"Finish thy task, Vittorio, nor let thy hand falter; it must not fail thee at the signature."

Obediently Vittorio bent to his careful writing again while Gonzago continued:

"My assailants were masked all and dumb, fearing, as I suppose, recognition. But one of these I had the misfortune to kill, for he was but a youth . . . and methought his young features, though something altered by death, were yet vaguely familiar. I have seen him—somewhere at some time. . . . Would you have known him I wonder? Nay—finish thy work of art, and let it be the most perfect of thy life."

"And, sir," cried Vittorio with almost wild fervency, "my life is—and shall be dedicated wholly and most faithfully to your lordship's service."

"Thy life, Vittorio? I shall take—and use it hereafter—mayhap."

Having at last finished his carefully written document, Vittorio sanded it and, rising, tendered it to Gonzago with bow even humbler than usual, and it was to be noted he smiled no longer.

Gonzago examined this manuscript line by line and word by word, scrutinized it closely, peered at it afar, turned it this way and that; finally, sighing almost rapturously, he looked up at Vittorio's lean, pale face, smiled and murmured:

"Vittorio, thou art a very artist, a master pen-man, a magician of the quill, for this is perfection of the writing craft! By thy peerless skill here is a lie that showeth for truth manifest! Here is absolute falsity made to seem so perfectly real it shall lie most triumphantly, blaring truth like shrill trumpet-blast or echo-waking clarions! Vittorio, thou art thine only peer. Ah, but canst thou as perfect be in—that is yet to do?"

"My lord, this I can promise."

"Art prepared? The—wherewithal?"

"Here, sir!" And from the breast of his rich doublet Vittorio drew an inch or so of thin, silken cord.

" 'Twill be sure, Vittorio?"

"Most certain, my lord."

"Then go see if he be come; if so—bring him hither. And, Vittorio, he is in affliction so—be thy kindest self." Now at this, Vittorio's lipless mouth widened to slow, quite terrible smile as with scarcely perceptible nod and no sound of foot he stole away, leaving Gonzago gazing after him beneath drawn brows until, hearing sudden hasty footsteps, he rose as Sebastian entered cloaked and booted as for a journey; of hat and cloak, very solicitously, Gonzago relieved him, saying:

"Sit and be right welcome, Sebastian."

And how woefully changed was this once proud man! Here was no stately dignified gentleman, but a cowering furtive misery, whose tall form seemed shrunken, whose noble features were drawn and pallid, whose once resonant voice was low and hesitant and in whose haggard eyes was agony of fear.

"Gonzago," said he, sinking feebly into the proffered chair, "I . . . I am here to thy bidding. 'Tis good in thee to aid thy . . . fallen friend. For here all . . . all is lost to me save thy friendship! I am alone . . . deserted . . . Fabriano and the others are fled and——"

"I know. 'Twas I warned them, Sebastian."

"Then . . . wherefore didst keep me here? Why . . . ah, why am I not . . . away . . . in safety also?"

"Because, alas, Sebastian, for such as thyself can be no safety—ever!"

"No safety—for me? How—why? Prithee, wherefore not—— Ah, what . . . what mean you?"

"Because, Sebastian, as I warned thee time ago, thou art thine own destruction. In thee is neither angel nor devil, thou art but a thing named Sebastian. If there be a God He never meant thee for villain, yet villainy thou hast attempted and so vainly that now thou art victim of thy most pitiful self. And, as this, I have used thee——"

"Gonzago . . . oh . . . Gonzago, in the name of friendship, what . . . what mean you with me?"

"Thou wert so feeble in thy villainy, so infirm in thy purposes, that I have used thee for mine own, made of thee my ladder, and now——"

"Gonzago . . . in mercy . . . what . . . ah—what——?"

"Wert thou more of a man, Sebastian, now could I pity thee. As 'tis, I can hope your God will do his best with thee and in another life remake thee to better avail. And so, Sebastian, fair thee well!"

Gonzago gestered slightly—then, unheard, unseen by Sebastian, the silken noose was about his throat and Vittorio's skilled hands dragged him down—and down—to death.

And, after brief while, Gonzago, gazing up at the richly painted ceiling and a certain, great, deeply-carved beam whereon, deeply chiselled in bold relief, were three cherubs' heads, pointed thitherward, saying:

"Yon amoretti, the midmost one, should support him, I think. Let us essay." Ensued now an interval of speechless effort and strain, then:

"Admirable!" said Gonzago, somewhat breathlessly. "Now his chair—on its side, this way—so! Ay, 'tis convincing! And—ha, now, my Vittorio, thy masterpiece—upon his table—thus—a little askew as witness of his perturbation— or should it lie upon the floor as loosed from fingers lax in despair? Nay, I choose the table and the paper a little crumpled—thus and so! Ay, 'twill serve; here is such evidence, such factual lie as none shall disprove. Thus, Vittorio, our several parts are done so well that tomorrow eyes and tongues shall crown our doing with positive and universal belief. Now, to thy well-earned rest; away and take with thee my veneration for thy so notable abilities, and, Vittorio—sleep well!"

It was some while later that Annibal, waiting at place appointed, beheld his master strolling towards him, but who paused in his leisured stride to bare his handsome head and gaze up at the sinking moon, saying as he did so:

"Hail, Luna, fair Dian, pale goddess of the night, as thou has sped and fortuned me in the last hours, do thou so aid and bless me in my wooing." Then gracefully he donned hat and continued his advance.

"Annibal," said he, as they went on together, "the man Vittorio Manucci hath sinned far too long. Doth this suffice thee?"

"Perfectly, my lord. He shall be translated ere cockcrow."

"How sweet is life, Annibal, at such hour as this, for this is verily time of promise . . . a new day; already I smell the dawn, Aurora's waking sigh! Well, I'll to bed, but as for thyself 'twill be cockcrow anon!"

Annibal smiled, laid finger on dagger-hilt and bowed himself away.

CHAPTER XXVII

TELLS OF THE DUCHESS, HER LOVE—AND HER PLEDGE

IN HIS sunny garden next morning Friar Clement, brawny arms bared and habit tucked high, was hoeing busily when someone tugged at him from behind and, glancing round, he saw this was the Duchess.

"Holy father," said she, in small voice unusually meek, "I have to confess that which, as I do think, must be my shame."

Starting erect, he turned and leant upon his hoe, surveying her beauteous, down-bent face very keenly, nor moved he nor spoke until head still bowed, she glanced up at him; and thus, seeing the stern anxiety of his regard, Jenevra smiled and blushed, though with no least shame in her steady gaze; wherefore the breath he had checked escaped in sigh of profound relief.

"Highness," he enquired, gently, "wilt thou confess as sinner—unto God, or as Jenevra unto me?"

"To thee, dear Father Clem, and to thee alone in all this world! Also I shall plead thy counsel and advice, though I may be pleased to agree or accept neither."

"So be it, my child. Come thou!" Hand in hand they went to sit beneath the shady mulberry tree. Here she nestled to him, but, instead of speaking, began to smooth and pat his rough, threadbare habit, not looking at him now until at last:

"Well—my loved child?" he demanded.

"Well!" she repeated. "Upon a day you sent me—a Jester!"

"Well, Jenevra?" he enquired again and in tone that was a caress.

"Well," she repeated for the second time. "I know him now for other than common Jester or any such poor, mere wretch."

"How, my child?"

"By his every word and look and gesture. The lilt of his voice, the high, proud carriage of his head, that maketh nought of foolish cockscomb and dignifies his motley. Wherefore—and therefore, I demand of thee, Father Clement, who, what and whence is he. Speak, Sir Friar; as thy Duchess I do command thee!"

"And, noble lady, I can but tell thee he came to me a forlorn and homeless wanderer."

"Ah, dear Father Clem," she murmured, nestling to him again; "knowing thee all my life, thy ever-loving care of me, sure am I such tender father would never have sent him to me had he (I mean thee) not known him (I mean him) for one much nobler than he seemed."

"Why, Jenevra, to be sure I judged him a worthy youth."

"And what more?"

"Well, an honourable man."

"And what more?"

"Eh? More? Well," said the Friar, floundering, "I suspected——"

"No, not suspected, you knew him for a gentleman in motley guise; I say you knew this! So I demand of you again, who, what and whence?"

"And, Jenevra, I tell thee again, he came to me poor and destitute—clambering over the wall yonder, this and no more," said Friar Clement and would have risen but that she clutched and hung to the cord that belted him, saying:

"Bide thou, reverend father, abide and strive not, for I desire thy counsel and crave thy advice, the which, as I say, I may neither accept or act upon. Now, have I thy most reverent and sagacious ear?"

"Yea, verily!" he answered, with a deep, soft chuckle, setting his arm about her loveliness. "Mine ears do both attend Your Highness."

"Then first I ask thee . . . can I and should I for mere love's sake stoop and shame myself by . . . loving this Jester that no Jester is, and would such love indeed be my shame?"

"Oh, Jenevra, I tell thee, 'twould verily be thy glory and love's triumph if——"

"Nay, 'if' me not, father, for this word doth mind me of most 'if'-ful verses and one—Bimbo! And what Duchess in all this world could ever love any Jester called—Bimbo? Not one——"

"Palter not, my daughter. For I tell thee love that by the mind reacheth the soul, this only is true love that endureth through life and beyond death. Is this the nature and measure of thy love?"

"Dear Father Clem, 'tis this I would have thee learn and discover for me."

"How so, Jenevra?"

"By thine ears, father, and thy dear wise head. For thus is the nature of this love.. When he is near, I know rest and comfort. When he is away, I miss and yearn for him. If he touch me, which hath been seldom, I would he touch me again. When he speaketh, I am deaf to aught else. When he looketh at me, I would fain look away, yet cannot for in his eyes is a light thralls me. Though I be mournful, the which is full oft, he, with word, can banish sadness. If I be angered, the which is very seldom, he shameth it from me with gentlest mockery. And . . . oh, my father . . . should he die or leave me, then should I be lost and desolate. Well, Father Clem, is this love? And if so, should I wed him, since wed someone I must and so hatefully soon, according to the vile old law! And if I wed him, think you he would be as good a duke as he was a Jester? Speak now and counsel me!"

Here she glanced shyly askance at the Friar's thoughtful face; and, seeing him thus perplexed, smiled. He was still mutely pondering these many awkward questions when the quiet was troubled by a hurry of approaching footsteps with excited voices, then the ponderous garden door swung wide and in strode Count Ippolito with Andrea and Manfred.

"News, Madame!" cried the Count. "Oh, my lady, wildest maddest tidings . . . and yet good—and yet again I know not if it be so indeed."

"What is your news, Ippolito? Speak, sir, and be done."

"Then, Highness, in a word, Sebastian is dead!"

"Dead?" she repeated, in tone of amazed disbelief.

"Your Grace," explained Andrea, saluting, "we found him in that small chamber called his cabinet——"

"And, my lady," Manfred added, "he'd hanged himself from the carved beam above his working-table."

"Killed—himself?" she whispered. "Oh, horrible and past belief!"

"Yet, Highness, upon his table he had left this for proof!" said Andrea, tendering a folded paper. Reluctantly she took it, but, instead of even glancing at it, gave it to Friar Clement, bidding him read it aloud. And so, unfolding this paper, he obeyed—thus:

"'Gonzago having discovered all, in mercy for past friendship and on condition of full confession, suffers me to die by mine own hand rather than the sword of shameful, public execution. Thus I pronounce myself guilty the death of Lord Fortunio by means of poisoned wine, this substituted by one Luigi for that sent by Her Grace the Duchess, whom God preserve, amen. Now with abhorrence of the crime for the which I am about to die in expiation, and humbly praying God may have mercy on my grievous, penitent soul, I here subscribe myself for the last time, the lost, bitterly remorseful

"'SEBASTIAN.'"

Friar Clement bowed his head and made a cross in the air, and thereafter for a space none spoke or seemed to move.

Then, turning from them, the Duchess walked a little this way and that as if impelled by some emotion too deep for words; yet at last back she came to say:

"Gentlemen, let these tidings be published this very hour in the city and throughout the countryside; go ye now and see to this."

So they bowed, saluted and hasted away to do her behest. But hardly were they gone than Jenevra, clasping her hands, turned to the Friar, sighing:

"Oh, father—Father Clement, the question is answered—the problem resolved for me!"

"Howso, my child?" he enquired anxiously, taking those clasped hands, protectingly. "What wouldst thou, loved daughter?"

"Weeks agone, father, in thoughtless moment I gave my word. . . . I promised to wed Gonzago should he ever discover Fortunio's murderer! And now . . . oh, Father Clement——"

CHAPTER XXVIII

WHICH IS MERELY TALK

"Angelo, wherefore gloom ye?" Pedrillo demanded as they stripped to bathe them in water fresh-drawn from the well. "Is not this right good tidings? Fortunio's murderer denounced and, which is better, dead and buried, the other rogue councillors fled, the State and thyself thus secure, and all—all the work of one man!"

"Why there it is!" replied Angelo, busied with the great leathern bucket. "That it should be—this of all men!"

"Well, is not Gonzago a very man, instant to see and bold to do? Strong as Hercules and lovely as——" Here he gasped, speechless, as Angelo emptied the bucket over him—then stood to gasp in his turn; and presently, their ablutions ended, they dressed and went indoors to breakfast with the Friar and Beppo, who, eating much, said little while his elders conversed thus:

PEDRILLO (*argumentatively*): I say again that of all these lords and courtly gentles none may compare with Gonzago! For is he not a joy for the eye? Is he not vigorous in mind as body? Is he not, though a Spaniard, a right valiant gentleman, ha?

ANGELO: He is all this. And yet——

PEDRILLO: What meaneth thy 'yet', Angelo?

ANGELO: That he is so much beside all this, I must needs wonder how much of him is real, for verily he seemeth too perfect for this finite humanity.

PEDRILLO: Howbeit, the Duchess hath given or loaned him thy castle of Fidena.

THE FRIAR (*sighing*): Alas—unwisely methinketh.

ANGELO: Not so, father! For—if things be as be they may, this shall be passing well in that I do know its every nook and corner, its every stone from dungeon to battlement.

PEDRILLO (*after a pause*): Well, what's for thee today, my Angelo; more gardening, ha?

ANGELO (*musingly*): I think the Jester shall return to go afooling.

PEDRILLO: Well, so he may with none to let or stay him now, since Cavalcanti and those would have killed thee be all driven into shameful exile by lord Gonzago, God bless him! Yet, prithee what's thy purpose, Angelo?

ANGELO: Haply to learn this, to wit: do gods, ay, or demi-gods, yet walk this earth.

PEDRILLO: Why now here is merest folly, Angelo.

ANGELO: Agreed! For the gods of the groves and fountains be vanished all, Olympus is a desert and these we hail as gods may prove to be——

PEDRILLO: What, man, what?

ANGELO: This only a fool shall answer thee, perchance, mayhap, hereafter.

CHAPTER XXIX

TELLS HOW FIDELIO WARNED JENEVRA OF THE DUCHESS

THE NAME and fame of my lord Gonzago seemed every-where; it buzzed from lip to lip at court, in the city and beyond; wherefore Messire Astorgio, as his known friend, basked in reflected glory and was, consequently, bowed to, smiled upon and courted by all such as, for their own present or future profit, sought the great man's favour by favour of the great man's friend.

Thus Astorgio was waited upon by noble lords and stately dames with such murmured pleas as: "When next thou'rt private with his lordship, bring me to his kindly notice!" And to all Astorgio, with gracious patronage, made much the same reply:

"We shall remember you."

Today he was his most·radiant and resplendent self, for his eyes were bright as the jewels that sparkled upon his ornate person; his small peaked beard was a jutting arrogance; his daintily-shod feet almost pranced, while his slim legs in their gracious posterings were eloquent of triumphant assurance.

From the wide palace garden, this place of courtly promenade with its bowery grottoes, its fountains and shady groves, rose the cheery babel of merry voices and laughter; thither Astorgio was tripping when he espied one who stood watchful and alone, which solitary he saluted graciously:

"Sir, as esquire to my noble friend Gonzago, I hail, I greet thee well and bid thee be welcome to Court, Master Annibal."

"Sir, your graciousness confounds me!"

"Yet go with me, sir, and I shall make thee familiar with myself, our courtly methods, manners and graces, together with divers lords and ladies—Valour richly manifest, sir, and Beauty graciously personified! By these, for my sake, thou shalt be welcomed. Come, sir."

Astorgio's entrance was greeted with acclaim; 'broidered gowns billowed in stately curtsies, plumed bonnets and velvet cloaks swept and fluttered at him, thus he was hailed joyfully, more especially by three ladies seated together in shade of a leafy arch.

"Oh!" cried Fiametta, slim hands lifted gracefully to shade mischievous eyes. "Oh, here is dazzlement! Astorgio, I protest thou'rt too glorious! Leonilda, Juliana, saw we ever such blinding vision?"

"Gracious loveliness," he retorted, with bow of many complexities, "I am but the poor, pale reflection of thine own transcendental refulgence! But, sweet ladies and right noble lords, I take honour to present for your amity Messire Annibal, esquire to my noble friend—Gonzago!" Ensued a ceremony of curtsies, bows and flourishes; which done, the lady Leonilda enquired:

"Astorgio, prithee tell us the yea or nay of this whisper that spreads of late, and ever louder, how that our Duchess shall soon wed my lord Gonzago——"

"The which I deny!" cried Fiametta. "I tell thee again, Leonilda, no thought hath she to wedlock with him or any other. And I should know, I being so oft her bedfellow."

"Yea, but," laughed Juliana, "it needeth two for a wedding, or so I've heard, and though Her Grace, being so truly feminine, may show unwilling and coy, his lordship, being so truly masculine, may be but the more ardently compelling. So now, Astorgio, thou, as his friend, should perchance know his mind in this——"

"Oh, verily and in truth, Madonna, this do I—living as 'twere in the very bosom of his most secret thoughts, hopes, desires and intents. Thus and therefore, I can tickle your dainty ears, pretty auricles, with tidings amative and warmly amorous as—to wit——"

"Oho!" cried a mocking voice from behind adjacent hedge.

> "Oh nay! Oh nay!
> (Like ass I bray)
> Yet to thee say:
> Thy wit's astray,
> Thy wits, my lord,
> Be all abroad,
> Since this is so
> Ass—tor—gee—oh
>   I
>   Cry
>   Fie!
>   Go to!"

And in among the startled company strode the Jester, his worn motley showing even shabbier by contrast with the splendour around him; instead of bauble he carried a short, stout bludgeon, one end of which he was cutting to the rough semblance of a grotesque face.

"Oh—oh!" cried Fiametta, with her pretty, lilting laugh. "'Tis the fool—my lady's 'fool of comfort!' Come, good Motley, be merry; make us laugh and I shall fee thee well."

"Nay," exclaimed Astorgio, pettishly, "nay, Fiametta, sweet lady, not so! 'Tis but sorry japing jackanapes; a most mopish mumming mountebank, and sorts not with such as we; 'tis very vulgar, vain fellow——"

"So am I the more fain to hear him——"

"Yet 'tis naughty knave, a clown contemptibly egregious and should be whipped hence for scurvy dog! I say whipped——"

"Oh, excellent!" laughed Fiametta, clapping her slim hands.

"Do thou lash him with thy nimble tongue, Astorgio; belabour him with the truncheon of thy wit until he flee thee for very shame. Come, Astorgio, thy schooled wisdom 'gainst his folly; at him now—to pleasure me!"

"Oh, fairest lady, thou aspect of Venus! Ah, Fiametta, I live but to thy pleasure; and yet—to bandy words with—this!" And he gestured disdainfully at the Jester, who chipped at his carving regardless of all else.

"Alas!" sighed Astorgio. "Oh, Fiametta, this were to debase the very gentlehood of mine intelligence!"

"Yet," sighed she, with look of tender languishment, "for my sake, Astorgio."

"Ah, so," he sighed, "thou heart-smiting allurement, for thy sake!" Then, turning to jut his little beard quite ferociously at the Jester, he demanded:

"Base fool of thy baser folly, tell me—what is wisdom? Pronounce!" And still chipping busily, the Jester replied:

"Sir, 'tis like to a dying fish!"

"Ha—fish, fool? Wisdom—a fish!"

"New caught, sir, and therefore adying. Such like is wisdom."

"How so, thou fatuous Folly? Preposterous mountebank—declare!" And without glancing from his busy knife the Jester answered:

"Being smooth, sleek, slippery and very nimble is shall ever escape your lordship's grasp."

Fiametta threw back pretty head and laughed joyfully. Juliana and Leonilda giggled; others of the gay company hid their merriment. Astorgio frowned, and the Jester went on chipping.

"Oh—oh!" gasped Fiametta. "A—fish!"

"S-slippery!" gurgled Leonilda.

"Nimble!" tittered Juliana.

"Alas!" gasped Fiametta, wiping tears of laughter. "Thy truncheon availed thee not, Astorgio, this first time. So prithee to it again! Bid him propound the nature of folly—"

"Or love!" sighed Leonilda.

"Or wedlock?" laughed Juliana.

But with magnificent gesture Astorgio fronted the Jester, saying:

"Base mime, remove! Begone, I say, nor dare to show thy fool's-head uswards hereafter—away!"

G

"No—no!" cried Fiametta, and others also; but submissively, with bow that set his bells jingling, the Jester turned and departed.

He went by sequested way, keen eyes questing and ears listening for sight or sound of the one he had come seeking, until at last he reached that most private garden, only to find it deserted. Seated dejectedly beside the sundial, he looked gloomily about him, and then, having nothing better to do, went on carving that grotesque face upon the bludgeon that was to serve not only as a fool's bauble but formidable weapon also.

And it was only after the Duchess had watched him some while that Jenevra slipped out from the dense leafage nearby.

"So," said she as he rose, "thou art back again—thou Bimbo, with thy half-dead fish! Oh, I was lurking behind the hedge. Fish, indeed!"

" 'Twas the best I could do——" he replied, gladdened by the smile that dimpled her cheek.

"It served!" said she, leaning against the sundial, so near that he might have touched her; and, yearning to, went on chipping instead, so that she enquired:

"What do you there?"

"Make me a new familiar. I shall call him Wyg."

"Show me!" And taking his unfinished handiwork, she viewed it this way and that, frowned, shook her head at it and said:

"He will be as ugly as his name, hideous almost as my Phantom." Here they were mute, she intent on the carving, he gazing as intently on her, of which she was perfectly aware, of course, and, waiting for him to speak, was silent until, thus compelled at last, he uttered the words for which she had waited:

"I hear the Duchess will certainly wed Gonzago." And still intent upon the carving, she answered:

"I heard this also."

"Well—Jenevra, what think you of this?"

"Well—Fidelio," she retorted, "what say you of this?"

"Nought but think the more."

"Then speak me your thoughts of my lord Gonzago. Is he not—handsome?"

"As Apollo."

"Or aspect—bold and valorous?"

"As Mars."

"Well then?"

"Well, then, God save thee, Jenevra!"

"From what?" she demanded, turning to look at him with that unswerving, deep-searching gaze of hers. "From what should God protect me?" And meeting her gaze with one as keenly steadfast, he replied:

"From the three, my lady; all three!"

"Here now is riddle you shall expound for me. Who are these three? What mean you?"

"That though Apollo be good to look upon and Mars valiant as himself, neither would be comfortable husband or fit to wed thee, Jenevra, and—ah, sweet soul for thy life's dear sake—beware of the Duchess!"

"How? Beware of—myself?"

"No, of the Duchess."

"Oh, be done with this wordy fooling!" said she, wearily. "Speak me plain now—what of the Duchess?"

"She is thy greatest danger being a merest duchess—a thing of cold pride, of vain pomp and empty state. Thus is she no fit companion for thee, Jenevra, thou sweet and lovely feminine thing, thou maid, thou woman, thou manifestation of nature's supreme artistry, thou——"

"Heaven's light!" she exclaimed. "Am I all this?"

"Being Jenevra, thou art infinitely more!"

"Indeed, Fidelio, I do mind how once thou didst protest me for 'the perfection of God's handiwork!' Dost still believe me so?"

"Ay, I do!" he answered fervently.

"Then I am so proud," she murmured, "I must needs be most truly humble."

"And so dost prove thy worthiness, Jenevra."

"Well now," sighed she, "let us talk of our Duchess, the poor creature, for she is so distressful I would have thee pity her as I do."

"Nay faith, Jenevra, she is far above the compassion of such humble souls as we."

"Yet, for my sake, give it. And now of Gonzago, this man that, unaided and alone, avenged my dear Fortunio's cruel death and freed us of hidden treachery. Was not this well and nobly done?"

"Ay, most truly! He hath well earned the honours bestowed by Her Grace and therewith the gratitude of all this duchy."

"And, Fidelo, thus it is the Duchess needs must wed him!"

"Oh, never! There be limits! This were beyond all reason——"

"Yet here is most compelling reason—her plighted word! For I must tell thee——"

"This I learned of Father Clement, and 'twas for this the Jester sought thee."

"Well, my fool of wisdom, what is thy counsel?"

"Nay," he murmured, "this must wait, for yonder mid the leaves be eyes that watch! Ho there!" he cried. "Ho Jack-a-peep peep forth and show thyself." A moment's delay, then Annibal appeared, hat in hand, to bow, flourish and say:

"Your Highness, I come to warn Your Grace that my noble master, lord Gonzago, entreateth audience."

"Then, sir, you may return and inform your master he shall speak with me tonight at the council board."

Annibal bowed again, flourished gallantly and departed with something of a swagger to hide his discomfiture; noting which, the Duchess wrinkled her shapely nose and murmured:

"I like not Gonzago's new esquire. How think you?"

"That he should be in buff and steel."

"A soldier!" she nodded. "And a spy!"

"And doubtless hasting to warn his master how Bimbo is returned and in favour with Your Highness."

"Then will my highness to my courtiers, being in no mood for my lord Apollo just now. As for thee, Fidelo, away, and farewell . . . and if my fool of comfort will vanish again, let my phantom haunt me in his stead . . . and . . . the moon will be at the full . . . tonight . . ."

Then she turned and left him gazing after her—and upon his knees.

CHAPTER XXX

TELLS OF SUSPICION AND OF A LADY OF SORROW

SEATED in that same great, cushioned chair had been wont to throne Sebastian's stateliness, Gonzago leaned back to gaze up at a certain cupid's head, one of three wonderfully wrought and deep-chiselled in mighty, gilded roof-beam.

"The mid-most one, my lord?" enquired Annabel, also regarding this work of art.

"Even so, Annibal. And 'tis marvellous well wrought . . . to the very life! See how those carven eyes smile down on us —the wanton curve of those wooden lips! In a moment they might laugh aloud. And . . . from this angle . . . yon lovely face . . . I have seen the Duchess smile so . . . ay, there is noble artistry, Annibal."

"Oh, indubitably, my lord! Though I was wondering how lord Sebastian could reach so high?"

"By means of this chair, thou dullard, and silken noose upcast. . . . But enough—harkee and perpend! Since the Duchess hath set the castle of Fidena in my charge, I have had it garrisoned and by trusty chosen men obedient to none but myself. For though, as Lord High Constable, all troops, save Her Grace's bodyguard, be in my command, yet I would now have bodyguard of mine own, and thyself, Annibal, shall captain it."

"Ha, my right good lord, now hear me swear——"

"Not yet, hear me instead! Fidena is small and so strong that twenty men might hold it, so will I have an hundred and these well paid and equipped. Now, therefore, thou with Rodrigo shalt 'list me these extra men, forthwith, but—not in the city, mark that!"

"Aha, I do, my lord; right well I do——"

"The countryside is full of disbanded soldiery of the late war, masterless, discontented rovers. Of these choose such as be in worst plight, for they shall be the more desperate and eager for hire. With these men, by night and by twos and threes will I garrison the castle and none aware till it be done. Is this understood of thee?"

"It is, my lord, it is! And hear me say and avow——"

"Not yet, Annibal . . . instead . . . tell me of that night at the Black Horse tavern and of those ye had to do with. As I remember there were two?"

"Ay, two, my lord, and——"

"What like were these two, their outer semblance, speech, bearing, gestures—be particular, Annibal."

"Why, sir, 'twas sunset when they came and the place dim-lit, yet light enow to note one for tall gentleman, fair-haired and ruddy——"

"So—this would be the Englishman! And the other, what of the other?"

"Younger, my lord, more instant of motion, dark-avised, and softer spoken——"

"And this, ah—this would be Count Angelo——"

"But, my lord, he wore neither cloak nor feather——"

"Ha, sayest thou? Well, which of these had the misfortune to die?"

"This, my lord, I know not, for as afore told, the business was dispatched right speedily and i' the dark."

"The—dark!" Gonzago repeated softly though his eyes, no longer slumberous, showed wide and so fiercely bright that Annibal recoiled, saying:

"Eh, my lord, what now?" And again in the same gentle voice Gonzago repeated:

"The dark! Annibal, except I know this—here is darkness yet! Think man, think! Which of these died that night?"

"My lord, all I can say is—one fell and that we brought his hat and cloak for proof."

"His hat and cloak," said Gonzago musingly. "True, these were as they should be . . . these were as expected . . . and yet . . . Annibal, have you ever seen or heard tell of a . . . Jester . . . a motley calling himself Bimbo?"

"Ay, sir, I saw and heard the merry wag——"

"Where, Annibal, and when?"

"This morning in the Palace garden, my lord."

"And 'tis now past two o' the clock!" From the many papers before him Gonzago took a sealed letter, enquiring:

"How many of your fellows are to hand?"

"Three, my lord."

"Is Vitry of them?"

"My lord, he was killed in your service some while since. Yet we have as good, to wit, Tito Vanni, Iago Bandello and Crespi—all devoted to your——"

"This is expected. Bid Crespi to horse with this letter; it must be delivered tonight." But, in the act of giving the letter, Gonzago paused, broke the seal and, having added certain words, resealed it carelessly. It was at this moment that the door began to open very slowly and with such noiseless stealth that it escaped notice.

"Must Crespi have this at once?" enquired Annibal, placing the letter in the wallet at his girdle.

"So long as it be delivered tonight. . . . But now—of this Jester! What did he, whither went he—be particular."

"Well, my lord, when he had befooled Messire Astorgio and had been by him dismissed therefore, I was fain for more of him and followed until, to my wonder, I saw the Duchess do likewise, though with sly stealth——"

"Ah, she followed him, Annibal?"

"Ay, sir, to the garden o' the sundial and there they talked——"

"Heard you ought?"

"Not a word, my lord, they stood close and spoke very low."

"Talked she long with—this Jester?"

"Sir, I know not, for he spied me amid the leafage and cried me forth."

"Then what did you?"

"Made obeisance, sir, and, being put to it, ventured to say your lordship craved audience."

"Well, and she——?"

"Stood a little frowning and said you might speak with her tonight at the council, and so I left her——"

"And with this—Jester!" Gonzago's voice was soft as usual, his handsome face serene, but in his eyes, no longer slumberous, was that which drew Annibal nearer and nearer until he could speak whispering.

"How, my lord? This motley now? Must he be—translated as the late Vittorio?"

"Mayhap. Yet first will I speak with him—and soon! Seek him out, Annibal, and, by force or 'suasion, have him to me——"

Here the door opened, closed, and, glancing up, Gonzago exclaimed:

"Carlotta!" while Annibal stepped back to flourish and bow.

"Carlotta, did I not forbid your presence here?"

"And therefore, here am I," she answered, tranquilly.

Frowning, Gonzago turned from her to say:

"Annibal, you may go—and remember, by force or 'suasion!" Annibal bowed almost hurriedly and departed, closing the door carefully behind him.

"So—'tis thus you disobey me, Carlotta!"

"For 'tis thus I love thee, Gonzago!"

"You become rebellious, and this must not be."

"I become more aware of that is yet to be, and do accordingly."

"It will not do to defy me, Carlotta. I warn thee 'gainst myself and the power, ay, the god within me that no thing in earth shall defy or withstand——"

"Except death, my Gonzago! And 'tis thus I do so fear for thee."

"Far better fear for thyself, Madonna."

"Wouldst kill me, beloved? Dost threaten me——"

"I warn thee!" he answered wearily. "For I say again, I swear nought in this world, not even thy beauteous self, shall let or stay me."

"And, Gonzago, I tell thee nought in earth or heaven, alas, can stay me from loving thee—thus am I above all fear."

"How came you hither?" he demanded. "How passed you my guards?"

"I showed the signature of thy letter—this!"

"So? And 'tis in that letter I forbade you the court!"

"And so, by this letter, I am here."

"By Venus!" he murmured. "Thou art ever thine own one and only self and my admiration! Well, what now?" With the smoothly supple grace that beautified her every movement, she sank into the nearest chair, put back the shadowy hood of her cloak and looked at him.

"Well," he enquired, lightly, "why this disobedience, thou essential feminine?"

And softly she answered:

"Thou art become so great the fame of thee was all about me as I came, 'twas so I heard thou art to wed the Duchess —and soon."

"This I told thee long since, Madonna."

"And long since I laughed to hear thee, Gonzago, but now when others so tell I could weep."

"Then, loveliness, hie thee away; here is no place for thy so precious tears."

"Nay, my loved one, I shall not weep—yet. For I do not think thy Duchess shall live to wed thee." Slowly Gonzago's languid form stiffened, his slender brows contracted, his shapely mouth thinned to down-trending line.

"Carlotta," he whispered, "make me so believe—and these hands shall wring the life from thee!"

"Then," she murmured, leaning near to smile into his fierce eyes, "dying I would strive to kiss thee, my beloved. For thou art so truly mine as I am thine—love hath made us one; apart we cannot live nor one find death without the other. So thou must not, canst not, shalt not wed the Duchess, my own Gonzago, thou part of me."

Rising from his chair, he took a leisured pace or so, then paused to touch the glossy midnight tresses that crowned her stately head, saying as he did so:

"So, when I have wed the Duchess and am_Duke, thou shalt be second lady in the State, though ever first in my heart; believe this, Carlotta, for——" He paused and frowned at a soft rapping on the door with Annibal's guarded voice:

"My lord, 'tis I with——"

"Come in, man!" The door swung wide, Annibal entered, beckoned imperiously and in strode the Jester; he glanced at Gonzago, but gazed at Carlotta, saying with grandiloquent flourish:

"Hail, Juno! Queen of night and high Olympus, hail!" Then, quick to heed the profound sadness of her look, bowed, saying and in quite altered tone: "Lady of sorrow, I salute thee." A moment of silence wherein they surveyed each other, then, faint-smiling, she spoke:

"There be eyes 'neath thy fool's hood!"

"Madonna," said Gonzago, reaching her his hand, "I will see you to the courtyard." Annibal opened the door.

"Dear my lord," she answered, tranquilly, leaning back in her chair, "you may better see me here." For once in his life Gonzago seemed at a loss, then he smiled, bowed, and Annibal closed the door, while the Jester, spying a stool nearby, perched himself thereon, crossed his legs, and enquired:

"How now, Apollo? Thy Mercury yonder, this thy solid Ariel, stooping like falcon seized and wafted me hither with touch, or clutch, such and much less like gentle Zephyrus than rude blast of blusterous Boreas! Urged thereby thus theeward—therefore thus perforce I perch perilously perchance, to plead thy pleasure."

Gonzago laughed, Annibal chuckled, Carlotta leaned nearer as the Jester repeated his question:

"Well, my lord, what would you?"

"Thyself!" answered Gonzago. "I would fain have thee in my service—of my household."

"Ay, but—for how long?"

"Let us say, Bimbo, as long as thy 'piece of rope' that could be cut asunder, yet first—hang a man. Dost remember?"

"Verily, Apollo! I mind also the Lord Sebastian was hanged."

"So? He was hanged! Sayest thou?"

"'Tis so I heard."

"Yet, Bimbo, 'twas everywhere reported how he was his own executioner and hanged himself."

"So, here, Apollo, here was the same with a difference, for, by self or no, he was hanged."

"In expiation of proven treachery, Bimbo."

"And thus was an end to both, Apollo."

"Ay, but, was it, Bimbo? I wonder! I begin to doubt! For, speaking of treachery, there was—or is—one, Count Angelo! Hast ever heard tell of him?"

The Jester's bells tinkled as he turned to regard Gonzago, and thus for a breathing-space they viewed each other, eye to eye; then nodding languidly, Gonzago repeated his question: "Hast heard of this Count Angelo—Bimbo?" And, nodding also, the Jester replied:

"Ay, that he was killed and thereafter proclaimed a traitor —and so let him rot."

"And yet I wonder!" said Gonzago, shaking his head. "Howbeit, I would have thee to my service, for as Jester I love thee, Bimbo, and as a man I esteem thee right well."

"Your lordship is marvellous gracious," sighed the Jester, rising to bow, "but, alas—I am bespoke of Her Grace. I am even now her Court Buffoon and shall pervade the palace. For, since by the law she must wed anon, she would have me jingle and jape to lighten wedlock's grim shadow, if such be possible. To this purpose I am engaged——"

"Since when, Bimbo?"

"Oh, sir, since the moon changed——"

At this moment a heavy fist pounded upon the door, which, being opened, in strode Manfred bulking large in his half-armour. "My lord," said he, saluting, "by your noble leave, yon fool is wanted. Come, Motley, and tarry not."

So, with a bow to that silent, impassive lady whose smile was sadder than tears, the Jester followed whither he was led, nor spoke they but once, and this softly:

"Came I in time, Angelo?"

"Ay, most aptly, brother." This only, until they reached a small inner chamber within the guard-room where Andrea and Count Ippolito greeted them with anxious question, where-to the Jester replied:

"He suspects that I am Angelo—and how should he, except by foreknowledge? So needs must I suspect him. Be warned therefore! Set a secret watch upon Fidena by day and night."

"Ay, and what now, Angelo—what will you?"

"Make trial of this bludgeon and Father Clement's mail-jack."

"Ha, by the nails—how so?"

"Woo Master Annibal to further action . . . he must needs rid his master of Angelo and . . . if he attempt this, I shall be sure . . ."

CHAPTER XXXI

CERTAIN MENTION OF "A BLACK HORSE", AND A DAGGER-STROKE THAT FAILED

MEANTIME, Gonzago sat frowning at the many papers that littered the table before him, while Carlotta watched him, seeming tranquil as ever; from him she glanced where Annibal stood testing his dagger point and edge, then set it back in the scabbard loosely as if for instant use, ere he coughed politely and ventured to enquire:

"Well, my lord, do I follow again?"

"Wait!" said Gonzago, softly and almost as if speaking to himself. "This Jester I like so well that . . . I must be certain as possible . . . have assurance absolute! For . . . upon my life— "

"Ah, my lord," sighed Carlotta, speaking at last, gently though with deep and moving fervour, "upon thy dear life I do conjure thee, beg and pray thee to forgo this mad design, check thy ravening ambition, rouse thee from this wild dream of that which can never be—take that which so truly is! Oh, Gonzago, with life and thy present greatness—be content——"

"Content!" he repeated, and laughed . . . and in this was such answer that she bowed her stately head at last and shrank like one utterly lost and despairing. And it was now that Annibal enquired again:

"Well, my good lord, do I follow? Is it to be . . . so?" And he laid finger-tip to dagger-hilt.

For a while Gonzago hesitated, then nodded.

"Ay, seek him out, question him, and, if assured—make sure! Then hie thee instantly to Fidena, nor venture abroad until I give thee word."

So Annibal, smiling and confident, went forth upon his quest, nor was it long ere he espied the Jester strolling aimlessly, who, at his friendly hail, paused, turned and saluted him with airy flourish of his bauble.

"Aha!" exclaimed Annibal gaily, "where away, Bimbo?"

"Nowhere, sir, for being here I am there already. But what's for thee, fair master, thou wingless Mercury?"

"I'd fain walk and talk with thee, Bimbo."

"Why then, so—ho, an this be so, then ere we go, a fee bestow. I say a fee that gold must be, since now in me, as told to thee, I am now Court Jester and therefore of consequence in consequence."

Annibal hesitated, then opened his wallet into which the Jester peeped instantly saying: "Ho, here behold, of lovely gold, a sum untold."

"Back!" cried Annibal indignantly. "Stand off! There, take thy fee!"

The Jester picked up this flung coin, pouched it, and nodded: "Now at thy service, gracious sir."

"Ha!" exclaimed Annibal, frowning. "I perceive thee for knavish, prying fool."

"Alack, sir 'tis most true!" sighed the Jester. "Such is my nature that when not prying I peep. Howbeit—since now this fool hast fee'd

What of fool is thy foolish need?
Ask me thy question, sir, and I,
Like fool, shall foolishly reply."

"Why then," said Annibal, after they had strolled some little distance, "I'll e'en question thee of—horses."

Now at this the Jester, glancing sidewise, saw Annibal watching him also askance and very keenly; so he enquired:

"Horses, Master Mercury? And wherefore of horses?"

"And wherefore not, good Motley? So what say you of the horse?"

"Ay, but what horse, which, what, where and whose?"

"What knowest thou of any horse, Bimbo?"

"That 'tis creature with four stout standers, two twirts up, a flurry and a whiskabout."

"Ay, and what more, friend Bimbo?"

"That horses be of different sexes and of divers colours."

"Name them, prithee, for thy loving friend, good Bimbo."

"Oh, sweet Master Mercury, thou art grown so kindly familiar I will rhyme and jingle them for thee, thus:

> "The Chestnut, dun, the brown and bay,
> The sorrel, white and dapple grey,
> Also the bald, that is a skew,
> The bald that yet a pie is too;
> Thus would I choose, friend Mercury,
> Though others' others choice may be——"

"Ay, faith," said Annibal, his tone and look even more engaging, "for Bimbo, dear my friend, here is one left out—hast made no mention of . . . the black horse." Here again they glanced askance on one another. "Didst thou forget the black horse, Bimbo?"

"Not so. 'Tis but that I love not your black horses."

"Ah? And wherefore not?"

"For that sometimes they be—dangerous."

"Howso, prithee?"

"I had a loved friend die of a black horse."

"A friend?" Annibal repeated; and then again, "A friend, ha? Wilt tell me the how and the—where of this?"

"Ay, though 'tis woeful tale! Hearken then—nay first do thou tell me how long hast served thy lord Gonzago?"

"Long enough to know him for the greatest man in all this duchy, ay, or any other!"

"I can well believe it. And thyself his Fidus Achates, his Mercury——"

"Nay, his esquire I, and proud therefore. Now tell me of this friend o' thine that died—of a black horse; was he thrown, kicked, or rolled upon?"

"Neither."

They had reached a place shaded by trees and shut in by dense thickets, a remote seclusion far from all chance observation, and here the Jester halted suddenly, head aslant as if listening intently while he gazed fixedly at the small, rough-hewn face upon his bauble.

"Eh," demanded Annibal, "what do you?"

"Hearken."

"What hear you?"

"A warning."

"How—who?" questioned Annibal, glancing round about them, "what's to do? Be plain!"

"Lo here, Esquire Annibal, see you this my bauble?"

"Ay, I do, and it shows more like clapperclaw's bludgeon than jester's toy!"

"Verily, sir, and 'tis thus so much the better. Now see you this head, this face, this carven visage?"

"Ay, and 'tis curst hideous! What of it, Bimbo?"

"He is my familiar, Wyg, being short for Pigwiggin, and he can foretell that is to be; even now he bids me——" setting this to his ear the Jester seemed to listen very earnestly while Annibal watched scornful of glance and contemptuous of lip.

"Well," he enquired, derisively, "what sayeth thy Wyg?"

"Hist! Softly! He warneth me of a perilous evil!"

"Ha, so? Doth he say what manner of peril threats thee, Bimbo?"

"Nay—alas, friend Annibal, 'tis thou art threatened!"

"Me?" exclaimed Annibal, his smile vanishing. "Me, sayst thou?"

"Alack, poor soul, thy very self—though of what or how or when——"

"What said thy—thy damned familiar?"

Bauble to ear, the Jester listened again, repeating slowly as if thus dictated:

> "If caput caput meet, then shall
> Prostrate lie Squire Annibal
> Bereft of sense. So let him flee
> While, sensible, the sense hath he."

"Pah!" exclaimed Annibal, positively spitting in contempt. "Arrant foolery, as I thought!"

"Why, so think I," nodded the Jester. "And yet thinks I there was some small sense, as for instance, since 'caput' meaneth 'head'——"

"Enough!" said Annibal. "No more o' thy foolery. I'll hear no more o' thy friend that died of a black horse——"

"And yonder," said the Jester, halting again, "yonder is the wicket of that most private garden wherein none may enter except——"

"Howbeit, Bimbo, thither we'll go."

"Yet 'tis most strictly forbidden!"

"Tush, fool! Who shall let or stay us? There we may sit, with none to see or hear, and talk as right friends should, so come thou!"

Thus side by side they reached this narrow gate and here, once again, the Jester paused to bow and flourish, saying:

"Enter, sir esquire, Folly needs must follow."

"Nay, to prove my friendship I give thee precedence—in with thee, Bimbo."

Then, nerved for that which he dreaded, Angelo turned his back, strode through the gateway, was staggered by the murder-stroke, steadied himself, swung round and smote in answer—a blow so utterly unexpected and truly aimed that Annibal plunged headlong to earth and lay mute and very still.

Now glancing from this sprawled shape of helplessness to the face on his disguised bludgeon, Angelo nodded grimly:

"And so caput caput meeteth—head to head!" said he; and as if in answer the underbrush nearby was burst asunder and Manfred came leaping through, followed by Andrea and Count Ippolito.

"Now by The Teeth!" snarled Manfred, gnashing his own, "I was afeared for thee, Angelo; this dog showed so murderous."

"Well so he is!" sighed Angelo, very conscious of his bruised back. "And I were now dead but for Friar Clement's stout mail. 'Twas the neck stroke I feared."

"So now," growled Manfred, "now am I minded to slit his villain throat——"

"But instead," said Angelo, kneeling beside prostrate sense-lessness, "you shall presently bear him to yon fountain and cherish him to his recovery. You shall speak him kindly and use him tenderly, for by him, as I do think, all shall be known at last."

"By the Pyx!" exclaimed Ippolito, taking the weapon from Annibal's lax fingers. "See, his dagger-point is quite turned!"

"The which doth prove the excellence of Father Clem's mail-shirt!" said Angelo, busied searching his still senseless

assailant; thus presently he rose with a letter in his hand.
Very carefully he loosed the seal, unfolded and, having
scanned this missive, read aloud:

"'To J.F. these. At the Castle of Fidena you shall be
heard three nights hence a ten.
    Come you alone.'

"Well now, my brothers, what say ye of this most precious
thing?"

"Ay, but who is J.F.?" questioned Manfred.

"Who but Juilo Fabriano, whom we know for traitor. And
who the writer but Gonzago. This man who, being unto himself a god omnipotent, can soar above all human rascality to
sin like Lucifer that was a glorious angel once! Howbeit, to
Fidena we go, three nights hence, we that do know the castle
its every nook and corner! To Fidena . . . where Fortunio
died handfasted with Jacomo! To Fidena, there to hear, perchance, and see that the which shall end Treason once and
for all. . . . Now a tinder-box, a heated dagger-blade to reseal
this most precious letter." And when Angelo had done this
he replaced the letter in Annibal's wallet, saying as he gazed
down into this pale, still face:

"Now God forbid I struck too hard!"

"Nay," replied Andrea, peering anxiously, "the foul,
accursed rogue, breathes easier, saints be praised!"

"Then," said Angelo, rising, "away with him to your best
care, for deliver yon letter he must and soon as may be. That
I may know of him, come ye at sunset to Friar Clement's
garden and bring my clothes with rapier and dagger, for my
fooling days are ended or soon shall be. And so, God love
and keep ye all."

CHAPTER XXXII

TELLS OF A WOEFUL HEART

"So?" EXCLAIMED Pedrillo. "Must thy wit be pointed with
steel now? Do Jesters go armed o' nights?"

"Ay, faith—this one shall," replied Angelo, belting on
rapier and dagger.

"Ha—a fight is it? A duello?"

"Nay, 'tis but precaution—for I feel the night is full of lurking evil, murder in the very air."

"Then by the Rood, I'll with thee! Haply shalt find my quarterstaff better than yon foining bodkin o' thine. Nay, frown not, my Angelo, shalt not adventure alone! What with this murderous Annibal out for thy life and, alas, Gonzago— though even now I can scarce believe such lovely man so evil! Howbeit, with thee I go this night."

"Then God love thee, Rillo, so be it—though 'tis my dear hope to have word with Jenevra tonight. Come then, let's away and—softly!"

So together forth they went, speaking seldom and then below their breath; and thus it was that as they entered the gloomy cypress grove they heard voices, the one harsh and deep, the other soft and huskily sweet.

Angelo drew his rapier, Pedrillo poised his staff and thus they stole forward until they could distinguish words and glimpse the speakers by light of the rising, full-orbed moon.

"Indeed, Rodrigo," said the soft voice, "I do not fear death, I never have or ever shall . . . only, before thy dagger stills this woeful heart, I would fair know—is it by—his will that I must die? Tell me, Rodrigo."

"Lady, speak thy passing prayer and be done."

"Wilt thou not, even in this my dying moment, show me this small mercy, Rodrigo?"

"Ha, lady, this I may not and therefore cannot. Instead, say thy prayer, then lift thy hand for sign 'tis spoke."

"Thou wilt strike true and make sure, Rodrigo?"

"Ay, lady, this I promise thee, I shall not strike amiss."

"Nor I!" cried Pedrillo, and down whizzed his heavy staff, crushing Rodrigo's stalwart form beneath it so that he lay with battered head at Carlotta's feet; so for a moment was stillness, then she touched this head lightly with toe of her shapely, daintily-shod foot, saying in that richly-sweet, tranquil voice of hers:

"Sir, I think he is dead."

"Lady," answered Pedrillo, "'twas so my intent, for here was murder manifest."

"Madame," said Angelo, and very gently because of the look in her wide eyes, "what is for thee, now and here-after——?"

Instead of answering, she clasped her hands, then slowly lifted them heavenward saying in a dreadful voice:

"Oh Mary. . . . Blessed Mother of Mercy, pity . . . oh pity me!" Then, wringing her hands as if in agony, she turned, and so dumb now and silent as poor ghost, went her solitary way until, like forlorn ghost, she vanished.

"Holy saints!" exclaimed Pedrillo, crossing himself piously. "Yonder went grievous sorrow, Angelo!"

"And tragedy!" he sighed, sheathing his rapier.

"Well now what o' this carrion?" said Pedrillo, stooping to peer at his handiwork.

"Is he dead, Rillo?"

"He should be . . . and yet he breathes, curse him!" Here Pedrillo knelt and by instinct began to minister with those skilled surgeon's hands of his to the man he cursed so heartily.

"Can he live, Pedrillo?"

"Ay, he might—with care. Yet why care for such bloody rogue?"

"This for thee to answer, Rillo."

"Nay, the good Friar shall! So saying, Pedrillo lifted and tucked his inert victim beneath mighty arm, then paused and stood frowning and hesitant, saying fiercely: "Shall I now leave thee, my Angelo, for this bundle of villainy? For verily 'twould seem the night is full of evil."

"Howbeit, Rillo, I go now to seek the loveliest, holiest, noblest thing 'neath all heaven!"

"Ah well, despite being all that, may she remember, for thy sake, that she is, first of all, a woman!"

CHAPTER XXXIII

TELLS WHAT BEFELL IN GARDEN OF THE SUNDIAL

THE MOON indeed was at the full, wherefore Jenevra, dressed and wide awake, lay upon her great bed looking up at it, and listening; presently the nightingale began its wonted song, whereat she frowned and listened the more intently until, at last, to bird-song was added another sound faintly sweet as bells of faerie suddenly heard and as suddenly hushed. Then swiftly Jenevra rose, caught up the hooded cloak that lay ready, and, light of foot, stole out and away.

In leafy shadows they met, amid shadows they went nor spoke until they reached the garden of the sundial. In this remoteness they paused to gaze upon each other, and because their eyes were so eloquent still neither spoke for a while.

"Wherefore a sword?" she demanded, at last. "This was not needed to prove thy true estate. Nor should I be here, and at such hour, but that I know thee for one so truly honourable."

"God make me worthy thy faith!" he answered, reverently.

Coming to the sundial she sank down upon the marble bench thereby and beckoned him beside her, saying:

"Fidelio, tonight, I shall make thee my councillor awhile, so—be seated! Now—have I thy profound and most complete attention?"

"As ever, my lady."

"Then today befell that the which greatly perplexes me concerning one Bimbo, a poor, wandering Jester, homeless and destitute. . . . Art thou listening, Fidelio?"

"And wondering, gracious lady."

"Well, this evening as I walked upon the terrace with Fiametta, there suddenly appeared to us a strange woman— cloaked was she and tall and of a dark, wild beauty, and when she spoke I knew her for person of degree, though what she said greatly surprised yet angered me far more—and no wonder! For she told me my Jester—yes, she said 'my Jester'—must be banished or wed to save his miserable life."

"Were these her actual words?"

"Well, not precisely. What she said was: 'Thy Jester is marked for death and must surely die except thou banish him to safety or wed him to such greatness as shall defy Murder.' Now, Fidelio, this seemed so preposterous that, naturally, I became furious."

"Naturally!" he repeated. "What said you then?"

"Bade her tell more."

"And how answered she?"

"With sad smile and shake of head and so left me— raging!"

"Very naturally!"

"Fidelio," she retorted, indignantly, "I do not rage naturally—I mean, 'tis not my nature to rage, and if I ever do

rage 'tis for most just cause and sufficing reason. And—how
dared she say he was 'my Jester' ?"

"Indeed 'twas vastly bold, Madame. And yet, I have
heard thee name him thy fool of comfort——"

"Why, so I did, for so he was when vile treachery seemed
all about me. But now, thanks to Gonzago, Treason is driven
away and tonight I sit in this peaceful security with thee.
So now, Fidelio, resolve me this great perplexity,—who would
seek the life, who trouble to murder a humble Jester? And
if so—wherefore? And did the cloaked woman speak truth?
And—oh, Fidelio, on thine honour as gentle man, answer me
this—is Murder seeking the life of my fool of comfort? Now,
answer me plainly."

"Then I must needs tell thee Murder hath struck at him
twice."

"Oh!" she whispered, clasping her hands. "Then the
woman spake truth indeed?"

"Indeed, most truly."

"And now, Fidelio, oh, now I . . . to save his life . . .
I must banish or—wed him? Well, thou shalt advise me . . .
which should I, shall I, must I do? Tell me, Fidelio, thou
faithful one, what is thy counsel?"

"Let the Duchess banish him."

"Oh!" she murmured. "So much for my Fidelio! Now
what sayeth my Phantom?"

"Let Jenevra's heart tell her."

"Now lastly, what, oh, what sayeth my fool of comfort?"

"Beloved, marry him! Give thyself to him—to love and
life and an abiding happiness, I hope and pray."

"Oh, dear fool of comfort!" she whispered, leaning nearer
—then she cowered away, for leaves were rustling nearby and
they started afoot as out from this nearby, rustling shadow,
into the moon's pale radiance, stepped Gonzago.

"Noble lady," said he softly yet with no gesture of salutation, "were you no more than Celonia's proud, young Duchess,
now should I laugh and crave pardon for this intrusion, but
knowing you for Jenevra, a lady of such unblemished fame,
I should, craving pardon, laugh not. Yet, Madame, as my wife
soon to be, I must now—persuade you, gently as may be, to
return to your palace and your bed. Madame—my hand!"
Now, as Gonzago advanced towards her, the Jester drew back,
leaving her to face him alone. So, for a breathless moment

none spoke or moved; then, throwing back her hood, she looked at Gonzago with that wide-eyed, unswerving gaze of hers.

"Madame," he repeated, "Jenevra beloved, I am waiting!"

"Vainly!" she replied. "Instead, my lord, I bid you leave me."

"Oh, impossible!" he sighed. "Love forbids and duty commands. For the promise you gave, binds you to me and me to your loving service henceforth and forever.",

"Gonzago, it was the Duchess gave that promise."

"It was indeed, Jenevra, and here in this garden. I rejoice you thus acknowledge it."

"Oh, I do?" she answered, gently. " 'Twas here beside this sundial the Duchess promised herself to thee, Gonzago. And now 'tis here I must tell how I shall never wed thee, since I that speak am no more than merest woman——"

"So?" he exclaimed, stirred to show of anger at last. "What Jester's trickery is here? What foolish mummery is this?"

"Truth, my lord. Tomorrow shall be proclaimed my abdication. Be not angry, Gonzago, for truly I hold thee in such high esteem that for thy disappointed hopes I grieve and pity thee, and 'tis said 'pity is akin to love'——"

"Pity?" he exclaimed. "Pity thyself and all the world save me. I'll none of it! Hate me rather—no tepid pity or insipidity of good-will! Give me love all demanding, to match my own, or hate inveterate that I'll out-match to hatred's last extremity! And so, Jenevra——"

"Not so!" said the Jester, stepping forward. "Fie on thee Apollo, to prate of hate—go to! A demi-god should seem less pettishly, pitifully human. An thou must vaunt thy hatred, go prattle of it otherwhere——"

"Ah—thou!" exclaimed Gonzago, turning on him in a fury more deadly for its restraint. "Thou motley thing of many deceits, thou furtive wooer, thou burrowing mole, thou nameless pest, thou that art yet art not, thou death in life that should be dead—this will I now endeavour. Thy life upon my rapier-point; draw and defend thyself and to extremity—one of us is due for death. Come now, my devil 'gainst thy God—out steel now and to it——"

"No!" cried Jenevra. "I forbid——"

"Madonna," said Gonzago, flourishing out his rapier, "thy word is said and now be dumb! Ha, motley wag, thou that I could name yet will not, come—end me or die in thy motley and be buried for japing fool—to it, I say!"

"Most readily, sir," said the Jester, advancing. "Yet first I must needs warn you I wear a hidden armour."

For a moment Gonzago stood mute, then he laughed, and removing his hat bowed, saying:

"Noble sir, your honour compels mine. Thus I in turn must needs warn you that I also go armed 'gainst the assassin's dagger. And, sir, by this I am now so sure of thee that kill thee I must or all's amiss. Thus, sir, we play for eyes or throat —come!" So saying, he tossed aside his hat and drew his dagger; and thus with both hands armed, they fronted each other.

. . . Clash and grind of death-darting steel, glittering flash of long rapier-blade with shorter gleam of dagger plied by hands well skilled in their deadly manage. . . . Shuffle and stamp of quick, ever-moving feet . . . sway and swing of supple bodies, with that ceaseless grind and clink of blades in lightning thrust or parry. . . . Speechlessly they fought and with a determination that allowed of neither pause nor respite, until, as he stepped back before sudden counter-thrust, Gonzago stumbled over his hat—in which moment his rapier was beaten from his grasp, and, sinking to a knee, he gasped, laughed and demanded breathlessly:

"Was this in faith thy God, or did my devil nod? Here is . . . my first and last . . . essay at rhyme . . . strike and be done . . . the loser pays . . . and . . . 'tis doubly just——"

But now, between him and the glittering point that menaced his life, Jenevra leapt, crying:

"Enough . . . have done! Oh, God . . . no more! This horror of steel . . . no more! Fidelio, stand back! Oh, now, Gonzago, up—up and away, take thy life and go."

"Nay, what saith my God-aided conqueror?"

"That the Duchess bids you to live, sir, and go."

Then Gonzago rose to say and with rueful smile:

"Most gracious lady, I should thank you for my life, though I had liefer it had been otherwise. Yet since I am to live I beg you to remember that I am—Gonzago! And now pray permit this question: what of your motley—gentleman?" And speaking like the proud young Duchess, Jenevra answered:

"My lord, he is the man shall wed me."

"Happy, happy man!" sighed Gonzago. "As for thyself, thou too well loved Jenevra, trouble not to un-duchess thyself—no need is there for thee to abdicate for, here and now, I free the Duchess of her plighted word. I give back her promise. Ah, but, Madame, the life you saved tonight is now thine till death, and so, Jenevra beloved, most gracious lady—be warned!"

Then he bowed, and, not troubling for hat or rapier, went from them with his usual leisured stride while Jenevra watched him very wistfully until he was out of sight; then she turned and saw how the Jester stood, armed hands crossed before him and head bowed.

"Well?" she enquired.

"But is it so, indeed?"

"You heard that I told him."

"And it achieved your purpose, he freed the Duchess of her promise."

"This was not my purpose."

"What then? I pray you."

"Nay, having said it once I will not repeat it."

"Yet except you do—I am not so presumptuous to dare believe such wonder."

"Indeed you are marvellous humble! Bimbo the Jester dared woo the Duchess—must Jenevra woo Fidelio? Whiles there you stand—like a stock, a stone, a wooden image——"

Down fell rapier and dagger and he sank before her on his knees to clasp his arms about her loveliness, yet when he spoke all he said was:

"Oh . . . my Jenevra!"

And now, yielding instinctively to his embrace, she put back his fool's-hood and with it his disfiguring elf-lock wig, and gazing down at this lean, dark-stained face lit by these adoring, luminous eyes, she murmured:

"So, my Fidelio, do I see thee at last?"

"Nay," he answered, "can you, ah—will you stoop to wed the man I seem?"

"Not stoop," she sighed, sinking also to her knees, "but here kneeling with thee in God's sight, I give myself to thee because I do love and honour the above all men. So tonight, 'stead of Duchess, I will be thy mere woman—thy wife, for, this night Friar Clement shall wed us . . . Nay, do not kiss me yet, beloved, lest we tarry here too long and be pursued, for Gonzago

warned me and he is indeed—Gonzago. So come, let us haste
to dear Father Clement and . . . happiness——"

CHAPTER XXXIV

TELLS HOW THE DUCHESS LOST HER FOOL BELOVED
AND JENEVRA FOUND ANGELO

THEY were breathless with haste when they reached the haven
of Friar Clement's fragrant moonlit garden, and together,
with bar and bolt, made fast the massive door; they were
breathless when, this done, they turned to gaze upon each
other with a rapture so far beyond mere words that they
could but look, and look, and sigh. . . . Then she was in his
arms, upon his heart and then he bore her to the shade of
the great mulberry tree, an aged tree so wise with years and
therefore so kindly that, although this glorious night was
so hushed and still, it yet contrived to make a faint rustling
as if, with its every leaf, it whispered a blessing upon these
humans who, close embraced, were kissing each other breathless again, until at last:

"Oh," sighed she, "I have always loved this old tree since
I can remember. I used to play under it, climb it years agone,
and so I loved it but never so much as tonight."

"And I," sighed he, "I have loved it, too, my Jenevra;
I think mayhap it has been waiting through the years for this
night, this wondrous night and us and our first kiss."

"For us," sighed she, when allowed speech, "and to bless
this wonder of our love——" Here she was silenced again
while the aged tree made gentle rustling reply.

"And the moon," she murmured, stirring in his embrace
to glance up at it, "showed never so lovely ere now!"

"And the night, my Jenevra, the night was never so fragrant,
or is it thine own sweetness—thy hair—thy breath——"

"Ah, this lovely night!" she sighed. "Would it might last
forever!"

"And," said he, "if it be thy will, this shall be our wedding
night."

"Oh!" she whispered, nestling closer. "And this is the
wonder of it—for when I knew I must be wed the thought

was hateful! When they paraded suitors for my choice I
detested them all and the thought of marriage was the more
loathsome . . . and yet . . . now, oh, tonight——"

"Tonight, Jenevra?"

"Thine am I indeed, for this is our wedding night and . . .
the thought is . . . joy!"

"So now," said he, after some while, "will I go wake our
Father Clement——"

"Nay, not yet. Be patient—a little while. . . . And thy
dagger irks me, the hateful thing! Take it off!" So obediently he unbelted his weapons and laid them by that he might
hold her the closer.

"Swords and daggers—how I hate them!" she exclaimed.
"Twice tonight I feared Gonzago would have killed thee."

"He is indeed a master of fence and that he should have
tripped is great pity."

"A pity?" she demanded. "And your dear life in such
peril!"

"But, dear heart, so was his. Truly I have seldom met
swordsman so able—a wrist of steel—foot, eye and hand so
instant. 'Tis marvellous great pity he stumbled and, of all
things, over his own hat——"

"He stumbled because I made him so do!"

"You, Jenevra,—you made him——"

"To be sure I did! While you and he were so hatefully
intent upon killing each other, I picked up his hat and threw
it so admirably true that it tripped him as I prayed it might."

"You—you prayed?"

"Most fervently. Not so loud, but with all my heart and soul."

"Now this," said he, greatly perturbed, "this was most—
irregular—very wrong and——"

"Wrong?" she repeated, and up went that proud young
head of hers. "Dare you tell me so?"

"I dare and I do! By this I might—ay, and should have—
killed him and 'twould have been murder!"

"How," cried she, forcing herself from his now lax embrace, "are you so bold, so wickedly ungrateful to suggest
I am a murderess?"

"Not so, my lady spitfire! All I know and say is that 'twas
'gainst all codes of honour and therefore wrong, but——"

"What care I for your man-made murderous codes of
honour?—nought, not a jot——"

"Howbeit these are what we must live by——"

"And die by, thou fool man——"

"Ay, verily, better die than live by trick dishonourable, say I, and——"

"And what I say to thee, thou too-hatefully virtuous wretch, is—thou'rt blind, gross, self-sufficing, prideful, ungracious, and therefore most detestable! And what's more, I'd do it again! I'd throw another hat, I'd throw thousands of hats to save the man I loved!"

"Merely because he was your love! So this was but selfishness and therefore——"

"So?" she cried angrily, leaping afoot. "To murder you now add selfishness!"

"Nought like this said I, and——"

"Thus now am I a liar also!"

Thus now, Jenevra, you are wilfully and most wantonly mistaking——"

"A wanton!" she cried wildly. "Lastly you dare pronounce me a wanton! It needed but this most vile accusation——"

"Now heaven aid me!" he exclaimed, with wild, helpless gesture.

"Ay, call on heaven!" she raged. "Cry on all the saints to aid thee, for never, oh, never again will I!"

"And yonder," cried he, leaping afoot, "glory be, hither cometh our Friar! Ha, Father Clem, surely heaven sent thee to my need."

"Nay, my son, thy so loud quarrelling waked me in no little troublous wonder—thou and Jenevra and at this hour! My wonder is now amazement!"

"Then, dear and holy father, hear me!" said she, taking the Friar's right hand.

"Hear me, Father Clem," said Angelo, grasping his left, "for lo—here is true love's abiding wonder, a great and noble lady that will stoop to wed such lowly wight as I——"

"And," cried she, "here, holy father, is lowly wretch that nameth this same love's wonder, this noble lady, a selfish murderess, a liar, and a wanton——"

"Never, ah never in this world, father!"

"Peace, my children! O' mercy's name, peace! Jenevra, sit thou here beside me and thou, my son, stand afore us i' this blessed moonlight. Now, beloved daughter, give me thy hand and speak."

"Well, dear my father, this Jester, this that was my fool of comfort, this man of men, in motley guise, won my love."

"Ha!" exclaimed the Friar, setting his long arm about her. "Oh strong, true spirit of love! Say on."

"So with him, father, hither came I that thou shouldst wed us this night——"

"Now God love us all and bless ye, children of my long love and care—this will I and with marvellous joy——"

"Nay, but, Father Clem, how may I wed one who, for that I saved him from peril of death, names me 'murderess', and 'liar' and——"

"Hush thee, dear child! Now, my son, speak thou and expound me this riddle."

And so, standing before them in full radiance of the great moon, a most heroic figure in his motley and ridiculous cockscomb, Angelo told briefly all that had been done and said this fateful night. Scarce had he ended than Jenevra took up the tale:

"Indeed, father, 'tis true I threw the hat and, by heaven's grace, with aim so exact that thereby I ended their murderous sword-play, saved the life of one, or both, and now await thy praise and blessing for act so instant and laudable."

Friar Clement, rubbing bristly chin, thus contrived to conceal his smile ere he replied:

"Verily, beloved daughter, this was right womanly deed, and so God bless thy sweet womanhood. And now tell me when and how didst find him out and learn thy Jester was Angelo?"

"Angelo?" she repeated, turning to stare in wide-eyed wonderment. "But Angelo is dead!"

"Then, oh Jenevra, loved daughter, art thou yet all unaware?"

"And this," said Angelo, "is love's veriest triumph—that, knowing me not, yet Jenevra for love's sake would have wed poor Bimbo the Jester, and——"

"Oh now," cried she, upstarting to her feet again, "what new mystery is this? Angelo is dead! 'Twas so reported and so believed that we, Father Clement, thou and I offered prayers for his passing soul!"

"And yet, Jenevra, by grace of God he 'scaped death, wooed thee in Jester's guise and now standeth here, Count Angelo of Fidena, to wed thee according to thy noble sire's will and decree. Here, 'stead of Bimbo the Fool is our Angelo, thy long-plighted lord and husband. So yonder in the oratory I will wed and bless ye to each other even now. Come ye——"

"No . . . and no!" cried she, and breathlessly again. "He that I loved was poor, humble and destitute, yet my dear fool of comfort. This lordly Angelo is a stranger! And thus am I deceived! And so—shame on ye both—yes, both! And now 'tis your Duchess speaks! Tomorrow I will back to court. . . . Now, Friar Clement, I'll to your bed, not to sleep but there to pray heaven's forgiveness on you for so daring to deceive your Duchess . . . and thy poor, woeful, too-confiding Jenevra!" So saying, she turned from them like the proud lady circumstance had made her, and then fled within doors like the overwrought girl she truly was.

"Now this," quoth the Friar, putting back cowl to rub tonsured crown, "this passeth my understanding, Angelo!"

"And small wonder, Father Clem, for this is the 'haviour of a Duchess spoiled by fawning courtiers and slavish flattery."

"Yet surely she loveth thee, Angelo——"

"Nay, God be praised, she loveth Bimbo the Jester or my wooing were vain."

"And yet again, Angelo, she will not wed Angelo! So here is perversity out of all sense and reason."

"Love is, above all, cold reason, father, and for this so unreasoned reason is reason why she, being faithful to Bimbo the Fool, shall wed Angelo, by love compelled thereto."

"How so, my son?"

"Father, this night, though unwed, she shall lie, and perchance sleep, in Angelo's arms——"

"Ha—what mad, unseemly words be these?"

"The words of thy Angelo, my father, that loveth her with such reverence—her sweet body shall be to him the most sacred thing in all this world. Canst thou believe this of me?"

"Whiles thou art Angelo and she herself—I do!"

"Then I'll with her to the wilderness! Ay, beyond the walls to the forest—the cave wherein I played as a boy and in this solitude talk her into reason. There with tomorrow's dawn thou shalt find us. Then, my father, do thou look us eye to eye and thou shalt know that, though we be man and woman, we are thy children still, true to thy teaching and all that is best in us."

Now Friar Clement raised his long arms heavenward, saying:

"Kneel, Angelo. To thy knees, dear son, for with the laying on of my hands, I implore and cry on God our Heavenly Father to bless thee for the man thou art and to keep thee ever true to thy noblest self."

"Amen!" said Angelo, fervently; then he rose and buckled on his weapons, enquiring:

"What of the little postern by the oratory, Father Clem, is it still guarded o' nights?"

"Nay, since the war ended 'tis but locked and I have the key thereby to visit the sick beyond the walls. So thou shalt find it open, my son. And now until the dawn, farewell."

Thus presently, armed and cloaked, Angelo entered the Friar's bare, little chamber just now radiant with moonlight flooding in through the small, unglazed window to show him Jenevra in the Friar's narrow bed, her eyes fast shut and covered up to her round and dimpled chin; and so he took this chin very gently between finger and thumb, saying:

"Woman, wake from idle dreaming to life's reality and a man named Angelo."

The chin was jerked away, the long-lashed eyes opened to glare up at him while the lovely though scornful lips parted to furious speech:

"Loathed man, begone, and instantly!"

"Beloved woman," he retorted, glancing about the little chamber, "where be thy clothes?"

"Count Angelo, I command you away—leave me! Ah, how dare you thus outrage——"

Twitching the bedclothes from her he saw she was fully dressed.

"Excellent!" he nodded. "Thou dear soul to be thus ready and waiting. Come then, let us go——"

"Oh—thou!" she gasped. "Thou base, vile, intruding wretch, never touch me——"

"Then rise, woman, or touch thee I must! Up, I say."

"Never!" she cried, but even then was plucked to her feet and walking out and away because of the compelling arm about her.

"Stay! What madness is this?" she demanded, struggling quite vainly, "whither do you take me?"

"To Bimbo thy so loved, happy fool."

"Stay or I'll scream!"

"Do so and I'll kiss thee dumb. So, I beseech thee, scream."

Thus in a little while they came to the postern gate that opened to his touch; and so, despite struggles, commands, entreaties and finally tears, this most compelling arm urged her whither it would.

CHAPTER XXXV

DESCRIBES A MOST ORIGINAL WOOING

DEEP-HIDDEN within the forest Angelo had lit a fire whose ruddy glow, putting out the pale moon, made of trees and thickets a gloomful mystery and the bush-girt cavern a place of furtive-lurking shadows. Seated by this fire, in nest of fern he had made for her, the Duchess, mindful of her unavailing plaints and tears, now turned to gnash her teeth at him instead, which done:

"Oh," she exclaimed, "how wise, how right was I to scorn and hate you so soon as I knew you for Angelo."

"Nay, most tenderly gracious of ladies, poor Angelo is left behind—here only is thy faithful Fidelio, thy gentle Jester, thy beloved Bimbo——"

"And," she continued, leaning nearer the better to frown at him, "I never thought I could so bitterly despise, detest, scorn and perfectly abhor any living creature as I do this abomination called Angelo."

"Alas, Madame, 'twould seem the poor gentleman is scarcely in favour, yet mayhap you shall come the more to love him anon. Meanwhile, to woo those so gently-ferocious eyes to kindliness, those sweetly scornful lips to smileful tenderness, your loving fool of comfort shall jingle rhyme for——"

"Nay, there never was true Jester, nor fool; these were but deceitful mockery and shameful sham!"

"Yet, gentle Madame, here he sits, as witness these foolish bells and ass's ears! So shall he jingle of a noble lady that was so wise as to love a fool:

There was a lady fair to see,
A lady proud, of high degree,

So truly, nobly proud that she
Could stoop a fool to wed.
Ah, but—alas for him and woe!
When this loved fool she learned to know
Was truly—merely Angelo,
Poor Angelo she fled.

Though Angelo's no fool, alas,
Yet mayhap it shall come to pass
That ere the dawn——"

"Oh, enough!" she exclaimed. "Instead, tell me why you have carried me into this dreadful wilderness?"

"That thy beloved fool may learn thee to better know poor Angelo."

"Then, Fidelio, you may tell me of him—what will he with me in this horrid desolation?"

"Look on thee and talk with thee."

"Well now, of him tell me this—wherefore came he to court like poor Jester?"

"To 'scape death, uncover treachery and bring to justice his loved brother's murderers."

"Well, Gonzago hath done this by compelling Sebastian to confess his guilt."

"Sebastian was but one."

"Who then the others?"

"Fabriano, Cavalcanti and, chiefest of all, Gonzago."

"Ah, never—never!" she gasped. "This cannot be! This I will nowise believe."

"Yet this shall be proved anon——"

"But he is one of the few I have dared to trust—and will yet! For Gonzago is such man that——"

"Ay, a man indeed, great for good or—greater evil, as Lucifer Son of the Morning, the archangel that fell—as Gonzago must and will! But this is yet to be. For us, thou and I in this lovely solitude, is now! This night that soon must be a memory, yet one that shall endure. For on this most wondrous night Jenevra would have wed her Fool Beloved but that the proud Duchess scorned poor, misjudged Angelo——"

"Nay, I but fore-judged him, and very wisely for the wicked wretch and brutal ravisher he is—to bear me into this—hateful

solitude! And I—I now at his mercy—nigh dead with shameful affright!"

"Yet never showed more quick with joyous life!" he nodded.
"All aquiver from lovely head to this small pretty foot apeep
at me 'neath thy cloak."

"Indeed," she continued, hiding the foot instantly, "I quake
with fear!"

"And thy beauteous cheeks aglow! Thine eyes so
bright——"

"With shame!" she retorted. "With dire and dreadful
shame!"

"So?" he demanded, and leaned towards her suddenly,
whereat she as instantly recoiled and with shudder almost too
violent for belief, as, leaning still nearer, he continued:

"Then, lady, the safest place for thee in all this world tonight is here—in the shelter of these arms——"

"Oh!" she gasped. "Spare me! Have mercy!"

"Mercy?" he repeated, then laughed so blithely that she
frowned on him in angry surprise.

"Hateful man!" she cried. "So now you will mock—
besides tormenting me with—with suspense?"

"Of what, noble lady, of what?"

"Your—brutality!" At this, and to her growing indignation,
he laughed again.

"Alas, poor lady! Doth thy womanhood vex thee? Then
forget it, as I have. For, this night, proud Duchess, despite
all thy peevish prudery, Jenevra shall lie here upon my heart
and there sleep secure."

"A most horrid thought! So shall I be ware and wakeful
all this fearsome night!"

"Then, thou poor, affrighted Duchess sitting there so bold
and fearless in thy beauty, now shall this brutal Angelo begin
his wooing!" And back on his shoulders went his wig and
cockscomb.

"Oh—now may all the saints of heaven be my protection!"
cried she, retreating yet further to gaze at him wide-eyed above
clasped hands.

"Amen!" quoth he fervently. "For, Duchess, here am I
fore-doomed as innocent child to become thy husband—and
thus in woeful plight and grievous case am I—since I must
avow to thee—I love not the Duchess nor ever shall, and yet
wed her I must perforce——"

"Never!" she cried, and breathlessly again. "Oh, never! I had rather choose the—the sorriest wretch that ever——"

"Ay, this sorriest wretch Angelo that must 'spouse thee in his own despite while with all his poor heart and yearning soul, ah, with his every thought and breath, he loved one infinitely sweeter than any Duchess, gentler, simpler and in every sense more worthy and lovable. Thus, your highness, though cruelly fated to be thy lord and husband, alack— poor Angelo shall never touch lips to thine, this night of nights, except thou beg, plead, sue, woo and entreat him to thy kiss."

"Oh vile! Rather would I die!"

"Ah glorious! If thereby Jenevra lives! She that I love for her quick mind as for lovely body. Indeed, I think, 'tis her strong, brave soul I do most love,—she that hath all my reverent worship and is to me the most precious and sacred thing in this world—she that, knowing all this, would never stoop to fear me, even in this solitude! So now—away, proud Duchess, and come thou, Jenevra, to this heart of mine that is and shall be thy home."

Now gazing into the eyes of one another, slowly they drew nearer until their hands met to clasp and cling; nearer yet until his arms were about her, until, at last, she pillowed that proud and lovely head of hers upon the breast of his shabby motley.

"Oh, Jenevra," he murmured, "I do so love thee that— tomorrow thou shalt wake here in my arms, unkissed."

"Oh!" she sighed. "Such love were of the angels!"

"And I am Angelo!"

"Yet—merest man. . . . And there be hours 'twixt now and tomorrow's dawn!"

"Thank all the saints!" said he, with fervour. "But how many of these precious hours shall we waste in sleep, alas! Sleep that is half-brother to Death."

"Ah, speak not of death tonight."

"Yet beloved, with each minute and every breath this dark Angel stealeth nearer!"

"Then let us bide awake."

"Art not sleepy, my Jenevra?"

"Nay, what foolish question!"

"And—art no longer fearful of this wilderness?"

"I—love it!"

H

"Or of me?"

"Never again," she sighed, nestling closer, "for here at last is peace."

And now they sat a while in a silent communion more truly intimate than speech, and no sound to trouble the all-pervading quiet except drowsing tinkle of the fire. But presently there stole a small, fugitive wind, a soft breath very cool and sweet to touch them like a caress and wake the dense leafage about them to a faint whispering.

"Hark!" she murmured. "It sounds as this dear forest were sighing for very happiness."

"Ay, the trees are bidding us good-night," he answered. "Soon all the world will be asleep . . . and at such times angels may walk the earth."

"Yet one sitteth here in the fire-glow—with me in his arms."

"Ay, faith," he sighed, "I am Angelo, thine own guardian angel! And yet, being Angelo, I am yearning for that 'sometime soon or late'."

"Which time and what?" she questioned.

"When, having learned to know your Angelo better and to love him as he now adores you—if this be possible, the which I doubt—you shall look him, eye to eye, and say: 'Angelo beloved, kiss me!' "

"And thus," she murmured, "thus make my Jester's dream reality—'in his dream world she cometh to meet him with love in her eyes and herself athrill with love'."

"Hast not forgotten then?"

"Nor ever shall."

"Truly, my Jenevra, thy Bimbo was boldly prophetic dreamer! For tonight, in this world of reality, mid this sleeping forest, his love is on his breast, her dear heart beating to his. How wondrous the dream, but how glorious the reality!"

The breath of wind had died away, the leaves were still and hushed, only the fire made soft, drowsy noises, and Jenevra so mute and still in his embrace that he thought she slept until, in voice soft as the drowsy fire, gentle as whisper of leaves, she spoke, at last:

"Angelo—kiss me!" And, breathless yet again, she waited, but he never so much as stirred; therefore she, being vastly surprised, somewhat angry and with new and quite delicious shyness, glanced up—to see him gazing down on her with such look that all other emotions were forgotten—except the one; yet, being her proud young self, she met his gaze with those clear, unswerving eyes of hers and said, more distinctly:

"Angelo . . . my beloved, kiss me!"

His response was instant and all-sufficing, so very much so that when at last she might speak it was in tone more breathless than ever:

"Ah, my . . . dearest love, was this . . . the kiss of . . . an angel?"

But now, before he could answer, came a vague, troublous stir, an on-coming rustle, growing ever louder, with snap of twigs that told of desperate movement. . . .

Angelo rose and his long rapier-blade glittered ominously red in the fire-glow; thus with one hand armed and ready and Jenevra's slim fingers in the other, he stood waiting, poised for swift action—while those threatening sounds grew ever louder, nearer—until out from the looming shadows strode Friar Clement, breathless with haste.

"Angelo . . . Jenevra," he gasped, leaning upon the long staff he carried. "Oh, beloved children, I grieve . . . thus to trouble ye. But trouble there is! Gonzago hath shut himself into . . . thy strong castle of Fidena . . . with many at his command . . . and is besides . . . in communication with Loredano the exiled rebel Count. So are ye needed for instant council."

Then Angelo sheathed his sword, glanced at the fire-lit cave, sighed regretfully, and, clasping Jenevra's ready hand, followed Friar Clement—to do, see, and suffer that which was to be; what time their deserted watchfire, soon to languish and die, blinked redly upon the gathering darkness.

CHAPTER XXXVI

TELLS HOW ONE THAT WAS DESOLATE WARNED AND PLEADED

IN THE Friar's garden beneath the mulberry tree now illumined by level rays of the sinking moon, they sat in council: the Duchess, Angelo and Friar Clement upon the rustic bench, with Andrea, Manfred, and Count Ippolito, in gleaming half-

armour, seated upon the grass, while nearby Pedrillo leaned
upon his ponderous staff, and all were listening to Manfred's
muted growl:

"Since setting secret watch on Fidena according to thy
command, Angelo, in these few hours we have seen much
coming but little going and suspect more adoing. First thither
rideth Gonzago with men thirty and five, men-at-arms and
archers. Then forth of the castle rideth one at speed, the
which horseman Ippolito presently followed as he shall tell."

"Verily," said the Count, "follow I did and secretly, as
might be, so I kept him in sight until he came to that solitary
inn called the Black Horse."

"I know it!" sighed Angelo.

"Here this fellow leaves his animal and takes a narrow
mountain path, so I hide mine and steal after him. And 'twas
now I recognized him as Gonzago's esquire Annibal. So, as
I say, I crept after him till, coming in sight of a small, desolate
hut, he halts and whistles and out into the moonlight steps
none other than Loredano himself——"

"Art sure 'twas he?"

"Most sure, Angelo, for I knew him well aforetime and saw
him plain, for, though completely armed, he wore no helmet.
Then presently, after some talk, Loredano calls and is joined
by Cavalcanti and Fabriano."

"Couldst hear aught was said?"

"Not at first, so I crept nearer, and thus I heard Cavalcanti
that is ever loud-spoken, and this said he: ''Tis all too soon
for me. Bid Gonzago wait until tomorrow night——' "

"Gonzago?" repeated the Duchess, woefully dismayed.
"Art certain—oh, are you quite certain Gonzago was named?"

"Indeed, Highness, sure as—death!"

Now even as he uttered the word, all were suddenly hushed
and every eye glanced in the one direction, for on the garden
door was a loud insistent knocking; so thither strode Pedrillo,
who, after brief parley, unbarred and opened this door—to
a soft voice huskily sweet yet plain to hear in the now breathless hush.

"If Count Angelo be here, now for God and thy life's sake,
bring me to him." But he was already afoot and coming to
that shrouded, lonely figure, reached out both hands to her,
saying gently:

"Lady of Solitude, be welcome."

"Count Angelo," she replied, as softly, "thou Jester with eyes to see so much, I am here to save him I love from defiling his poor, proud soul beyond redemption . . . and to implore thine aid."

"Then, lady, go with me and pray let us hear."

With unhurried grace she followed whither he led, there to stand regarding the company with her great, sad eyes, and so pale in the level rays of the sinking moon that her face gleamed upon them from the shadow of her hood. Then with slow, weary gesture, she put back her hood that all might see her features, and spoke in that richly soft voice of hers:

"Gracious lady and gentle sirs, first you shall know that in all save word, and of this deceived, I am the lord Gonzago's wife. In our dear Spain we loved as children and later were betrothed. Tonight I am desolate and he so powerful that by his potent will shall come war; at his bidding Count Loredano with all his vengeful exiles and outlaws shall suddenly assail your city and, alas, by Gonzago's will and command. I alone can stay him from thus bringing ruin and bloodshed upon your duchy. But to stay him from this great evil, this that shall be his own soul's destruction, I must see and speak with him though by him forbidden. Thus, now Count Angelo, Lord of Fidena, if there be any way known to thee, any secret entry into thy castle, I do now implore thee—tell me or bring me there, that I may save him from this wickedness, and for sake of those many innocents that must surely die except I win speech with him." This said, she stood, head bowed and pale hands folded as if in prayer; and for a moment none spoke.

Then the Duchess, frowning in troublous perplexity, leaned nearer to gaze very keenly at this so beautiful, woeful face, while the others muttered and whispered uncertainly.

"Tell me," said the Duchess, imperiously, "how are we to know, how be sure of the truth of thee? Thou—coming at such hour—to plead a traitor's cause, and he—thy love!"

"Ah, my lady, I plead not his earthly cause; I would, instead, preserve his soul from the damnation of God . . . by witholding him from this abomination, as I surely can . . . as I must, and will . . . if only I be brought to him and soon."

"And thus," said the Duchess, coldly, "thus learn the secret of this castle!"

"Oh!" cried Carlotta, wringing her hands as if in bodily anguish. "Trust me! In God's name, trust me! Have faith in me! Believe I mean no evil but the good of all . . . to save him from the anger of God and this sinful doing . . . ravished women, murdered babes, slaughtered men! 'Tis for this I plead . . . for these innocents I will give my life— gladly. . . . Oh, Mary, sweet Mother of Mercy, Blessed Mary of Heaven, let them believe me!"

"Lady," said Angelo, "this night you shall to your Gonzago in Fidena, and may God shield and prosper you!"

"And yet," cried the Duchess, "I am all suddenly atremble, and why? Wherefore should I shiver thus? Is the night so chill, or is this some dreadful omen . . . foreboding of evil to be? Come, let us within-doors for I'm acold—come!"

Rising, she gave her hand to Friar Clement and so led them from fading moonlight into the house where a fire smouldered and candles beamed.

"Bide you and rest, lady," said Angelo, "for soon we must away; I go but to rid me of this motley." And away he sped, leaving profound disquiet behind him; until the Duchess, beholding the tragic sadness of this beautiful face, drew Carlotta to the great oak settle, bidding Pedrillo bring milk and food, which done, she persuaded Carlotta to eat and drink, herself making pretence to do the same; but all at once Carlotta choked and looked at Jenevra through painful, slow-gathering tears.

"And, oh," she murmured, brokenly, "once I . . . so hated thee!"

It was now that Beppo, rosy with slumber, made his appearance, in the briefest of night-shirts, and who, rubbing sleep from his eyes and thus beholding the company, fled to hide behind Pedrillo.

"Why, Rillo," laughed Jenevra, "what rosy Eros is this? 'Tis either the little God of love or Astorgio's page boy."

"That same imp, gracious lady, saved by Angelo from murderer's dagger and hither brought for safety since he hath no kin. 'Twas by this good urchin we learned so much of past treasons. Beppo, make thy reverence to the Duchess, salute Her Grace." Sleepy but obedient, down to a knee went the boy to bob curly head and have it kissed, to his bashful surprise.

"And solitary is he, Rillo?"

"Ay, my lady, his folk be dead."

"Then he shall with me to court for my page——" Here
Angelo returned, clad like an Englishman from spurred heels
to ruff, which garments became him so well that Jenevra
for the moment forgot all else. Meeting her look, he smiled
and drew her aside to say, ruefully:

"So, my Jenevra, thus is our wondrous night become a
memory, yet one I shall cherish. For now must I away with
this woeful lady; we shall take horse at the palace——"

"Angelo, my dearest, think you she is to be trusted?"

"Ay, I do indeed."

"Yet she is creature passing strange! One that seeming
gentle is, I fear me, vastly otherwise—like sleeping volcano!
Thus am I all adread—for in her very shadow is peril."

"Howbeit, dear heart, for chance to prevent war needs
must I adventure whatso I may. And what of thy beloved
self, this night?"

"I shall bide here and pray for thy safety."

"And surely prayer of thine must be answered. And so
until we meet again, my loved Jenevra, fare thee well."

CHAPTER XXXVII

TELLS HOW THEY CAME TO FIDENA

THE SINKING moon was low when, leaving their horses tethered
in shade of trees, they turned aside from the road and
followed a little-used, bush-grown path until, before them,
throned upon a rocky eminence, grim and stark against
a luminous heaven, rose the embattled walls, towers and
mighty keep of this small and hitherto impregnable castle of
Fidena; here, screened by underbrush, Angelo paused to
scan wall and tower where armour flashed and pikehead
glittered.

"Ay, truly," he whispered, "the place is garrisoned for
war! Now, lady, give me thy hand . . . be silent and stoop
as I do, for there be many watchful eyes yonder."

Thus together they stole forward and up until they were
stopped by a great, bush-girt crag that rose sheer above them;
in its deep shadow, amid thorny tangles and jagged rocks,

Angelo parted dense leafage, beyond which a narrow cleft gloomed into blinding darkness.

"Now," said he, as they entered, "we are beneath the castle; before us thirty-five paces shall bring us to steps twenty and one with above a flagstone I shall lift whereby you may enter the great hall. But," said he, halting in this darkness, "when I mind your jeopardy in the cypress grove, the dagger at your breast . . . I fear . . . perchance death may meet you in the hall——"

"Well," said she in soft, untroubled voice, "what is death? If it be to live again in this troublous world, I am prepared—if it be blessed reunion with those loved and lost a while in death, I shall be glad. Howbeit, I go unfearing. So, I pray thee, lead on."

"Come then, noble lady," he sighed, "thou valiant soul."

They traversed the thirty-five paces, they mounted the twenty-one steps. Fumbling in the darkness, Angelo found and pressed the lever he sought; a flagstone rose above them and then—as he blinked to the sudden glare of torch and candle light, the hall rang and echoed with his companion's full-throated cry:

"Gonzago! Gonzago—hither to me!"

A rapid tread of spurred feet and Angelo, blinking up at Gonzago's astounded face, saw his eyes widen as in horrified disbelief, saw his shapely lips part to a quick-drawn hissing breath, and when at last he contrived utterance it was to gasp:

"Car—lotta?" But she replied gently as ever:

"Indeed, beloved! I am no ghost to haunt thee."

"But what . . . what miracle is this?"

"Love!" she answered. "The love that dieth not! The love that no power may kill! Then how should Rodrigo's dagger avail? Am I welcome, my Gonzago?"

"Oh, Carlotta, beyond the telling!" he replied with an unwonted fervour. "Without thee I am—not myself. Never will I part with thee again!" And now, as if aware of Angelo for the first time, he saluted him with smiling, airy grace.

"Count Angelo, this is a joy wholly unexpected! Enter, my lord, and be right welcome!"

Followed by Carlotta, he obeyed and saw this once grim hall now luxuriously transformed; in place of battered arms and armour its walls were hung with rich tapestry, its stone floor covered by rugs and carpets of the Orient, its long table hid 'neath white napery brave with glittering crystal and silver, as for a banquet—only Fortunio's ponderous arm-chair remained and the great clock, upon the wall telling the passing moments with its deliberate tick-tock as it had once ticked Fortunio's life away. . . . . Thus, as he listened, Angelo's hand dropped instinctively to grip the hilt of his rapier. Gonzago, quick to heed this smiled, then gestured towards the secret stair, saying lightly:

" 'Tis well to be ware of this, sir, for where one hath entered, many others may. It shall be duly watched and warded. . . . So thus, Count Angelo, thou most lovely Jester, we meet again and, I fear me, for the last time,— thou'rt armed, I see, and this is very well. For truly I esteem thee so highly and with such warm regard that 'stead of calling my rogues to—rid me of thy too-dangerous self, I shall do this myself for myself and thus in more selfish though honourable fashion." From the high, carved back of Fortunio's great chair hung his belt with rapier and dagger; this he now took, enquiring:

"Shall it be rapier and dagger, Count Angelo?"

"As you will!" he answered.

"Then let it be rapier alone, for I'd prove if thou'rt as much master at the one as two. . . . And yet . . ." With blade half drawn, he paused, then inch by inch resheathed it, saying as he did so: "Having all things in my grasp, why should I run peril of Angelo for sake of that lovely fool Bimbo? Fool indeed were I!" Uttering the word, he struck sheathed sword to an Oriental gong that stood hard by; which summons was answered, and almost instantly, by Annibal, followed by two other armed men, whom Gonzago beckoned, with the command:

"This noble lord to the chair yonder! Bind him and be gentle as ye may."

Back stepped Angelo, hand on dagger, but this hand was clasped by two others, slim, strong hands, while in his ear was a faint whisper: "Wait!" Next moment he was seized, disarmed, led unresisting to the chair and, yielding sub-missively, was there fast bound.

Dismissing his servants with a gesture, Gonzago began to pace the long hall with his graceful, leisured stride while Carlotta, throned on cushioned settle, watched him, what time Angelo in his bonds listened to the slow tick of the clock which, as it seemed now, was measuring the last hour of his life. Presently Gonzago halted to look down on him and say in that oddly wistful tone of his:

"Angelo, the Jester Bimbo so won me that for his sake I now offer thee life and freedom—back in England or whereso be thy desire—except in this duchy of Celonia, the which is too small for such as we—together. Give me thy word to go and never more return and thou art free. Come, thy promise and I free thee now."

"Sir, 'twould be death in life. So rather will I abide the event and suffer that which must be."

Sighing, Gonzago turned, struck the gong and ordered wine; when this was brought he filled a goblet and tendered it to Angelo, who merely turned away.

"So?" murmured Gonzago. "Instead, if thou wilt suffer thyself to live, I will pledge long life to thee . . . for indeed I find it hard to think of thee as mine enemy."

"Then, sir, remember how, in this hall, my brother Fortunio drank with thee, or of thee, and died!"

"Ay, true!" sighed Gonzago. "Alas that this should have been—for of all men I honoured him most——"

"Yet murdered him."

"Though marvellously 'gainst my own will—believe this of me, if you can! . . . Fortunio died of his own greatness, by Sebastian's long cherished desire and my sudden act . . . because his great work was nobly done and mine to do. He freed Celonia; I will make her great. To this one end I have wrought and for this I will live and die. Thus how shall any man's life or woman's tears—ay, or other earthly power—stay me from achievement so god-like?"

"God Himself!" murmured Carlotta. "'Tis so I·pray——"

"Do so, my Carlotta, for what is thy God but a remoteness, a phantasm, deemed omnipotent by His deluded worshippers. My god is within me, a living power, the inspiration of my every thought and act. Thus I am the god of my destiny and therefore above all weakness or sense of failure, for to doubt myself were to be false and unworthy the god that is myself."

"Alas!" sighed Carlotta. "So never did I grieve or fear so much for the man that is Gonzago!"

"And thou wert ever prone to grieve, but wherefore to fear?"

"Lest God this night summon and require thy soul of thee."

"Nay, my summons will be the brazen clarions of my lordly devil, Sathanas, Prince of Acheron and ruling monarch of this world. . . . Angelo, we talked of this when thou wert Bimbo—ha, but for spite of cursed circumstance we should have been good friends, thou and I! Perchance we were, in some foregone life and mayhap shall be again in some hereafter. Thus I am bold to ask thee again—to live, Angelo, to give thy promise nor doom thyself to death so untimely. Come, thy promise and life—a nod shall suffice." But seeing Angelo neither moved nor spoke, he turned to glance up at the clock.

"At the least," he sighed, "thou shalt live to see me Duke and the Duchess Jenevra my wife."

"Then, sir, God send I live forever!"

"Nay, alas, but scant half-hour or so, for I expect her very soon——"

"You . . . expect her?" gasped Angelo, stirred at last. "Here . . . tonight?"

"Ay, I do indeed. I have had all made ready, this table set for our wedding feast, a reverent and holy son of the Church waiting below to voice the needed mummery shall make us one and myself her lord and Duke——"

"Oh, God—now God forbid!" cried Angelo, struggling instinctively but without avail against his bonds.

"Thy God again, my poor, deluded Bimbo? See how He hath left thee in the lurch! Tonight, as ever, my Devil is victorious! Ay,—hark, Angelo, hark how he serveth me even now!" A distant stir growing louder . . . heavy footsteps, clink and clash of armour, a heavy knock upon the massive door. . . .

"Come ye!" cried Gonzago, rising. The door swung wide, in strode armed men, and in their midst, pale, distraught and trembling like the fearful girl she was—Jenevra.

CHAPTER XXXVIII

TELLS HOW GONZAGO TRIUMPHED

IN THIS first dreadful moment she was aware only of Angelo in his bonds and would have gone to him but that rough hands stayed her until a commanding voice spoke and she was free; then feet tramped, door closed and so came silence except for the loud, deliberate ticking of the clock.

And now, as if waking from a daze, she glanced at Gonzago, gazed upon Angelo and spoke to that ever silently watchful figure on the cushioned settle:

"So, Jezebel, this was your faith? May our Holy Mother of Mercy forgive you, for I never will. As for yourself, Gonzago, smiling hypocrite and arch traitor, speak your evil mind and be done."

"My mind," he answered, lightly, "is to save thee and thy duchy from ruin, if it be so thy will, Jenevra."

"My—will?" she repeated, utterly bewildered.

"Thine only, Jenevra. I had thee carried hither to plead the cause of thy loving people, to beseech thee—save thy innocent townsfolk and noble city from ravishment and horror of war. Their fate, for much good or great ill, lieth with thee; thy word shall bestow life or death."

"You must speak me plainer, Gonzago."

"Noble lady, to be explicit . . . within an hour's march of us is Count Loredano with his wild, outlawed companies and other exiles, lusting for vengeance and pillage. He waits but my command, Jenevra."

"Your command? Dare you pronounce yourself such—such monster of perfidy?"

"Gracious lady, I dare all the powers of heaven and earth to come at my desire——"

"So, Gonzago, you must proclaim yourself in league with this most vile rebel lord?"

"Say rather he is in league with me, as truly he hath been this long while——"

"You—you of all men are Loredano's friend and ally?"

"I am, except thou make me thy husband and his enemy for thy dear sake——"

"My . . . husband?" she repeated, and in the same passionless tone. "Gonzago, I would not believe you faithless, but now I can believe all and any evil of you . . . 'twas you poisoned my loved Fortunio . . . well, show me such poison and I will drink and die as he, rather than wed such inhuman iniquity as Gonzago!"

"Then alas," sighed he, "for thy selfish perversity that for such whim can thus doom thy people, these many innocents, to death and worse——"

"Not so, thou traitor. My city is warned ere this, thank God; my soldiers posted and ready."

"Again, alas, Jenevra! For thus shall the onset be the more bloody and Loredano's vengeance the more pitiless when the city falls, as it assuredly will!"

"Never believe it!" said Angelo, calmly. "The city withstood and drove back invasion ofttimes ere now."

"True!" replied Gonzago. "But then Fortunio was at his mightiest to defend—now is Gonzago to attack and lead! And I have not lived so long within the city but I know its strength—and weaknesses. Thus while Loredano assaileth gates and walls, I shall win entry by postern and culvert—so must the city fall, Jenevra, and thy miserable people perish except their Duchess save them, as she alone may, or woe to these innocents! Think, Jenevra, think of them —the screaming women, the little children, the tears, the blood and anguish! Think, and I implore thee take pity on them! Canst not see them in their shame and agony, hear them crying on thee to spare and save them? Think——"

And now he described such horrors that Jenevra covered her ears and yet must listen . . . until her proud spirit quailed at last and she cried, agonized and weeping:

"Ah, no—no! This must not be! Oh, God of mercy, help me! What . . . what can I . . . Ah, what must I do? Angelo, my love . . . help me, be strong and counsel me! Angelo, how may I save my people? Oh, Angelo . . . beloved . . . tell me what I must do . . . speak!"

And in voice agonized as her own, he answered:

"Remember only . . . thou art . . . the Duchess . . . and thy first duty to thy people. . . . Duty and service . . . the grievous price af thy noble heritage. . . ."

"My duty!" she repeated, and for a moment stood utterly

still and mute; then swiftly she came to helpless and now despairing Angelo.

"This!" said she, kissing his furrowed brow, "this is for so truly advising me! And this," she murmured, kissing his tearful eyes, "is for thy so unselfish wisdom! and this," she sighed, kissing his tremulous lips, "is for my undying love and farewell, for now, my beloved man, I go to my duty praying God I may die unsullied." Then passing Carlotta's still form, nor heeding her shyly furtive touch and whispered word, she confronted Gonzago with head back-thrown.

"Traitor and murderer," said she, "with loathing and praying for death, I will wed thee here and now. . . . This I do to save my people."

"Jenevra and Duchess," he retorted, clasping her nerveless, unresisting hand, "thus I take thee and in all gentleness. . . . And this I do to make thy duchy great, in hopes to win thy love, in thine own time, and mayhap found a dynasty shall endure and be a glory."

And now once again he struck the gong, whereat was a stir, a murmurous chant growing louder, the great door was set wide and, attended by choristers and acolites, a mitred cleric entered. With melodious chant and fragrant censers aswing, they advanced down the great hall—then halted and were silent as the officiating priest stepped forward, a pale, uneasy man despite splendid vestments, who performed his office in low, hurried murmurs, which done, he lifted hand in perfunctory blessing, turned hastily, his choristers struck up their chanting and this reverend company departed in cloud of incense.

Scarcely had the ponderous door closed than, sinking gracefully to a knee, Gonzago kissed his new bride's cold, lifeless hand, saying:

"Beloved wife and noble lady, thus doth thy Duke salute thee——" He paused and rose, as from courtyard, battlement and tower drums sounded, trumpets blared and hoarse voices cheered lustily.

"Hark, how these men o' mine acclaim their Duke! Dogs of war every one and marshalling even now. For soon shall I loose and lead them to Loredano's destruction, Jenevra—for in my duchy shall be no room for such as he!"

And now the great hall was athrong with liveried serving men to set forth and attend the banquet, thus all was stir and

bustle. It was now also that the Lady Carlotta moved at last
and became busied . . . while Gonzago loosed his prisoner,
saying:

"Thus now, Count Angelo, thou'rt free to go or bide in
our duchy at thy pleasure. And I would gladly have thee sup
with us and thereafter ride with me 'gainst Loredano—an it
be thy will." But seeing Angelo neither stirred nor spoke,
he turned where came a portly steward bearing two crystal
goblets which he proffered on bended knee.

"My lord Duke," quoth he, sonorously, "lo thy bridal
possets!" Taking these, Gonzago tendered one to his Duchess
who, mutely scornful, turned away—in which moment it was
taken by Carlotta with movement so unexpected and sudden
that some of its contents spilled, staining the white napery
red as blood.

"My dearest lord," she murmured, "suffer me!"

"Faith, it seems I must," he laughed, "now as ever!"

"Now as ever!" she repeated. "And for ever!" Speaking,
she raised the goblet to her ruddy lips, gazing above it at
this man of her devotion; and now her gentle eyes, no longer
sad, held in their glowing deeps the light of love and a great
happiness; also when she spoke in her richly deep voice
was a lilt of joy ineffable:

"Gonzago, my lord Duke, I pledge the with three effs—
the Future, Forgiveness, and Love's Fulfilment."

"Carlotta," said he, and with unwonted fervour, "always
I have loved thee, yet never more than now as Jenevra's
husband and Duke of Celonia. Thus I honour thy pledge
with all my heart, and most especially—Love's Fulfilment."

Then lifting goblet to lip, he quaffed deep while she, sipping
daintily, watched him with that same adoring look.

So Gonzago drank, sighed, caught his breath, and, in the
act of setting down the empty goblet, shuddered violently
and let it fall to gaze down at it with eyes that widened to
dawning horror while his hands gradually clenched themselves to quivering fists . . . and so again was silence except
for the slow, fateful ticking of the clock; when at last he
spoke it was in voice dreadful as his look:

"Carlotta, what . . . what have you . . . done——?"

"Saved thy soul, I pray sweet Jesu!"

"Ah, damned murderess, is this . . . death?"

"Nay, life eternal, I pray sweet Jesu."

Gonzago sank backwards into his chair uttering a gasping cry, a wail so terrible to hear from such a man that Angelo shrank appalled and covered his face; when he ventured to look again it was to see Gonzago struggling desperately against the agony that convulsed him; the spasm past, he mastered failing body, glanced from Angelo to Jenevra—and smiled; he even contrived to laugh.

"Madame my wife," said he, thickly, "rejoice in thy soon widowhood . . . get thee to thy new lord and master yonder . . . for I thy present lord shall presently be . . . carrion for speedy burial! Ha, Angelo, behold thy vengeance . . . be content." Here again he was convulsed and again a despairing cry broke from him:

"Failure! I die . . . a failure! Oh, Satan, accursed fiend . . . hast mocked me . . . a failure! Carlotta . . . I fail by . . . thy doing——"

"Alas, my beloved," she murmured, "there was none other way! Thou wouldst have brought ruin and death upon so many. From this great sin I have saved thee to God's mercy. And now I go with thee to plead thy forgiveness and salvation." Here she emptied the goblet and, setting it by, sank before the dying man upon her knees, gasping:

"How is it . . . with thee . . . my Gonzago? Ah, never did I love thee . . . so tenderly as now! Speak . . . speak to me!"

"Failure!" he repeated, bitterly. "Now . . . now fades the light . . . and in this darkness . . . whither go I——?"

"With me, Gonzago! The Angel of Death hath united us . . . with him we go that same dark way that . . . by thy will . . . Fortunio trod. Yet, my beloved, through this darkness I am with thee . . . before these deepening shadows to life again and . . . nobler doing. Canst hear me?"

"Oh . . . Carlotta, I . . . am blind . . . lost and lonely . . . in the dark——"

"Then, Gonzago, come to my heart and . . . take me to thine. . . . But a little while now . . . a brief season of pain to . . . an everasting joy, I . . . pray sweet Jesu. . . . Hold me . . . on thy heart, beloved, and let us . . . go thus . . . to God's mercy together."

Slowly, feebly, with his last strength, Gonzago reached forth his arms and, sinking in her embrace, sighed deeply and was still. . . .

So, once again came a hush save for the ticking of the great clock—and then a broken murmur:

"Sweet Jesu . . . of our . . . redemption . . . we come——!"

And presently Angelo set his arm about Jenevra's shaking body, and together they stole away—down the stair and out through glooming dark to the sweet freshness of dawn, leaving behind them an awful stillness.

For now in the great hall was no sound of life or movement except the ticking of the clock.

CHAPTER XXXIX

(AND LAST)

To FRIAR CLEMENT, busied in his grimy laboratory, came Pedrillo, an anxious man, with the question:

"Think you, wise master, that any may die of a broken heart?" And without pause or glancing up from the work that engaged him, the Friar answered:

"Not I, though others do, and 'tis a moot question. But this I do know, that grief may kill such as, having no desire for life, will themselves to die."

"Then alas!" groaned Pedrillo, with hopeless gesture. "If Angelo be dead, as all do now believe, thus will our lady Jenevra die also!"

Now at this Friar Clement looked up to enquire:

"Hast seen her at last?"

"Nay, she will see none save the Lady Fiametta, her chosen gossip. 'Twas this lady told me how she is surely pining to death—knowing Angelo slain in the late battle, as now do we all believe, to our common grief."

"Eh, thou, too, Pedrillo?"

"Master, needs must I, by reason of Manfred's tale——"

"Oh ye of little faith, to mistrust the mercy of God!" exclaimed the Friar reproachfully.

"Yet, holy father, God suffered Fortunio to die——"

"For that his work was done. But Angelo's is yet to do, wherefore I believe he will be spared to our need."

"Would I might so believe, good master. But, yonder i' the garden sitteth Manfred growling of his wounds and

groaning lamentably, ay, and with tears, being so sure Angelo
is dead and his comrade Andrea also, for he saw them both
unhorsed! Ah, couldst thou but hear him——"

"I will. Go bid him to me." Away strode Pedrillo to
return presently half-carrying a much-bandaged Manfred, who
limped painfully, growled fiercely, sighed woefully and, being
seated, told of the late desperate battle thus:

"They outnumbered us three to one, holy sir, and for
some while was close affray very bitterly bloody! Ah, but—
thanks to Angelo—we routed them, for d'ye see, he out-
thought and quite out-manœuvred Loredano. He posts me
to command our main and midmost battle, pikes and mus-
keteers to maintain our ground what time he and Andrea with
our horses charged and assailed them o' both flanks—but—
at the precisely right and proper moment! And so was the
field ours. Ay, faith, in Angelo we might have had another
Fortunio were he not now, too—like Fortunio, cold in bloody
death."

"But, my son, wherefore so sure God hath not preserved
him?"

"Reverend sire, I saw him borne down amid shock o' lances!
I saw his charger killed and himself fighting afoot, ay, and with
Andrea beside him and both close beset and furiously assailed,
and hard beside them the Count Ippolito sore stricken . . .
then smoke and dust hid them. I cried a rescue and ordered
my pikemen to advance, but even then I was struck down,
trampled senseless, and when I waked the battle had rolled
away and I alone and helpless along o' the dying and the dead.
But when methought to die likewise, came divers of my
company and bore me away. So—there's my tale, holy sire,
and I right woeful therefore. And thus, d'ye see, with Andrea
now no better than worm's meat along of our noble Angelo,
I am the sorriest dog that ever howled—ay, a shotten herring
were happier than I."

"Saw you them dead, my son, their bodies?"

"Nay, holy father, but I saw them ringed by death, nay a
hundred deaths as lance-points, swords, axes, spears and shot!
Since when hath been five woeful days and nights and never
a word of either!"

"Mayhap their messages went astray."

"But, holy sire, how may the dead send ever a message, for
dead I must needs know them to be, alas!"

"My son, rather know them to be alive, as I do and shall so long as I may."

"Ah, good Friar, I fain would, yet cannot, and so I mourn."

"Manfred, dost believe in God?"

"Certes, father; I do my best thereto."

"Then, go say thy prayers, my son, seek comfort of the Lord Almighty and shalt surely find it."

Manfred shook bandaged head, gestured feebly with bandaged arm and, uttering sound between growl and sobbing groan, limped dejectedly away.

"Tell me, Rillo," said the Friar, bending to his work again, "how do our new patients today?"

"The most of them so im-patient, master, that they do well and ever better, thanks to thy new lotion and the salve."

"Praise God!" murmured the Friar. "This afternoon, I'll with thee to them. Ha, and what's more, I'll see the Duchess. I'll speak with our sorrowing Jenevra, poor child, whether she will or no and despite her armed guards and lordly court physicians."

"Father Clement, I am here!" She was leaning in the doorway, her lovely face the paler by contrast with the long, black cloak that draped her. "I come," said she in awful still voice dreadful as her look, "for that I am . . . so lonely . . . They tell me Angelo is killed . . . so would I were dead . . .without him life is so hateful. And indeed I think my heart died when I heard the news, for I cannot weep, or feel, or think of aught beside. And I dare not sleep . . . in dream I hear him cry on me . . . I see him bleed and die. I have tried to pray and . . . God is so remote. Oh would I were dead . . . or a little child again to weep and forget. When I was a child and anyways hurt I would flee to thy care. So come I now to thee . . . but now, alas, a grievous woman with a sorrow beyond even thy comfort. So would I were dead or little child again——"

"Beloved daughter," sighed he, reaching out his hands appealingly, believe Angelo alive—as I believe——"

"Oh, death!" she repeated, heedless of words and gesture. "Oh, hateful death! I saw Gonzago, that arch traitor, die so cruelly that I pitied him . . . and then his noble lady . . . that I named, 'Jezebel'! For this I grieve now and ever shall. And today it is Angelo! Ah, hateful death, be kind this once and take me also——"

"Nay, Jenevra, thou art the Duchess and must live for thy people!"

"Then let them find some other . . . for I am all weary of life. . . . Oh, father, an I must live, what—what is there now left for me?"

And very gently, he answered:

"Work, Jenevra! Today thou shalt with me to help tend our many sick and wounded, to soothe their pain. Service to others is the only solace for our own griefs."

Now at this she turned to clasp those outstretched, appealing hands, and, drawing his arms about her, pillowed her head upon his breast, saying meekly:

"Then, dear, holy father, I'll with thee now. Let us go."

"Nay, child, first I will have thee sleep a while."

"Ah, no—no! Sleep is becoming my dread."

"Yet it shall be thy blessing!" said he, taking from crowded shelf a little phial, one of many. "Beloved daughter, here is that shall soothe thee to dreamless slumber, so shalt wake anon refreshed and more able to do and hear whatso God in His wisdom shall ordain. Drink this, thou child of my love."

Meekly she obeyed, then with her slim, cold hand in his warm clasp, like a child, followed whither he led.

Then, presently, outstretched upon his pallet with him seated thereby, she murmured:

"Oh, my father, thou dear, wise Father Clem, never did I love thee as now!"

"Then to prove this, my Jenevra child, close thine eyes and —sleep."

"Wilt not leave me, father!"

"Nay, I shall bide within call. Now—sleep, daughter, sleep!" He watched expectantly until her deep and regular breathing told how grief was soothed awhile in the blessed forgetfulness of slumber; then, sighing a wordless prayer, he returned to the laboratory where Pedrillo, packing medicines for their sick and wounded, glanced up with the anxious question:

"Sleepeth she at last, father?"

"Yea, my son, and should do till sunset. Howbeit, I cannot leave her."

"Ay, truly, master, she seemed marvellous strange and all

distract! And small wonder, for all's amiss since Fortunio
was killed—and now—our Angelo, alas and woe——"

"Enough!" sighed the Friar wearily. "Stint thy gusty
dolour, this mopish repining! Thy clamant mourning is all
too previous, I hope and pray—so have done! Get thee to
our patients, say I shall see them tonight, each and every.
Meantime, I'll to the compounding of my new salve, then
there's the lotion and cordial elixir. I shall be too busied for
grieving ere I must, or conjuring up imagined woes. Off with
thee now and do likewise."

So taking up his burdens, away strode Pedrillo to his
ministry, leaving Friar Clement to those labours that were to
end only with his devoted life. . . .

Thus the busy day passed while Jenevra slept and the
Friar worked, though often pausing to listen prayerfully—
only to hear distant clocks tell the passing hours until, as the
sun declined, back trudged Pedrillo, who, in answer to the
Friar's eagerly questioning glance, shook his head dejectedly
and replied in groaning voice:

"No news, my master, never a message, not a word . . .
only . . . the Count Ippolito hath ridden in wounded and
saith he saw Angelo . . . borne down and trampled. . . .
So, alas, master, 'twould seem God's will is not ours and
that . . . 'spite our prayers . . . Angelo is surely dead."
The Friar's busy hands faltered, his head drooped at last and
sank while he murmured:

"Now Almighty God . . . Father of us all, if this indeed
be Thy will, show me how to comfort her, Thy so afflicted
child, this woeful Jenevra. . . . Endure me with thy healing
power that I may save not only her body from death but her
mind from that most——" The prayer was hushed, and he
stood rigid and still—listening, as did Pedrillo.

Horse-hoofs approaching at rapid gallop . . . clash and ring
of heavy armour . . . a loud, persistent knocking on the garden
door.

"Oh God . . . news!" exclaimed the Friar brokenly. "Tidings . . . at last."

"Ay," gasped Pedrillo, "but of what . . . of which . . .
life or death?"

Then they were out in the sunset glow, with great leaps
Pedrillo reached, unbarred, threw wide the door, and into the
garden, on foam-spattered charger, rode one sheathed from

head to heel in dusty and battered armour, one who, lifting
vizor with weary gesture, showed a face haggard and sweat-
streaked. . . .

"Oh, sweet saints and angels!" cried Pedrillo, throwing wide
his great arms.

"Angelo!" exclaimed the Friar. "God is merciful——"

"Ay, we thought thee dead!" laughed Pedrillo. "So we all
grieved . . . but now, oho, all the city will rise to acclaim
and welcome thee, Angelo!"

"Wherefore I rode helmed and with vizor down," he answered, "for I hasted to warn thee, Father Clem, hard behind
me they bring Andrea sore wounded. 'Twas for him I tarried
so long, as my messenger informed thee."

"My son, there came no messenger——"

"And thus," cried Pedrillo, "we grieved thee dead, all save
my wise master! Ay, he alone believed God would preserve
thee to the future weal of us and the duchy—ay, and so shall
our bells ring anon for joy thou art alive!"

Here Angelo doffed his helmet to gaze down on them and
say, like one greatly awed and mystified:

"Ay, truly I am alive . . . e'en I that should be dead am
all unscathed, not so much as a scratch, thanks to God and
. . . this . . . this that is now my wonderment and ever will
be. And my glad wonder is that . . . Fortunio seemed beside
me in the battle, warding me from death! Thrice in the
closest fray it seemed my loved brother fought beside me!
Once when our ranks wavered, I seemed to hear, loud and
unmistakable above all that clamorous tumult, Fortunio's
rallying cry! When my horse was killed, and I down and
helpless, a hand of power bore me up amid that trampling
press to front, unharmed, the shock of blows! A lance
that should have been my death, splintered on my corselet
—lo, here is the dint of it! Thus, and thus only, am I
alive!"

"There then was a miracle!" exclaimed Pedrillo.

"There," said Friar Clement, "was the very hand of our
Almighty God!"

"Moreover," added Pedrillo, "he weareth Fortunio's harness, and 'tis armour o' proof! Hark! I hear horsemen!"

"At last!" sighed Angelo, turning. "Yonder they bring
Andrea, and direly hurt, Father Clem!" So saying, Angelo
dismounted with Pedrillo's ready help and, leading his charger,

went forth where seven grim-looking men-at-arms were halted about a litter.

Now, looking down at this pale, still face above which Friar Clement was leaning, Angelo enquired:

"Lives he yet, Father Clem?"

The Friar nodding, beckoned Pedrillo, who raised this inanimate form in mighty arms, and together they went to fight their battle with death.

Then Angelo gave his horse in charge of these seven grim fighting-men, saying:

"Ye veterans of Fortunio's company, right worthily have ye borne yourselves, wherefore in Fortunio's name I thank ye. Later I shall parade the whole Guard that our Duchess may reward and the citizens show their gratitude. And so, good comrades all, God keep ye." And when they had saluted and jingled away, Angelo clanked wearily into the garden, closed the door and, coming to that rustic seat beneath the great mulberry tree, sank thereon to lean back and close tired eyes, for he had ridden far and slept very little of late.

So Angelo closed his eyes and was upon the very brink of slumber when—she stepped forth into the sunset glory. . . . Her light feet trod silently, her silken robe made only the very softest of whispers; but the old tree stirred—its every quivering leaf found a small voice singing together like chorus of faerie, to welcome, to hail and warn—until—Angelo opened his eyes, and in that moment sleep and weariness were forgotten.

Her white hands were folded upon her bosom, her stately head was bowed, and thus she would have passed him unseeing but that he hailed her, and in the voice of Bimbo the Jester:

"Woman, whither goest thou?" She stopped and stood rigid and still, as if doubting her ears; therefore he hailed her again:

"Oh, woman, thy fool o' comfort waiteth to be kissed. Come thou!"

She turned to gaze wide-eyed and mute, as though disbelieving her eyes; but when he rose and she heard the clash of his armour, fearful doubt was banished by such rapturous joy that, uttering an inarticulate cry, she fled to his embrace, nor heeded steel-clad arms or sweat-streaked face—for these arms drew her to lips sweet and warm with passionate life. . . .

And now again this aged and therefore very knowing tree quivered as it had done once before to the ecstasy of that kiss.

At last, remembering his armour, Angelo exclaimed:

"Oh now, fool that I am—did I hurt thee?"

And clasping him ever closer, she sighed:

"Oh, dearest fool that thou art, I am most direly bruised, but—ah, beloved, hurt me again. Ah, fool beloved to be so foolishly tender of me; for though in steel thou'rt ever and always my fool of comfort, so for my comfort thou mayst hurt me—a little."

"Why so I shall anon, so pray help me to unarm."

"Gladly, my Angelo—nay, but all these straps and buckles and hooks and rivets—must show me how—— Why, surely this is Fortunio's armour?"

"Ay it is, and this his sword . . . I have tried to be worthy of them. . . . Let us to the oratory; there will I unarm and leave them, for, being indeed Fortunio's, they are to me very sacred."

So came they to the little chapel, and here Angelo drew this famous, battle-notched sword and, holding it in both hands above the altar, said very reverently:

"Fortunio, loved brother, thou bright angel of God, here now I give back thy sword, praying there shall be no need for it hereafter. With it, by God's help, came victory . . . and . . . oh, Fortunio, by thee as I do think, I was inspired and my life saved—and to ever better purpose, I hope and pray. Thus now upon this holy altar I lay thy sword in memory of thee that, being dead, live on with God for ever."

And now Jenevra said, very gently:

"Indeed, God is very merciful! For, Angelo, but a little while since, I was on my way hither to pray for thy soul . . . and also . . . because I can nowise endure life without thee . . . to implore our Almighty Father would unite us in death, thou and I, beloved."

"In death!" he repeated, and sank to his knees as if he would have worshipped her. "Oh, my Jenevra," he whispered. "Now I pray only to be worthy of thee in life . . . all my life."

Then, kneeling beside him, she folded reverent hands, saying:

"And now my prayer is—that we together, Angelo, may rule this duchy to the glory of God and the welfare of our people. For here, in this holy place, I pledge myself in faith and love to thee that shalt soon be my lord and husband and Duke of Celonia."

"Amen!" said a dearly-familiar voice, and to them came Friar Clement saying he had good hope Andrea was to live; whereupon Jenevra clasped his nearest hand to cherish it, though when she spoke it was as the Duchess, imperiously:

"Well now, holy father, since you have saved yet another life, 'tis my will you shall unite and perfect other two lives by wedding me to my so long betrothed lord——"

"Forthwith!" quoth Angelo, grasping his other hand.

"Nay, but," said the Friar, glancing from one to other, "this should be matter of high estate for my lord archbishop and bishops, with nobility attendant, all pomp and pageantry."

"Yet shall it be here," said the Duchess, "here in thy little chapel."

"Indeed!" said Angelo. "Thou, and only thou, my father, shalt bless us to each other. And what better estate than Jenevra in her own loveliness and I in Fortunio's armour? He, I think, would be glad."

So, hand in hand, down they knelt again before the altar, in which moment a level ray of the sinking sun flamed upon the long, bright blade of Fortunio's sword and made of it a glory.

And when Friar Clement had wed and blessed them, he turned to go, but Angelo stayed him, saying:

"Wait, dear my father! Come now, help me to unarm." But the Friar shook that wise, grey head of his and answered, smiling:

"Not so, my son! Heaven forbid that I should come betwixt man and wife! Bid thy Duchess do this for thee." So saying, he left them and this tender smile was still curving his shaven lips when he met Pedrillo who, quick to heed, enquired:

"Good master, how now?"

"Now, Pedrillo, ay, even now, in the oratory I leave a man and wife, our Duke with his Duchess."

"Glory! Glory be!" exclaimed Pedrillo.

"With all my heart!" sighed the Friar, happily. "Wherefore, Rillo let us now 'give thanks unto the Lord, for He is good!'"

"Ay, truly!" quoth Pedrillo. " 'For His mercy endureth for ever!'"

Meanwhile, in the little chapel, two stood looking upon each other quite speechlessly; but at last:

"Wife," said he, "help thy husband do off his armour."

Mutely she obeyed, nor looked at him now, perhaps because her eyes were needed for those same buckles, hooks, and rivets though her busy hands trembled—as indeed so did his, yet between them it was done at last.

Coming into the garden, they found it a place of dewy twilight, sweet with the blended fragrance of herb and flower. . . . Slowly they walked together amid this glimmering dusk, and still neither spoke, for theirs was a rapture too deep for any words. But at length, coming within the magic shadow of the mulberry tree, Angelo drew her near, saying:

"Well, dear my lady, thou art a very silent wife—so far!"

"And thou," she retorted, a little breathlessly, "thou, my lordly husband, art nowise talkative—as yet! Ah, but . . . when a poor Jester dared woo me . . . he was so marvellous eloquent, so . . . so sweetly speechful that, despite his foolish cockscomb, I . . . could not but . . . love him. And so, my lord, I would fain know of thee . . . am I to love my jingling fool more than the Duke, my husband, Angelo?"

"This," he murmured, drawing her nearer yet, "is now to prove. Oh, my own Jenevra—come!" Then she was in his arms, and with her thus high upon his heart, Angelo bore her to that rustic seat within the deeper shadow. . . .

Now, though this great, old tree was to live on and endure the passing of many years, as some trees will, yet surely never again was it to hide within its gentle-rustling shadow a deeper ecstasy, a truer love, or more lasting happiness than now.